THE NEW HEROES
THE CHASM

MICHAEL CARROLL

MaxEdDal Publications
www.quantumprophecy.com

ISBN: 1547067799
ISBN-13: 978-1547067794

First published 2017

To the memory of my inspiration, my hero, my friend
Harry Harrison

Acknowledgments

I would like to thank everyone who ever supported these books. Innumerable thanks to every teacher, book-store employee, librarian, copy-editor, publisher's employee and of course every reviewer.

Well, every reviewer except *one*... ;)

Special thanks to my amazing friends Danielle Lavigne, Richmond Clements and Paul Tomlinson for their help!

Ultimate thanks as always to my wonderful family and my amazing friends, and double-infinite thanks to my darling Leonia for putting up with me for all these years. Honestly, she deserves a medal!

And thanks to *you*, too. Yes, you, the person reading this right now. You're awesome, and don't let anyone ever tell you otherwise. If they don't think you're awesome, then they're wrong and that's *their* problem, not yours! Right? Right!

Thank you all for your support over the past decade and a bit... If you've enjoyed the ride even half as much as I have, then I can rest easy knowing that I've done my job well!

The Registry of Utter Awesomeness:
Mayumi Aldam, Francesco Alexiou, Luaan Anaya,
Sukie-Jane Aniston, Nana Argyros, Augie Aries, Reuben Austin,
James Bacon, Sam Baskin, Catherine Batts, Irna Baustaedter,
Henry Beniades, Anastasia Beth, Brandon Botset,
Mitch Bragdon, Yukio Bryans, Quenton Buteau,
Francel Capellari, Ben Carter, Charmayne Cataldo,
Shenagh Chaney, Josh Chapman, Maryanne Cheetham,
Elton Choy, Tracey Cicerchi, Nial Claridy, Maddox Cleaver,
Caleb Clements, Ewan Clements, Dominique Cockersell,
Rony Combeer, Jami Connors, Jovi Cordara, Luther Corless,
Elizabeth Cross, David Court, Tara Elizabeth Court,
Bryony Curtis, Rowena DeClaire, Viea Depies, Stanley DiCristina,
Shenah Dilmore, Cody Dostman, Suzette Eddington,
Peter Elmore, Brehn Etheridge, Farley Ewings, Dan Evans,
Dave Evans, Izzy Evans, Julie Evans, Tom Evans, Vicente Fallis,
Niven Faranda, Tamara Farrar, Paxton Farthing,
Sydney Fermenick, Alice Ferreira, Seru Frye, Waylon Glaude,
James Gowans, Sooki Greshock, Kitty Guariello,
Eamon Guillaume, Dylan Hall, Logan Harvell, Mallory Hatfield,
Amanda Heap, Floyd Henry, Emma Hickey, Luke Hickey,
John Higgins, Marc Hiler, Saswat Hoang, Nunzio Hum,
Anthony Hughes, Emma Hughes, Sally Jane Hurst, Naomi Ibarra,
Natalie Ibarra, Nikayla Ibarra, Zachary Ibarra, Casto Iceton,
Tom Inniss, Salisa Jatuweerapong, Pragti Jorgensen,
Hetty Jorgenson, Owen Jow, Hettie Kants, Sagar Kashyap,
Luke Kavanagh, Aidan Kirk, Justine Kligman, Tyler Koestner,
Rolando Kripac, Judge Kris, Marcelo Kristen, Paula Kronenberg,

Anna Langton-Connolly, Rashid Lawlor, Waylon Leavy,
Nic Lemos, Debbie Leventhal, HyeSeung Lipin, Lennie Lissner,
Vere Looby, Lancelot Lullo, Ferris Luna, Farid Mathis,
Geraldine Manning, Colton Maursky, Alison Mazer,
Joe McKinney, Emily McMillan, Angus Mahon, Finn Mahon,
Sacha Mahon, Kendra Medak, Andrew Milo, Zachery Mimbs,
Dr Lynn Moran, LeMoyne Morina, Hugo Murphy,
Naoise Murphy, Sinead Murphy, Greg Mysogland, Heidi Nacco,
Gary Nakadate, P. Thai Nance, Frances Nofield, Lily O'Higgins,
Jude O'Neill, Jude O'Sullivan, Ruby O'Sullivan, Eudora Oaks,
Kira Ogden, Bernhard Oka, Joseph Opoku-Akymong,
Lennie Peckover, Alexandra Peel, Arran Persbrandt,
Darlene Pino, Carmen Pivaro, Suzana Pressey, Adriann Pusich,
Elle Rabilwongse, Lottie Raja, Eden Raucci, Bernardo Raymonde,
Colby Rego, Blossom Repecka, Ethen Ritmanis, Jason Rosen,
LaFaye Rosenstock, Nazrin Rosette, Janssen Roy, Lenora Sajak,
Dub Sarkar, Meghan Schiereck, Barry Schoenbrun,
Josh Schwaner, Earl Schweitzer, Michael Scott, Mona Scott,
Dominic Shaw, Wilson Siemer, Masaki Silberston, Dheeraj Sills,
Sarah Simon, Lee Small, Lon Spiteri, Craig Springett,
Annalise Stankowski, Jerome Stark, Daniel Stout, Michael Stout,
Seán Stout, Valentin Strickler, Noby Suh, Aurora Taylor,
Leigh Taylor, Caoimhe Teeling, Alverne Teffer, Malay Thakkar,
Quinby Thor, Shari Tian, Deni Totten, Anya Tuthill, Kurtis Viner,
David Vivsik, Daria Voronca, Peter Wakely, Terry Wandel,
Chuer Zhang

And finally...

(AKA Yet Another Note from the Author!)

We made it! Hooray!

The New Heroes: The Chasm is the ninth and final novel In the series. It's also the longest, at over 100,000 words.

Long-time readers might recall that at one stage I was toying with the idea of ten novels—*Crossfire* would have been followed by a novel called *Overkill*—but in the end I decided to combine the final two books. Partly this was because there was no clear point at which this last phase of the story could be split, but mostly it was because even though I do love these characters and I've had tremendous fun playing in the sandbox I've created for them, I realized shortly after I'd finished *Crossfire* that it was time to wrap everything up. (So if I *had* written *Overkill* then the title would have been deliciously self-descriptive!)

My earliest notes on the series are from 2002, so that's fifteen years these characters have been living in my head... I need to let them go. (Also: I've been sitting on the ending for all those years, unable to share it with anyone!)

Now, some notes... First, if this is your first experience of the *New Heroes* universe, well, I *strongly* suggest that you stop right now and read the earlier books in the series because you've got a lot of catching up to do!

But if you insist on charging ahead with the idea that you'll pick it up as you go along, here's a brief "catch-me-up" to fill in some of the blanks...

Twenty-eight years ago the first superhuman—Krodin, an indestructible immortal—was taken from his time (four thousand years in the past) by some very bad people who wanted him to take control of the human race. This was prevented by some youthful superheroes, who—after some very exciting adventures—managed to strand Krodin on Mars. About fifteen years after that, a villain called Ragnarök created a device that stripped every superhuman—hero or villain—of their abilities, forever.

But the device had no effect on those who were destined to become superhuman when they reached puberty. Among such people was a young man called Victor Cross, who grew up to be a superhuman genius with far-reaching but devastating plans.

Cross triggered a world-wide war that was only stopped by the intervention of a new generation of heroes led by Colin Wagner (son of the former heroes Energy and Titan), Renata Soliz (a time-locked survivor of Ragnarök's power-stripping device), and Danny Cooper (son of the hyper-fast superhuman Quantum).

In *Crossfire*, Victor Cross unveiled part of his plan: he has created clones of Colin Wagner with the specific goal of finding a superhuman with ability to teleport Krodin back from Mars. That particular plan failed, but Cross had a back-up plan... Now, Cross and most of the surviving clones have been imprisoned, but the most dangerous clone—Shadow—has traveled to Mars in a powerful rocketship: he will physically bring Krodin back to Earth.

As for Cross's ultimate end-game... Well, all is revealed within, I promise!

The prologue for *The Chasm* is a short story that first appeared in *The New Heroes: Superhuman* short story collection, so if it seems familiar, that's why! And if you've read

Crossfire, you'll recognize a chunk of a chapter in here as one of that book's epilogues.

All the answers and secrets that have been teased and hinted at for so long can finally be found in this book! Not least of which is implied by the title...

They've been talking about it for many years, but what *is* The Chasm? Read on and find out!

Take a deep breath, folks...

Here we go!

Michael Carroll
Dublin, Ireland, June 2017

Michael Carroll

Prologue

One million years in the future...

For the last class of the year, I arrange for all the students to gather in the old museum's auditorium. A lot of them—actually, *most* of them—don't bother to come. I can understand that: they've already received their final grades, it's often a long way for them to travel, and they have their minds on other things.

They've heard all the lectures, read all the papers, watched the old recordings. They've submitted their essays, completed all the quizzes. They think they've learned all that there is to learn.

They think it's not going to be worth their while traveling all the way to a dusty, decrepit old museum just to hear me throw out a few final words.

They're wrong, of course.

This year the turn-out is the lowest yet. Forty-eight students out of almost five hundred. And I know that some of the forty-eight are only here because their parents forced them to come.

I can hear them now, trying to settle themselves in the auditorium's uncomfortable seats.

They arrived an hour ago. Few of them had ever met in person, and I watched from the darkness of the balcony as they tentatively checked out each other, recognizing one another from their profiles on the Link. Groups of two and three formed and split, merged with other groups, dissolved into individuals.

Now they're beginning to quieten down.

The overhead lights dim, and the murmuring rises with anticipation, then dissipates as I walk out onto the stage.

I stop at the podium and look out at the students. "Good morning."

A hesitant, almost embarrassed, "Good morning" rises from the assembled.

I smile. "I want to thank you all for making the journey here today. I'm sure that some of you would rather not be here, but I promise that you will find it all worthwhile." I press a key on my Pad, and a hologram appears behind me, filling the stage with seven familiar faces.

"You will I'm sure recall the discussion we had at the start of the year. Why are these people still known as the New Heroes when it was so long ago? One of you—Ms Tayner, I believe it was—made the valid point that New Harbor is still called New Harbor even after all this time.

"We've already covered the facts about the New Heroes. History tells us who they were, and what they did. Facts. History gives us facts." I pause for emphasis. "But there is more to the story of the New Heroes than is covered in the course. Much more. More than I could ever impart to you in a life-time of lectures. After today, after this short talk, I'm hoping that some of you will decide that you want to continue your study of the New Heroes. I teach another course that is not advertised."

At that, all of the students' interest is engaged.

"The second course is completely voluntary. There are no examinations. No qualifications for having attended. No papers, grades, quizzes. No homework, no study work, no penalties for failure, no rewards for success. And best of all there are no fees."

There is some mild laughter at this last point.

I continue: "To get a true sense of the New Heroes and the time in which they lived, you will need more than the facts. You will also need the *flavor*."

I leave the podium and walk back to the floating heads, point to one in particular. "The facts tell us that this young man almost destroyed the human race. We know this to be true. We've covered the details. His birth, the discovery of his abilities, the tragic death of his sibling, his part in the war... We know everything there is to know about him. Except we don't know *why*. Why did he do it? What made him believe that he was right? What were his justifications?"

I return to the podium and stare out at the faces. "They're all dead now, of course." A hand shoots up. I ignore it. "The New Heroes lived and died so long ago that it's almost impossible to imagine their world. Despite the population being greater than it had ever been before, the human race was on the edge of extinction. Most of them didn't realize that. Understandable, because memory is like walking backwards down a street. We cannot see where we're going, only where we've been.

"Today, we have the advantage of greater vision. We can look back and see exactly what the Earth was like in the twenty-first century. Our technology allows us to record the past. Does anyone know how this is done?" The lone hand is lowered. No other hands are raised. As I expected.

"I see. Like so many people, you accept the benefits of technology without understanding how it works." I hit another key on the Pad and the image is replaced with a picture of the Earth as it was. "In a vacuum, light travels at almost three hundred million meters per second. In a year, it travels exactly one light-year. Not a huge surprise there, given the name."

This raises a few wry smiles.

"A starship that is one light-year from Earth and is equipped with a powerful telescope can look at the Earth and see it as it was one year ago. A starship that is further out will be able to see further into the past. In the first years after faster-than-light travel was developed, all of human history was recorded. As you might expect, that led to the rewriting of quite a few of the history books." I turn and point to the image of the Earth. "But this is not a recording. This is live. There is a starship that is currently almost one million light-years from Earth. We are seeing the Earth as it was in the time of the New Heroes."

That *really* grabs their attention. I adjust the Pad's controls and the image zooms in on one of the smaller continents. "The land mass formerly known as America. Part of this land was called the United States, a conglomeration of sub-nations that—in theory—operated as a whole. At its center is the city of Topeka, in the state of Kansas. And if we look closer..." The image grows; the details clarify to show a devastated landscape pock-marked with kilometer-wide craters. A square object comes into focus and grows to fill the stage behind me.

"Interpolation allows us to adjust the angle..." The image shifts and warps, and the square becomes a flat-topped pyramid.

"This is where they lived, where many of them died. This is Sakkara."

A collective gasp from the audience.

The image grows larger still, and clears to show three figures sitting on the edge of the roof. Two boys, one girl. They are talking, but we cannot hear them.

"Colin Wagner, Renata Soliz, Daniel Cooper," I say, though such an introduction is hardly necessary. "Sound doesn't travel through a vacuum, of course, but again technology comes to our aid. The soundwaves cause minute vibrations where they strike solid objects. Our instruments can detect these vibrations and re-construct the voices of the founding members of the New Heroes." I hit a key on the Pad and Colin Wagner's voice is suddenly audible.

Naturally, the students can't understand a word of what he says. No one speaks the old languages any more.

Another key on the Pad switches to a live translation.

Colin says, "Your father doesn't much like us, does he?"

"Can you blame him?" Renata replies. "He's been through a lot. After what happened to me and then Robbie, he's never going to trust any of us again."

The boy with one arm—Daniel Cooper—scratches at the ragged, thin beard on his youthful chin. "We did what we had to do."

Renata fixes him with a stare. "You keep saying that. You weren't there, Dan. You don't know what it was *like*."

Colin begins, "Mina said—"

"Shut up about her!" Daniel Cooper yells. "She's gone, all right? Just forget about her. She ruined everything."

They fall into silence, and I use this time to address the students.

"I've watched this before. Many times. This is one of the most important moments in human history. Many of my colleagues don't agree with me, but it's my belief that the next seven words shaped our entire civilization."

Colin turns to Daniel. "No. It wasn't Mina. It's *your* fault."

Then I pause the image. The students are all sitting forward now; mouths open, staring past me to the frozen hologram.

I say, "You've all studied the text. You all know what happens next. But as you've just seen, the history books tell us *what* happened, but not necessarily *why*. I'm hoping that you're now intrigued enough to sign up for the second course. I will now answer one question."

Every one of the forty-eight students raises a hand. I pick a dark-haired girl from the nearest row. I know what she's going to say.

The girl points to the frozen image, "But... That's not—"

I cut her off. "I know. But they didn't know that then." I clear the image, and step back from the podium, walk to the edge of the stage. "They didn't know that then," I repeat. "That is the point of this talk, and it's at the core of my second course.

"Thank you all for coming here today. I know that some of you have traveled all the way from the outer edges of the Virgo Cluster, a distance that was almost unimaginable in the New Heroes' time, and I know that some people will argue that this short talk could have been presented just as well over the Link... But I believe that a teacher should meet his students face-to-face at least once.

"I hope that what you've seen here today will be enough to encourage you to continue your studies of the New Heroes. There are many hundreds of courses about them, but—without disparaging my colleagues and their work—most of those courses are rather dull, chiefly concerned with the facts and figures. But I believe that history is not about facts and figures. It's about people."

I look around at the wide-eyed faces. "Despite everything the New Heroes did, and everything that happened to them, and the world-changing consequences of their actions, first and foremost they were people. They were young men and women doing what they believed to be necessary.

"The history books and the other courses will tell you how they died...

"I am going to show you how they *lived*."

Chapter 1

"The world changed when you appeared. Nothing was ever the same again. Nothing." The man looked down at his mottled hands. He was clenching the edge of the park bench to stop them from trembling. "I have nothing to apologize for. I've done nothing wrong."

"Is that really what you believe?"

"It is. You have no right to harass me like this. No right. I should call the police!"

"Go for it," Brawn said. "Call them." He had been down on one knee, crouched in front of the old man, and now he straightened up a little, looked to the left. "There's a cop over there, beside the bandstand. He's been watching—he knows I'm here. Call him over. Report me."

Pastor Cullen looked away from the blue giant's colorless eyes. "You have no right." His voice was little more than a whisper.

The pastor was an old man now, and Brawn was torn between finally getting this off his chest, or letting the matter drop. For days he had been debating what to do, but whichever way he twisted the arguments in his mind, he kept coming back to one thought: some things you just don't let slide. "You lied about me," Brawn said. "Accused me of killing Gethin Rao."

"You attacked me! Broke my arms and legs, fractured my skull. You almost *killed* me!"

"That was an accident. You know that."

"But I *didn't* know—"

"You couldn't know that I *was* Gethin. That's not why I'm here. Pastor, you thought I was a monster and you screamed, 'Not me, not me... Take the boys instead!'"

The pastor immediately blurted, "You *crippled* me!" and

Brawn knew then that he was not going to get through to the man.

He sighed, then stood up. "Give me a break. Less than a year later you ran the half-marathon! It was in your book, all about your brave battle with the monster and your struggle to walk again."

"Nearly thirty years you've been gone," Cullen said. "Now you come back just to taunt an old man who can't fight back?"

"No, I came back because this was my home town. You think *your* life changed that day? I was twelve years old. I lost everything. And your actions—your *lies*—only made things worse. I was hounded as a monster, imprisoned, beaten, starved. You were supposed to be a man of God, Pastor. You think that when you meet him he's going to be happy with the way you've behaved?"

Pastor Cullen shifted further along the bench before he pushed himself to his feet. "So you're here to lecture *me* about the Almighty?"

Brawn looked around again. Aside from the police officer and a cluster of young men with nothing better to do, the small park was almost empty. The locals were now used to seeing a thirteen-foot-tall hairless blue giant. But two weeks ago, when he'd arrived in the small Vermont town and climbed out of the back of the truck, things had been very different.

Brawn closed the truck's doors then patted on its side with the flat of his hand, the universal signal that lets the driver know it's safe to move on.

Before the truck rumbled away, he could already hear screams from someone behind him.

He hoisted his over-sized backpack onto his shoulder and walked slowly in the direction of the local police station.

Lance McKendrick had told him, "People are gonna *freak*. You know that. Best thing to do is contact the cops first. Actually, let *me* do it—I know the right people to talk to. We clear your name and let them know you're coming, and the rest will be smooth sailing."

That approach hadn't felt right to Brawn. He'd asked Lance to make sure that he wasn't wanted for any crimes, but that was all. "I want to do this my way," he'd said.

Now, he wasn't so sure that had been the best idea.

Motorists slammed on their brakes and ran from their cars. Pedestrians darted down side-streets or ducked into stores. Within two minutes he was facing three police cars, all with their front doors open and the cops taking cover behind them.

"Stand where you are!" The police sergeant roared at him. She had a bullhorn raised to her mouth but had neglected to turn it on. Her voice was loud enough without it. "I mean it! Don't take one more step!"

"Why not?" Brawn asked. He had stopped walking anyway.

"You're under arrest!"

"On what charge?"

The sergeant hesitated. "Resisting arrest."

Brawn raised his eyes and shook his head. "You can do better than *that*. How about causing a panic?"

"The military has been advised and are en route!"

"Yeah, you might want to check that."

A few minutes later, standing in front of Brawn and wearing a slightly embarrassed expression, she introduced herself as Sergeant Irena Rosenblum. "I'm sorry about all that. It's just that everyone *knows*..."

"I get it," Brawn said. "I have done some bad things, but I did my time. I've paid my debt to society."

Rosenblum nodded. "So... why are you here? What brings

you to our town?"

"I lived here. My real name is Gethin Rao."

Rosenblum dropped her bullhorn and didn't notice. She stared up at his giant blue face. "You've gotta be kidding me."

"I'm not."

"So you didn't kill that kid when you first showed up. You *are* that kid, and you changed into this."

"Yeah."

"Well, *that* sucks!" The sergeant stepped back. "All right, then. There's no law against being big and blue. Stay out of trouble and we won't have to talk again. Though we probably will, because my mom lives on the same street as *your* mom. If you're going to visit her, better let me go first, so I can explain your situation."

"She already knows what happened to me," Brawn said. "But she doesn't know I'm coming today, so..."

"You should have gone straight home, then, because word's gonna reach her before you do."

"Yeah, well, I wanted to check in with you guys first." He smiled down at Sergeant Rosenblum. She was about forty, his own age. Strong build, nice smile, a kind of no-nonsense look about her. He liked that. In a different life, maybe...

"Come on, I'll walk with you. Folks'll be less jittery if they see you're with a cop."

"OK," Brawn said, "but the sidewalk's a little too narrow for me. If I walk on the street, will that be considered jaywalking?"

Rosenblum nodded. "Yeah, but I'll let it slide." She started walking, and Brawn fell into step beside her.

Around them, the other police officers climbed back into their cars and drove slowly away.

"So is it like this everywhere you go?" the sergeant asked.

"Mostly. Sometimes they open fire first." He shrugged.

"Though it has been a long time since I was out in public on my own."

"You were in that prison in Kazakhstan, right? It was on the news. The New Heroes saved everyone."

"That was Lieberstan, but yeah, that happened." Brawn ducked under a power cable that had been strung across the street. "That's too low. You'd wanna check the town's regulations on power-lines. Get them to raise it. Trust me, this is the sort of thing you know about when you're four meters tall."

Sergeant Rosenblum looked up at him. "So... awkward question..."

"I can't change back. I'm stuck like this. I don't know how my eyes work. And aside from my height, skin color and lack of hair, I'm pretty much normal. I eat, I sleep, I go to the bathroom just like everyone else. My skin's a lot tougher than the average human's, but that's a result of the initial change..." He stopped. "Sorry. That was rude. Most people ask the same questions so I tend to jump the gun."

"I *was* going to ask where you intend to stay while you're here. Your mom's house doesn't have a lot of space for a thirteen-foot-tall visitor."

"I'll buy a tent, live in the garden. Trust me, that'll be five-star accommodation compared to Lieberstan." Brawn looked around. "Everyone's staring. That's what bothers me most about being like this. I could cope with never being able to fit through doors or buy shoes again if only people would stop *staring* at me."

"Well, my daughter was born without legs so you'll understand if I don't sympathize."

They walked on in silence. At the next junction, while they waited for a very slow-moving car to make the turn—the driver couldn't look away from Brawn—he began, "Listen..."

"Don't apologize. You didn't know. And I shouldn't have snapped at you like that."

"Yeah, you're a real monster," Brawn said.

They laughed, and after that the conversation flowed a lot more smoothly.

When they reached the street on which Brawn had grown up, he asked, "How old is your daughter?"

"Amita's ten."

"Any others?"

"No, just the one. She's going to flip when she finds out I met one of the New Heroes, though. She's got a little crush on your friend Danny Cooper."

Brawn laughed. "She's not alone there. Girls *adore* that kid. More than half the mail we get at Sakkara is for him."

"You get Amita his autograph and a certain officer of the law will turn a blind eye to anything you want to steal. Actually, get her a signed photo and I'll let you do a *murder*."

"It's a deal."

They stopped outside Brawn's childhood home, and he stared up at it. All along the street, neighbors were peering through their screen doors or windows, or had found excuses to be on the front lawn.

"Tell your mom I said hello," the sergeant said.

He nodded, then stepped over the closed gate. In two more steps, he was in front of the door. He reached out to knock, but the door swung open.

"Hey, Ma."

The old woman smiled up at him, then peered past him to wave to Sergeant Rosenblum. To her son, she said, in a not-very-quiet whisper, "That's Patsy Rosenblum's daughter. She's *divorced*, you know."

*

"What do you *want* from me?" Pastor Cullen asked, looking back over his shoulder.

Brawn was following a few steps behind him. "Ever since I came back you've not stopped talking about me, but you don't want to talk *to* me. You're too ashamed to admit that you were lying all those years ago so now you're attacking me every chance you get. Every sermon, you're denouncing me. Calling me a murderer, a terrorist, a monster. You even called me 'The Cerulean Satan'—which I admit was a good one. You've turned the pulpit into your personal soap-box. You're spewing so much bile that it's a wonder there's anything left of you."

The old man fumbled a cellphone out of his pocket. "I'm calling 9-1-1!"

"I don't care. Look, Pastor... What happened to you made you the biggest noise in this town, but that was almost three decades ago, and it was built on a foundation of speculation and lies. You're a Christian. You're supposed to follow the Ten Commandments. Including 'Thou shalt not bear false witness.'"

The pastor stopped, and looked back. "I... I'm not..."

"You're not strong enough. I understand. But..." He crouched down in front of the pastor. "If you don't believe that people can change, then what's the point of contrition? That's the crux of your religion's entire dogma, isn't it? That the truly penitent can atone for their sins. So maybe your *next* sermon could be about something better than hate. It could be about forgiveness."

"You're looking for my forgiveness?"

"No. I'm offering *mine*." He reached out his hand.

Tentatively, the old man shook it, and—for a little while—all was right in the world.

Chapter 2

In the heart of the ghost-town, Renata Soliz called for an equipment check.

"We just did it, like, *twenty minutes* ago!" Mina Duval said.

Renata glanced at her brother, Robbie, who was leaning back against the side of his car, watching. He glanced at his wristwatch. "Almost two hours ago, Mina."

Renata said to Mina, "And even if it *had* been twenty minutes ago, the point is you do it again. Because I said so."

As an experiment, Renata had split Team Paragon into pairs. The twins—Alia and Stephanie—were already perfectly matched so she'd paired Stephanie with Roman and Alia with Cassandra. Nathan was paired with Danny, and Alex with Mina. They quickly and efficiently checked each other's armor and weapons. The process took a little under five minutes.

Not good enough, Renata said to herself. "Let's go again. And mix it up: different partners."

The town was Greenville, on the western edge of Kansas. Before the Trutopian war the population had been almost nine hundred. Now, it was zero. It had sustained so much damage in the war that none of the survivors had wanted to return. For the past four months the New Heroes had been using it as a training ground.

Robbie had found the abandoned town and helped secure it for them. Renata was proud of him, but still wasn't sure how to treat him. At twenty-two, he was five years older than her, but he was also five years younger: the decade she had spent in her crystalline form—immobile and unageing—had really messed up her life.

The first time she met him after she'd recovered, she hadn't known what to say. The skinny nine-year-old boy whose head didn't reach up to her shoulder had become a broad and strong adult and *her* head didn't reach up to his shoulder. And he was no longer Bobby: at some point in his teenage years he'd decided that Robbie sounded more grown-up and had insisted that everyone call him that instead.

Robbie said, "Ren, it's been fun, but I've gotta go. It's a long drive back and Dad's on the edge as it is. He's still living in fear of the middle-of-the-night phone-call that tells him you've been crushed by an alien dinosaur or shot in the head with a poisoned harpoon gun. So if he asks, I spent this whole weekend trying to persuade you to quit the superhero business and go back home, OK?"

"Sure. Thanks for coming out." She gave him a quick hug.

"And phone Mom before she explodes. She says she doesn't know what it is that you imagine she's done to upset you, but you haven't spoken to her for months."

Renata raised her eyes. "I was on the phone to her for an *hour* last Wednesday."

He grinned as he opened the car door. "What can I tell you? You've still got ten years of not being there to make up for. Be good, sis." He nodded towards Danny Cooper, then climbed into the car.

As he was driving away, Renata asked Danny, "What was that about?"

"What was what?"

"The nod."

Danny force a grin. "After you went to bed last night we stayed up talking and your brother very casually recited a long list of horrible things that he's heard can happen to unfaithful or disrespectful boyfriends."

"Oh, that was nothing. You ever get to meet my aunts and uncles, you're not going to know what's hit you." Renata turned back to her team. "All right... So, you've all checked and double-checked and triple-checked. Everyone's armor is fine, right?" Without waiting for any of them to answer, she said, "No, wrong. What have we missed?"

Alex raised his hand. "No one has checked *your* armor yet."

"Well done, Alex. You get to do that."

The boy stepped forward and examined Renata's armor. "Seals intact... No major battle-damage or stress-damage. Weapons... check. Flares... two missing. Radio is clear." Then he stopped, and smiled at her. "You can't fool me. Your coolant-pack is almost empty, but you've fudged the read-out to make it look full."

"How could you know that?"

Alex pointed to the computer display attached to the left wrist-piece of Renata's armor. "Because we've been out here for four hours. Unless you've topped up the coolant yourself, it should be no more than eighty per cent full. And you can't have topped up the coolant yourself because you'd have to remove your armor to do that."

Renata asked, "Or...?"

"Or your coolant isn't draining because you've not got it switched on. But in that case you'd be stewing in your own sweat right now."

She nodded. "Good work—well spotted. All right, everyone. We're heading back to Sakkara. Danny, how far is that?"

"Five hundred and forty-two kilometers, as the fly crows."

"Which will use up *how* much fuel... Alia?"

The girl checked the computer display on her own armor. "Actually, that's cutting it close. We should *just* about be able to make it back without eating into our reserves, as long as nothing slows us down."

Nathan, the smallest—and in some ways the youngest—

member of the team said, "Uh oh. This is gonna be another test, isn't it?"

Next to him, his brother Roman let out a low groan. "Aw *man*... Renata, give me a pass, huh? My leg is killing me and I got, like, *no* sleep last night! I'm exhausted."

Renata knew what was coming next, and she suspected that the others did too.

Danny stepped up to Roman and said, "Oh, your leg is sore? This would be the leg you broke when you were trying to kill Renata? Yeah, you've been back to *that* particular well a few times too many, Roman. You want to be part of this team, you learn to follow orders without question."

Roman sneered. "This from the guy who disobeyed Impervia's direct order not to intervene in Lieberstan?"

To herself, Renata said, *Yeah, he's got a point there.* Aloud, she said, "That's enough. Roman, for this exercise you're out of commission. The rest of you... you have only enough fuel to get yourselves back to Sakkara. So you choose: do you leave a man behind, or figure out a way to take him with you? And bear in mind that he's injured. You have ten minutes. *Yes*, Mina?"

Mina said, "But Roman can fly on his own!"

"For this task we're assuming that he can't."

"If your brother had waited a bit longer, he could have given Roman a lift."

"Just get to work!" Renata stepped back and watched them trying to figure out what to do.

She knew that Stephanie Cord was holding back, but not because she didn't have anything to contribute. Steph was by far the most effective member of the team, and the others would never learn anything if she kept taking control.

Danny, too, was taking a back-seat, but that was mostly because he knew he was only here to make up the numbers. As soon as Kenya returned, he'd step down again.

For a moment she found herself wishing that Grant Paramjeet had stayed with the team. When his parents first discovered that he was working with the New Heroes they had been more than happy to allow that to continue, but their doubt set in when his grades began to suffer, and when he was almost killed by a band of enraged Trutopians in Berlin, they had demanded that Lance discharge him from the team.

As she waited for the others to figure out what to do, Renata removed her left glove and examined her bare hand, clenching it into a fist, flexing her fingers individually, holding it up against the sun. Nothing, yet. But she was sure that it wouldn't be much longer before her powers returned. Earlier that morning Colin had told her that his enhanced hearing was starting to come back.

It had been a tough eight months since the battle at Victor Cross's base inside the glacier at Zaliv Kalinina. Without their superhuman abilities, the New Heroes' only advantage was their armored division, Team Paragon.

But their powers *would* come back, she was certain. Cross had said that his device had only stripped them of the energy that made them superhuman, not destroyed whatever it was that allowed them to use that energy.

Not for the first time, Renata silently thanked the gods that Cassandra had stayed behind on that mission to the Arctic. If she'd been with them, Cross would have used his machine on her and the team would have lost its greatest early-warning system: her telepathy.

And she was thankful for Roman, too. He could be annoying at times, but he was the only one of Victor's clone army who still retained his abilities, though he was severely hampered by his damaged left leg. He could just about walk on it now—he'd constructed a splint from carbon nano-tubes; the only material strong enough to keep his shattered femur in place while it healed—but preferred to fly.

Roman had been trapped in Sakkara during the New Heroes' assault on Cross's base; unlike his clone-brothers, he'd not had his powers stripped by Cross. Now, he was technically the most powerful member of the team, but few of the others trusted him.

They liked Alex, though, and Nathan. The other clones— Tuan, Eldon, Oscar and Zeke—had so far resisted the deprogramming system designed to shatter their loyalty to Victor Cross. Right now, they were being held captive in Sakkara's basement, but Renata spoke to them every day, tried to get them to understand that Cross's way was wrong.

Tuan was the worst. After Shadow—the first of the clones, and their leader—Tuan had been closest to Cross, and with his surrogate father now imprisoned, he was stubbornly refusing to believe anything negative about him. He was particularly hostile toward Renata, whom he blamed for Warwick's death.

The thought of Warwick still brought a cold sweat to Renata's back. The clones had been trying to kill her, and she'd fought back with just enough force to put Warwick out of commission. He might have survived if Cross hadn't ordered the others to leave him there in the Arctic snow.

Nine clones. Warwick was dead, Shadow was missing. Three had defected to the New Heroes... that left four. If their powers recovered before everyone else's, they would destroy Sakkara and kill everyone inside the building. And then they'd move on to the Cloister, and free Victor Cross.

There was some hope, though, horrible as it was to contemplate. Oscar and Zeke's loyalty to Cross was wavering, but only because they now had unshakable proof that he had lied to them.

As Colin Wagner made his way down the unpainted concrete stairs into Sakkara's basement, the thought occurred to him that he really didn't know the building as well as he should. It was home now, and had been for a few years, but there were still corridors and sub-basements he hadn't visited.

Walking alongside him was ten-year-old Niall Cooper, who as always was talking about his favorite cartoon show. "So the Magnus goes to X-Roy and says, 'Defend ye not the mighty castle, for it is forever doom-ed!' That's how he always says it. 'Doom-ed' not just 'doomed.' And then guess what X-Roy says?"

"I've no idea," Colin said.

"He says, 'I stand always for truth! Doom-ed or not, I *shall* defend the castle until my dying breath!' How cool is that?"

"It'd be a lot cooler if they weren't all bunnies," Colin said.

Niall looked annoyed. "They're not bunnies! They're just people who evolved from rodents instead of primates!"

They reached the bottom of the stairwell, and Colin said, "OK, you know the deal. You're not allowed on this level."

Niall was standing on the bottom step, and pointed down to the floor. "I'm not *on* that level." He stretched out with his left foot until the toe of his sneakers was an inch above the floor. "Almost... but I'm still not standing on that level." He lowered his foot a little more. "*Almost* breaking the rules... Still not in trouble."

Colin said, "Yeah, *that's* not annoying."

"I've already been on this level, like, a thousand times. *And* the one below. And I worked out a way to get from Ops down to the machine room without ever once walking on the floor. See, if you're up on, say, the second level, 'kay, and you count the steps up to the first, then you measure the height of each step, then multiply them—"

Colin put up his hands. "Niall, stop, please! I've got things to do. Will you just go back?"

"I'll wait here until you're done."

"No, it's cool," Colin said, gesturing back up the stairs. "I'll catch up with you later."

"I don't mind. I can tell you the rest of the episode then."

"That's what I'm afraid of," Colin said. "I could be down here for hours. Go on."

"Aww...!" The younger boy began to very slowly walk backwards up the stairs. "I might wait for a bit. Like, an hour. Will you be done by then?"

"I don't know. Go and find my mother—*she'll* give you something to do."

Niall groaned, then turned around and trudged up the stairs, calling back, "Yeah, she'll make me take care of your little sister again."

When he was sure that the boy wasn't going to follow him, Colin strode away from the stairwell. Further along the corridor, two of Sakkara's guards—wearing full body-armor and holding assault rifles—stood on either side of a closed steel door. They nodded at Colin as he approached.

"Anything?" Colin asked.

"Just the usual," the guard on the left said. Corporal Kaye LaPenna was in her early twenties, Colin guessed, but no taller than him. She always smiled when she saw him and he couldn't understand why that made him feel guilty. "Complaints about the food, demands to be set free, threats to kill us all and destroy the world. Nothing unexpected." She turned to the door's control panel and entered a lengthy code.

Something inside the door's mechanisms hissed and clunked, then the door slid open. It hissed closed again the moment Colin stepped through.

The well-lit room was about the size of a four-car garage, and contained four sets of bunk-beds at one end, and a pair of large couches at the other, both facing a small TV set. Eldon and Zeke were watching the TV, which was currently tuned to the local news. Tuan was sitting on his bunk playing with a hand-held video game, and Oscar was lying in bed, huddled up with what looked like every spare blanket piled on top of him.

"How is he?" Colin asked.

"Dying," Tuan said, without looking up from his game. "What do you care?"

From the sofa, Zeke said, "Give it a rest, Tuan."

Colin looked around the room. It was like seeing into his own future. Tuan looked to be about a year older than Colin, and Eldon about a year older than that.

Victor Cross had cloned them from Colin's own DNA, and artificially accelerated their aging process: superhuman abilities usually kicked in at puberty, and Cross hadn't wanted to wait twelve or thirteen years for that to happen.

He'd promised them that their artificial aging would slow down and soon they'd age at the usual rate. Another one of his many lies.

Now, Zeke looked—and moved—like a man in his thirties.

Colin walked over to Oscar's bunk. The clone was barely visible beneath the blankets. He peered up at Colin, staring at him through gray eyes that were not yet two years old, yet looked to be a century or more. What was left of Oscar's hair was now white, his skin was so thin Colin could see his veins and tendons.

"So cold..." Oscar said.

Standing beside Colin, Eldon said, "He's got two electric blankets under there, both of them switched on all the time, and turned up full. Put your hand on his head. Go on."

Colin reached out and gently touched the backs of his fingers against Oscar's forehead. "He's freezing!"

"Yeah. I don't know what else we can do for him."

On the next bunk, still with his attention on the hand-held game, Tuan said, "A bullet in his head will solve everything."

"He's your *brother!*" Colin said.

"No more than you are." Tuan tossed the game aside, and stood up. He was three inches taller than Colin, with a much stronger build. "When are you going to let us out of here?"

"When we can trust you."

Tuan snorted. "You people are *pathetic*. If I had my powers I'd siphon the life-force out of every single one of you morons and not think twice about it. Look what you've done to him— and to Zeke!"

"Keep me out of it," Zeke said from across the room.

"I didn't cause this," Colin said. "Cross did. You know that. He made you. And don't forget that *you* attacked *us*."

Tuan clenched his fist and held it an inch away from Colin's face. "If I had my powers..."

Colin said, "If I had *mine*, you wouldn't have the guts to make threats."

A few days earlier, during the weekly meeting, Colin had again raised the problem of the clones. "We can't keep them prisoner forever."

Lance McKendrick had said, "They wouldn't survive in the real world, Col. They've got no experience. I mean, they've never used money. They've never interacted with people who don't look like you, Victor Cross or Evan Laurie. They don't know how to act or react to the world. Take away the fact that they look grown-up, and they're still infants. Your *sister* has a better grasp of the world than they do. And she doesn't have the power to destroy the human race. Well, not yet, anyway."

"How long before we get our powers back?" Colin had asked him. But there had been no answer to that. The only person who had a good understanding of superhuman abilities was Cross, and he wasn't talking.

Now, as Colin and Tuan stood glaring at each other, Zeke got up from the sofa and strode over to them. There was gray in his beard, his hair was starting to thin, and lines creased the skin around his eyes.

That's me in twenty years, Colin thought.

Zeke said, "I keep thinking that it's slowed down for me, but it hasn't, has it? I figure I've got maybe seven months before I look like Oscar."

Colin began to respond, but Zeke cut him off. "I'm not spending the rest of my short life locked up in this room. If I'm going to die so soon, I want to have *lived*. You tell that to your people upstairs, Colin. Even if my powers come back, I'm not going to run off and rescue Cross from wherever you've got him stashed. I want to do at least some of the things that real humans do. I want to walk on a beach. I want to drive a car. Have at least *one* date with a woman. Look at *this*." He pulled his t-shirt off over his head. From his throat down to his naval, a thick white scar was visible beneath the thick black hair on his chest. "I almost *died* when Brawn attacked me, so I'm going to make the most of the time I have left."

Colin said, "I understand that. But you were trying to *kill* Brawn—don't blame him for defending himself."

"We were under Cross's control," Tuan said. "We had no choice."

Zeke nodded. "Right. Even *Nathan* did whatever Cross ordered, and Nathan despised him."

"None of you are under his control now, so why is it that

only Nathan, Alex and Roman have signed up with us?"

Tuan said, "Because we might have all come from the same source, but we're not all identical. You should be able to understand that, Wagner, considering that *you're* the source."

"You always make it sound like I did this to you! Why are you blaming *me*?"

Zeke said, "And we're back to that again. Colin, with Victor gone and Evan dead, you're the closest thing we have to a relative. When Oscar goes, you have to make sure he's taken care of."

"You trust him to do that, after what happened to Warwick?" Tuan asked. "They left him to die in the snow!"

"No, *you* left him to die in the snow," Colin said.

Zeke said, "We were ordered to leave him. *We* had no choice—your people *did*."

Then Eldon said, "He's gone."

Colin froze. "What?"

Eldon stepped away from the bunk. "Oscar's dead. Just now. He... he just stopped."

They stood there for a long minute, then Zeke said, "I'll be next."

"We'll find a way to reverse the aging process," Colin said. "Or slow it down, at least. Danny can manipulate time—maybe when his powers come back, he'll be able to do something."

Eldon pulled one of the blankets up over Oscar's head. "Colin, you should tell someone. There'll be a funeral, I guess."

Colin found his mother on the building's uppermost level, in the room she'd designated as a classroom. She'd insisted on four hours of lessons every day for the teenagers.

Now, she was sitting at her desk reading through their homework assignments, and glanced up at him as he entered.

"I'm busy, Colin."

"I know. But... Oscar died."

Caroline Wagner dropped the book and walked over to her son. "Are you all right?"

"Yeah. I... Well, I didn't like him much, but it was the *way* it happened. No two-year-old should die of old age!"

"How are the others coping?"

"Nathan and Alex and Roman don't know yet—they're on patrol. The others are, well, upset. I supposed that's understandable."

His mother said nothing, just watched him steadily, and he knew that she wanted him to keep talking. She'd always been a strong believer in not keeping things bottled up. "It was like watching *myself* die. Like a premonition or something."

"That's Danny's area of expertise." She smiled warmly and stepped closer to him. "You too big now for a hug from your mother?"

"Kind of. But I don't mind."

As she wrapped her arms around him, Colin said, "Nathan's going to need this a lot more."

"I know."

Nathan had been the first of the clones to switch sides— Cassandra had used her telepathy to check that he wasn't lying—and he'd bonded almost instantly with Colin's mother. None of the clones had had a mother of their own. Caroline had told Colin, "Nathan reminds me of you before this whole mess started. Before you got your powers and our lives got turned upside-down, back-to-front and inside-out."

Then Colin pulled back from the hug. Something was wrong.

"Colin—what is it?"

"Something's coming," he said.

"Your super-hearing's back?"

"No, not yet—it's getting stronger, but it's nowhere near back to full power yet. Mom, sound the alarm!"

"You're certain?"

"Just do it!"

He ran for the door, raced along the corridor toward the armory. He didn't know what, exactly, was wrong, but something felt out of place.

Then the alarms ripped through the building, sirens blaring, lights flashing. The floor trembled as every interior door slammed shut.

Seconds later, the alarms fell silent and the lights blacked out. Colin slowed to a walk as he waited for the emergency lighting to kick in, knowing that it shouldn't take more than a few seconds. But the seconds dragged past. Five. Ten. Twenty.

That's not good.

This corridor ran through the heart of Sakkara, with no external windows: he was moving blind. When he had his powers, he could see in almost total darkness, or he could generate his own light. Now, he was creeping forward with his arms outstretched.

Something flared to his left as he passed a side-corridor, and he turned to see Roman standing outside the armory. He was on the verge of asking what was happening when he noticed that the light was coming from Roman's fingertips.

Roman can't do that. And he's too big to be Nathan or Alex.

The clone smile at him, a wide, dangerous grin. "Hello, brother!" He raised his clenched fists and a powerful arc of electrical energy jumped from one to the other. "Remember me?" Shadow asked.

Chapter 3

Colin turned, racing back the way he had come.

Running from Shadow was futile: if the clone wanted him dead, there was nothing he could do about it. Without his powers he was no match for *any* of them.

But he wasn't willing to roll over and die. The alarm would have been automatically transmitted to Team Paragon, to the Substation, the Cloister, and the nearby military base. If he couldn't fight back, his job was to stay alive and learn as much as he could about the situation so he could inform the others when they made contact.

The emergency lighting finally flickered on, bathing everything in a sickly yellow glow—but it was enough.

Ahead was the door to the Operations room—the room was empty right now, but he could see his reflection in the door's glass panel: there was no one behind him. Shadow was letting him live, for now.

He knows I'm no threat.

Was Shadow alone? Who had he come for? Was this an attack, or a rescue attempt?

Had he already been to the Cloister and rescued Victor Cross?

No—any attack on the Cloister would have triggered alerts here in Sakkara.

Colin rounded a corner and almost collided with a tall, very thin, very pale man. He had long ragged hair, an unkempt beard, and was wearing only a pair of shorts.

The man had his mouth full and a half-eaten sandwich in one hand, a whole pineapple in the other.

Colin tried to dodge around the stranger, but the man dropped the sandwich and grabbed Colin's arm, his bony fingers like steel trap.

The man looked down at Colin in one hand, and the pineapple in the other, as though debating which was more important.

He chose the pineapple. He bit into its spiny husk, chewed and swallowed, then drew the back of his hand across his mouth. He grinned at Colin. "I have not eaten for a long time." His accent was thick, his words pronounced with care, as though he was not very familiar with the language. "You are the... original. The Colin. The mold from which Shadow and his brothers were cast. He tells me that you are my enemy."

Colin gave up trying to pull himself free. "Who are you?"

"I am Krodin. Your ruler."

In Sakkara's gymnasium Colin sat cross-legged on the floor, a few meters away from his mother. She looked unharmed, but the same could not be said for everyone present.

The guards at Sakkara had shot at Krodin, but their bullets couldn't penetrate his skin. They hit him with a prototype high-powered plasma-gun, but all it did was scorch the walls around him. They detonated a blackout bomb at his feet, but within seconds his eyes had adjusted to compensate.

In less than twenty minutes, Krodin and Shadow had defeated every obstacle and taken control of Sakkara.

Shadow had freed his clone-brothers, and now the entire staff of Sakkara—conscious, unconscious or dead—had been dragged into the center of the gymnasium. Colin counted thirty-eight—but there was no sign of his sister Abigail or Niall Cooper.

"Stay seated," Krodin ordered. "Or die. Your choice."

Shadow walked over to Colin, and glared down at him. He had found an over-sized sword—one of the weapons Brawn had been offered but had declined to use—and was carrying it over his shoulder. "You brought this on yourself."

Colin said nothing.

"You're a joke, Wagner. Pathetic. All that power you had, and you did *nothing* with it. You could have changed the world."

"Yeah, well, that's kinda our motto: Just because you *can* do something, doesn't mean you *should*. That's the difference between us. You care about nothing but yourself."

"I'm going to kill you," Shadow said. "But only after I kill the others. You'll get to watch them die."

Krodin called, "Shadow. Enough."

Obediently, Shadow returned to Krodin's side, where Tuan, Zeke and Eldon were already waiting.

"I have come to rule," Krodin said. "Which is the one called Lance McKendrick?"

There was no answer.

Krodin pointed to Corporal LaPenna, the young woman who had been on duty outside the clones' room. "Shadow. Kill that one. Then perhaps the others will talk."

Shadow lowered his sword, dragged it behind him as he strode toward the kneeling woman. The tip of the sword carved a deep groove in the floor.

Colin jumped to his feet. "All right! We'll talk! Lance isn't here right now."

"You telling the truth?" Shadow asked.

"Yes! I swear!"

"Good." He swung the sword, and Corporal Kaye LaPenna's head fell from her body.

Krodin said, "Every answer that is withheld, or delayed, or displeases me, will invoke the same penalty." He pointed to an older male technician whose name Colin didn't know. "That one will be next. Is there anyone here who does not understand these rules?"

"We understand," Colin said. "What do you want?"

Krodin looked at him as though he was confused by the question, then walked toward him, stopped only a few feet away. "I told you. I have come to rule. Did you not listen, or not comprehend? Either would displease me."

"I meant, what do you want from *us*?"

"You will serve me, all of you." Krodin looked down at Colin for a few seconds, his lips pursed, then he turned toward Shadow and the other clones. "I expected stronger resistance. You told me they were formidable warriors."

"They were," Tuan said. "Victor Cross stripped them of their powers. Us too. Uh..." He briefly glanced toward Shadow, before looking back. "Do you know about Victor Cross?"

"Yes. The super-human who created you. His hope was that one of you would develop the ability to... teleport me back from the other world. From Mars." Krodin turned back to Colin. "It was Lance McKendrick who sent me there. His death will be slower than he can imagine."

Colin knew Krodin had been the first superhuman, born five thousand years ago. He was said to be immortal, and indestructible. He had been hundreds of years old when he'd conquered most of the known world, but then at the peak of his power he had been destroyed in a column of fire. His followers learned of a prophecy that he would one day return from the dead and fulfill his destiny to rule the human race.

They called themselves the Helotry of the Fifth King, and twenty-five years ago their descendants had put their plans into action. They used a superhuman called Pyrokine to snatch Krodin out of the past, seconds before he was struck by the column of fire... But Lance McKendrick, then only a teenager, had realized that Krodin had never died: what his followers had witnessed was not his death, but the energy that pulled him through time. They had caused the very anomaly they had been trying to prevent.

Lance's friends—including Brawn—had fought Krodin to a standstill, but his ability to adapt his body to resist any danger meant that they could never win... Until Pyrokine had sacrificed himself, burning up his entire body—and taking Krodin with him.

Some time later Brawn and Lance and the others discovered that the world around them had suddenly changed. They eventually learned that Krodin had not been killed by Pyrokine's sacrificial blast. Instead, he had been cast back in time, no more than six years—but that had been long enough for him to work his way into a position of power. He had amassed huge, powerful armies and was on the verge of conquering the world. In that horrifying alternate reality, only Brawn and his friends knew the truth.

They defeated Krodin again, but this time by using his own technology: the teleporter he used to wage instant war against his enemies. Krodin had believed himself immune to the effects of the teleporter, but Lance had realized that it could be used to pull objects out of time: he set it to lock onto Krodin the moment he'd arrived in the past, six years earlier... And instantly the world resolved itself.

Lance had sent him to Mars.

That was Victor's original plan, Colin thought. *To get Krodin back from Mars. But he told Danny he'd abandoned that because he hadn't been able to make a clone who could teleport over long distances.*

Cross lied, of course. The missile we thought was going to destroy the world... When it seemed to randomly shoot off into space we just let it go. What harm could it do out there?

It hadn't been a missile at all. It had been a rocket destined for...

A sudden memory jumped out at Colin and he fought hard to suppress a shudder.

Two years ago in Romania, back when Cross had been disguised as Reginald Kinsella, leader of the Trutopians... Colin had been with him when he made TV broadcast denouncing the New Heroes. At one point, Cross had said, "Just in case some of you have been living on Mars..."

He was telling *us! Right from the start that arrogant jerk was bragging about his plan!*

Chapter 4

Kenya Cho liked the Substation a little more now that the main construction was finished. It didn't seem quite as crowded as on her previous visits, but it was still too noisy, much too dark, and she missed the open air.

"I don't like it here, Lance," Kenya said. "I'd rather be at home."

"You mean home in Madagascar, or in Sakkara?"

"Madagascar. Or Africa, at least. I still have a lot of work to do."

"But look how *awesome* this place is!"

They were riding in the clockwise cable-car as it slowly trundled its way from the north end of the station to the east. The Substation had been designed as the world's largest particle accelerator, a subterranean tunnel twenty-four kilometers in circumference. The project had been abandoned due to lack of funds shortly after the construction began.

Now, the tunnel had been completed, and its bore—the distance between the inner and outer walls—had been doubled to sixty meters. It was home to almost one thousand people, many of them refugees from the prison camp in Lieberstan.

With the loop now complete, Lance had insisted that he and Kenya try out the Substation's public transport system, an open-topped cable-car that was suspended fifty feet above the station's single curved street. There were two lines, one running clockwise, the other anti-clockwise, with stations at the north, east, south and west.

"We definitely do need more stations," Lance said, peering over the edge and waving to the people below. "The circumference is eighteen miles, and with only four stations that's..."

After a second, Kenya realized he was waiting for her to supply the answer. "One every four and a half miles."

"Correct!"

"You're not a teacher, and I'm not your student."

He turned to her, grinning. "Ah, but it could be argued that everyone is a teacher, and everyone is a student."

Kenya said, "It *could* be argued that the moon is a giant paper plate that someone glued to the sky. That doesn't make it true. Lance, I don't even know why I'm here! I should be training with the others."

"You, young lady, are here because you have a very special gift." Lance stood up and grabbed hold of the car's hand-rail. Ahead, the eastern station was approaching. "Here we are..."

"We're not going all the way around?"

"Not yet. Got someone who needs to meet you."

The cable-car swayed to a stop, and Lance stepped out onto the platform, where Warren Wagner stood waiting.

"How'd it run?"

"Pretty smooth," Lance said. "But these cars are a death-trap. We need fully-enclosed cars, with doors that only open when it's stopped. Otherwise kids'll be daring each other to hang on the outside as it goes around."

Warren said, "The kids aren't *that* stupid, Lance."

"Yeah? If *I* was thirteen I'd be first in line to see if I could go all the way around just hanging on with one hand."

Kenya followed them down the stairs to the ground level.

"It's a wonder you've lived this long," Warren said.

"It really is," Lance agreed. He patted the hand-rail as they reached the bottom. "Stairs aren't enough. We need elevators. Not everyone can *manage* stairs. I'm surprised you didn't think of that, Warren. Surprised and, y'know, a little disappointed."

Warren Wagner pointed to the left. "You mean, like *those*

elevators?"

Lance looked toward the elevator doors for a second, then back to Warren. "That was fast. Well done."

Kenya tried not to smile as the two men resumed walking. She liked Lance, but sometimes it seemed that he lived in his own world. He was arrogant, but with just enough self-deprecation to make his arrogance more entertaining than irritating. He was smart, too, and had a great way with people, but he was sometimes blind to their needs. Since he had taken over the running of Sakkara, everything had to be done *his* way. He was happy to listen to other people's advice, and always seemed to give it a fair amount of consideration, but he rarely heeded it.

Warren, on the other hand, was less fun. He was pleasant enough, and always treated everyone with respect, but Kenya always had the feeling that he was a man you did *not* want to be around when he was angry. He didn't seem to have much of a sense of humor and hated not being taken seriously.

When she first met them Kenya thought that Warren and Lance despised each other, but she gradually realized that their constant sniping was just how they preferred to communicate.

She became aware that Lance was looking back at her. "You OK back there?"

"I'm fine. It's a bit dark, though."

They slowed a little, allowing her to catch up. They knew that Kenya's night-vision was very poor. Warren said, "Before he left, Razor was talking about light-enhancing contact lenses. What do you think, Kenya?"

"I don't like stuff going near my eyes. But it's a nice idea."

Lance said, "Well, we'll be putting in a lot more lighting. This far down we get most of our electricity from geothermal energy so it's practically free."

The first time Kenya had visited the Substation she'd hated it, but now she was merely uncomfortable at the thought of being a thousand feet underground inside a closed loop. She had been assured that the tunnel wasn't going to collapse, that it could withstand a direct nuclear strike, and that even if all the entrances and vents were sealed and the air-recycling was turned off, the inhabitants could survive for months without suffocating.

Ahead of her, the street curved very gently to the right, but in this part there wasn't much else to see. In time, there would be homes here, and stores. The northern side of the Substation felt like a busy city street at night, but now that the loop had been completed the people would spread out more.

"Did I tell you about the artificial windows?" Lance asked Kenya. "See, the idea is we get a bunch of giant screens, all around the outer wall, and onto them we project images of the outside. In real-time, too, not just static images. We can have a really high-resolution three-sixty-degree camera set up in a field somewhere, and we transmit the images back to here and project them onto the screens. So that way it feels more like we're on the surface. What do you think?"

"I think that the first spider that crawls across the lens is going to scare the pants off everyone."

Warren laughed, and Kenya wasn't sure how to react to that.

Ahead, Kenya could just about make out three people in a small cluster standing in the middle of the empty street. They all seemed to be looking straight up.

She looked, too, and spotted another person suspended from the ceiling next to one of the inverted pylons that kept the cable-car's cable in place. The beam of a flashlight flickered about near the base of the pylon.

One of the people below shouted up, "Anything?"

The woman above shouted down, "No! Wait... yeah, I see it. Whoever installed this one put one of the locking bolts on the wrong way around. So it's secure, but not tight to the ceiling. That's what's causing the rattle. Hold on..."

As she got closer, Kenya saw that the people below were holding tight onto a rope that was strung through a series of small loops set into the tunnel's ceiling: the woman above was suspended from that rope.

A few minutes later the woman was lowered to the ground, moments before the anti-clockwise cable-car rumbled past.

Warren said, "You cut that one close, Sorcha. What'd I tell you about the health and safety protocols? If that car had hit you..."

"I'd have been knocked aside and maybe got a bruise." The woman glanced at Kenya, then to Warren she said, "This is her?"

Lance said, "No, this is a completely different girl we brought along as a substitute. Kenya, Sorcha here is the build supervisor. And..." He looked around at the other workers, then put his hand on one of the men's shoulders. "This is Herizo. He is, apparently, an absolute genius when it comes to electronics."

The man was in his early forties, stocky and balding. He grinned at Kenya as he approached, but the grin faded for a moment when he saw her scarred face.

He regained his composure quickly. "Herizo Rakotoniaina," he said, and bowed a little.

Warren said, "Herizo is absolutely *useless* with languages. But he kept pointing to Madagascar on the map so we're guessing he's speaking Malagasy."

"*That's* why you brought me here? As a translator?"

"Yep. Why, what did you think we wanted you for?"

"Malagasy!" Herizo said, then added, more to himself than

anyone else, "I wish I knew what was going on here."

Speaking in her native language, Kenya said, "You don't speak English?"

Herizo's grin grew even wider, and for a second Kenya thought he was about to hug her. "No. I've never been able to learn another language. I figured out that they can't bring in a translator because they want this place to remain a secret."

"How did they hire you if you can't speak English?"

"I was in Lieberstan, in the platinum mine. I was there about five years, I think, when the New Heroes came and rescued us. I can't go back to Madagascar because... there's no one to go back to. Not now. Everyone I knew was killed in the war with the Trutopians."

Kenya's stomach clenched. *Oh Lord, no.* She didn't want to ask him, but she knew she had to. "Where were you from?"

"Ambovombe-Androy."

Relieve washed over Kenya like a flood. She had never been to that part of her homeland. "I'm from Fianarantsoa."

"How are we doing?" Lance asked. "Sounds like you can understand each other."

"We can," Kenya said. "But I don't think that this is the best use of my skills."

"Until your powers come back what else are you going to do?"

In Malagasy, Herizo said, "I have a thousand things to tell them... Another thousand to ask. You'll help me, won't you?"

Kenya stifled a sigh. "Sure. I'll help you."

"Thank you! First, why does this place exist? What's wrong with living in a normal town?"

"I have no idea." She nodded toward Warren and Lance. "They make the plans, but they don't always explain why."

Then both Warren and Lance pulled out their cellphones at

the same time, glanced at them, then at each other.

"Aw no...!" Lance said.

Warren was already running, heading back toward the cable-car station.

Lance said, "Kenya, stay put—Sakkara is under attack!" Then he, too, was gone, racing into the darkness after Warren.

"I can help!" she shouted after them, but they didn't stop, and she knew why. *No, I can't help. Without my powers—or my armor—I'm useless.*

Herizo watched them go, then turned to Kenya. "That was abrupt. Anyway... the food! Can you please explain to the chef that I don't like corn? Every day, he offers me corn and I shake my head but he gives it to me anyway. I never eat it but he still doesn't get the message."

"Sure," Kenya said. "I can do that."

The moment her visor's display showed the alarm from Sakkara, Renata ordered the team to head south-east toward Wichita. As they flew low and fast over the landscape, she told them, "We don't have enough fuel to make it back to Sakkara *and* defend the place. There's a hidden cache of fuel in Wichita. And there are weapons."

"Who's conducting the attack?" Stephanie asked.

"Unknown. The alarm cut off after a few seconds. No signals in or out since."

Alex asked, "Could it be Tuan? I can feel my own powers starting to come back—maybe he got a head-start?"

"It's possible," Renata said, "but speculation won't help us now. Steph, switch to a closed channel."

A moment later, Stephanie Cord's voice said, "I'm here. So, how bad is it really?"

"I don't know," Renata said. "It could just be a false alarm, but then they'd let us know. Once we refuel I want you to take everyone but Roman and Cassie to the Substation. But ditch your armor twenty kilometers out and go the rest of the way on foot—just in case someone's tracking us."

"So the three of you are going to face whatever it is without me? No chance."

"I'm in charge, Steph. Follow the chain of command."

"I can fly rings around you. And I know Sakkara inside out."

"This is not a democracy. Hold on—I want to bring in Cassie." Renata glanced back toward Cassandra, then tapped the side of her helmet with her index finger.

She heard Cassandra's voice inside her head. "What is it?"

Can you reach Sakkara from here? Find out what's going on.

"I'll try... Hold on..." A moment later, Cassandra said, "Oh no... It's Shadow."

The clone who went missing? How is that possible?

"I can't read him directly... but Colin is there."

Good. Patch him through.

"I'm not a switchboard, Renata! I can't link his mind to yours! Let me talk to him."

A few minutes later, Renata ordered the team to land. They touched down on the edge of a quiet country road and gathered around her.

"Sakkara has been compromised. There's been a few deaths, a lot of injuries. The assailants are Shadow and a superhuman called Krodin. Some of you will know that name. If you don't, well, we don't have time to go into it now. But he's dangerous, and ruthless, and practically unstoppable. If we go to Sakkara, we'll be killed. Just on his own, Shadow could wipe us out. We're going to need another plan of attack, another way to get to them."

Alia Cord asked, "What about the Substation? Is it safe?"

"Yes, so far. Cassie's been in contact with Warren and Lance. That's where you're heading next—from now on, that's our base of operations. So far, Krodin hasn't made any demands—when he does, we'll see if we can open a dialogue. But right now, we're not retaliating."

"This is crazy," Mina Duval said. "We can't just let his guy walk in and take over!"

Cassandra said, "I can't get inside Krodin's mind, but I saw Lance's *memories* of him. Believe me, going up against him is suicide. Even if everyone was at full power, we wouldn't be strong enough."

Renata said, "Tuan and the others have sided with Shadow. They know about Cassandra's telepathy so it's safe bet they're going to want to shut down that link. That means our top priority right now is keeping her alive."

"So we go into hiding?" Danny asked. "For how long? If we're waiting until our powers come back, then the others will get their powers too. We'll be no better off."

Mina turned to him. "When your powers return, you can alter time so that *our* powers come back before the clones'. The *other* clones, I mean," she added, looking toward Alex, Nathan and Roman.

Danny shook his head. "It doesn't work that way."

"All we can do right now is lie low," Renata said. "If we take the fight to them, we'll die."

Alex said, "This is bull! I didn't sign up to be a *coward*! We have weapons, and there are *eight* of us—we only have to take down Shadow and this Krodin guy!"

Cassandra said, "You're just not getting this, are you? Krodin is smarter, faster and stronger than all of us combined. They've already murdered six of Sakkara's guards. And *you* know what

Shadow is like: you can't reason with him. How favorably will he look on you when he learns you've defected?"

"We can't do *nothing*."

"We're *not* doing nothing, Alex," Renata said. "Cassie and Roman, you're with me. Stephanie, get everyone to the Substation and rendezvous with Lance. You too, Danny."

"My brother is trapped in there," Danny said. "I'm coming with you!"

"No, you're *not*. This is not a debate."

They flew in over Topeka, coming from the west on a high trajectory, with the setting sun behind them. Sakkara was on the east of the city, nestled among the hills. Once, only a few years ago, its existence had been known to only a handful of people. Now, three separate bus companies offered tours of the region that promised views of the fabled New Heroes' headquarters. Travel agents in Kansas featured the once-secret building on their posters.

Five hundred meters away from Sakkara, Renata slowed to a stop, and Roman and Cassandra fell into place on either side of her.

Into her radio, Renata said, "Lance. We're here."

"What can you see?"

"A lot of activity on the ground, on all sides. Looks like the army are preparing for a siege. They've got spotlights on the building..."

"They can't do anything until the hostages are clear," Lance said. "And Krodin knows that."

Roman grabbed Renata's arm, and pointed toward the building. "That's got to be him. On the roof."

Lance said, "You have better eyes than anyone else, Roman. How does he look?"

"Strong. He's carrying something... A football, I think. He's just standing on the edge, on the south side. He's put the football down at his feet and he's looking down at the tanks."

"OK. Cassandra, stay put. But keep trying to get inside his mind. Renata and Roman... Move in."

Shortly after they had moved into Sakkara, Solomon Cord had told the New Heroes, "Every mission could be your last. Every punch could be the one that kills you. Any bullet could have your name on it. This job is walking a tightrope while juggling chainsaws. In the dark. Do you understand that? You do *not* go into battle unprepared, or with your mind elsewhere. When you're fighting, there is *only* the fight. You set your everyday troubles aside. Put a pin in them for later, because moping about a broken heart is no defense against a psycho with a rocket-launcher, and worrying whether you left the stove on isn't going to help you find vital clues or defuse a bomb."

Later, Cord had simplified his message: "Anything you bring into the fight that isn't a weapon or a shield becomes a weapon or a shield for the *other* guy."

And now the "other guy" was Krodin. A legend. And possibly the first ever superhuman. Renata briefly wished again that her powers had returned, then set the thought aside as she and Roman drifted closer to the roof of the building.

"Slow and steady," she told Roman.

"I know. He needs to see us coming."

Now, she could see the man on the rooftop, illuminated by the army's spotlights from below. He was a little taller than average height, with long dark hair and a thick beard. He was bare-chested, wearing only a pair of jeans: his torso was slim but muscular, and seemed to be flawless.

He turned to watch them approach, and when they were five meters away they slowed, and hovered in place.

Renata unsealed her helmet and removed it. "Mister Krodin."

"Just Krodin," he said, peering at her. "And you are Renata Maria Julianna Soliz. You are seventeen years old, a superhuman. Though at this moment your powers are gone. You have come to plead for the lives of your friends and colleagues." He turned to Roman. "And *you* betrayed your brothers. I don't yet understand the technology that created you, boy—it might as well be magic to me. But then that's probably true for most people. We don't need to know how everything works, just trust that it does." He looked back toward Renata. "I've already spoken to McKendrick. Why should I speak to you? Or..." Krodin smiled. "Perhaps you're not an envoy, but a gift?"

"Wait, *what?*"

"When I ruled in Egypt it was common for enemies to offer me potential brides. You are magnificent, Renata Soliz, but several thousand years too young for me, I think!" He smiled at that.

Was that a joke? Renata wondered. "I'm asking you to stand down, Krodin. These are different times. We elect our leaders. No regime that was built on blood has ever lasted."

"*All* regimes are built on blood, girl. If you don't understand that, then you are not qualified to speak for your people. I was destined to rule, and so I shall."

Roman asked, "How? *How* were you destined to rule? I mean, where did that *come* from? Did you just wake up one day and think, 'I should rule the world.'? Or did someone *tell* you?"

"I am indestructible, indefatigable, and immortal."

The clone shrugged. "Well, me too. So far. *Anyone* who's still alive is immortal so far."

"Amusing." Krodin reached down and picked up the round

object next to his feet. He held up, making sure that it was in the beam of the brightest spotlight. "This woman is no longer immortal."

Over the radio, Lance's voice said, "What is that?"

Renata swallowed. "I.. I think it's Corporal LaPenna. He's holding her severed head."

"You're done," Lance said. "Get out of there."

Krodin said, "I see that you people do not comprehend this situation. There are no terms to discuss, no negotiations to be held. As of now, I rule. Anyone who fights me *will* die. This is a certainty. Renata Soliz, you and Cassandra Szalkowska will return to the Substation. If any of you approach me again, I will kill another hostage. Is that clear?"

"Yes," Renata said. "But if you understand people at all, you'll know that we will always resist a dictator. That's how the human race works."

Krodin smirked. "No. That's how the human race likes to *see* itself, as the noble underdog. The reality is that humans are craven, avaricious warmongers. At best. You understand only strength. In this time, strength comes in the form of fame or wealth. In my time, it was strength of command, or sometimes it was physical strength that the people respected. Such as *this*." He hefted the woman's head in his hand for a moment, then drew back his arm.

He threw Corporal Kaye LaPenna's head faster than Renata could see, but the result was clear.

It struck Roman in the chest with so much force that it tore straight through his armored, superhuman body.

Roman lived long enough for Renata to see the expression of shock on his face, then his body dropped, struck the sloping sides of Sakkara, and left a long, dark smear of blood as it half-tumbled, half-slid to the ground far below.

Chapter 5

"This is not hard to comprehend, McKendrick," Krodin said into the cell-phone. "I am sure that Renata relayed my message. It was quite clear. If you attack Sakkara or in any way interfere with my plans, every hostage here will die, instantly. Then we will come for you, and kill everyone in the Substation. I will start with the youngest, and force their parents to watch."

"I want to speak to Colin Wagner," Lance said.

"I'm sure you do. You may not. Now, I will ask you one more time, and if I don't get the right answer, another hostage will die. Do we have an understanding?"

"We do," Lance said. "But I'd like to meet you, so we can discuss this man-to-man."

"I've read the files on you, McKendrick. You have a gift for persuasion and coercion. It's unlikely that your charms will work on me, but I'm not stupid enough to take that chance." He ended the call, and tossed the cellphone to Shadow. "Walk with me."

They left the Operations room and made their way toward the gymnasium.

They passed Zeke on the stairs, and he hesitantly said, "Um... Krodin?"

The immortal stopped and turned back to him. "Yes?"

"You... I... Shadow told me that happened to Roman."

"I ended his betrayal," Krodin said. "Those who show me obedience and respect have nothing to fear, Zeke. Go about your duties."

The clone nodded, and continued up the stairs. To Shadow, Krodin said, "He allows his fear to rule him. And he is not alone in that."

"They lost their powers—that's unsettling for them. They'll

be all right in time. Assuming that they *have* time. Zeke's aging by the day."

"What about the missing children?" Krodin asked.

"The boy is Niall, Daniel Cooper's brother. He's hiding in one of the lower levels. He has the little girl with him. She's Colin's sister."

Krodin stopped walking. "His *full* sister?"

Shadow turned back to face him. "Yes, I think so."

"Then, like Colin, both of her parents were superhuman... Let her live, Shadow. The boy, too. Right now they pose no threat, and it will be interesting to see what abilities they develop. In time they might be strong allies."

"Or strong enemies," Shadow said.

"They live. Understand?"

Shadow nodded. "Sure. Yeah."

"And let them believe they are still hidden." Krodin resumed walking. "Caroline Wagner is highly intelligent so it suits us that she's preoccupied with concern for her daughter. Now... It's imperative that we eliminate all of the New Heroes before their abilities recover. Colin *should* be first, but he's the most well-known of them all so we'll save his death for when it will have the greatest impact... And for that, we will need someone who understands how things are done in this world."

"A politician? I could bring you the president..."

"No, not a figurehead. Someone who has experience with *real* power."

"You think it's time we freed Victor?"

"Not yet. Find a man called Maxwell Dalton."

Caroline Wagner whispered to her son, "She's safe. She must be. Otherwise they would have told us."

Colin wasn't sure whether his mother was trying to reassure

him or herself. He had wanted to talk to Shadow, to explain that his sister was missing, but he knew how much Shadow wanted to hurt him. The clone would be inclined to find Abigail and kill her in front of him.

Niall Cooper, too, was still missing. Caroline had said that Niall had been playing with Abigail when Krodin and Shadow attacked. "He adores Abigail—he'd never abandon her. And if he had, Shadow would have mentioned. We have to assume that Niall still has her, and they're safe."

Colin whispered back, "You're saying this because you don't want me to get killed trying to find her, aren't you?"

"Yes."

He looked at her for a moment. "I thought you'd be, y'know, more *scared*."

"You're forgetting that I was a superhero too, Colin. This not the first time I've seen someone I love in danger! Yes, I'm scared. And if anything happens to my baby—to *either* of my babies—I'm going to kill both Krodin and Shadow with my bare hands. But right now, I know you're safe, and I'm hoping that Abigail is. Until I know different, that's the way things are."

"Cassandra says that Dad's trying to find a way to get to us without them knowing."

From the far side of the gymnasium, Shadow called over, "And what way would that be? A secret tunnel? Hidden doors? Coming at night in a stealth helicopter?" He strode over toward Colin, and some of the other prisoners shuffled out of his way. "Did you forget I have enhanced hearing too?"

"Yeah, I did. Shadow, I don't understand why he's doing this. What does Krodin hope to gain?"

"The world."

"Why?"

"I don't ask questions."

Caroline said, "Maybe you should. He's already killed one of your brothers—maybe you'll be next. Do I have your permission to stand for a moment?"

The clone frowned at her. "OK..."

She got to her feet, and stepped up to him, so close that Colin had to suppress the urge to grab her arm and pull her back.

"You really are clones," Caroline Wagner said, peering closely at Shadow's face. "It's astonishing. It's like looking at Colin a year or two from now."

"Step back, you stupid woman," Shadow said.

"Genetically, I'm your mother. I might not have carried you to term, but half of your DNA comes from me so you will show me some *respect*, young man!"

Shadow looked as though he'd been slapped across the face, then he turned and walked away.

Caroline sat down next to her son.

"Well, that was a risk," Colin said. "You used your mom voice and your teacher voice at the same time. I didn't know you could *do* that."

"Neither did I."

Lance McKendrick got to his feet as the stern-looking woman strode from the car toward the Substation's north-west entrance. He had been sitting on an old wooden crate, watching the approaching cloud of dust kicked up by the car's wheels.

He hadn't slept more than a few hours since the attack on Sakkara, and right now it was all he could do to keep his eyes open.

The woman stopped in front of him wearing an expression that, it seemed to Lance, was daring him to say the wrong thing. She was dressed in crisp military fatigues and he tried to remember from her files whether she had ever officially left the army.

"So. Tell me everything," Amandine Paquette said.

"They arrived three days ago. Near as we can tell, Shadow remotely disabled Sakkara's defenses. He has almost identical abilities to Colin Wagner—he can control electricity."

"And they came from Mars?"

"*Returned* from Mars would be more accurate, but yes."

"How is that even possible? We should have detected their ship coming in."

Lance gestured toward the small building that housed the elevators leading down to the Substation, then followed Paquette inside. "I know. And I'm sure that Shadow knew that, too. There was a meteorite strike in Arizona three days ago. I've got people on the way to check it out now. I'm guessing that was their ship."

As the elevator doors closed, the woman said, "You're saying they didn't bother adjusting their craft's angle to slow its descent?"

"Either that, or they ditched the craft before it hit the atmosphere and Shadow flew them down. As far as we know, flight was never one of Krodin's abilities. Or Shadow just dropped him from orbit."

"You think Krodin could have survived that?"

"I threw an asteroid at him, and then sent him to Mars. A fall from orbit would barely bruise him."

"You should have sent him farther. Pluto, maybe. Or into the heart of the sun."

"Yeah, well, I was a kid. Besides, we were a bit preoccupied dealing with his personal army. The one *you* were leading."

She glared at him. "That wasn't me."

"Sure looked, smelled and *sounded* like you. Why are you

here, Amandine?"

"You're one of only a handful of people who've witnessed Krodin in action. That makes you our number-one asset right now. I want you to round up the others."

"I see what you're getting at, but no. I won't be doing that."

"That wasn't a suggestion. That was an order."

"I don't care. Hesperus and Cord are dead. Thunder and Roz are both off the radar now and I'm not going to put them in harm's way for no good reason. Same goes for Brawn. But you can have your old boyfriend Max if you want him."

Paquette flinched at that, and Lance said, "Oh, sorry. I forgot that was supposed to be a secret."

"No one knows where Max Dalton *is*. Do you?"

"Of course I do. Finding superhumans used to be my specialty, remember? I know exactly where he is, but the problem is that I know *what* he is, too."

"Meaning?"

"He's a liability. Max spent a huge portion of his adult life controlling other people's minds and he has never managed to shake the notion that he's destined for greatness. He believes that everything is still all about him, and that every idea he's ever had is a stroke of genius, that every choice he's ever made was the right one. You know he still stands by his decision to activate his power-siphon? If the kids hadn't stopped him, you'd be talking to a corpse right now."

The elevator gently bumped as it reached the bottom of the shaft. The doors opened and Paquette stepped out. "Get Max, bring him here."

Lance stayed inside the elevator. "I don't work for you."

"Then do it as a favor. For a friend."

"We were never friends, Amandine. But I'll do it anyway." He reached out toward the elevator's buttons. "You haven't seen

Krodin in action... He moves *fast*. And I'm not talking about his fighting skills. Things are going to change on this planet, and those changes are going to start happening *very* soon." The doors began to close, and Lance put out his hand to stop them. "I'm going to say something, and I want you to give it serious consideration."

The woman regarded him for a second, then said, "Go on."

"Krodin's greatest advantage over us is his ability to adapt to danger. The first time he was shot, the bullet wounded him. Next time, his skin was impervious to bullets. This is why Cross had to send someone to physically retrieve him from Mars: I used a teleporter to send him there, so it wasn't likely to work again."

"I know this. I've read the files. What's your point?"

"He's never experienced a nuclear explosion."

Chapter 6

"Lance!"

He snapped awake. "What? What is it?" For a second, he had no idea where he was, or what was happening. He blinked and looked around. He was in the New Heroes' StratoTruck, and from the sound of the engines it was moving at top speed.

Danny Cooper was crouched in front of him, a concerned expression on his face. "Thought you were never going to wake up!"

"What's happening?" Lance asked.

From the cockpit, Danny's step-father, Façade, shouted over his shoulder. "Bad news... Joshua Dalton has been attacked. Both legs shattered, almost choked to death. He's in critical condition, but he's expected to live."

Lance unclipped his seat harness and made his way forward. "How? And who?"

"He said it was Colin Wagner—he didn't know about the clones, so it must have been Shadow. Lance, Josh said that Colin was looking for *Max*. That's all the paramedics got out of him before he passed out. He's in surgery now—it'll be hours before he's conscious again."

"In Krodin's alternate reality Max was his right-hand man. So Krodin wants him too."

Danny said, "Lance, there's no way Josh knew where Max is hiding. You're the only one who knows that."

"Max could have *told* him. He always loved an audience, and Josh is pretty much the only person left on the planet who doesn't despise him. So Krodin guessed that Josh was Max's weak spot."

"But... *this* version of Krodin didn't know Max at all."

"Victor Cross did, and he would have told Shadow." To

Façade, he said, "We need to go *faster*."

"I'm already way past the red line, Lance. Our ETA is eight minutes, twelve seconds."

"OK..." Lance nodded as he absently chewed on his bottom lip. "Danny, tell me you brought your armor."

"It's right here. Want me to suit up?"

"Yeah. Load up its weapons, and make sure your jetpack's tank is full."

The moment the StratoTruck crossed into Doña Ana County, New Mexico, Danny threw himself out through the open hatchway and hit the thrusters on his jetpack.

The jetpack didn't have the range of the StratoTruck, but for short periods it could reach almost twice its speed. Danny hoped that would be enough.

He knew he wasn't the most proficient user of the Paragon armor. In fact, everyone else had more experience with it than he did.

He had just about mastered flying and landing. Using the weapons was a different matter.

The armor's in-built computer projected his target onto the inside of his helmet's visor, along with a grainy photo of what Max looked like now: he'd lost weight, allowed his hair to grow out and stopped coloring it, grown a beard, and was sporting thick-rimmed spectacles.

How does that fool anyone? Danny wondered. *He* looks *like he's wearing a disguise!*

Max was living under the identity of Conrad Kahale, a retired cosmetic surgeon. That occupation explained how he could afford such a large, expensive home.

Danny followed the computer's route at the fastest speed he could manage, though he knew that was a lot slower than

Stephanie Cord would have flown. *Should have brought her with us*, Danny thought, then corrected himself. *Should have brought them* all *with us!*

Max's home was a ranch a few miles to the east of the city of Las Cruces. It was a house large enough to be a hotel, surrounded by perfectly-sculpted gardens the size of football fields.

Danny dropped down to twenty meters as he neared the house, and slowed to half speed. It looked intact. If Shadow or some other superhuman had attacked, there would surely be signs of a struggle.

He circled the house twice, then slowed to a hover when he saw someone emerging through the front door.

Danny checked the figure against the image projected onto his visor. Into his communicator, he said, "Lance, I've got eyes on the target."

"He's seen you?"

"Yeah."

"All right. We'll be there in three. Tell him what's going on. But keep it vague, OK? Just enough that he understands the danger he's in."

"Will do."

Danny descended toward Max and set down directly in front of him. It was easily the smoothest and most professional landing he'd made so far, and he wished that Renata had been there to see it.

Max Dalton said, "So, the thing about going into *hiding*, Daniel, is that it only works if everyone involved keeps a low profile."

"I'm sorry, Max, but you're in danger and we need to get you out of here. Now."

"I'm not going anywhere. I'm done. And I'm not Max

anymore. Call me Conrad, or Doctor Kahale."

"The StratoTruck's on the way, and you have to come with us. I can't tell you why. Not here. But trust me, this is serious." He hesitated for a moment, then said, "They attacked your brother. He's in critical condition, but he's expected to pull through."

Max scratched at his gray beard. "How bad are we talking?"

"Broken arms, possible fractured skull. But he was conscious when the paramedics—"

"I mean, how bad is the danger to *me*? If they were only after Josh, what's that got to do with me?"

Wow, Danny thought, *he really is a self-obsessed jerk*. "We believe they were looking for you, and tortured Josh to find out where you were hiding."

Max shrugged. "Josh knows where I am but he'd never tell." He gestured back toward the house. "Besides, I've got weapons in there that could take down a charging elephant wearing body-armor. Who am I supposed to be scared of?"

Danny sighed. "All right. You *really* want to know? It's Krodin."

The color drained from Max's already-pale face, and for a second Danny thought he was going to collapse. "Please tell me that's not true."

"I wish I *could* tell you that. He's back, and he's taken Sakkara. We lost our powers when we fought Victor Cross, and they haven't returned yet. There's no one on the planet who has the power to stop him. But you spent time with him in the alternate reality—that's not much, but it's all we have."

They turned toward the house as the familiar whine of the StratoTruck's engines grew louder, and in seconds it had passed over the roof and was coming in to land ten meters from them.

Max said, "Give me five minutes to gather some things."

"For all we know, we don't *have* five minutes," Danny said.

Lance was already making his way down the StratoTruck's ramp, and he called out, "Let's go! *Now*, Max!"

Then he stopped, staring at something past Max.

Danny turned to see one of the clones drifting slowly toward the ground, coming toward them.

"Daniel Cooper," Shadow said. "So how's that broken jaw of yours?" He settled down on the lawn and walked up to Danny. "New teeth, huh? Nice." He looked toward the StratoTruck, where Façade was now standing next to Lance. "Let's see if I can remember the files in Sakkara... You're Hector Miller, otherwise known as Paul Joseph Cooper, otherwise known as Facade. And you're Lance McKendrick. Which means that this old guy has to be the man I'm looking for, Max Dalton. Yeah..." He smiled at Max. "Your brother sold you out. He resisted at first, played the hero, but the human body can only take so much pain. So, you're coming with me."

Lance said, "No, he's not."

Shadow turned back to him. "Oh, you have a gun! Well, unless you've got special magic bullets in it, don't waste your time. I could kill all of you quicker than it would take for me to blink. And I blink *fast*, believe me. But the boss says that you all get to live for now, so that's how it is." He almost playfully punched Danny in the shoulder. "But you *will* be dead before your powers return."

"I know why Krodin wants Max," Lance said. "We can't let that happen."

"You're going to *fight* me for him?" Shadow asked, grinning. "Good. If you get killed in battle Krodin will understand."

Danny said, "You're terrified of doing anything to upset him, aren't you? Coward."

"It's really not like that. You haven't met him. Krodin was

born to rule this world. Sure, so far it's taken him four thousand years longer than it was supposed to, but ruling was always his destiny." Shadow turned in a slow circle, looking toward the horizon. "Just think where we'd be now if he hadn't been taken out of his own time, if he'd been allowed to rule." To Max and Lance, he said, "You two understand that, right? In that alternate reality, Krodin had only been there for six years and he already had machines that were far in advance of *this* primitive culture. All it takes is one ruler, with the right vision. Max here gets it, don't you? Victor Cross did, too. And so did Ragnarök. See, the universe *wants* someone like Krodin because the human race is supposed to be united under one leader, not fractured into two hundred countries, each with its own separate laws and customs. *That* is so unbelievably stupid and pointless it makes me think that maybe you actually *deserve* extinction."

Max said, "I do get that. But—"

"We're done here," Shadow said. "You're coming with me whether you want to or not. But it'll be a lot simpler and much less painful if you cooperate."

"I'm with you," Max said. He turned back to Lance. "In that other reality... Yes, Krodin was a despot but we never saw the finished product. We didn't see how his world would have turned out after the war. And it would have been the *final* war. Picture that, Lance. A united world means no more wars, no more armies. Peace, at last."

"No matter how many people have to die to achieve that goal?"

"Yes! It's horrible, but sometimes the innocent have to suffer, for the greater good. That's why I sided with Krodin then, and why I'm going to do it again. He has the vision and the will—and the power—to unite the human race. That's something that no one has ever managed to achieve."

Façade said, "Max, look at the people who came the *closest* to that goal! Stalin, Pol Pot, Mussolini, Hitler... Their idea of a united human race meant exterminating the parts they didn't like. Krodin is worse than all of them, and once he's in power, there's no getting rid of him. He can't be assassinated, and we won't even have the luxury of knowing that one day he'll die of old age!"

Lance raised his gun, and aimed it at Max's head. "You side with Krodin and I will shoot you right here and now!"

Max let out a long sigh. "Seriously. Lance, you need to grow up and see the real world. We know we can't beat Krodin, but maybe we can guide him in the right direction. Didn't that occur to you? You all think I'm an egotist, but you're wrong. My job is to safeguard the human race by any means necessary. If that means I'll be signing a contract with the devil, then hand me the pen."

"Don't make me do this, Max."

Danny said, "Lance, come on! Just let him go. We don't need him."

"Krodin wants Max on his side because he used to be a telepath," Lance said. "Sure, it's been thirteen years since he lost his powers, but before that he'd spent a lot of time with people who were massively wealthy or politically important."

"Yeah, but you're not going to shoot someone just because he knows other people's secrets!"

"Danny, the rich and powerful got that way because they know how to hold on to their money and power—and most of the people Max worked with are still around. That means that all their dirty little secrets are still relevant. With the information that Max picked out of their brains Krodin could take down a dozen of the world's most powerful nations within a week."

Danny shook his head. "No, you can't justify it like that! There are no secrets that that are so important they're worth more than a man's life!"

"This is not about some politician having an affair," Lance said, "or which executive embezzled money from their company. We're talking about things like nuclear codes and the whereabouts of the last surviving doses of the smallpox virus."

Max laughed. "You think *that's* why Krodin wants me on his side? No, it's because he knows I can make the hard choices when I need to. Lance, you and I never have seen eye-to-eye, and maybe we never will, but I do *know* you. You're not a killer. You won't shoot me because you know there'll be no going back. That would be opening a door that can never be closed again."

Lance said, "This is your last warning."

Max smiled. "I'll take my chances with Krodin. Maybe one day we'll meet again, under better circumstances. We'll look back at this and laugh."

"No. We *won't*. Come on, man! Don't force my hand."

"I thought you already *gave* me my last warning. You won't shoot me, because you *can't*. And that's where you and I differ. If I thought I could save a hundred people by killing one, I'd do it, because *somebody* has to have the guts to make that sort of decision. Does that make me a monster? Maybe. But I can live with that. I can *be* that monster if that's what's best for humanity."

Lance said, "And so can I." He squeezed the trigger and the gun boomed.

Shadow staggered backwards, stared down at his blood-splattered clothing as Max Dalton collapsed to the ground.

No... No, please... Danny thought. *He might be all right—*

maybe the bullet just wounded him! Danny saw the blood seeping through Max's shirt, the pool of blood on the ground spreading out from under him. Max's dead eyes staring up at the sky.

"Straight through the heart," Lance said. "He wouldn't have felt it."

Shadow glared at Lance, his fists clenched. "You... I am going to kill you so *slowly*—"

Lance put his gun away. "Your boss wants us alive, for now. You said so yourself. So fly away, kid. Go tell him what just happened here."

The clone looked around at them all a final time, then darted up into the air. In seconds he was gone.

Danny fell to his knees next to Max's body. *I can't believe he did that... He just murdered Max!*

Behind him, Façade said, "You didn't have to kill him."

"Yeah, I did. And you know it." Lance turned back toward the StratoTruck. "Losing Max will slow Krodin down, but it won't stop him. If we're to survive this, we're going to need a miracle."

Chapter 7

"You look busy," Brawn said to Sergeant Rosenblum. Half-way between Brawn's new accommodation and the town, she was leaning against the side of her car, staring at her cellphone.

She looked up at him. "I was waiting for you. How's the new place?"

"It's OK." One of the sergeant's friends had agreed to let Brawn live in an old barn in exchange for his help around the farm. His initial plan—to live in a tent in the back garden of his family home—quickly proved to be a bad idea. Everyone knew where he lived and the house was quickly besieged with souvenir hunters. "I've repaired the roof, filled most of the gaps in the walls. It's not quite a palace yet, but it's getting there."

Brawn crouched and peered into the patrol car's back seat. "Aw, no Amita today?"

"It's ten in the morning, on a school day. The school board tends to frown on fifth-graders making their own schedules."

Brawn rolled his eyes and tutted. "Fascists."

"*I'm* on the school board."

"Of course you are. It wouldn't be Tuesday without me putting my foot in my mouth."

"It's Wednesday."

"See?"

The sergeant's smile didn't last long. "I'm not just here for a chat. Something strange is going on and I figure you might be able to make some sense of it. Flights over the mid-west are being canceled or diverted, and there are rumors of media blackouts and troop movements. Officially, no one is saying much, but *off* the record... there's a name that seems to have a lot of important people panicking: Krodin. Does that mean anything—"

"Irena, you need to leave," Brawn said. "Not just the state— you need to leave the *country*. As soon as possible. Take Amita and your mom. And *my* mom. Go to Europe, or maybe Africa would be better."

"You're serious?"

"I've seen what Krodin can do. He is relentless and merciless. Within a couple of months this entire country will be under his control."

Sergeant Rosenblum shook her head. "Gethin, I can't *leave*— I have a duty of care!"

"Then send our moms away, with Amita." He frowned for a moment. "If money's a problem I can talk to someone. He'll cover all the costs. He owes me, anyway. Actually, I'll get him to transfer you overseas. Somewhere you'll be safer."

"OK, now you're starting to sound crazy!"

Brawn knelt down in front of her and put his hands on her shoulders as he stared into her eyes. "I wish I was. Krodin is the most powerful and dangerous superhuman who ever lived. If you thought that the Trutopian war was bad, well, that was nothing compared to what's coming next."

Moving in almost complete darkness, Niall Cooper squirmed through the conduit. He was upside-down: the conduit's smooth metal floor didn't offer much in the way of handholds, but its ceiling was lined with small, regularly-spaced bolts that he was using to pull himself along. His shirt and jeans were had been torn almost to shreds from sharp edges and protruding studs within Sakkara's countless conduits and ducts, and were covered in a thick black oil from squirming under and around— and sometimes through— the building's machinery.

He'd loosely tied a thin but strong nylon rope around his left ankle. He'd knotted the rope every half-meter, and the other end had been secured to a strong water-pipe. When he reached the conduit's exit, he'd tie this end of the rope to something else. That way, next time he had to use the conduit, he'd be able to pull himself along the rope.

Resting on his stomach was a plastic water-bottle—half-full—and a slowly-thawing frozen burrito. He wasn't sure that it was safe to eat the burrito without heating it up again, but he didn't care. It was food and he and Abigail hadn't eaten since the previous morning.

Several days ago—he wasn't sure how much time, exactly, had passed—when the alarms sounded, he'd known what to do: find a safe place and stay hidden until someone he knew and trusted came to find him. He'd been in the playroom, watching TV, with Abigail carefully drawing on a nearby wall with a crayon. The playroom had originally been a medium-sized office, but Caroline Wagner had baby-proofed it and bribed the teenagers to paint cartoon characters on the walls. They'd brought in a pair of comfortable old sofas and a box of toys for Abigail. Niall didn't love the place, but it was better here in Sakkara than in the Substation where his mother lived. Officially, he lived there too, but Rose Cooper understood that it was important for Niall to spend time with his father and brother. He knew she wouldn't have been happy to learn that most of that time he spent wandering alone through the building, or up on the roof flicking peas over the edge, or trying to avoid Colin's mother, who seemed to have an endless supply of baby-sitting jobs or homework.

Then the lights and power went and the alarms blared so loud and suddenly that Abigail burst into tears. The playroom was one of the few rooms with a window, and for that Niall had been grateful because the emergency lighting hadn't kicked in.

He'd scooped up Abigail and held her tight as he ran through the corridors. He took a chance with the stairs, racing down them two at a time, all the while trying to comfort the two-year-old.

Months ago, he'd discovered that the door to one of the computer rooms on level three didn't quite lock properly. He pushed hard against the door with his left shoulder while pulling up on the handle, and the door clicked open.

The room was a maze of shelving units packed floor-to-ceiling with computer boxes, all linked to each other with so many cables it looked like the lair of some giant robotic spider. Usually, the computer boxes were alive with flashing lights and the occasional click or beep on top of the normal constant humming sound. Now, they were silent and dark. But he'd chosen this room for a reason: all the shelving units bore individual numbers that had been applied with luminous paint to better enable the technicians to find their way around and swap out different components without having one hand hindered by holding a flashlight.

Niall had set Abigail down and whispered, "We're playing a game, OK?"

She said, "OK," but he wasn't sure whether she understood or was just copying him.

"We have to be quiet, and you have to do exactly what I say. Every time you do, you'll get a star. But if you make too much noise, or you run away, or you don't do what I tell you, you lose a star."

In the bright-green glow of the luminous paint, he saw Abigail smile and nod.

"Good girl." He reached up to her face and wiped away a tear. "We got a little fright, didn't we? You know what we should do? Later on, when your daddy gets back from work, we should tell him that the alarm bell is too loud."

"*Very* too loud," Abigail said.

Niall scooped her up again, and cautiously began to move forward. "That's right. Now... should we go exploring? No, don't try to grab the cables! We really don't want two tonnes of computer stuff crashing down on us, do we? Over this way there's the entrance to a, uh, a magic tunnel that's called a maintenance duct."

Abigail said, "Quack!"

He held back a laugh, and said, "Not *that* kind of duck, Abby."

Now, as he forced his way through the conduit back towards the forgotten room, he tried not to think about what might happen if either he or Abigail became ill.

So far, he'd managed to keep her occupied and fed, and reasonably clean—she had been toilet-trained very young, and for that he would be eternally grateful—but they couldn't stay in the hidden room forever. Eventually, he'd be too big to fit through all the access panels, conduits, ducts and maintenance shafts.

But before that happened, they'd run out of food. The plastic-wrapped burrito he was now pushing ahead of him was the last of a package of twelve he'd found in the kitchen's largest freezer. He could open another twelve-pack, but there were only two left. If the assailants were paying attention, they'd notice that the food was disappearing faster than it should be.

The final leg of his journey was the climb. He hated this part, and not just because if he fell he'd break a leg, if not both. If he fell here and was trapped, there was no way anyone would hear him calling for help. And that would mean that Abigail... He didn't allow himself to finish that thought.

He calculated that this shaft ran down through the very

center of Sakkara. If that was correct, it meant this was the main pylon around which everything else had been built. It was a concrete cylinder three meters in diameter, with a meter-wide hollow core.

He wasn't sure *why* the core was hollow, and he didn't care. What was important was that at some stage someone had cut a large hole through it on level five, and there was a similar hole near the bottom. Niall had found a long rope and tied one end to a girder near the hole on level five.

That first trip down, lowering himself hand-over-hand into the darkness and with Abigail tied securely to his chest, was something that Niall would remember for the rest of his life.

But it had worked, and down there, beneath the lowest basement in Sakkara, they had found a small, forgotten cluster of rooms. Niall supposed that they had been used as living quarters by the builders: all of the rooms were empty, but the largest was big enough for several bunk-beds, and there was also a small kitchen and several offices.

A dozen trips back up the central core—climbing the rope so often had given Niall's hands rock-hard callouses—to retrieve blankets and pillows enabled him to create a reasonably comfortable hiding place for himself and Abigail.

He knew this couldn't go on much longer. As he eased himself down through the central core yet again, he thought, *If I can get to the roof, I can signal for help. There's bound to be someone watching.*

But I'll have to take Abby with me. If I get shot or something no one will ever find her.

The thought of Abigail being trapped forever inside the forgotten rooms was one Niall didn't want to contemplate. *We can climb up, and wait near the top until I'm sure it's night-time. Then we can sneak up to the roof and hide up there. Yeah.*

That's what we'll do. Tomorrow. We'll eat tonight, get some sleep, and we'll go tomorrow.

Or maybe the day after.

On the eleventh night of the occupation of Sakkara, a small team led by Amandine Paquette attempted to storm the building.

Information provided by Cassandra's mind-scans told them the location of every person in the building, and Paquette was familiar with its layout. She was convinced that her people could use the sewer tunnels to gain access.

Once the hostages had been freed, the military would engage with Krodin's forces long enough for the nearby city of Topeka to be evacuated.

And then Sakkara would be obliterated by a nuclear strike.

Lance first learned about Paquette's plan on the morning of the twelfth day, when her body and the bodies of every member of her team were tossed from the roof of Sakkara.

The sick feeling in the pit of his stomach hadn't eased since the incident outside Max Dalton's safe house, and only grew stronger as he read the reports on the attack.

Warren Wagner was waiting for him in the Substation's briefing room. "You heard?"

"Yeah," Lance said, tossing the reports onto his desk.

"This is your fault, Lance."

"What? I warned Amandine not to go near Sakkara!"

"You killed the man she loved. Why would she ever listen to your advice? If we'd had Max with us—"

"If *nothing*. He would have been useless. Worse, he would have advocated switching to Krodin's side. You know what he was like."

Through clenched teeth, Warren said, "My wife and my son

and my *daughter* are trapped in there! You're in charge—you get them out!"

"Krodin is riding a thin rail here. He knows that if he pushes too hard—say, he sends Shadow to wipe out Congress—then we're going to start hearing the term 'acceptable losses.' They will nuke Sakkara with all the hostages still inside. And if things look bad enough, they won't even wait to evacuate Topeka. So he understands that. If he wants to seize control he has to attack everything at once, take down the entire infrastructure in one go. He can't do that until the other clones regain their powers. But if he waits that long, *our* people will regain theirs. I'm sure he's already figured out that he needs someone who understands how the powers work."

"You're talking about Victor Cross," Warren said.

"Correct."

"There's no way that even *Krodin* can get to him in the Cloister, so—"

Lance raised his eyes. "What? Are you *kidding* me? What do you mean, there's no way? Krodin survived three decades alone on *Mars*. What makes you think that *anyone* on the planet is safe from him?" He forced himself to calm down. "It's a moot point, anyway, because Cross isn't in the Cloister any more. I moved him."

"Where to?"

"Somewhere no one but me knows about. Victor Cross is the mastermind behind bringing Krodin back, so there's no way I'm letting those two get together to swap plans."

"You shouldn't have done that without informing us, Lance."

"I've told you before. This is not your show. It's mine, and I'm doing things my way."

Lance looked again at the reports on his desk, and wondered how long it would be before the story reached the media. When that happened, he might as well hand Krodin the world on a plate. He dropped into his chair.

He needs an army he can control. The quickest way to get an army is to hire one. For that, he needs money. He would have got billions from Max, but that's *out the window. So what does he do?*

What would I do if I was an immortal tyrant?

He could take out the government, but that's not enough to put him in a position of power. There'd be chaos on the streets and I don't think he wants that.

Aloud, he said, "He wants them to love him."

Warren asked, "What was that?"

"Just trying to get inside Krodin's mind. If I can think like him then I can *out*-think him."

We need to give Krodin just enough leeway that he thinks his plan is working... So we keep trying to negotiate, make him believe that we might be willing to compromise. Otherwise he'll lose his cool and go on a rampage. Then there might be no stopping him.

He was aware that any plans he made could—and possibly would—be subverted by the authorities. They didn't like handing power over to Lance any more than they wanted to hand it to Krodin.

Again, his thoughts returned to the option of a tactical nuclear strike. There was no guarantee that it would actually kill Krodin, and that was probably the only reason the government hadn't yet ordered it.

Lance sat back. "Huh."

"What now?" Warren asked.

"I wonder... does Krodin actually want to *have* power, or does he just want to *acquire* it?"

"What's the difference?"

"It's like... going fishing but throwing everything back. Some people love the thrill of the hunt a lot more than they care about whatever it is they're hunting. This is just an idea, but, well, suppose we go to Krodin and pin a badge on his chest that says, 'Leader of the World.' Would that satisfy him?"

"Would it satisfy you, if you were him?"

Lance shook his head. "Probably not, no. Might be worth a shot, though. We have to do *something*."

Chapter 8

On the edge of Sakkara's roof, Krodin stared at the multitude of vehicles below, a sea of green-painted metal illuminated by the dawn light. He had yet to personally see such machines in action, but Shadow had shown him what he'd called an "awesome war flick" so he understood the principle of munitions.

Now, he'd had enough of waiting. His old life was long gone, and his long isolation on Mars was a memory he'd prefer to replace.

This was a poisoned, crowded world but it *could* be made right again. The humans had repeatedly demonstrated that they were incapable of ruling themselves, so he must rule them.

The dead clone—Roman—had asked him how he knew that he had been destined to rule. Krodin hadn't been able to answer at the time, but he had since given the matter a lot of consideration.

He knew in the same way that he knew the sun was warm on his face, in the same way he knew which way was up and which was down. He knew because his heart told him that was how things should be. The human race needed a leader, and the universe or the gods or what some of them called "Mother Nature" had brought him into existence to *be* that leader.

But a ruler needs the people to fear him or love him. And to reach that point, the people must first know him.

In times past, news of a warrior's deeds could travel no faster than a galloping horse. It would take weeks or even months for the news to reach every outcrop, every island, every tiny village.

But this electronic world was faster, so much faster. Shadow had told him that a man could fall from a ladder and news of his falling would reach the far side of the world before the man had hit the ground. That was an exaggeration, of course, but it served to illustrate the truth.

I will give the humans a reason to know me.

He peered down, over the edge. Below, the blood-smear left by Roman's body was starting to fade. Beyond that, a wide disc of empty land surrounded by a ring of military vehicles, all with their weapons aimed at this fortress.

Then Krodin smiled, and said, "Little boy, I could sense your presence the moment I emerged through the doors. You've been hiding in the lower levels, believing that we didn't know you were there. And now you're wondering how you will get away from here. There's no easy way down." He turned, and looked toward the StratoTruck's hangar. Huddled just inside the doorway was a ten-year-old boy. He was shoe-less, sitting cross-legged in the shadows, his arms around a sleeping infant. Their clothing was filthy and torn. "You are Niall Cooper, and the girl in your charge is Abigail Wagner. You must be hungry. Go inside, eat, wash, rest. My people will not stop you."

"Will you let us go? *All* of us?"

"No. If I do, your armies will attack."

"So what? You're supposed to be indestructible. They can't harm you. Let us go and this will all be over."

"You are too young to understand. Just take the girl inside and feed her."

Niall started to move towards the stairs, then stopped. "Mister Krodin... Sometimes the good guys have to do bad things, if it'll get rid of an even worse thing. There's a show I watch, and one time X-Roy had to hurt his friend the Magnus so that he could stop The Reality Welder. He's this really bad guy who wants to turn everyone into mushrooms. OK, I know it sounds stupid when you say it out loud, but the thing is, the soldiers out there might decide that it's better to lose the hostages than let you go free."

"I'm aware of that. But you humans are so poorly governed that such a decision will take weeks or months. Laws must be drafted, opposed, re-drafted, debated about endlessly... That's why you *need* a strong leader." Krodin again looked down over the edge. "Go inside, Niall Cooper. In a few moments it won't be safe for you out here."

He jumped.

Sakkara's basic shape was a truncated pyramid. An ordinary human would not have been able to clear its sloping sides and land on the ground, but to Krodin such a jump was second-nature.

He landed heavily, on his feet, and was striding toward the tanks before the dust-cloud had settled.

The first shell struck him square in the chest and exploded with such force that it slammed him back against the side of the building.

Before he was back on his feet, he'd been hit eight more times.

He closed his eyes and began to run.

Bullets peppered his skin, and he shrugged them off. A pair of soldiers launched a high-arcing bomb that detonated at his feet and drenched him with a white-hot burning jelly. He was impressed with the substance that he later learned was napalm. But he was even more impressed with the next weapon, a fast-burning powder called Thermite. Two canisters of Thermite struck him as he reached the first of the tanks, and he watched with fascination as the powder actually burned through the tank's shell.

A man with a hand-held pistol leaped from the burning tank and took a moment to pause and shoot at Krodin, but he barely noticed him.

Nearby, a second tank was racing toward him faster than a team of the finest Arabian steeds. Krodin stood his ground, and watched it approach. He had never been struck by a tank before so this would be an interesting new experience.

It hit him hard, crushed him beneath its metal treads, then, before he could recover, it reversed its direction and passed over him again. On its fourth pass, Krodin rolled out of its path, grabbed hold of one of the tread's links and wrenched it free. The rest of the tread unspooled itself and lay dead on the ground like a giant metal worm. The tank itself could no longer move in a straight line. He was almost disappointed to see that such a formidable machine could be so easily crippled.

Individual soldiers shot at him with all manner of projectiles. Flying craft shredded the ground around him with their cannons, or dropped powerful explosives in his path. Tanks attempted to shoot at him or crush him.

He fought on, mostly oblivious to the shouts and screams and gun-fire and rumbling engines, always moving west, towards the city.

He hadn't actually decided yet what he was going to do when he reached it, but he was sure it would be spectacular.

In his time, a city was a gathering of perhaps two thousand people. Shadow had told him that Topeka's population was over fifty times as many. "And Shanghai in China has about twenty-four *million* people. That's about twice the entire world population back in your day."

"You say that with *pride*, Shadow," Krodin had replied. "Unfettered population growth is not an achievement. It is a failure."

Ahead of him a wide ribbon of gray stone stretched toward the city. He'd seen this road before, when Shadow had carried him down through the atmosphere towards Sakkara. Then, the road had been dense with vehicles of all colors. Now, there were far fewer vehicles and they were all green.

For a moment, he toyed with the idea of continuing to fight the humans just to see how long they'd keep fighting back. *Perhaps they never* will *stop*, he thought. *Perhaps they'll keep fighting for as long as even one of them can carry a weapon.*

He vaulted over the barrier at the side of the road and strode on, ignoring the continuous rattle of bullets against every part of his body, and the soldiers darting out from between the vehicles and targeting him with their flame-throwers.

Before he had left Sakkara, Shadow had handed him some clothing. "Part of the New Heroes' uniform. The pants. They're bullet-proof, fire-proof, resistant to tears."

"Why would I need such a thing?" Krodin had asked.

"Because the scariest thing humans can imagine is their children seeing a naked adult body. You want them to follow you, don't go walking around in the nude."

"That does not make any sense."

"What can I tell you? Individually, they're usually OK. But collectively, they're *insane*."

Gradually the attacks from the aircraft stopped, the tanks were firing less and less often, and even the gunfire faded, until the soldiers simply abandoned their transports and Krodin found himself walking alone on the road, with few military vehicles ahead.

On the edge of the city, a soldier carrying a sword jumped out at Krodin from behind a large, eight-wheeled vehicle and swung the weapon at him. He caught it by the blade and twisted it out of the man's grip. "I will keep this."

He walked on a few steps, then turned back. The soldier—a young, brown-skinned man—had remained where he was. "You have not run away."

"I..."

For the first time, Krodin looked back the way he had come. The sky to the east was dense with smoke—fires from the burning tanks.

"Speak," Krodin said to the soldier.

"I... I was ordered to stop you."

"Why?"

"Because you are a threat to the United States."

He smiled. "Yes, I am a threat. Your united states..." He sighed. "The name is a contradiction, one country composed of many separate smaller countries. You humans *always* seek out the thorniest path, don't you? Your united states—and all other states—will be one nation. One world, under one ruler."

Another human approached. This one was female, and the insignia on her collar suggested that she held a higher rank than the male. "Captain Corrinne Salconi, United States Infantry, ETD. Sir, you are trespassing on US soil and you are hereby ordered to depart immediately."

Krodin looked toward the city. It was silent, and felt abandoned. This was not what he wanted.

To the woman, he said, "You know who I am, so you know that I am not of this time. I don't understand much of what happens here... But my young associates have shown me television, and the internet. Where are the cameras? The reporters?"

"That's what you want?" The woman asked. "An audience? The city has been evacuated and we've initiated a blanket-ban on all media coverage." She stepped closer to him, and in a tone that he guessed was supposed to be intimidating, she said, "We do not give in to terrorists' demands. Private Endoso!"

The young male soldier barked, "Sir!"

"Show this man the door."

"Sir?"

"Take out your sidearm, soldier, and blow his diseased head clean off his shoulders."

Krodin said, "That won't work. And it's clear that I've not yet done enough to gain the world's attention. If I kill you all, your superiors will find it harder to ignore me."

Captain Salconi said, "You might be indestructible, but you'll find *we're* no pushover."

Krodin put his hand through her neck.

As her body collapsed to the ground, the male soldier turned and started to run: he managed four steps before he was sliced in two with his own sword.

Krodin smiled to himself. It had been a long time since he'd used a sword. He again glanced back the way he had come. Countless soldiers waited between here and Sakkara. He would introduce the sword to every one of them.

Chapter 9

The general and her team had arrived in the Substation at midnight and demanded to see Lance. He was surprised to find that the general was younger than him. Her uniform bore no insignia but the stars at her collar. She had a slim folder tucked under one arm.

She shook his hand. "General Anna Mendes, ETD." She sat down opposite him without being asked, and kept the folder on her lap. "Where is Victor Cross?"

Lance smiled at her across his desk. "That's need-to-know only, General."

"Believe me, we need to know. You saw what Krodin did in Kansas this afternoon."

"I've read the report. What action are you taking?"

"That's above your clearance level."

"I figured," Lance said. "I'd say there's a lot of important people in expensive suits or sharply-pressed uniforms shouting at each other and panicking right now, because no one knows *what* to do. I'm guessing that's where *you* come in. The report said that the first soldier he killed was Captain Salconi, ETD. General, I know a little about the military and I've never heard of ETD."

"Extraordinary Threat Division. We keep a low profile. The division was established twenty-five years ago in response to Krodin's first appearance. It was put on ice twelve years later after the battle with Ragnarök. Revived three years ago following the incident in California."

"And where was your division during the Trutopian war?"

"We were on the *battlefield*, Mister McKendrick." She paused for a second. "Where were *you*?"

Lance raised his left leg and pulled back the cuff of his jeans, revealing his prosthetic leg. "I think you'll find that *this* is a good excuse for not being a soldier."

The general raised her right leg and did the same. Her own prosthetic was almost identical to Lance's. "I know a lot of veterans who would disagree with you." She lowered her leg again. "We had spy-drones watching Krodin for the entire attack. In the four hours and twenty-three minutes between killing Captain Salconi and returning to Sakkara, he did not stop moving."

"Yeah, he's pretty relentless."

"No, Mister McKendrick, you don't understand. We've analyzed the footage in detail. Krodin was in constant motion that entire time. Didn't stop to take a breath, to eat or drink, or look around. He moved in the fastest and most efficient path through our soldiers. Even when *they* were moving. That is an incredibly complex series of calculations. Do you know of the Traveling Salesman puzzle?"

"Remind me."

"You're a salesman with a route that takes you to a dozen different places. How do you work out the most efficient route that visits each location only once?"

Lance shrugged. "I'd start with the nearest location and then move on to the next nearest. But you're going to tell me that's not necessarily going to be the shortest or most efficient way... And, I guess, it gets harder if the target locations are moving because you have to take into consideration each one's speed and vector. Plus they sure won't be moving in a straight line..." Lance straightened up. "General, are you about to tell me that Krodin somehow worked out the perfect path to inflict the greatest number of deaths in the shortest time?"

The young woman nodded. "Yes. But I don't think that he worked it out. I think he just *knew* it. Instinctively."

"The report said that more than four thousand—"

"Four thousand, eight hundred and seven men and women died yesterday. Almost all of them killed by a single stab-wound with the same weapon, a ceremonial sword that belonged to one of the soldiers. We've estimated that Krodin was hit by gunfire over two hundred thousand times. There is now so much lead on that battlefield that it's in danger of seeping into the water-table."

"That... doesn't sound like it should be your highest priority right now."

"It's not. That was just to illustrate the extent of the situation. To prepare you for something that so far is known only to a very select number of people." The general placed the slim folder on the desk removed a photograph and pushed it over to Lance.

It was an aerial photo of what he first thought was the crater-marked surface of the moon. And then he looked closer. "Wait... those lines at the edges... they're *roads*." He raised his head and stared at the general. "What scale is this? What did you *do*?"

"The official report ends with Krodin returning to Sakkara. For reasons that will become clear, it deliberately omits the next phase of our retaliation. Krodin and Shadow began to loot the bodies of the fallen for weapons and supplies. The president signed the order for the obliteration of Sakkara and its surrounding regions through the use of high-yield non-nuclear weapons. Each weapon is designed to inflict maximum damage with no radioactive fallout: you don't poison your own breadbasket."

Lance jumped to his feet, still staring at the photo. "The hostages..."

"The city of Topeka is *gone*, Mister McKendrick. Because it had been evacuated, no civilian lives were lost in the process, for which we can be thankful. Now look at the picture again. About two inches right of center."

Lance saw a tiny intact square in the picture. "It's still there."

"Sakkara was designed to withstand a direct attack. It's the only building still intact in the region. Our drones took long-range photos of the building after the attack. The hostages are clearly visible inside Sakkara's gymnasium, alive and unharmed." She handed him a second photo. "This one was taken at the same time."

The second photo showed Krodin was standing on the roof of Sakkara, looking out across the devastated landscape.

Lance said, "So you missed him."

"No, we didn't. Krodin was *outside* when we launched the missiles. He was at ground zero for at least three direct hits."

Lance slid the photos back. "You destroyed an entire city for no reason. I *warned* you that he was indestructible."

"Yes, you did. We cannot kill Krodin, or harm him. Or even scratch him. If we could somehow trap him, we wouldn't be able to starve him out: he survived for thirty years in the freezing Martian air, with no food, oxygen or water."

"So where does that leave us?"

"It leaves me right here, telling you to hand Victor Cross over to my people. That's not a request, Mister McKendrick. That's an order."

"If Krodin gets his hands on Cross we are *finished*," Lance said. "Right now, Cross is more useful than he's a liability. The second that changes... Well, you know what happened with Max Dalton."

"I do. And when this is over, you'll answer to a murder charge. You have one hour to tell me where Cross is."

"And if I don't?"

"I'll shoot you myself. Cross is more important than you are."

"An hour's not enough. Give me two."

"This is not a negotiation, McKendrick. One hour."

"Ninety minutes, then. Seriously, it will take that long to find him."

"You don't *know* where he is?"

Lance shook his head. "Not as such, no. But I know how to get in touch with the people who *do* know where he is. See, if Krodin had come here looking for him then he could have tortured the information out of me. My people have instructions to not hand him over to anyone else without specific key phrases, and if they have any doubts they're to disappear with him."

General Mendes' chair scraped back across the floor as she stood up. "Then you have your ninety minutes. One second more, and everything ends for you."

For eight days, Victor Cross had been tied to the same wooden chair in the same dark, wood-paneled room. He was freed three times a day to use the bathroom, and for meals one hand was untied. Eating and sleeping were the only times he wasn't gagged.

His four identical captors wouldn't answer any questions. When they spoke to each other, it was in scant monosyllabic words. They all wore body-armor and were equipped with handguns. Whenever one of them came within four meters of him, he removed his weapons first and the others held theirs in readiness.

Cross had always prided himself on being able to out-smart anyone, but that skill wasn't much use this time. Each of these four men looked like they could kill him bare-handed.

He had already worked out who they were, but that didn't

The New Heroes: The Chasm

help him in any way. It seemed clear that the only way he'd survive this was to ride it out and see what happened.

Right now, judging by the weariness of the four men, he guessed it was a little after midnight. Two of them stood watch while another paged through a movie magazine. The fourth was asleep on a sofa, his back to the rest of the room.

Victor heard a sharp beep, then the man reading the magazine pulled a cellphone out of his pocket and examined the screen. "It's time," he said to the two guarding the doorway.

All three of them looked over toward Cross.

Their hands aren't moving closer to their guns... None of them are looking at the others for confirmation or reassurance. They're not going to kill me.

While one woke their sleeping colleague, another moved behind Cross and unclasped the gag around his mouth, then crouched at his feet and snipped the cable-ties that had bound him to the metal chair. "Stand."

Victor obeyed. "My hands...?"

"Remain tied." The man pointed to the room's only door. "Walk."

The two men closest to the door stepped aside to allow him to pass, while the fourth man opened the door and walked out backwards, constantly watching Victor.

"McKendrick's behind this, isn't he? He wants to scare me. Perhaps he has a good reason for that." Victor stepped through the doorway, and looked around. "Where are we?"

"No more questions."

"OK. Then I'll provide my own answers." The corridor outside was as dark as the room. Bare walls, bare floorboards, a single yellowing bulb suspended from the ceiling. No windows, no other doors. The corridor turned to the left, but there was nothing to indicate where it might lead.

"Move."

"In a minute. This is a hotel," Victor said. "Built in the nineteen-seventies. The woodwork around the door-frame is indicative of that era, and the drywall sheets have a faded Aftab-Russert stamp. Aftab-Russert was a small Kansas-based company that went out of business in the seventies. The floorboards are... alder, judging by the color and grain-patterns. That tells me that this was *not* a high-end hotel." He sniffed the air. "There's also a hint of old, burnt wood... There was a fire nearby, a very large one, but it was some time ago. A couple of years. The burnt timbers haven't been removed. No decent hotel manager would be happy with something so distressing nearby that would upset potential guests, so I think it's pretty certain that the hotel has been abandoned." He smiled and looked back towards the two men behind him. To the one on the left, he said, "How am I doing so far, James?"

The man exchanged a look with his colleagues, and Victor's grin grew wider.

"We're in Greenville, Kansas," Victor said. "The town was almost destroyed during the Trutopian war, and most of the population died. This is the Starshine Hotel. And we're on the fourth floor." Ahead of him, the two men slowed as the approached the corner. "I know we're on the fourth floor because every other floor would have doors to the bedrooms. The fourth floor is the attic. The shape of the roof allows for one room, slightly wider than usual but with a lower ceiling. Many of the rooms below us have quite high ceilings, which explains why there aren't even any storage rooms up here. The fact that the corridor's walls and floor are unfinished strongly suggests that the room was never used by guests."

He felt a gloved hand on the back of his neck, and was shoved forward. He stepped out and the two men ahead of him began to walk backwards, constantly watching him, while the other two followed.

They rounded the corner. Ahead, a dark-lacquered wooden door featured the word "Stairs" in faded gold paint. To the man he'd called James, Victor said, "You and your brothers have been wonderful hosts, Mister de Luyando, but I'm afraid I can only give you one star for the accommodation and food."

The door opened before they reached it, and a man not much younger than Cross stepped through. He was handsome with an average build, tightly-cropped blond hair and a neatly-trimmed beard. "Thanks, guys. You take off."

One of the men said, "He knows who we are."

"It won't be a problem, trust me." The stranger stared at Victor. "Mister Cross understands that you were protecting him as much as imprisoning him."

The men looked at him one last time, then exited through the door.

Victor raised his hands towards the stranger. "Untie me."

"No. We'll wait here until our friends have left."

"Because you don't want me to see the manner in which they leave, in case that helps me to identify them? What's the point of that? I already know that they're Solomon Cord's brothers-in-law."

"And they know that you killed him."

Cross said, "Hmm. Last time I checked on them, they didn't know anything about Cord's real life. Nor did they know that their late sister was Hesperus. Clearly McKendrick is reaching deep into his bag of tricks if *they* are the people he's resorted to using. What's happening in the world, then? Some disaster that has the New Heroes on their toes?" He paused. "But their powers won't have fully returned yet... So it's up to Team Paragon to save the day. Why was I secretly spirited away from the Cloister?"

"You really do like the sound of your own voice, don't you?"

"And who are you?"

The man smiled. "Shouldn't that big brain of yours have deduced everything about me already? You're slowing down, Vic. I thought that by now you'd have worked out my social security number to thirteen decimal places." The man tilted his head to the side for a moment, listening. "OK. We're clear to leave."

He reached out behind him and pushed open the door, then took hold of Victor's upper arm and pushed him through. On the other side was a brightly-lit stairwell with a window overlooking the abandoned town, visible now only through moonlit shadows and reflections.

Victor said, "I was right. The Starshine Hotel in Greenville, on the western edge of Kansas." He glanced at the blond stranger. "We're four hundred and thirty miles from the Cloister. Surprised I know that?"

"I have no idea what the Cloister is, so no." He gestured down the stairs. "Move."

"You're lying... You *do* know," Victor said, glancing back at him as they descended. "So that means you're directly connected with Max Dalton or the New Heroes. Maybe both. But you just flinched a little at Max's name, so you know him but you don't like him enough to willingly work alongside him. Your apparent age, race and gender eliminate a few possibilities... Leaving us with one. You are Garland Lighthouse, also known as Razor. And I see that I'm right. Did you know that you're a proto-superhuman, like Solomon Cord and Lance McKendrick? You specialize in building machinery that is far too advanced for someone of your level of education and experience."

Outside, tiny eddies of dust brushed the ground and Victor turned in a slow circle, then looked up at the stars. "Nice to be outdoors again. This place is the pits, but it's better than in there." From what he could see, the lot next door to the hotel contained nothing but piles of charred timber and rusting girders. "As I recall, this was a pleasant little town before the war. Pity."

"You're the one who *started* that war, Cross."

"*Au contraire, singe monolingue*—I was officially dead at the time. This was all Yvonne's doing. She liked you, you know. I mean, she had a crush on you strong enough to knock over an elephant." He stepped back and peered at Razor for a second. "I wonder if she'd prefer you like this, all neat and groomed, or as you used to be, in your hedge-backwards days?"

Razor said, "Yeah, keep talking. They're coming for you. You've got about two minutes left of freedom."

"*This* is freedom?"

"It is compared with what's coming next. You're in for a world of punishment."

Victor's eyes grew wider. "Oh. Oh... I see. He *did* it, didn't he? Shadow succeeded! He brought Krodin back!" He couldn't help grinning. "*That's* what this is about. Lance put me into hiding because he didn't want Krodin to find me. And Krodin needs me because... the clones. I stripped them of their powers before I fled the base. So right now Krodin's only functioning superhuman ally is Shadow. What about Roman, is he still alive? No, you won't tell me and it doesn't matter. Some of them will have sided with the New Heroes. Probably Alex. Certainly Nathan. Maybe one or two more. So there's a race, isn't there? On one side, Wagner and his friends, on the other side, his clones. And they're all waiting for their abilities to power back up..." Then Victor nodded. "And they want me because no one knows more about the superhuman energies than I do. That makes me the world's most valuable commodity."

A truck was approaching from the north, at considerable speed, its headlights bobbing and weaving as it navigated the cracked asphalt. "Your transport's here, Victor," Razor said. "The chances are I won't ever see you again, but I'm resisting the temptation to take a swing at you for calling me a monolingual ape. Why would you assume that I can't understand French? Don't bother answering—I *know* why. It's because you're an intellectual snob. You think you know everything."

The truck skidded to a stop, its rear doors burst open and four soldiers carrying assault rifles jumped out. Without a word, two of them grabbed hold of Victor's arms and half-carried him into the truck.

As they forced him into a seat he looked out at Razor, who shouted in, "But I know something you don't, Victor! Something about *you*."

One of the soldiers approached Victor with a gag, but before it was put into place he shouted to Razor, "And what's that?"

"You were dreaming about your plans. And you talk in your sleep."

Chapter 10

Lance assembled the members of Team Paragon in one of the least-used areas of the Substation, at three-thirty in the morning when the cable-cars were no longer running. It was the best time to avoid being disturbed.

"The military are taking over. From now on, this will be their base of operations. They're bringing Cross here. They refuse to believe that this will be a big mistake. Krodin will come here looking for you guys *and* for Cross. It's my guess that the word 'carnage' is going to feature heavily when the historians come to write about this place. We're evacuating the civilians, which is a good thing, but in the morning the general will order you all to stay put. She believes that Cross can be persuaded to return your powers to you. So... *I'm* thinking that you guys have got to go. Eggs, basket, that whole thing. Go, hide, and *stay* hidden until your powers return."

This can't be happening, Danny thought. Aloud, he asked, "Where should we go?"

"Best if I don't know. But do *not* choose friends or relatives or anyone who knows you. And I advise you to split up, too. Three teams of three, no communication between the teams if at all possible, for obvious reasons."

Alia said, "Lance, our *mother* is here! We can't leave without saying good-bye to her. How much time do we have?"

"None. You leave now. I'll talk to Vienna—she'll understand. The evacuation of the civilians will begin at dawn and I want you to be long gone by then."

Renata stepped forward. "We have no money, no food... Our armor is on the other side of the Substation! You want us to go out into the night with nothing more than the clothes we're wearing right now?"

"Yeah." He reached into the pocket of his jeans and pulled out a wad of twenty-dollar bills. "There's three hundred here. It's not going to get you far, but it's all I can do."

"You said three teams of three..." Cassandra said, "but you really want *me* to stay, don't you?"

"I'd like that, yes. I know you haven't been able to get inside Cross's mind before, but you might be the only hope we have."

"And you think that Krodin will kill me when he gets here."

Lance nodded. "I won't force you to stay. If you want to go, then I completely understand."

"I'll stay."

"Thank you." He looked around at the others. "Man... I hate this but the general is under the delusion that the Substation is the safest place in the world, and she's very wrong about that. So this is how I think you should split up..." He handed five twenty-dollar bills to Danny, another five to Stephanie, and the remaining five to Renata. "You three are the leaders. Pick your teams wisely."

Danny glanced at Renata. "But Renata and I should—"

Lance interrupted him. "This is not a romantic adventure, Danny. This is about *survival*. And not just yours—there's no one else who can stand up to Krodin. So you keep your heads down, don't take any risks, and wait for the powers to return. If they don't, then find new lives for yourselves. I'm assuming you all understand the seriousness of this situation. If you have any doubts or questions, raise them now because you might not get another chance."

The teenagers looked at each other, but no one asked any questions.

Lance said, "Good... Cassandra, which of them are secretly planning to go stay with relatives?"

"Don't make me answer that!"

"Which of them intend to sneak back here and maybe collect their armor or a weapon?"

Renata said, "Enough, Lance! We get it!"

"Be sure that you do, because this is not a game. You use your brains, keep your heads down and you might just make it." Still watching them, Lance began to walk backwards, into the darkness. "A hundred meters ahead you'll find a ladder. It'll take you straight to the surface, and it's the only exit that's not currently monitored. If you head directly south and keep up a steady pace, you'll reach a highway about an hour before dawn. Cassie? Say your good-byes."

The young telepath looked around at her friends. "This *is* real. I know you were wondering that, Alex. Lance is serious. He thinks that the general will probably court-martial him for letting you go. But you have to do it. He's sure that Krodin would rather lose Cross than allow him to work for us."

Danny said, "That... That's familiar."

Inside his head, Cassandra's voice said, "Danny, the others don't know about Max Dalton's death. You *can't* tell them—it'll shatter their trust in Lance if they learn what he did."

But you know?

"Lance can't keep secrets from me. We've talked about it... And I understand why he had to do it."

Well, I don't understand. But I won't say anything.

Renata said, "Kenya, you're with me. Danny, you take Nathan and Alia. Steph, you've got Mina and Alex. Are we all happy with that?"

Kenya asked, "Any reason you chose the teams that way?"

"Because when our powers do return, each team will have a good balance of abilities."

"OK, but Alia and Stephanie aren't superhuman. So they probably don't even need to come with us."

Alia asked, "You think Krodin will slow down his killing spree so he can check? You're not leaving us behind!"

Danny thought, *Cassie, are you still listening?*

"I'm here."

You'll watch out for us, won't you? You'll tell us if anything happens in Sakkara?

"Of course." Aloud, Cassandra said, "I'll walk with you to the ladder."

As they walked, Renata said, "Danny, I know you can't climb ladders very fast, so you should go first."

"No, I should go *last.* Otherwise I'm slowing everyone down, not just my own team."

"He's right," Nathan said. "You guys go on." He nodded toward Alex. "Don't get killed out there in the real world."

"You either," Alex said. "Good luck, little brother."

When they reached the ladder, Danny, Alia, Nathan and Cassandra stood back and watched the others climb.

Then it was Alia's turn, then Nathan's.

Danny turned to Cassandra to say good-bye, and then froze for a moment. *This is the last time we'll all be together.*

Cassandra said, "You can't know that for sure."

That wasn't just a thought—that was a premonition.

"Well, that might mean your powers are coming back."

He smiled. "You're good at finding the positive in every situation." He took a deep breath, and looked around at the Substation for a few seconds before grabbing hold of the ladder. "What do you think our chances are?"

Cassandra hesitated for a second, then said, "They're better than zero."

Danny laughed. "Right now, I'll take that. Good luck."

"You too."

*

At dawn, when they reached the highway, they split up. Renata and Kenya crossed the quiet road and continued south. Danny's team followed the highway to the west, while Stephanie and the others went east.

In the days that followed, Cassandra regularly sent telepathic reports. She guided them to where they might find food and shelter, and on occasion Lance was able to arrange parcels of food and money to be dropped off at prearranged locations. But soon they realized that the drops had to stop: for their own safety, Lance could not know where they were. Cassandra ceased communicating with them shortly afterwards, for the same reason.

Stephanie's team caught a Greyhound bus on their first morning. By the end of the week they had traveled all the way to Minneapolis.

At the start of the second week, Danny Cooper's team happened upon a huge, litter-strewn field, the site of a recent music festival outside Boise, Idaho. Among the discarded items they found were six intact two-person tents, a dozen pairs of rubber boots and four cellphones. At the next town they sold everything but two of the tents to a shifty-looking man outside a bowling alley for two hundred dollars.

Renata and Kenya had spent a month in the wilderness when they found a day-old newspaper. That was how they discovered that Krodin had put the next phase of his plan into action. He now had an army.

Chapter 11

Brawn wiped the blood from his mouth with the back of his hand as he turned on the spot. On a normal day the shopping mall's parking lot would be packed with cars and minivans. Now there was nothing but twisted wreckage smoldering on cracked asphalt, the result of a fourth failed attempt to take control of the town.

Defending the town was a full-time job now. Sergeant Rosenblum had taken command of two dozen police officers and twenty members of the National Guard and, along with more than a hundred volunteers, they had sealed off every road leading out of town and established hidden watch-points in trees and water-towers.

This time, the antagonists had been members of Caucasians for Christ, a small but well-armed group who believed that they had been chosen to "Lead the Way to a Glorious Future – White, Protestant and American!"

They had arrived shortly before dawn, driving dump trucks stolen from the local quarry, crashing through the barricades that blocked the Northern Cross road. The blockade was clearly a weak spot in the town's defenses, which is why the locals hadn't shored it up. All four bands of raiders had attempted to breach the same spot. And all four had realized too late that it was a lot more heavily defended than it looked.

Now, a few surviving attackers were fleeing for the woods with Brawn's colleagues in pursuit. Sitting on the ground close to him was the raiders' leader, a fifty-year-old pot-bellied man called Douglas Munton-Pryce. He stared down at the ragged, scorched, blood-oozing remains of his trembling hands and whimpered softly. When he saw Brawn approaching he looked up. "You maimed me!"

"You maimed yourself."

Munton-Pryce had raced towards Brawn's group with a lit Molotov Cocktail in his hand, ready to throw it. But as he drew his arm back, Brawn had hit him with a weapon of his own: a sixteen-pound bowling ball.

Brawn couldn't help grinning. "You got to admit, that was a good shot!"

Brawn's bowling ball had hit Munton-Pryce square in the chest. If he hadn't been wearing body-armor the ball would have shattered his ribs and cracked his sternum. Instead the impact knocked him backwards and his Molotov Cocktail—a large glass soda bottle filled with gasoline and stuffed with a burning strip of cloth—had arced up into the air and crashed down next to him, dousing him with gasoline that instantly burst into flame. In his panic-filled attempts to put out the fire he had managed to roll around on the broken glass.

"Could have been a lot worse," Brawn said. "The fire cauterized the wounds." He crouched down next to the man. "All of your people are down or running. At least five are dead. And right now, there's no one watching. You get that? No one. I could crush your head in my fist and none of your people would ever know what happened to you. None of *my* people would care. Now..." He shuffled a little closer and leaned his head down so that it was only a hands-breadth away from Munton-Pryce's face. "You came here to kill us and plunder our supplies. Give me a reason to let you live."

Munton-Pryce dry-swallowed. "You... you can't win. They say Krodin was stronger than you back when you were still a superhuman. He's already destroyed this country's infrastructure. There's no going back from that. Sign up with him, Brawn. That's the only way you're going to survive."

Brawn laughed. "I know about you and your sad little cult.

How's it feel to be subservient to someone like Krodin? How does that fit in with all your bull about you being superior because your skin happens to be a lighter shade than some other people's?"

"It's not about skin color!" Munton-Pryce snarled. "It never *was*. It's about cultural and genetic purity! The white man was *chosen* to lead and it is our *destiny* to lead because we *are* superior and—"

Brawn had heard this circular, self-feeding argument before and really wasn't in the mood to go through it again. He clenched his fist and slammed it into the man's face. He knew that an act of violence was rarely an effective solution to racism but sometimes it was immensely satisfying.

Munton-Pryce collapsed onto his back, unconscious, and Brawn grabbed his leg and dragged him backwards through the debris-strewn parking lot towards his own people.

Before he reached the shopping mall the sergeant was striding towards him. She stepped to the side a little and looked down at Douglas Munton-Pryce. "Uh... Brawn?"

"Yeah?" He stopped.

She nodded towards the unconscious man. "You might wanna..."

Brawn looked. Somehow, on the journey across the parking lot Munton-Pryce's body had flipped over. Judging by the blood trail, for the past thirty yards or so Brawn had been dragging him face-down.

He let go of the man's ankle and used his foot to roll him over onto his back. Munton-Pryce's face was a mess of scrapes and deep cuts. "Oh, that's nasty. Looks like he's been trying to shave with a cheese-grater. On a trampoline. Yeah, that's not gonna heal any time soon, is it?"

"Doubt it," the sergeant said.

"Well, he deserves it. He's the sort of moron who fights new ideas with bullets."

"Brawn, we've heard from your friend."

"McKendrick?"

"We think so. But he wouldn't use his name. He said there was no point using a fake name either, because you wouldn't know it."

"Yeah, that sounds like the sort of thing he'd say. So what's the word?"

"They want you to keep a low profile until they bring you in."

They both looked out across the devastated parking lot, and Brawn shrugged. "No point now, is there? Everyone knows where I live anyway. If Krodin wants me, he'll find me. I say we keep going as we are." He hesitated for a second, then added, "Unless you think I'm putting you and everyone else in danger."

She put her hand on his arm and smiled. "So far, no, I think it's the opposite. Your reputation is keeping some of the worst of them away. But when the time comes..."

He nodded. "I got it. If Krodin sends his people for me, I'll leave. In the meantime... You see that trick with the bowling ball? We need to get more of those!"

Sakkara's gymnasium was more than large enough to accommodate all of the hostages, but after two weeks trapped in the same room, nerves were frayed and tempers rising.

Colin woke to the sound of an argument between his mother and one of the guards. In an instant he rolled off the exercise mat and was on his feet, running toward them.

The guard was Corporal Kurt Severns, a tall, wiry man in his thirties, and he looked only seconds away from punching Caroline Wagner in the face. Around them, the other hostages were either keeping well clear or pleading with them to calm down.

At the doorway, Zeke and Eldon were watching with interest, and showed no indication that they wanted to stop the fight.

Caroline was saying, "She's only two years old, for crying out loud!"

"That was *my* chocolate she stole—if you can't control her, then I will!"

Nearby, Colin saw Niall Cooper holding Abigail in his arms. She was sobbing so hard she was almost silent.

"What happened?" Colin asked, stepping between Severns and his mother. "What'd he do?"

Through clenched teeth, Caroline said, "He hit Abigail!"

"I did not hit her! I saw her taking the last of my chocolate and I just nudged her out of the way! It was a little shove at the most. She didn't even notice until *you* came screaming over here like some demented harpy! I was *saving* that piece of chocolate. It was my last one and that little brat stole it! So you keep her out of my way or I'll give both of you a *real* reason to cry!"

Colin stepped up to him, wishing he was six inches taller so that they would be face-to-face. "Threaten my mother and sister again. Go ahead."

The guarded leaned closer, tilting down toward Colin until their noses were almost touching. "You don't have your powers any more, kid. Don't push someone who can push back harder."

From the doorway, Eldon shouted, "Get him, Colin! Smash his head in!"

Zeke said, "No way, my money's on the other guy."

Colin ignored them. Still glaring at Severns, he asked, "If that was your last piece, why does your breath smell of chocolate?"

"You calling me a *liar*?"

"Yeah, I am."

The guard stepped back, his hands spread in a gesture of surrender. "OK. I've had it. I *quit*. I've been working in this nuthouse for nearly two years, guarding these little New Heroes punks and what do I get for it? Half of them don't even notice I'm there, the other half think I'm their slave." He looked around the room. "You're all in the same boat. We're supposed to treat them like they're royalty just because they can shoot lasers out of their eyes or fireballs out of their butts? They've got powers? Big deal! That doesn't make them special—they're just *lucky*. Last year that jerk Butler got killed and they were all, 'Oh no, boo-hoo, one of us got killed in the line of duty.' The kid's bigwig father got him a military funeral, with full honors! He didn't deserve that, and he sure didn't earn it. He was a *moron*! Nobody liked him! But these kids decapitated Corporal LaPenna and took her *head* somewhere and I don't see you guys weeping for her!"

"Are you *done*?" Caroline asked.

Severns said, "Not even close! My own kid and my girlfriend were in Topeka and I was supposed to be on *leave* this whole week. Now our entire city has been wiped out and I don't even know where they are! And if I *did* know, I couldn't tell them what's happened. They don't even know that I work here because it's supposed to be a secret, even though *everyone* knows this is the superhumans' HQ. So they think I'm a grunt in the military base and they've no idea what I have to put up with. Blue giants and girls who can control minds, twelve-year-olds who are smarter than Einstein, and Cooper's big brother who can run to the moon or whatever. And now this psycho Krodin comes here just when all those powers are gone and he takes over and butchers nearly five thousand people outside and the army tries to blow him up with the biggest explosions I've ever *seen* and he's still not got a scratch on him!"

At the doorway, Zeke inhaled sharply through clenched teeth. "Ooh... you did *not* just call Krodin a psycho, did you?"

Severns turned pale, and swallowed audibly.

Colin said, "No, he said *psychic*."

Zeke said, "He's not actually psychic. At least, I don't think he is. But he is smart and he has great instincts."

Eldon looked disappointed. "So there's not gonna be a fight? Aw." He turned and walked out into the corridor.

Kurt Severns looked down at Colin, his eyes wide, his hands trembling. "I... Thanks. I didn't mean to let rip. I was..."

Caroline said, "You're under pressure. We all are."

"I'm sorry I upset Abigail. My own son is the same age. I'd go insane if anything happened to him."

"You're forgiven." She turned to Colin. "And you... You have no powers. Corporal Severns would have *flattened* you. Colin, nobility is one thing, stupidity is something else entirely."

"But mom!"

"And I don't need you to fight my battles for me, thank you very much. I was a superhero for a lot longer than you have been, remember." She walked over to Niall, and lifted Abigail out of his arms. "It's all OK now, sweetheart." Looking back at Colin, she added, "Everything will work out all right."

But he could tell from her expression that she didn't believe that.

Outside, the bodies of thousands of soldiers lay untouched because no one knew whether it was safe to bury them.

Krodin and Tuan stood side-by-side in Sakkara's operations room watching the monitors. The clone pointed to the screen on the left. "OK, so *that* map shows all the known locations of the New Heroes. Each one is represented by a flashing red dot."

Krodin peered closer at the monitor. "There is only one

flashing red dot. And it's here."

"Exactly. That's Colin, the only one who's location we're certain about. This is not a good thing, but we can't change that right now. We're getting reports that the others left the Substation very early this morning. Apparently General Mendes is spitting *bullets*."

"Spitting bullets?"

"I mean, she's enraged. It looks like McKendrick encouraged them to leave in the middle of the night, and he helped them to go. Turned off a few sensors and cameras so they wouldn't trigger an alarm. So he's in trouble with the general, which is good for us. They're less of a threat divided."

"That's debatable," Krodin said. "These other displays?"

"The current deployment of the United States military," Tuan said. "That's if Sakkara's techs aren't lying to us about patching into the satellite feeds."

"The technicians are aware of the penalty for subterfuge."

"Yeah, you *really* don't know enough about the American people," Tuan said. Then he quickly added, "Yet. I mean, I don't know that much myself, but I've seen a lot of movies and it's pretty clear that if you tell an American, 'You are not permitted to do this' he or she will say, 'Oh, is *that* so?' and then try to do it. The more you lock them down, the harder they squirm to get free. It's not in their nature to ever believe that they're beaten."

"Then we will *show* them."

Tuan sighed. "No, seriously, you're not getting this. Even if the chances of success are one in a hundred, they're going to think that it's a risk worth taking. They will lock onto the slightest crack in the cage and see it as proof that they can get free."

Krodin said, "Then we will seal the cracks."

"Man, it's like I'm talking to a brick wall here! Krodin, if you reduce their chances of success from one in a hundred to, say, one in a *million*, that will spur them on even more. When it comes to something like this, the American people value their freedom above anything. Or their *perception* of freedom. That's the angle we should be taking. You don't conquer America by forcing your way in and telling the people that they're now your subjects. You do it by persuading them that you're their liberator and they are now free. Do you see what I mean?"

"I do. We show them the chains that they didn't even know were constricting them, then we snap those chains."

Tuan grinned. "Exactly!"

"You are wise, in some ways, Tuan. But you insulted me."

The clone took a step backwards. "I... I did. I'm sorry. That was just the heat of the moment. I didn't mean any disrespect."

"It won't happen again," Krodin said.

"It won't, I promise."

"You misunderstand. It *won't* happen again, but not because you have made a promise. It won't happen again because there will never be the possibility of it happening again."

Tuan suddenly found himself on the floor, on his back, with Krodin's left hand around his throat, squeezing.

The immortal superhuman was saying something to him, but all Tuan could hear was the rush of his own blood, the panicked beating of his heart. And then a final, life-ending *crack*.

Chapter 12

"Another body tossed from the roof of Sakkara," General Mendes said, passing a blurred photograph across the desk to Lance. She leaned back against a filing cabinet and crossed her arms. "Looks like Colin Wagner."

"But it's not," Lance said. "It's one of the clones."

"And how can you be certain of that?"

"Because you've already talked to Cassandra and she's confirmed that Colin is still alive."

Mendes drummed her fingers on the edge of the filing cabinet. "I ordered her not to communicate telepathically with you."

"She didn't. I was guessing." Lance picked up the photo and looked more closely at it. "Hard to say which one it is... The one throwing the body has got to be Shadow, but the dead one could be any of them... Cassandra will find out from Colin. Me, I've got my fingers crossed that it's Tuan."

"Why him?"

"He can steal other people's life-force—they get weaker while he gets stronger. He almost killed Brawn that way. He's one of Krodin's most dangerous assets."

"Speaking of assets..." The general moved towards the door. "Victor Cross should be in his cage by now."

Lance followed her out onto the gantry. "Do you want me to tell you—again—how stupid it is to have him here? You haven't finished evacuating the civilians yet!"

"And you were stupid to let the kids escape, McKendrick. With them gone, your usefulness is at an all-time low."

"Your use of the word 'escape' is troubling, General. They weren't prisoners. Or were they? If so, all the more reason for me to let them go. If they weren't, then, hey, it's currently a free country so why shouldn't they leave?"

The general ignored all of that. "You've met Cross before. And you've studied him. So you're conducting this first interview. My advice is—"

"I know how to talk to him. *My* advice is that you greatly restrict access to him. Physically, he's no fitter or stronger than the average person. As far as we know his superhuman abilities only affect his brain. And that's what we need to be clear about. Victor Cross is smarter than all of you combined. Including me. So if you have any soldiers who can't understand English, or—better still—are completely deaf, then use them when you need to clean out his cell or feed him."

"I've dealt with geniuses before, McKendrick."

"Not like this guy. There's a friend of mine who's got total recall. He can remember absolutely everything that ever happened to him. Picture that ability combined with a brain that's a thousand times faster than yours. Remember what you said about Krodin instinctively knowing the most efficient way to kill all those people? Well, Cross would be able to do that, but it's not instinct, it's mathematics. He can mentally run hundreds of processes at the same time, maybe thousands, and he's almost impossible to second-guess. I managed it, once, but that only means that he'll be more focused on me now. It's not going to be easy to do it again."

"We don't need you to second-guess him. We need you to persuade him to work for us, to show us how to recharge the superhumans' powers before the clones' powers recharge naturally. You are free to use any method you think will work. Bribery, threats, subterfuge, torture. Whatever it takes, I'll back you up."

"No you won't. You want me as a scapegoat in case it all comes crashing down. But I'll give it a shot." Lance pointed ahead, to a small, prefabricated metal room. "He's in there, right? General, I know you're going to want to listen in, but I'm asking you not to do that. Cross doesn't have my skills with persuasion but he *is* highly manipulative and he's going to say things deliberately designed to shock just to put us on edge."

"I can deal with anything he says."

Lance stopped outside the door of the metal room. "Yeah? Well, let's meet here in an hour's time and we'll see. Just remember that I warned you." He looked around. "Keep the guards back. They really shouldn't be in earshot."

"Just get it done, McKendrick."

"They're going to execute you, Victor. In their eyes, refusing to help us is tantamount to helping Krodin. They consider that to be an act of treason."

Victor Cross nodded. "I expected as much."

"So what will you do?" Lance asked.

"I'll wait for Krodin."

"Doubt he'll be interested in a corpse. Besides, what makes you think he needs you?"

"Because I know what his ultimate purpose is. The reason for his existence."

Lance leaned back against the metal room's door. "To rule the world."

"No, to *lead* the world. There is a difference. Are you smart enough to understand that difference, McKendrick?" Victor was perched on a metal stool in the center of the room. His hands and feet were unbound, but a thick chain led from the ceiling to a metal collar around his neck.

"A ruler tells his people what to do. A leader *shows* them."

"Very well put. I'm not sure I could have phrased it better. Krodin's job is to lead the human race."

"And what does that mean, exactly? Lead us to where?"

"Now, don't make needless assumptions," Victor said. "Assumptions are the limescale buildups on the water-pipes of the imagination. People can be led *from* something as well as led *to* something. If I tell you that I own four hats and three of them are blue, what color is my other hat?"

"I don't have the time or the patience for your smug little puzzles. What is Krodin's purpose?"

"To lead the human race."

Lance turned and opened the door. "Then we've come full circle and we're done. Have fun being tortured."

"Wait... Come on, admit you're enjoying this. You're the only one who's ever out-smarted me, McKendrick. You're not even a full superhuman, yet you managed to do that! You've got to understand how fascinating that makes you to me."

"Give me something, then. Give me a reason to keep playing."

"What do you want? Questions, answers, ideas, notions, calculations, formulae... Name your price."

"All right. You say I'm not a full superhuman. A long time ago a man called Daedalus said the same thing. Some of us are changed by the superhuman energies but we're not actually superhuman. What does that mean?"

"To answer that, I'll have to tell you what it is that *makes* someone a superhuman. Are you ready for that?"

"Of course."

"No, consider this for a moment. There are certain truths that might not sit comfortably in your brain and you can't unlearn them. Paul Cooper, for example, actually *was* a superhuman and the truth gradually drove him insane. You remember him, don't you? Quantum. Danny's real father. His visions... his memories of the future, I should say... showed him the truth but it wouldn't all fit in his head. Not without nudging a lot of other things out of the way first."

"Just tell me. What is it that makes a person superhuman?"

Victor tapped the center of his forehead with his index finger. "I have a node on my brain, right about *here* on the frontal lobe. It's a very rare condition. So rare that it doesn't have a name. The node grows up through the *Pars triangularis* from the *Posterior ramus*. It's so small that it's almost invisible to the unaided eye, and exactly *how* it works, I don't yet know. My research has shown that the node doesn't exist in normal humans, but every superhuman I've examined has that node. From what I can tell, when puberty kicks in and the body is swamped with hormones, that node becomes active. It reacts to a certain form of energy and can help the body *store* that energy. Now, I'm not going to tell you exactly what that energy is, because that's a different question, so let's—"

"The blue lights that only a tiny number of people can see."

Victor said, "Hmph. Yes. The blue lights. Anyway. That extra node seems to occur mostly at random, but the chance can be skewed by genetics. Colin Wagner, for example, has two superhuman parents so he stood a much greater chance of developing that node. And once it's there, once it's part of a person, any copy of that person will also have the node. Hence Yvonne and Mina Duval, and of course Colin's clones. Now, for someone like you, or Solomon Cord, or your son... I believe that the node exists but it almost immediately dies on exposure to the superhuman energy. So you were changed, but you can no longer use the energy. With the right equipment the energy can be taken from a superhuman and stored. Danny Cooper experienced exactly that when he destroyed my power-siphon in California. It also completely drained him and it was months before he built up enough energy to use his powers again."

Lance said, "So that's why he couldn't move as fast when his powers returned as he had before he lost them? Your power-siphon damaged the node?"

"Close. The energy burst from the power-siphon overloaded it," Victor said. "It's the same for Renata... Well, almost. She lost her powers when she turned the entire world into crystal to stop the Trutopian war, and then turned it back. She burnt herself out. She later recovered some of her powers but not all. Would you like to know *exactly* what happened to her?"

"Go ahead."

"I'm hungry. Feed me, then we'll talk. Trust me, you'll like this one."

"I don't know. You said this was going to blow my mind. It's fascinating—if it's *true*—but my mind remains unblown."

Smiling, Victor said, "You know, I've been sitting on all of this for a long time and I've never been able to tell anyone. It's kind of nice to finally get it all out in the open."

Lance reached out behind him and opened the door again. "All right. Food's on the way. But time is short, Victor. You might not have heard, but Krodin attacked the US military forces stationed outside Sakkara. He killed all of them. Four thousand, eight hundred and seven people. Each one with families, friends, colleagues... That's on *you*, because you brought him back. I hope for your sake that your superhuman brain allows you to block out pain, because these people are going to hurt you. I don't have the words to even begin to explain *how much* they're going to hurt you. I promise you this: you will be *begging* them to kill you, to put an end to it. But they won't. They're going to keep on hurting you so that every day you're going to look back on the previous day's agony as though it were a cozy sleep-in on a rainy winter's morning."

Victor laughed. "Yes, sure. I know how this works. I can avoid all that suffering if I just answer the questions."

Lance looked puzzled for a second. "What? Oh, I see. No, that's nothing to do with the *questioning*, Victor. They're going to do all that regardless of whether you answer. You could give them the secret of turning dirt into diamonds, the formula for immortality and the keys to the kingdom of Heaven and they're still going to make you suffer like no one has ever suffered before."

He stepped, and then looked back in at Victor. "And I want you to understand that if Krodin comes for you and it looks like he's going to take you away, the very first thing we'll do is put a bullet in your brain." He tapped the center of his forehead with his index finger. "Right here."

Chapter 13

After the massacre outside Sakkara, Shadow and Krodin had begun collecting the soldiers' weapons and supplies and loading them into a truck. When it was full, Shadow had carried the truck to Sakkara's roof and stored it in the hangar. He had been about to return to the battlefield when the missiles struck.

Two days later, Shadow dropped down in the center of a compound in Nevada and lowered the truck to the ground. He spotted the same grizzled, bearded man he'd spoken to last time. "Just like I promised. Weapons and ammunition. And you can keep the truck, too."

The man was Dougie Albano. Sixty years old, short but strongly-built. He was missing his left eye and the smallest finger on his right hand. His bare arms were covered in tattoos, many of which were crisscrossed with scars. "Knife-fights," Albano had explained when Shadow first met him. Shadow had said, "Don't worry, you'll get better with practice." Albano hadn't like that. In an instant, he had drawn one of his knives and slammed it into Shadow's chest. Shadow had leaned down and picked up the shattered blade, and simply handed it back to him.

Now, Dougie Albano walked wordlessly past Shadow and opened the back of the truck, then jumped back as hundreds of handguns and rifles spilled out.

Shadow said, "Yeah, they're not in boxes or anything. Do guns even *come* in boxes? Anyway, they're yours. All you have to do is follow our instructions."

Albano picked up a Glock from among the pile, and turned it over in his hands. "So when your boss said the guns would be delivered by truck, we was thinkin' he meant comin' over the roads. Not carried through the air by a flyin' kid. How do we know you weren't tracked?"

Shadow shrugged. "I guess you're going to have to trust us. Besides, why would we trick you? We *need* you."

"You need us to go to war."

"That's right."

"With the guvmint."

Shadow thought about that. "If you're trying to say 'government' then yes, that's it exactly. See, we're going to build a whole new society here, and the best way to rebuild something is to dismantle the old one first. You guys bring the chaos, then we bring the peace. Everyone gets what they want."

Albano nodded slowly. "Now, just so's you know, boy, when all this is over we ain't knockin' back your Kool-Aid or settin' foot on your spaceship, understand?"

"Not even slightly," Shadow said.

"We ain't joinin' your cult or bowin' to your leader."

"Oh, right. Yeah, sure, we're cool with that. And he'll respect that, too. Krodin doesn't like yes-men. He prefers people with principles who aren't afraid to defend them." Shadow looked around the compound. Forty men, most of them around Albano's age. They'd cause a lot of trouble and draw a huge amount of attention, but they were not going to be an effective force. Most of them wouldn't survive their first clash with a real army. "I know you've got an ongoing feud with Dagmar Sidoriak's gang. Well, you need to know that we've armed them, too."

Albano suddenly had the Glock in Shadow's face, its muzzle an inch away from his left eye.

Shadow pushed the gun aside. "Please, don't embarrass yourself. Sidoriak's an anarchist too, and he hates the establishment as much as you do, so you'll work alongside him and his people. Then, when it's all done, you can wipe them out if that's what you want to do."

"Suppose we wipe them out *first*."

"And make your job a lot harder? That's not a smart move. If you're gonna execute a man, you don't shoot him here and then carry his body into the woods and then dig the hole yourself, right? You make *him* walk there, dig his own hole, then all you have to do is blast his brains out and fill in the hole. So what I'm saying is you let Sidoriak think all is cool with you. He and his boys will do most of the heavy lifting, then when it's done you blow him away and take the spoils."

"We can do that," Albano said.

"I know you can." He patted the man on his shoulder. "Now, go bring me some dead cops and soldiers."

Albano smirked. "Heh. How many would you like?"

"All of them."

Colin knew that the New Heroes' databanks had files on every known criminal gang operating in the United States, Canada and Mexico.

He also knew that Shadow and Krodin had forced some of the technicians to give them access to those files.

And now he knew why they wanted them.

"Your enhanced hearing is definitely returning," his mother whispered. It was mid-morning. They were sitting side-by-side with their backs against the gymnasium wall. Abigail was asleep in Colin's arms, wrapped up in a blanket.

They could only converse like this when Shadow wasn't around to hear them, and even then it was risky: Zeke or Eldon's super-hearing could be coming back too.

Colin said, "It's taking its time. You remember when my powers first appeared? It was, like, almost overnight."

She smiled. "Well, it wasn't quite *that* quick. I seem to recall your powers being very unreliable for the first few months."

"Even so. This time it should be faster. You know what I'm thinking? I was the first one to be zapped by Cross's power-zapping thing, so..."

"So logically you should be the first to recover. I thought of that too. I hope you're right." She lowered her voice a little more, and said, "If... no, *when* your powers are restored, don't rush out and take on Krodin. Go for the weakest of the clones and put him out of commission fast and hard. You keep hitting him until he can't get up again because he's unconscious or dead."

"Mom! I'm not going to kill someone!"

"Usually I'd agree with that. But Shadow cut off that woman's head right in front of us as casually as if he was hitting a golf-ball. Krodin murdered thousands of people right outside this building—their bodies are still out there. So you'll fight dirty if you have to. With luck, Shadow won't be around. You take down both of the clones if you can, then you get back here and you take Abby and Niall away. Not to the Substation. Somewhere safe that only you know about." She shrugged. "I'm sure you'll think of somewhere. But you do *not* attack Krodin, whatever happens. Understand?"

"Yeah, but—"

"You can't beat him. He's thousands of years old and he's indestructible. If you can't stop the clones, and you can't get back here, then you forget about us and go." Caroline reached out and gently stroked Abigail's forehead with the backs of her fingers. "*One* of us has to survive, Colin. There are countless stories of people who have drowned because they tried to save someone *else* who was drowning."

"There are more stories of people who *didn't* drown because someone managed to save them."

She laughed softly and said, "You really *are* a proper teenager now, aren't you? Always arguing."

"No I'm not!"

Caroline leaned back, resting her head against the wall, and closed her eyes. "Want to know something?"

"Sure..."

"When you were born I prayed that you wouldn't get any powers. Then we all lost our abilities and I thought it was all over. I prayed again."

Colin frowned. "Why would you still pray when you'd already *got* what you wanted?"

"Don't you think that God would sometimes like to receive a thank-you note among all the countless begging letters?" She opened her eyes. "Krodin's followers, the Helotry of the Fifth King... They thought *he* was a god. Maybe not in recent centuries, but back in his day some of them believed it. I suppose from their point of view he probably was."

"Wait..." Colin said. "Here's something that I keep forgetting to ask Lance. The Helotry worked for centuries to bring about Krodin's return, then they succeeded twenty-five years ago. Krodin fought Brawn and the others... Hesperus and Thunder and Roz Dalton."

"And Lance."

"Right. And then there was all that stuff with Krodin being sent back in time a few years and the time-line going wonky and everything. Then Lance used Krodin's teleporter to grab him from the moment he appeared twenty-five years ago. So that means Krodin doesn't remember the battle with Brawn because it didn't happen for him. He—"

Caroline said, "No, Lance took Krodin from when he went back the extra six years, from *thirty-one* years ago. So for Krodin the battle *did* happen."

"Oh, right." Colin thought about that for a moment. "Time-travel makes things really tricky. Anyway, what I'm getting at is *this*... The Helotry took Krodin out of the past, then as far as they know he was killed. They don't know that he got blasted back in time. So what happened to them?"

"They were all arrested. And I remember Lance saying something about all their money being tied up in a complex web of companies that stretched back for centuries. It was supposed to be a *lot* of money. Billions of dollars."

"So all that money could be sitting around somewhere, waiting for someone to..." Colin stopped, and slapped his forehead with the palm of his hand. "So *that's* where the Trutopians got their money from!"

"You could be right. And it would explain how Cross was able to build his base in the Arctic."

"He was one step ahead of us at every stage. At *least* one step."

Caroline looked at her son. "Makes you wonder if maybe *everything* that's happened was part of Victor's plan, doesn't it?"

"That's... a scary thought," Colin said. He looked around the gymnasium, at the weary guards and technicians, at Eldon sitting by the doorway flipping through an old music magazine, at Niall Cooper over by the bars attempting to do chin-ups. *She's right. Everything and anything could be part of his plan. Cross is that smart. He could be...*

Colin shuddered, and briskly shook his head in an attempt to shake off the disturbing image. But it wouldn't budge. *If Victor Cross is as smart as everyone says he is, including himself... Smart people tend to know the truth, because they're able to figure it out or because they know how to recognize it when they see it.*

Maybe Cross's plans are working out for him because he knows exactly what he's doing and maybe that's because he's right.

"How many?"

"It's difficult to say," Zeke said. "Fifty, maybe."

Krodin let out a sigh of exasperation. "Not enough. I was expecting thousands."

"I know. But..." the clone shrugged. "Even if there had been thousands of them, the Helotry weren't fighters. They were administrators, for the most part."

"I remember soldiers. I remember a fast-moving, vicious woman called Slaughter."

"Yeah, *she* was a fighter, but she lost her powers a long time ago. The soldiers were mercenaries. And we can't hire mercenaries without money."

"So we need money. How much?" Krodin asked.

Again, Zeke shrugged. "I have no clue. Ten thousand dollars each? I don't even know where we'd *find* mercenaries. Shadow's the one who's watched all the war movies—he'll have a better idea of how all that works."

"Then we will get Shadow to acquire money, and hire mercenaries. They will augment the gangs..." Krodin examined the large map of the USA projected onto the wall. "We start on the outside borders, I think, and move in. If we were to start here in Kansas and move outwards, we'd be thinning our forces rather than concentrating them. We would also be fighting on an expanding front rather than a shrinking one."

Zeke nodded. "Right. Plus, if we start here they could take out all of our people with a couple of nukes, and we don't want that."

"Once America is ours, we move on to Canada and Mexico,

at the same time. And then we go further..."

Krodin glanced at a calendar pinned to the wall. "It has been three weeks since I returned to Earth... Every day increases the likelihood of the New Heroes regaining their powers. We need to find and eliminate them as soon as possible. The war will drive them out of hiding."

"Krodin, we have one of them right here! I don't want to question your judgment, but keeping Colin Wagner alive is a risk."

Krodin smiled. "He's still alive because you and Eldon are identical to him. When his powers return, I'll know that the return of yours is imminent. Wagner is a barometer, that's all."

"OK..."

"You still believe that it's unwise to keep him alive."

"He might be able to kill me and Eldon *before* our powers return."

"Yes, he might. But he won't be able to kill *me,* and that's what's important." He slapped Zeke on the back. "Now, we have a huge war to plan and New Heroes to find. Get to work: I want to see this world in *flames.*"

Chapter 14

After they'd fled the Substation, Danny, Nathan and Alia had followed the highway to the west. At first, it had been kind of fun, especially when they left the road and went cross-country. Their journey took them into the southern foothills of Idaho's White Cloud Mountains, and it was entertaining because Nathan had never been immersed in the countryside before.

The young clone had been particularly impressed with Danny's ability to name every wild-flower, tree and insect until Danny accidentally used the same name twice and Nathan realized he'd just been making them up. After that, it had become a game to come up with the funniest or silliest name. Alia had laughed longest at the large gray moth Danny had insisted was an "I-Can't-Believe-It's-Not-Butterfly."

She hadn't liked sleeping outdoors much, so after they'd found the tents at the site of the music festival things were a lot more comfortable.

Alia had always hated the idea of living off the land—if it didn't come wrapped in plastic, then bugs might have crawled on it or laid eggs in it, so no thanks—but by the end of week two, she was making mental plans for her own remote cabin in the woods.

It was around that time that Nathan asked her if she still missed Grant. It was early morning, and they had camped near a small river.

"Well, sure, yeah," she'd said. "Of course I miss him. He was my boyfriend."

Danny was standing knee-deep in the river failing to catch a fish with his hand, and he looked up toward Alia. "Really? I was never sure about you two."

"Well, he was. And then his parents took him away." She

shrugged.

Nathan said, "You don't seem *that* upset about it."

"He wasn't my first boyfriend. Anyway, he had a thing for Steph and only settled for me because she's in love with Colin."

"*Is* she, though?" Danny asked. "Whatever's going on there is complicated."

Alia said, "Only the *boring* relationships are uncomplicated."

In the middle of their third week, they found an old map and worked out that at some point they had passed into Oregon. They climbed a small mountain to check out the view.

That was when they saw the thick column of smoke on the horizon. "What *is* that?" Nathan had asked. "Which direction are we facing?"

Alia glanced down at their shadows. "It's about mid-day, so we're looking north-west. Anything in that direction, Danny?"

Danny consulted the map. "If we are where I think we are, then there's not a lot between here and Portland. That's, like, two hundred and fifty miles away."

"If that's Portland then the whole *city* must be on fire."

Five days later, they got separated from Danny.

They had found an abandoned gasoline station and set up camp on its forecourt, and next morning were woken by the brake-squeals of eight large flat-bed trucks. Each of the trucks pulling up outside was packed with exhausted-looking people and tied-together supplies.

The driver of the first truck jumped down from its cab. She was a sixty-year-old woman and reminded Alia of a strict hospital matron she'd seen in an old British comedy movie.

"How do we know you aren't with *them*?" the driver asked Danny, pointing back towards the west.

"We don't even know who they *are*."

One of the woman's colleagues approached from the second

truck, swinging a rifle onto his shoulder. She said to him, "Ten minutes, Dex."

The middle-aged man stepped back, cupped his hands around his mouth and roared, "Folks, we're moving on in ten! You gotta pee, pee now!"

As Dex and some of the others explored the gas station, Alia asked the woman. "Can we get a ride? We can't pay you back with anything, but we'll work for it. See, we were hiking with some friends when suddenly—"

"Oh, I *really* don't need to hear your carefully-constructed fake background story, my dear." She pursed her lips. "We don't have a lot of space... But I do like your tents. Swap you the tents for a ride?"

"It's a deal," Danny said.

"Excellent. I see you're missing an arm... You don't want to be riding in the back with that. The roads can be bad and sometimes you'll need two hands to hold on. You head on back to the very last truck there. That's Tom's truck. Tell him Viv said to let you ride in the cab with him." She glanced at Nathan. "You look familiar."

"Yeah, my mom tells me that all the time."

Viv laughed, and to Alia she said, "He's a smart one. Pack up your stuff, kids."

A few minutes later, just as they had finished dismantling their tents, the man called Dex emerged from the gas station empty-handed. "Nothing in there but hungry-looking spiders," he told Viv. "Place was cleaned out years ago."

"Then we're done," Viv said. She opened the cab door and to Alia and Nathan, said, "Climb on top. Folks up there'll make space for you."

Dex said, "Whoa... Just a minute. You packing? Because yesterday we were on a run and picked up a guy who had a gun and he tried to steal one of our trucks. So I'm not letting you ride with us if you've got guns or knives."

Danny said, "No weapons, I promise."

"Then you won't mind if we search you? Just to be sure."

"Go ahead."

Alia estimated that between the eight trucks the convoy was carrying about fifty people. Two of them helped her and Nathan load their tents onto the truck, then they climbed up.

The trucks drove without stopping for hours. A couple of times she heard someone on the second truck playing a guitar, but the noise of the engines was too loud to make out the music. It was certainly too loud for normal conversation.

Alia fell asleep at some point before sunset, and woke to find Nathan leaning over her, his face barely visible in the darkness. "Alia, we've stopped."

"Why are we whispering?" she whispered back.

"Because some people are still asleep." He straightened up, and held out his hand to her. She grabbed it and he pulled her to her feet.

The trucks had parked inside a high-walled compound. Two large spotlights shone down from high towers, and it seemed to Alia that the place might have been a farm until recently. A few of their fellow travelers were climbing down from the trucks, looking exhausted and dazed.

Nathan climbed over the side of the truck and dropped to the ground, and Alia followed him. Nearby, the man called Dex said, "Smoothly done. You two are clearly agile. Strong, fit. You'll do well here."

Alia yawned. "Where are we, anyway?"

"You don't get to ask *questions*, little miss. You just keep your mouth shut and do what you're told."

The woman who seemed to be in charge, Viv, climbed down

from the cab. "No, Dex, we can answer that one. Kids, what we have here is a stronghold. A little place that a few of us put together after the Trutopian war. With this new war making *that* one look like a playground tussle, we've got to protect ourselves. When they come here—and they will—they'll find we're no pushovers. They'll have a fight on their hands like they've never imagined. But until then, we need workers for the fields, and to keep the trucks going, and to dig trenches and build new walls. So the deal here is that we feed and shelter you, and you work."

Nathan said, "Then we're not interested."

Dex said, "You don't understand, kid. You don't have a choice." He pointed off to the left. "See the wall? See those fine men in the towers? They're armed. No one in, no one out without our say-so."

"You're slavers," Nathan said.

The woman considered that. "Overseers is a better word. You're minors, after all. Someone's got to take responsibility for you."

Alia looked around. "Where's Danny?"

Dex laughed. "You mean your one-armed crippled friend who's not going to be worth feeding? Yeah, we left *his* sorry butt back at that gas station." He swung his rifle down from his shoulder, aimed it straight up, and let off a shot.

The noise woke up the rest of the sleeping passengers, and Dex shouted out, "All right, folks! Apologies for the subterfuge, but we figured you weren't gonna be willing to join us if you knew what was really going on. Fact is, we got guns and you don't. That means, for the *idiots* among you, that we got the power and you got *squat*! Now you folks have had your rest, so it's time to get to work! First, you unload the trucks. The boys here'll tell you where everything goes. You'll know which of us are in charge because they'll be the ones with the aforementioned guns." He turned away, and as he passed Nathan and Alia he snarled, "What are you two lookin' at? Get to work!"

Alia had been assigned to the wheat field, cutting the wheat with a small curved knife. At the end of every day, she had to clean and sharpen the knife before returning it to one of the overseers.

She guessed that they were still in Oregon, because almost all of the cars and trucks had Oregon number plates, but there was no way to narrow down their location.

Nathan had been put on trench-digging duty and Alia only saw him at the breakfast line in the morning and the supper line at night. Sometimes they managed to exchange a few words before the overseers stepped in: they discouraged the workers from talking to each other.

Even at night when the workers were all crammed into the "dormitory"—an old, rotting barn with moldy straw bales for beds—at least one overseer kept watch, always with a loaded rifle and wearing an expression that very clearly said, "Don't even *think* about it."

Alia's make-shift bed was very close to the front, in full view of the overseer. Nathan was nearby, on the edge of the second level, about two meters above ground. At night, sometimes Alia would roll into her back and look up, and Nathan would be lying on his side, looking back at her. He'd give her a brave smile, and mouth, "You OK?" Most of the time she'd nod, but not always.

They were fed on bowls of cereal and water, sometimes with a little freeze-dried fruit mixed in, and given a small cup of reconstituted orange juice every other day. "That's so's you don't get scurvy," Alia was told by the old woman doling out the cups.

They worked from dawn until dusk, without stopping.

On the morning of the eighth day a woman whose name Alia never learned attempted to escape by running toward one of the trucks as it was returning through the gates. At the last second the woman threw herself to the ground and skidded between the truck's front wheels. As the gates closed, Alia had a last glimpse of her behind the truck, rolling to her feet and running.

Then the gates closed, and there was a single gun-shot.

The following week, a man working next to Alia in the field threw down his scythe and said, "I can't take this any more." He strode towards their overseer and said, "Shoot me, then. Kill me in cold blood if you're that much of a monster."

The overseer, a woman in her twenties, raised her gun and pointed it at his head. "Back to work."

"Go on!" the man screamed. "*Do* it! Murder me and condemn yourself for all eternity!"

The overseer swung her gun to the side, aiming it at Alia. "You work, or *she* dies. You want that on your conscience?"

The man returned to work, but Alia had seen the look on his face. He had hesitated. He had taken the time to consider that just maybe he *could* live with her death on his conscience. She hated him for that, for being so cowardly and selfish.

Later that night, as she lay in the barn unable to sleep, she realized that if the circumstances had been the other way around, maybe she would have hesitated too.

We have to get out of here!

The next morning, she passed Nathan in the line for breakfast and whispered, "The overseer called Cale falls asleep on duty. Think he's on tonight. Watch me."

But there was a different overseer that night, and the next

night, and the next. Then it was Cale's turn again, but Alia fell asleep before he did.

Their first chance to escape didn't come until their fifth week in the compound. Cale was on night-watch duty, and the sky was moonless. Alia had noticed when he settled down he clicked on his rifle's safety—just in case he twitched in his sleep and shot someone.

She spent hours that night lying on her side, watching Cale, until he finally nodded off. The rifle went slack in his hands.

Alia rolled off her hay-bale and barely breathed as she approached him.

Nathan had been watching: he dropped down from his level and stopped next to her. He gestured towards the overseer's rifle.

She reached out and carefully pulled it free from the sleeping man's loose grip.

Nathan took the rifle from her, hefted it in his hands for a moment, then jabbed the rifle's butt hard into the side of the Cale's head. Hard enough that Alia was sure she heard his skull crack.

Nathan slung the rifle over his shoulder, took Alia's hand in his, and silently they ran for the wall.

She knew that there could be sensors on the wall, or that one of the guards in the towers might glance their way at the wrong moment, but there was no going back now.

The wall was four meters high. She ran ahead of Nathan, stopped with her back to the wall and her hands clasped in front of her. He placed his left foot into her hands and jumped as she hoisted him up.

Nathan grabbed the top of the wall and pulled himself up, then lay flat, face-down along the top and stretched his arm down.

Michael Carroll

Alia took a few steps back, ran, jumped, and caught his arm.

On the other side of the wall they knew that they couldn't run: the sudden movement would attract the overseers' attention. So they crawled away from the compound through the long grass, slowly, carefully, and Alia couldn't stop thinking about something her father had told her many years ago. "You never hear the bullet the kills you. So if you *do* hear a gunshot, that means you're still alive. You keep going."

After what she guessed was half an hour, Alia caught up with Nathan, and they looked back toward the compound. From here, all they could see were the watchtowers and the roofs of some of the larger buildings.

"What now?" Nathan asked. "If we're going to find Danny we'll have to figure out where *we* are first, and I was asleep when we were brought in."

"We can't go looking for Danny. Not yet, anyway. We have to help free everyone *else* in there."

"Are you crazy? The overseers outnumber us thirty-to-one and they have guns!"

"You're a superhuman, Nathan."

"Not right now, I'm not." The young clone shook his head. "Alia, there's no way in without being seen. What *can* we do to help the other slaves?"

"We have to do *something*. If we walk away and don't even *try* to help the others, what does that make us?"

"It makes us still *alive,* that's what."

The people moved slowly but steadily along the interstate highway, a constant trickle of shattered lives marching on blistered feet. They walked with their heads down, and their stomachs empty. They had been on the road for so long that they no longer looked for food inside the wrecked cars they passed, or reacted to the far-off explosions, or stopped to help when one of them collapsed.

Danny Cooper *had* stopped to help, at first. He thought that might have been a week ago, when he first encountered this band of refugees.

They were marching east, towards the Great Lakes. Everyone knew that the borders were impassible but some said that there was a way to get from Michigan into Canada. There, the Canadians were welcoming people with open arms. The people behind this didn't want Canada, it was said. They only wanted the United States.

Some people said otherwise, that this great migration was destined for Elizabeth City in North Carolina where boats were waiting to take them across the Atlantic to Europe and Africa.

Danny knew that it was all a fantasy, that there was no salvation at the end of the journey because the journey didn't have an end. This was a ragged group of starving people who were fleeing the war and had collectively invented a more attractive reason for their migration than fear.

From ahead came a soft, steady rumbling sound that he first took to be far-off thunder. But it was persistent, and a few minutes later he saw what it was: people walking over a fallen highway sign. Though it was now buckled and scratched and smeared with dirt, he was just about able to make out the words "Lincoln" and "Airport."

Nebraska, he said to himself. *How did I get this far into Nebraska without realizing?*

Ahead, he thought he could see the city. *If this* is *Lincoln, Nebraska...* He turned to the right, looking south-west. *Then Sakkara is about one hundred and forty miles that way.*

He fell back into step with the other shuffling refugees.

A hundred yards past the sign, a man had fallen and the

woman with him was trying to help him up. She pleaded with Danny, but he wouldn't look her in the eye. *Don't stop. The others will see it as weakness and then next thing they're begging you for food or water or to carry their children.*

He kept marching, and the woman's voice followed him.

I've only got one arm.

I'm starving too.

I've been on the road longer than you or anyone else.

I can't help you.

Someone else will come along.

It'll be all right in the end.

Someone else will be here to save the day and...

He stopped, forcing the man behind to walk around him muttering, "Jerk."

There isn't going to be someone else, Danny said to himself. *There's me. I'm here. And I can help, I just don't want to be dragged into your world and feel obliged to solve your problems too.*

But I will.

Danny turned back toward the woman, and eased his way through the downcast crowd.

The woman shrank away from him when she saw him returning, but he crouched next to her and said, "I'm sorry. I only have one arm, but between us I think we can get him on his feet."

With some effort they hoisted the man up, but he was too weak to walk unaided. Danny tucked his right shoulder under the man's left arm and tried to support him, but neither of them had the strength to go more than a few yards.

"Leave me," the man said to the woman, his words breathless and rasping. "Pneumonia, I think. Just leave and go on."

"I'm not leaving you!"

"There's nothing out there for us, Fran." He gestured to Danny to help him over to the side of the road.

Danny helped him to sit in the shade of a smashed up white Toyota, and the man gasped his thanks. "How'd it happen so fast, huh?" he asked when he'd recovered a little. "I used to hear people saying that the most civilized man was only three missed meals away from barbarianism, but I thought that was just one of those things. You know? People say stuff that they hear and they never check if it's true, they just believe it because it's a good story and they *want* it to be true."

Danny said, "Like the one about dropping a penny from the top of the Empire State Building. It'll hit the ground with the speed of a bullet."

"Hah, yeah. It's nonsense... But the one about the three missed meals?" He looked up at the stream of refugees. "I think we've got an answer on that one."

The woman lowered herself down next to the man. "We'll rest here for a while. Thank you for coming back to me. No one else..." She cut herself off. "No. I can't blame them. *We* passed people too, ignored their tears."

Danny said, "Me too. I *want* to do more. I used to be able to do more, a lot more, but... I'm waiting for something to kick in. I thought it would have happened by now." He shook his head. "I'm sorry, that probably doesn't make any sense." He stood up, turned to face back the way he had come. "I *will* do more. I'm not going to give up just because I'm powerless."

At his feet, the woman said, "You're right. We don't have to do everything. But we do have to do *something*."

The man smiled at Danny. "Good luck to you, son. What *will* you do?"

He took a deep breath, and turned towards the south-east,

towards Sakkara. "I'm going to kill Krodin."

The woman asked, "Who?" and Danny realized, for the first time, that only a handful of people even knew what this war was about.

Chapter 15

In the small town of Klarfeld, Wisconsin, Stephanie Cord and Mina Duval rummaged through a thrift store and approached the teller with eight dollars' worth of old clothes, plus a pair of thick-framed glasses for Alex: he looked identical to Colin so a disguise was necessary. They'd left him at their campsite on the edge of a field, two miles outside the town. This time they'd made sure to note the landmarks they'd passed along the way: the previous week, a hundred miles from here, they'd managed to miss a turn on the way back to their campsite and it had taken them an extra four hours to find Alex again.

"Costume party," Stephanie explained to the teller.

The teller—a girl about her own age—said, "Yeah, totally," and rang up the items on the antiquated cash register.

As they were leaving, Mina whispered, "Did you see that?"

"See what?" Stephanie was stuffing the items into her backpack.

"You gave her a ten, she gave you two back, but she only entered *five* dollars into the till! She ripped you off!"

"No, she ripped off whoever owns the store."

"We should report her."

"Good idea. Bring attention to ourselves." Stephanie looked along the street, then turned around and looked the other way. "No cops to be seen. Oh well. *Next* time, we'll report her."

Mina's response was drowned out by the scream of a north-bound low-flying US Air Force jet, then another, and a third.

They were almost immediately followed by loud, wavering siren that brought everyone in the stores out on to the street. An old man with the long strands of his comb-over haircut not yet plastered back into place emerged from a barber's shop, followed by an even older man with obviously-dyed black hair and a barber's smock.

"Air-raid siren," the first man said.

The barber said, "Nope. That's the flood warnin'."

"Same siren, you old fool." The man turned to Mina and Stephanie. "You girls mind you get home. Double-quick, too."

A US Army jeep roared along the street, following the path of the jets.

"Does this happen a lot?" Stephanie asked the old men.

"Been a couple of years," the barber said. "I'll see if there's anything about it on the radio." He ambled back into the store just as four more jeeps raced after the first in quick succession.

Mina said, "Steph, we need to get back to Alex." She looked north. "And he's in *that* direction."

The old man said, "You two on the run? I saw you earlier. You don't know this town and you don't seem to got a car. You were looking in the window of the bakery like starving dogs, now you're shopping at the thrift store."

Mina asked, "So?"

"So I'm just wondering where you took your low-profile lessons, because maybe you can get your money back."

Another string of jeeps, another two jets. By now, it seemed like the whole town was on the street, watching.

Then a final jeep appeared, and riding in the back, standing up, was a soldier with a bullhorn. The jeep stopped in the center of the street and the soldier roared into the bullhorn, "Attention, people of Klarfeld! A state of emergency has been declared! You need to get off the streets and into your homes—immediately! We have a situation developing in La Crosse so for your own safety you will comply!"

The old man called out, "What kinda situation is it, Lieutenant? Are we talkin' sandbags or storm-cellars?"

The soldier lowered his bullhorn. "You serve, sir?"

"Three tours and proud. Silver star."

The soldier glanced down at his driver, who looked back and nodded. He jumped down from the jeep and approached the old man, then glanced at Mina and Stephanie. "These girls with you, sir?"

Stephanie said, "He's our grampa. We're staying with him for the summer."

The old man nodded. "*That's* the truth. Eatin' me out of house and home."

The soldier stepped closer. "Sir, I can't tell you what's going on, *officially*, because then you'd know you oughta stock up and prepare for a siege and barricade your doors and windows. You got hardware at home?"

The old man said, "I brought back some souvenirs, yeah. How bad are we talkin', son?"

The soldier suddenly looked weak, exhausted. "They're everywhere. Half of Minneapolis is in flames, and I just heard we lost Madison. The enemy are... In the city, they're gangs. In the country, they're survivalists. In between... Biker gangs, the Klan, all the hate groups. They've stopped fighting each other and they're taking on the cops and the military. And it's not just here. It's *everywhere*. They're destroying bridges and blocking roads and taking down power-stations and cell-phone towers. They're picking off the cops and the National Guard and the fire department. I saw action during the Trutopian war but that was a cake-walk. *This*... this is *hell*. On the way here we saw a cop car on the freeway. Seems they'd stopped to assist at an accident. They were gunned down. Ambushed. There are similar reports all over the country. I heard that just outside of 'Frisco the gangs stormed a *school* and lynched the teachers. Half the country is without power and in Mississippi someone poisoned a reservoir. Before the cell-phone towers went down my sister told me she'd seen a bunch of guys attack a girl because she was in a wheelchair. They said that America is for the *strong*, and that the weak should be weeded out."

The soldier looked away for a moment, and shook his head. "I love this country. But... There's no going back from this. I can no longer put my hand on my heart and say that this is the greatest country in the world. The United States of America is dead."

Kenya Cho returned to the campsite with good news for Renata: "There's a whole bunch of rabbits over that way—we're not going to starve!"

Renata emerged from their tent and said, "I'm not sure I can kill a rabbit."

"I'm not saying we kill one. I'm saying that tomorrow we follow them and eat what *they* eat. I'm assuming that they're not cannibals, so we should be OK."

Renata dropped to her knees next to the small campfire and poked at it with a stick. "Sounds good. What do we have left?" She tossed the stick into the fire and lay back.

"One can of peaches in syrup," Kenya said. She looked up at the sky. "We've got about an hour until sunset. So don't add any more fuel to the fire."

"Because we want it to die out before it gets dark. Got it."

Kenya dropped down next to Renata She didn't want to admit it, but she was quite enjoying herself. Life out here under the stars was better than in Sakkara or the Substation. Here, she could more easily imagine that the world was at peace. In the Substation she had always been conscious of how deep they were underground, and in Sakkara there had been the constant military presence.

She noticed that Renata was holding her hand up against the

sky, and said, "Still nothing?"

"No. It's taking too long. When Danny lost his powers a few years back, Colin saw him pass through one of the blue lights, and very soon after that Danny's powers came back. Then when *my* powers were gone, Colin brought me to a place where the blue energy was stored, and cracked it open. My powers came back instantly. So that's what we need. One of those mysterious blue lights."

"Which most of us can't see. And of which there are apparently very few."

"Right." Renata let her hand drop onto her stomach. "I wonder what the others are doing right now?"

"Probably in a five-star hotel suite eating... what *do* rich people eat? Whatever that is, and lots of it, from gold plates."

"A hotel suite with a giant bath!" Renata sighed. "A bath would be luxury. Or even a nice long shower. Or a short one." She let out a short, harsh laugh. "Let's be honest. Right now I'd settle for a freezing cold shower as long as the water was clean."

"Well, as long as we're wishing... I wish Cassandra would get in touch and tell us what's going on. For all we know the Substation isn't even there any more. That thing in the newspaper... You think it's real?"

"I hope not. But, yeah, it could be."

"An army of the disenfranchised," Kenya said, slowly shaking her head. "I've got to say, it's a smart move. Every culture develops its own clusters of psychopaths and hate-mongers, and your country seems to have nurtured way more than its fair share. All Krodin has to do is work them up into a frenzy, give them weapons and let them loose. They rampage across the country and the infrastructure collapses. Then he establishes himself as the new ruler."

"In school they told us that Mussolini may have been a merciless dictator but at least under his rule everything was efficient. Like, the trains ran on time. *That* one was apparently a big deal back then. I mentioned that to my dad once and he said, 'Sure, the trains ran on time... *if* you were the person responsible for scheduling them and you had to give a full report to the ruling party every week.'"

Kenya sat up and reached out behind her to grab her backpack. "I do kind of like the idea of a unified world." She lifted the backpack onto her lap and opened it. "No countries, no borders. Full freedom of religion and all that. That's what we had in the Trutopian community in Madagascar." She removed their last can of peaches, handed it to Renata, and began to fish around inside the backpack for their can-opener. "Or that's what we *thought* we had. But it was all a lie. Victor Cross making the world dance to his tune. But better him than Krodin."

"I wouldn't say that in front of anyone else, if I were you," Renata said. She sat up and took the can opener from Kenya. "You never met Solomon Cord."

"Yeah, I know."

"Cross is a murderer. I know Krodin is too, but in a way he's just... a wild animal. Or a tornado, that might be more accurate. He's a force of nature. Cross took my family hostage, did you know that?"

"I did. Sorry, I wasn't thinking."

Renata passed the open can to Kenya. "That's OK. Maybe when this is over you'll get to meet them. They'd like you a lot."

Kenya smiled. "Thanks, but you know how I am when it comes to meeting people." She waved her index finger in the direction of her own face. "The scars put them off." She spooned a half-peach out of the can and stared at it for a second. "I hate my face."

"I know."

They took turns in eating the peaches, then shared the syrup, and when they were done Kenya said, "Thanks for not saying something like, 'But people can see your inner beauty shining through.' I hate that dippy 'everyone is born equal' rubbish."

"Yeah, me too. If there's inner beauty, then there should be inner ugly as well. Or even just inner mediocrity."

Kenya laughed at that. "Ah, life is weird and complicated and sometimes horrible. But considering the alternative, I'll take it." She reached into her backpack and pulled out their map. "Where *are* we...? OK, so, we're about eight kilometers—that's five miles to you American Luddites—north-west of a place called Duck Creek Village."

"Still in Utah, then?" Renata asked.

"Oh yeah. We've got a long way to go before we reach Arizona." Kenya folded the map. "So we don't know where we're going, but we'll know when we get there... It's getting dark." She stood up and kicked dirt over their campfire until it went out, then, in the semi-darkness, she said, "Renata..."

"Yeah?"

"I think we should start heading back. To the Substation, I mean."

"Any particular reason?"

"I just kicked a bunch of dirt over the fire."

"Well, duh. I know. I was right here. I saw you do it."

"But did you *hear* me do it?"

Renata grinned. "No, I did *not*! Your powers are coming back!"

Kenya returned the smile. Maybe things were finally starting to turn around for them.

Chapter 16

The old man allowed Stephanie and Mina to carry his grocery bags for him, and as they walked along the quiet road leading out of Klarfeld he told them that his name was Brendan.

"My wife's passed these four years, and our daughter's got her own life in Georgia. So, you girls and your friend can stay with me awhile, as long as you help out around the house. The gable-ends gotta be painted and I don't do heights any more. Doctor's orders. And the garden's getting overgrown. Stuff like that. And my Jenny was a *preserver*." When Mina had asked what that meant, he said, "Spent her life makin' jams and jelly, pickling fruit and vegetables, that kinda thing. It was her hobby. It used to be that she gave it away. But most of our friends and relatives are gone now. We got a basement full of that stuff. If there is a war coming then we're gonna be glad of the supplies."

When they reached a narrow side-road, Brendan said, "My place is just along here, on the left. See there between the trees? That white rectangle? That's the chimney block." He took the grocery bags from them. "You go get your friend." He handed them two twenty-dollar bills. "And pick up some more food on the way back, OK? There's no way of knowing how long this thing is gonna go on for."

They walked side-by-side back into the town, and already people were boarding up windows and doors, and everyone they passed seemed to be regarding them with suspicion.

"This place was a *lot* more friendly a couple of hours ago," Mina said. "What do you think? Should we really go stay with that old guy, or should we move on?"

"We should stay. At least until we have a better idea of what's happening."

When they reached their campsite in the woods forty

minutes later, there was no sign of Alex, and their packs and equipment were gone.

For a moment, Stephanie thought that they'd just come to the wrong location, but there was a specific tree she'd noted as they'd left for town, and a small scorch-mark in the ground, the site of the previous night's campfire.

Mina turned in a slow circle. "So... this is unsettling. Where do you think—" She stopped. "What was that? A noise?"

Stephanie shook her head. "I didn't hear anything."

"Something *crawling...*" Mina turned to the left and briskly marched away.

"Mina, wait! Come back!" Stephanie watched her for a few seconds, then muttered, "Stupid girl!" under her breath. She set off after Mina, and found her a minute later, staring down at something half-buried under dead leaves and twigs. "What is that?"

"It's Alex," Mina whispered. "He was... he was moving—twitching—and then he stopped. Just now."

Stephanie took a step back. The young clone was lying on his side, facing them. His sweater and jeans were torn, his face bruised, his hand and arms covered with fresh cuts and scratches.

Mina crouched down beside him. "So... I'm thinking that someone found him, and they tried to take our stuff, and he fought back."

She reached out to push Alex onto his back, and Stephanie called out, "Mina, don't!"

"He's not going to get any *deader*, Steph." Mina pointed to Alex's stomach and chest. "Multiple stab wounds."

Stephanie put her hand on Mina's shoulder and tried to pull her away. "We have to call the sheriff. They'll want to collect evidence, and you're contaminating the scene."

Mina jumped back. "Oh, you're right. I've seen some of those shows." She looked back at Stephanie. "So, I'll stay here with him and you... Steph, are you crying?"

"He's *dead*, Mina! He was our friend and someone just murdered him!"

Mina frowned. "But... We didn't know him that well. And, well, he's just... I'm not saying he's not a real person, but, you know. He's a *clone*."

"So are you!"

"Yeah, I know, but I'm my real age. Alex and his brothers were grown in a vat." And then Mina said, "Ahhh... I see. You're upset because he looks just like Colin so this makes you think of *Colin* being dead. That makes sense. This *is* what Colin would look like if he was dead."

Stephanie was shaking, but she wasn't sure whether it was from grief or fury with Mina. "Just... just stay here and don't touch him! I'll get help!"

She ran, and had reached the town's main street before she realized what she'd done: she'd left Mina behind, on her own, in the woods where someone had just murdered Alex.

But turning back now would be a worse mistake: she ran on, faster, until she saw the sheriff's office—and the sheriff and her deputies speeding away in their cars, sirens blaring.

Inside, a shaking, pale receptionist told Stephanie that there was a state of emergency and she should be at home.

"Seriously, get outta here." The young man was kicking an empty plastic crate ahead of him, towards a vending machine.

"Someone attacked my friend! We were camping..."

"I can't help you. I'm sorry." The receptionist used a key from his belt to open the vending machine and began to load the crate with bottles of water.

"They *killed* him!"

The young man paused, then resumed loading his crate without looking at Stephanie. "I'm sorry to hear that. I really am. But this is a bad situation. Everything is coming apart out there." He scooped up his crate and darted into a side-office.

A few minutes later, she glanced out through the building's glass doors and saw the same man run past, then there was the screeching of tires as he drove away, and she was alone in the Sheriff's office.

From somewhere far away there came the sounds of a gunfight, and shortly afterwards the power in the entire town blacked out.

It was dark by the time Stephanie made her way back to the woods, where Mina was still waiting next to Alex's body.

They returned to Brendan's house, resolving to go back the next day and bury their friend. But the next day the town was overrun with strangers, all carrying weapons and forcing their way into the stores and homes.

For what seemed like hours Victor Cross listened to the battle raging through the Substation. It started far away, possibly on the opposite side of the station. Sound didn't carry as far as it would have in an empty tunnel of the same dimensions; he presumed that was because much of the Substation was packed with living quarters and storage areas.

He had to make such presumptions because he still hadn't see anything of the Substation beyond the few square meters of curved metal wall on the other side of his prison's doorway.

There were gunshots and screams and explosions and shouted orders, some muffled, some sharp. More unsettling were the tremors. Most were fairly mild, but this deep underground any tremor was worrying. A big enough explosion could weaken the structure enough that it started to collapse.

Then the sound of the battle stopped, abruptly, and Victor allowed himself to relax. *OK. It's over for now. So whichever side won, they'll be coming for me. All is well.*

Seconds became minutes, and minutes became hours. There was no sound from outside.

They're all dead. They're all dead and I'm the last one alive and I'm trapped in here!

A secondary part of his brain automatically took control and herded the panicky thought processes into a quiet corner. *You're not going to suffocate—you'd die of old age long before that happened.*

But you might starve to death or die of thirst if there really isn't anyone else alive out there.

His hands and feet were uncuffed, and for that he was grateful. The only thing keeping him inside the metal room was the chain between the metal collar around his neck and a strong-looking loop in the ceiling. The chain was two meters long, which allowed him to almost reach the door with his out-stretched foot.

So how do you free yourself, Victor?

There was nothing in the room aside from the small metal stool. At night—or what he presumed was meant to be night-time; down here there was no way to be certain—his guards brought a flimsy metal cot into the room so that he could sleep without the chain choking him.

He realized now that until he managed to get himself free he wasn't going to be able to lie down.

That was worrying.

He put his hands up to the collar and—as he had done many times before—felt all the way around it, inside and out, searching for cracks or flaws in the metal. There was nothing but a neatly-welded seam. He suspected that the weld was stronger than the collar itself. It would not be easy to break. The metal felt like steel, and the chain was attached via a loop welded to the collar.

Pulling it off over his head was the first thing he'd tried, but it was just too tight. If the collar's inner diameter had been two centimeters larger, he'd have been able to slip it off.

But the collar was still loose enough that he could turn it all the way around. And the loop in the ceiling was fixed. As he turned the collar, the chain began to twist around itself and he had to move away from the center of the room to avoid the links wrapping around his neck.

A few more turns and it was taut. And that was all he could do with it. Victor imagined that a superhuman with physical strength would have no trouble snapping it, but he was no stronger than a normal person.

He spun around a few times to relax the chain again, then picked up the stool. *If I can break off one of the legs it might be possible to wedge one between the chain's links and force them apart.* This seemed feasible. There was a lot of links, and all he needed to do was find one that was weak enough.

But how to break the stool? That's the question.

I could wrap the chain around it, keep turning the chain until it crushes the stool. Yeah, that'll work, and then I'll have a bunch of metal shards but no way of even sitting down.

He looked around the cell again. It was large enough that the chain only allowed him to make contact with the floor, but even if he had been able to reach the walls it wouldn't have been much use. They were metal panels fixed together with heavy bolts. He doubted he'd be able to unscrew any of the bolts bare-handed, and even if he could, what would be the point?

If I could remove enough of the side panels then the rest wouldn't be able to support the ceiling. It'd collapse. And then I could...

Victor looked up. The ceiling was also composed of similar metal panels bolted together.

All I have to do is unbolt the panel that the chain is attached to.

He stood on the stool, reached upwards and judged the distance between his fingertips and the ceiling panels. *That can't be more than forty centimeters.*

He jumped, and the tip of his ring finger brushed the ceiling panel.

Victor spent the next hour jumping up from the stool, grabbing the chain, holding on with one hand while he tried to undo one of the bolts with his other hand.

He slipped four times, but each time managed to hang onto the chain, aware that if he fell all the way to the floor he'd probably break his neck.

When he could take no more, he collapsed onto the stool and sat there staring at his bloodied, blistered fingers.

It was pointless. He hadn't managed to budge the bolt even the smallest fraction of a degree. And even if he were somehow able to do it, to detach the panel he'd need to undo sixteen bolts.

And then the panel would crash down on me and probably cave in my skull.

"I can't do this," he said aloud. "Someone's got to come for me!"

He forced himself to stand, took a few deep breaths to steady himself, then bellowed, *"Help!"*

From immediately outside his metal room, a man's voice said, "What kind of help would you like, Victor?"

He froze. Then, tentatively, he called, "Hello?"

The voice came back. "Hello."

"Who's out there?"

"*I* am."

"That... that's not making things any clearer."

The door swung open, and a tall, strongly-built man stepped through. "So, Victor Cross. Why didn't you shout for help sooner? I've been standing out there for *hours*."

"Who are you?"

"My name is Krodin. I believe I have you to thank for my rescue from Mars."

"You've been standing outside *waiting* for me to ask for help?"

"No, I was wondering whether your legendary intelligence would enable you to think of a solution. Evidently, it didn't."

Victor said, "I think it did, in the end. You're here. Why has it taken so long for you to find me?"

"McKendrick is wilier than I'd realized. We knew he'd moved you when the Substation was evacuated, but we couldn't find you. And believe me, we *searched*. For a while we even began to wonder whether you might already be dead."

Victor leaned to the side a little and peered out through the open door. "So we *aren't* in the Substation?"

"No, we are. He hadn't moved you at all."

"And you didn't *think* of that?"

"Of course we did," Krodin said. "But McKendrick is devious. He planted fake evidence that told us you *were* still here. We discovered that the evidence was fake before we actually investigated, so we concluded there was no need for an investigation."

"*Fake* fake evidence. Yeah, that has McKendrick's fingerprints all over it. Why did you come now?"

"We were looking for McKendrick himself. He and his pet telepath have completely disappeared. We've checked every possible location, interrogated *hundreds* of people, and there is nothing. The trail is cold. So we decided to start the search from the beginning. We came here and discovered that a platoon of soldiers was left behind. Presumably to protect you. Or to ensure that you wouldn't escape."

"So you've raised an army and gone to war."

"Correct. Now the dust is settling." Krodin paused for a second. "But the problem is that it's settling on blood, and that does not make for a solid foundation. Many of the New Heroes are still at large, and their powers are starting to return."

"And you need me to help the clones get back to full power first."

Krodin slowly shook his head. "No, I don't. Shadow is still extremely powerful, as am I. The New Heroes are no threat to me. Not directly. But it's logical for a gardener to destroy the weeds before they overrun the flowers."

"So you've taken America, or you're about to. What's the *next* part of your plan? The rest of the world?"

"Of course."

"And *then*...?" Victor asked, failing to mask a slight smile.

"There is no further stage. Conquering the world is the ultimate goal. What more *can* there be?"

"And that's why you need me just as much as I need you, Krodin. You are the strength, I'm the imagination. We're going to make a good team."

The immortal smiled. "No, we are not. I don't need you, Victor. There's only room for *one* arrogant, egotistical superhuman in charge of this planet, and that position has been filled."

"Then... then why did you come to rescue me?"

Krodin moved backwards towards the door. "Whoever said that this was a rescue?"

Victor felt his heart racing. "No... Please! You can't leave me here to die!"

"I'm just leaving you here. It's not up to me whether that means you'll die. There *is* a way for you to escape, Victor. But if you can't see it then you're not as clever or as courageous as you believe you are, and that means you're no good to me." He stepped out through the door, and as he pushed it closed he said, "Consider this an audition. If you can get out, come find me. Perhaps we can strike a deal."

Victor Cross screamed until he could no longer stand, then he collapsed onto the stool.

He didn't realize he was crying until his tears stung his cut and blistered hands.

Eventually, the tears subsided and his body submitted to exhaustion.

But every time he dozed into sleep, he slumped to the side and the chain became taut and tugged at the collar around his neck.

Chapter 17

In Sakkara, Shadow walked in a slow circle around Colin Wagner. They were in the center of the gymnasium, and all of the hostages watched from around the walls.

"Tell me you understand how this works, Colin."

"If I resist you, you'll kill my mother, my sister and Niall Cooper."

"That's right." Shadow smiled. "You believe me?"

"I believe that's what you *intend* to do. But you won't be able to do it if I kill you first."

Shadow slowed, and looked Colin up and down. "Power-wise, you're at about forty per cent of maximum, Krodin says. He can see it, somehow." The clone shrugged. "He could be making that up for all I know. So what's your job, Colin?"

"To defend Sakkara when the New Heroes come."

"That's right. And you have some experience fighting your friends, don't you? In Lieberstan you almost killed them. But you were under Yvonne Duval's mental control then. You couldn't stop yourself from obeying her orders... *except* for her order to kill. You hurt your friends, but you were able to resist the kill order. See, that's interesting to me. You're under my orders now, and I'm telling you to kill your friends when they show up. Are you going to do it?"

"No."

"Then your little sister will die." Shadow put out his right hand, fingers splayed and palm-down, and slightly waggled it from side to side. "You're on shaky ground there, Col. You don't love your sister, is that it? Little Abigail not as close to you as, say, Renata is?"

"Of course I love her."

"But you'd let her *die*? What kind of a monster *are* you,

Wagner?"

Colin raised his eyes. "Oh, you really are such a smug little *jerk*, aren't you?"

Shadow looked over towards Caroline. "Is he allowed to speak to people like that?" He didn't wait for an answer. Instead, he poked Colin's upper arm. "You'll defend Sakkara even if it means killing your friends. Simple as that. But to make it even simpler, we'll be moving all of the hostages—including Caroline, Niall and little Abigail—to somewhere else. Just in case you get the idea that you can break them out of here."

"What about Zeke and Eldon? Are their powers returning too?"

"Slowly, yes. You're a little ahead of them... But not for long. Like you, Krodin can see the blue lights." Shadow smiled. "You understand the implication?"

"If your brothers can absorb the blue energy that might boost their recovery."

"Krodin and Zeke and Eldon are out there right now, using your StratoTruck to search for your friends, and they'll be looking out for the blue lights along the way. If they see one... Zap! They're recharged and the chances of your friends surviving are decimated."

From the side of the room, Caroline said, "Decimated means reduced by one in ten, Shadow. Avoid using words that you don't fully understand."

"You're not my teacher," Shadow said, "*or* my mother. So shut up."

"Don't speak to my mother like that," Colin said.

"Why? What are you going to do about it?"

Colin leaned closer. "I'm going to remind you that you're alone. Your boss and your brothers aren't here to back you up."

Shadow started to laugh, then immediately launched a

vicious punch at Colin's head.

Colin dodged the blow, caught Shadow's wrist in his left hand, and slammed out at the clone's jaw with his right fist.

He wanted to say something like, "Looks like your boss was wrong about that forty per cent," but this wasn't the time. Still holding on to Shadow's wrist, he hit him in the face again, and again.

Don't give him time to recover! Again!

He was vaguely aware of his mother and the other hostages rushing out of the room, but refused to let himself even think about how they were going to escape from the building.

The only thing now was Shadow.

The clone's face was a mess of blood, and the only reason he hadn't yet collapsed to the floor was that Colin was still holding his wrist.

He continued to hit, over and over, barely taking the time to breathe.

He felt something crack and he wasn't sure whether it was a bone in his own aching hand or part of Shadow's jaw.

Another blow, and two of Shadow's teeth shot out and rattled across the gymnasium floor.

Niall Cooper's voice beside him said, "Colin!"

He didn't turn to look. He didn't stop punching. "What?"

"Use this!"

Colin briefly glanced at Niall. The ten-year-old boy was holding out a thick, half-meter-long metal bar that looked almost too heavy for him to lift.

Colin grabbed it from him. "Good work. Now, get going, Niall!"

He was surprised to discover that the metal bar seemed to inflict less damage on Shadow's face than his own fists, but it did mean that his fist now wasn't taking any damage at all.

He became aware that Shadow had stopped flinching with each blow, and wondered whether he'd gone too far. *Maybe he's dead.*

I always swore I'd never kill someone.

And then he realized that he was still hitting Shadow.

He let go of the clone's right arm and let him slump to the floor.

Shadow's face was a mess, but his chest was rising and falling, his breaths rasping but steady.

For a second, Colin looked at the blood-dripping metal bar and wondered whether stopping was a mistake. *This guy is going to recover, eventually. And then he'll come for me and everyone I know and* he *won't stop. He won't show mercy.*

He tossed the bar aside, and flexed his right hand. It hurt, a lot, but everything still worked.

Colin had known for over a week that his powers were returning. He'd found himself sleeping less and less, and realized he hadn't been hungry for days. He was starting to once again sense the flow of energy in his surroundings. His senses sharpened, his strength returned. And one night, one of the rare nights when he did sleep, his mother shook him awake to warn him that he was floating five centimeters above the floor.

He knew he was a long way from being back to full power, but right now this was enough. He had the strength to get the hostages down from the roof—he could hear them up there now—but he didn't know where they could go from there.

Worry about that later, he told himself.

He looked down at Shadow once more. *How long before he recovers? What can I do to delay his recovery besides killing him?*

If Renata was here and she had her powers, she could turn

him solid and just leave him.

Colin smiled. *I can't do that, but I can do something similar.*

He dragged Shadow's unconscious body through the building, leaving a long smear of blood behind him, as he tried to remember exactly where Niall Cooper had told him he'd found the entrance to the massive hollow concrete pylon that led down to the lowest levels.

When he found the entrance he hoisted Shadow up to it, pushed him through, then listened for the satisfying *crump* as he hit the bottom.

Then Colin climbed through the entrance himself and dropped down, not caring when he landed feet-first on Shadow's stomach.

He dragged Shadow out of the pylon and threw him across the floor, then found one of the water-pipes running across the ceiling. He ripped the pipe open: the water burst out in a continuous spray almost strong enough to knock him over. In seconds, Shadow was floating.

Colin waited until the water was up to his waist, then shut off the flow of water by crushing the pipe. The water sloshed around him as he waded back to Shadow, then he began to absorb its ambient heat into his own body. He made sure that Shadow was on his back, with his mouth and nose clear of the surface as the ice began to form around him, holding him in place. Then the clone's breath began to mist. The moisture in the air condensed on his skin, and the blood around his mouth crystallized.

Colin rose himself out of the water, and continued to siphon the heat until he estimated the temperature to be about minus eighty degrees Celsius. *That'll keep him out of commission for a while.*

Colin returned to the pylon and drifted back up through it.

It felt good to have his powers back, though he knew he wasn't strong enough yet to take on Krodin.

And from what he understood of the immortal's powers, he might *never* be strong enough. All of the New Heroes working together might never be strong enough.

From the outskirts of Lincoln, Nebraska, Danny had turned north towards Sioux City, Iowa: the opposite direction to Sakkara.

Several times every day he tried to initiate telepathic contact with Cassandra, but he knew it was probably futile. It was like picking up a telephone handset in the hope that the person you wanted to speak to just happened to be on the other end.

The roads were too exposed, so he stuck to following the banks of a slow-moving river. It was quiet, and peaceful—certainly more peaceful than many parts of his journey—and as he skirted around a town called Oakland he unwittingly walked straight into a hidden camp.

Forty heavily-armed men and women were staring at him an expression of surprise that he knew matched his own.

He said, "Uh... Sorry?"

The muzzle of a handgun was in his face, and on the other end of it was a man wearing a tattered and blood-stained US Air Force uniform. "You lost, son?" The man was stocky, a little shorter than Danny, and sporting a thick brown mustache.

"I think this might be the most lost I've ever been," Danny said.

"Now, we can do this one of *two* ways..."

"I'll choose the easy way."

"Never said one of the ways was going to be easy. Who are you with?"

"No one."

"Well, you're too young to be a soldier, so that makes you one of Krodin's."

"I'm neither, I swear."

"How'd you get past Cliff if you haven't had training?"

Danny shrugged. "No idea who that is. I was just walking, came around the bend and suddenly all you guys were here..." He looked around. This was clearly more than a temporary camp: there were campervans and tents, a large fire-pit, recently-washed clothing strung out on a line between the trees. And then he spotted a young man hurriedly carrying a toddler into one of the campers.

He turned back to the man with the gun and the mustache. "Trust me, I'm not one of Krodin's people. My name is Danny Cooper. I was one of the New Heroes."

A woman walked up to him and frowned at his face through cracked glasses. "Yeah. He does look like Cooper." She grabbed the loose right sleeve of Danny's jacket. "And he's got the one arm, too."

The man with the gun said, "I see. Now, don't go thinking about moving, son. I'm an excellent shot. Seriously, I've won *medals* for sharp-shooting. You do anything without my say-so and I'll put a round in the back of your head. Tell me that you comprehend."

"I understand. I won't run."

"If you *are* Cooper, maybe you can tell me why you people didn't fight back? Isn't that your *job*?"

"We all lost our powers. Temporarily, I hope."

"Too much of a coincidence that you all happen to lose your powers and then Krodin shows up."

Danny said, "It's not a coincidence if the man who took our powers away is the same one who brought Krodin here. He wanted us out of the way to smooth the path."

"Fair enough." The gun still hadn't wavered. "So... what do we do now? Where does this leave us?"

"I haven't eaten in days," Danny said.

"As you can probably guess, we don't have a lot to spare. So why would we share some with you? What can a one-armed ex-superhuman offer us in exchange for a bowl of soup?"

Danny shrugged. "I know some great stories?" he suggested.

The man put his gun away. "Yeah, that'll do. Amy, show the kid where he can wash up, then find him something to eat."

Chapter 18

Stephanie Cord held her breath and stared at the trapdoor above her head. Next to her, Mina Duval was doing the same thing. And on the far side of Mina, the old man was lying on his back, snoring gently.

Mina put her hand over Brendan's mouth and pulled it away instantly. "Ew!"

Stephanie mouthed, "What?"

Mina made a face and pointed to the string of drool that was dripping from the palm of her hand.

"I don't care!" Stephanie whispered. "Just make him stop snoring!"

She didn't need to: a heavy footstep on the trapdoor above woke the old man up. He opened his eyes and Stephanie and Mina were both glaring at him with their index fingers pressed against their lips.

A man's deep voice echoed from the kitchen above. "Nothing. You check the attic?"

"Yeah. Well, Vinnie did."

"All right... But the photos on the wall tell me that this guy's a veteran. So there's a strong chance he has a gun."

"Yeah, but he's not here, so he prob'ly took his gun with him." Another set of footsteps across the trapdoor. "If he—"

"Hold it," the first man said. "You hear that? The floor's hollow right there. Lift up the rug."

Shuffling sounds from above, then, "You weren't wrong. Trapdoor." The trapdoor rattled. "But it's locked."

"From the inside or the outside?"

"What do you think? From the outside. If it was locked from the inside that'd mean there's someone in there and I'd have *said* that. Look. Big bolt, heavy padlock."

"Find the key."

"Easier to shoot the lock *off*, Brian."

"Oh, really?" the first man said. "Is it *really*? Go ahead, then, Mister I Get All My Education From Action Movies. Go ahead and shoot at the hardened steel lock with your soft lead bullets and see if that works! Go on!"

"So it won't work, is that what you're telling me?"

"You'd have more luck climbing up a fire-escape while wearing skis."

"Well, there's an ax in the trunk. I'll get it."

"There's no time. Look, there won't be anything in there other than the old guy's collection of fifty-year-old newspapers or rotting dogs' heads or some other weird crap. My grandmother used to collect old postcards. Thousands of them, she had." The man's voice was beginning to fade as they moved through the house.

"A lot of people collect old postcards. Some of them are worth a fortune."

"Yeah, but grandma used to collect the *blank* ones, not the ones with the pictures."

After a few minutes, Stephanie said, "OK. I think we're safe now." She stood up and pushed on the underside of the trapdoor. It had been Mina's idea to leave the lock in place but remove the screws from the hinges: the trapdoor appeared to be locked but in fact it now opened the other way.

For extra realism, the old man had cut the heads off the screws and glued them into place on the hinge-plates.

As Mina followed Stephanie out, she said, "I'm glad they *didn't* try to shoot the lock off."

Brendan hoisted the ladder into place and used that to climb out of the cellar. He grunted with each step. "Not as young as I used to be... So, what did they take?"

Stephanie looked around the kitchen. The drawers had been pulled, their contents scattered across the floor, and the cupboards were open, and bare. "There wasn't much *to* take."

Brendan lowered the trapdoor into place. "Next time we might not be so lucky. We're going to have to find somewhere else to hide."

Mina said, "No, we should be fighting back! We can't keep going like this! Or, no, you know what we should do? We should leave the door open all the time. That way the next bunch will see that it's open and assume the house is abandoned. They won't rob us then."

"Suppose we do that," Stephanie said. "And suppose they're looking for somewhere to sleep for the night. They'll think, 'Hey, great, abandoned house—let's sleep there!' So we won't be doing that."

"All right, then... We get a pile of broken bricks and burnt timbers, and we pile them up around the front of the house to make it look like there's been a fire. No one's going to bother searching a burnt-out house. We could even get some black spray-paint and paint scorch-marks and smoke-damage around the windows."

Brendan nodded. "Oh, she's a smart one, this one. I like that idea. But make sure it's water-soluble paint so it'll be easier to wash off when all this is over."

Stephanie and Mina exchanged a glance at that. Stephanie said nothing, but was too late to stop Mina. "Brendan, things aren't going to go back to the way they were. Not *ever*. Those days are gone."

He pursed his lips as he stared back at her. "Well, they are with *that* attitude."

Stephanie began, "Mina..."

"I know, I know. We're guests here." She turned to the old

man. "I'm sorry."

"You're not forgiven."

"Yes I am."

"OK then." He up-righted a chair and sat down at the table. "Your idea is a good one. But I think maybe Stephanie is right. We should move on. There has to be someone around here who has a nuclear bunker that's seriously lacking an old man and two teenagers." He was silent for a moment, then said, "I never thought I'd see the day. Girls, you remember that lieutenant the first day I met you? All the things he said?"

Stephanie began scooping up the fallen cutlery. "We remember. If it hadn't been for him, there's no telling *where* we'd be now."

Mina said, "But Alex would still be alive."

Stephanie and Brendan said nothing, and Mina added, "Well, he *might*."

Stephanie left the kitchen on the excuse of checking through the rest of the house, but they all knew that right now she couldn't be in the same room as Mina.

I don't blame her, Stephanie told herself. *She's had a sheltered life. She doesn't really understand yet what death means. She wasn't around when Butler died and by the time we got her back he was long gone.*

But Alex...

Finding the young clone's body was the worst experience of Stephanie's life. Even worse than seeing her father's body being brought back to Sakkara.

Solomon Cord had been a fighter. He had chosen the path that, ultimately, led to his death. But Alex never had a chance, or a choice.

Someone—and she was certain that she would never learn who—had found their campsite and had decided that their belongings and equipment were worth more than Alex's life.

That had been over a week ago, and it hadn't yet been safe to return to the woods.

After a few minutes, she returned downstairs to the kitchen. Brendan was sitting on his own at the table, reading a newspaper that was so old the edges of its pages had turned yellow. He looked up at her and said, "Mina's resetting the early-warning system."

Brendan had set up a very thin copper wire across the narrow lane leading to the house, a few centimeters above the ground. The wire was looped to a nine-volt battery. If the wire snapped, interrupting the current, an alarm beeped inside the house—giving them a minute's heads-up on whoever was approaching down the lane.

"I know she's... odd sometimes, Stephanie, but she has a good heart. And she's been telling me about her sister. Now, *there's* a nasty piece of work." He carefully folded the newspaper and handed it to her. "Something to wrap your mind around, when you get a chance. In the meantime, there's got to be somewhere more secure than this old place." He looked around the room. "My Jenny would *not* have liked all these strangers going through her stuff. She was kind and gentle but if you pushed her too far she'd hit you with a stare that made you feel like you were six inches tall and made of glass. She'd have loved you, you know. And she'd have had plenty to say about Mina, too. Much of it complimentary. Well, *some* of it."

Stephanie asked, "Where *can* we go?"

"Depends on *why* you're going. If you just want to be safe from other people, you go to the remotest part you can find. If you want to *help* other people, then you probably need to go wherever they are. And if you want to fight, then you follow the gunfire. Soon enough, you'll find someone willing to fight you."

Brendan placed his hands flat on the table and pushed himself to his feet. "Look at the paper, Stephanie. Go on. Read the headlines."

Stephanie unfolded the old newspaper. It was a copy of the Wisconsin State Journal, almost thirty years old, and the headline read, "Jet-powered Hero Rescues Trapped Climber."

Brendan patted Stephanie on the shoulder as he passed. "See, Mina *has* been talking to me. Paragon was your father, wasn't it? And heroism is hereditary. You need to be where people can avail of your skills, where you can do the most good. Both of you. And you don't want an old man like me slowing you down. So as your acting commanding officer, I'm ordering you to leave me behind. I'll be OK here. You take anything and everything you might need, got that?"

"We're not leaving you!"

"I'll be in more danger on the road than I am here. Leaving me is the right choice. Now, look behind you."

She turned. Resting on the kitchen counter was a plain wooden box she hadn't seen before. It was about the size of a breakfast cereal box.

"Open it."

She opened the box. Inside was a handgun.

"That's an AMT Hardballer," Brendan said. "Courtesy of a friend of a friend. Though I suppose it doesn't matter any more how it ended up in my possession. Semi-automatic, stainless steel throughout, not the *best* gun in the world but it's reliable and it'll stop a charging bull in its tracks."

"Brendan, I can't take this!"

"Sure you can. Look, if you don't take it, then one day someone's gonna break in here and I might not be able to defend myself, and *they'll* take the gun. So if you don't take it, you'll be responsible for whatever they do with it."

"Yeah... that's not going to work on me."

"Just take the gun, huh? You won't be leaving me defenseless. I've got more." He paused. "A *lot* more. And believe me I know how to use them."

When they left Brendan's house the next morning, Stephanie had the gun tucked into her jeans. Mina didn't know about it— she wasn't sure she could trust Mina not to mention it to every person they met.

They were laden with supplies from Brendan's food cellar, almost three hundred dollars, and rough directions to Chicago, over two hundred miles away.

"So, what's in Chicago, anyway?" Mina asked as they walked.

"Us, in about a week."

"And we're going there because...?"

"Because there's something there I have to collect. It's a surprise, so don't keep asking."

"OK," Mina said. After less than a minute, she said, "I can't wait that long! What's the thing you have to collect?"

"You'll see."

"Is it something cool? Something dangerous? Something we're not supposed to have?"

Correct on all three counts, Stephanie thought. But she just smiled at Mina and said nothing.

Chapter 19

As they trekked north through Utah Renata realized that more and more often she had to turn around to check that Kenya was still behind her. Her powers allowed her to move in complete silence and she tended to automatically turn on that ability.

Now, as they followed an old, long-abandoned railway track, Renata once again looked back, but this time Kenya wasn't there.

She waited for a minute, thinking that her friend had probably gone foraging for berries, nuts and mushrooms again. The time she'd spent in Madagascar and Africa after the Trutopian war had made her an expert in living off the land.

Renata sat down on the track and pulled the bag of emergency candy from her backpack: a mixture of chocolate-covered raisins, M&Ms, and peanut butter Reese's Pieces.

It had been a long journey, but she figured they were on the downhill part now, so she could treat herself. *Kenya's powers are almost completely back, and I'm sure I'm getting stronger.*

She still wasn't able to turn her body crystalline, but there were three hundred miles to go before they reached the Substation. Plenty of time.

She dug into the bag and fished around until she found a green M&M, then put the bag away. There was no way to know how long it would be before they encountered another store that hadn't been looted or burned to the ground.

Five days earlier, they'd found a trading post: really just a wheel-less Winnebago stocked with dried foods and canned fruit. The men guarding the post had told them, "Three cans for a box of shotgun shells."

Kenya had said, "We have no shotgun shells, but... I can show you how to make nettle soup. It's a lot tastier than you'd think, and really good for you. There are nettles all over this area—that's basically free money."

The elder of the traders, a man sitting on a deckchair on top of the Winnebago with a pair of binoculars on his lap and a rifle by his side, had shouted down, "Nettle soup? Had that when I was a kid. Tastes like it's already been eaten. What have you got in the backpacks? Anything to trade?"

"We have chocolate," Renata said.

"Well, so do *we*. What have you got?"

Kenya produced three Hershey bars from her backpack. "What'll these get us?"

"Can of peas."

"That's all? *One* can?"

"It's a seller's market, kid. Look, where's the rest of your group? Maybe they've got something better?"

Renata pointed back the way they'd come. "Back that way. Steve and Donnie found an abandoned car, and all the dads are trying to get it started."

"Three cans of peas and a box of Fruitiflakes for a gallon of gas," the old man said. "Best I can do. *Unless...*" he looked down at them.

Renata felt an all-too-familiar knot in her stomach. "*Not interested. Kenya, let's go.*"

"But what about—"

Renata grabbed her arm and pulled her away from the Winnebago. "Just keep walking. Don't look back. If they come after us, run."

"What's going on?"

"You didn't see the way they were looking at us?"

"What about it?"

"Two teenage girls, on their own, no law and order any more, half the country is at war... They don't see us as customers. They see us as *product*."

The men from the trading post hadn't followed, and in the days since Renata had wondered if maybe she'd jumped the gun. Maybe the old man's comment had been innocent, maybe she'd just imagined that look on his face.

The cold metal of the train track was numbing her backside, so she stood up and looked back the way she'd come. The track was straight, and relatively clear of debris. There was no sign of Kenya.

OK, now I'm worried.

In a large, clear patch of dirt next to the track, she used the heel of her boot to mark a square inside a circle, a symbol she and Kenya had earlier decided would mean, "I'll be back: stay put!" Then she hoisted her backpack onto her shoulder and began to walk.

When was the last time I saw her?

Renata remembered the crumbling railway bridge that crossed the fast-moving river: Kenya had run ahead to ensure she spent as little time as possible on the bridge itself. *After that... There was the old waterwheel. We stopped there for a break.*

She scanned the undergrowth on both sides of the track as she walked. *Should have been more careful, Renata! It's your own fault. You know what she's like. A slow walker who gets distracted easily and moves in silence.*

Ahead, Renata spotted a section of the track where, long ago, someone had dug up the wooden sleepers. Fifteen in a row were missing.

OK, when we saw this bit Kenya asked me why anyone would want to take old railway sleepers. So somewhere after this, she disappeared.

She made another mark in the dirt, a triangle with two

horizontal lines through it that meant, "I've moved on: keep going." She walked back, taking her time, trying to see what it was that might have led Kenya away.

Then Kenya's voice right beside her said, "So there were soldiers over that way."

Renata jumped. "Aaah! Don't *do* that!"

Kenya was pointing into the woods. "Sorry. So I saw these guys and I guess they must have crossed the track shortly before we got here. I followed them for a bit. Renata, they don't look like the American soldiers, or any of the gangs. They're wearing black uniforms with a blue and gold symbol on the arm. And the uniforms look new. I mean, *really* new. First time out of the box."

"How many?"

"Thirty or forty. And I *think* they're looking for us. I heard one of them speaking into his radio about 'Cooper's people' and 'the resistance.' That could be Danny."

"It's a common name..."

"I know, but if *anyone* was going to organize a resistance, it would be Danny. What should we do?"

"We ignore them and keep going. And from now on, either stick beside me or you're taking the lead, OK? At least that way I'll *see* you wandering off."

Four hours later the railway line ended in the middle of a construction site. The tracks and sleepers had been dug up and were piled to the side, next to an abandoned excavator, two huge trucks, and a pair of prefabricated buildings. Beyond the construction site a freshly-laid road replaced the railway line.

"What do you think?" Renata asked. "Stick to the road—it *is* going in the right direction—or do we move into the woods? That's slower, but safer."

"I say we stick to the road," Kenya said, looking back at the construction site. "*After* we see if there's anything good in those prefabs."

The first prefab was locked, but Kenya was strong now: the lock snapped on the first kick.

Inside, there was nothing but a desk covered with blueprints and a filing cabinet stuffed with incomprehensible documentation.

The second prefab was clearly a rest area for the workers. A dartboard on the wall, a fridge containing three cans of soda and a green mass that might once have been a sandwich, and a rack of tools.

Kenya stuffed two flashlights, a hammer and the darts into her backpack, then hefted a long crowbar in one hand. "Nice. You find anything?"

Renata held up a set of keys. "Any cars out there?"

"I didn't see any."

"Hmm. Then what do *these* belong to?"

A few minutes later, Kenya pulled open the excavator's cab door. "Yes! Now, if it has any fuel in the tank, we could be in luck. You can drive, right?"

"No. I can fly a StratoTruck, but I've never driven a car. You?"

"Don't know yet." She climbed into the driver's seat. "There's enough room for two in here, and it'll be easier than walking."

"It'll be louder, though," Renata said. "Like, a hundred times louder."

Kenya poked and prodded at the excavator's levers. "OK, so there are five levers on the left, four on the right. Three pedals. And a steering wheel. At least we know what *that* one does. There's a slot here in the control panel. I mean, the cockpit. Or is that only for planes? Anyway, the keys must go in here..." She inserted the key into the only matching slot. "Aw. Nothing."

"Did you *turn* the key?" Renata asked, backing away.

"Am I supposed to?"

"I think so."

"OK then. Which way?"

"It probably only turns *one* way. Try clockwise."

Second later, the excavator's massive engine rumbled into life. Renata didn't know whether to run and hide—in case the noise attracted attention—or grab their bags and jump up into the cab and see whether they could make it go.

She noticed that Kenya was almost giggling with excitement as she played with the steering wheel and pushed and pulled on the levers, and she couldn't help smiling. "All right, then." She scooped up their backpacks, and threw them into the cab behind the driver's seat, then grabbed hold of the door handle and climbed up. "Let's go."

"I'm trying. The levers don't move very far."

Renata looked down at the floor. "What about the pedals? Which one is which?"

"Well, from what I remember, going left to right, the pedals are una corda, sostenuto and sustain."

"Those are the pedals on a *piano*," Renata said.

"I know, but that's the best I can do."

"Try holding one down and *then* moving the levers."

It took them almost fifteen minutes to figure out enough of the excavator's controls to get it to move, but soon they had left the construction site far behind. One of the prefabricated buildings was now missing an entire side, and several small trees had been inadvertently felled, but at least they were lurching awkwardly in the right direction.

The excavator's cab had only one seat, so they had to share it. Kenya steered and sweated while Renata panicked and shouted at her to watch out for things.

The road was relatively straight, having been built on the railway track, but still Kenya's knuckles were white as she gripped the wheel.

They had traveled about ten miles before Renata began to relax. "I suppose this *is* marginally faster than walking."

Kenya had her gaze fixed straight ahead. "Do not talk to the driver."

"And we're out of the rain. Or we would be, if it was raining."

"Renata, please...!"

"You're doing fine. And there's nothing ahead for miles."

"Are you crazy!? Look! There's a *tree* lying across the road!"

"That's a branch. Just ride over it. It's barely *even* a branch. It's a twig with ambitions. A hundred bucks says we won't even feel a bump."

As they trundled closer and closer to the branch, Kenya took a series of short, sharp breaths. "If we crash..."

"We're not going to crash," Renata said. "That branch weighs about ten pounds. The excavator weighs, like, forty tons. Probably."

The excavator rolled over the branch with some rustling and a slight *snap*.

"What did I tell you?" Renata asked.

Kenya relaxed a little. "OK... But when we tell people about this, it was a massive tree-trunk and we had to take a run at it. We had to build a ramp and *jump* over the—"

Renata said, "Kenya, slow down."

"I'm just saying."

Renata pointed ahead. "Slow down. That's a *real* road-block."

Two hundred meters ahead, a series of huge concrete barriers had been erected across the road, and behind each one was a man with a gun, taking careful aim at the excavator.

"OK, well, there's a problem. Slowing down is not something we've learned how to do," Kenya said.

"Ah." Renata examined the multitude of controls, switches and levers. "Is there a button marked 'Brakes'?"

"Not that I can see."

"Well, we're only doing about four miles an hour. We could jump out. It'll probably stop when it hits those barriers." Renata reached out to open the cab door, and realized that a camouflage-wearing man with a gun was walking alongside them, shouting orders at them.

"Sorry," Renata shouted through the open door. "Didn't hear you!"

"I said, shut down your engine and get out. Hands where we can see them!"

"We don't know *how* to shut it down. We only learned to drive it an hour ago."

The man muttered, "Oh, for cryin' out *loud*!" and launched himself at the cab. He squashed himself in next to Renata, reached over to the keys, and removed them from the dashboard.

The excavator's engine died, and the man jumped down. "All right, out. Leave your stuff where it is. Out, hands where I can see them. And bear in mind that you're surrounded."

As she climbed down after Renata, Kenya asked, "Are you the good guys or the bad guys?"

The man ignored her, and spoke into a walkie-talkie. "Sarge. Got a situation at the south roadblock. Two girls riding an excavator. Teenagers, not a lot of stuff with them."

A static-filled response came back, but Renata couldn't make it out.

The man looked at them and said, "One Latina, I think. The other's, I don't know, Hawaiian, maybe? Or some sort of mixed-race combo, like African and Japanese." He lowered his voice a little. "*Lot* of facial scars, that one."

Renata heard the next response clearly: "That's them. Bring them in."

Chapter 20

The man with the thick brown mustache introduced himself as Duke Tansey, and it was immediately obvious to Danny that he was the self-appointed leader of this small band of rebels.

On his first morning with the group, Duke had taken him aside and explained the situation: "I got out of Sioux City before the siege, but we're not strong enough to take them on. We know there are other pockets of resistance out there. There *must* be. But we need a way to communicate with them. The cellphones and landlines are down. Radio seems to be jammed. So we need runners. People who can physically run between the different groups and pass messages back and forth. You in?"

"If I still had my powers, sure. But then if I did, I'd have sorted this whole mess out by now. Duke, Krodin's people are looking for me and my friends. I'm easy to recognize." He patted the stump of his right arm.

"Well, you've got to do *something*, son. You can't keep running forever. You're welcome to stay with us but you gotta do your share. I know you can't hold a rifle so unless those powers are going to switch back on soon, you're dead weight."

"I understand."

"So, when the powers do come back, what'll it be like? All at once, or kind of gradual?"

"There's no way to know. The last time they went away, they did come back pretty quickly, but that was really only by accident. My friend Colin can see the blue lights and he saw one pass right through me, but, like I said, that was an accident. Just a coincidence."

Duke frowned at him. "The blue lights."

"Yeah, I know. But Colin swears they're real, and apparently that's where the superhuman energy comes from."

"And *you* can't see them?"

"Very few of us can."

Duke nodded his head in the direction of their camp. "Time to get back." As Danny fell into step beside him, he asked, "So what does your friend say these lights look like?"

"Bluish balls of energy, just floating around. When my girlfriend lost her powers, Colin tried to help her find one, but they're scarce. Instead he took her to a place where the same sort of energy was stored." Danny shrugged. "Long story."

"So... Yesterday you said that there are three kinds of people. Ordinary folks like me, superhumans like you, and folks who are in between, like your friends Razor and Lance. Have I got that right?"

"That's right." Danny picked up a pebble from the ground and tried to skim it over the surface of the slow-moving river.

"And folks like Razor and Lance have some skills, like they're really smart or good with machines."

"Yep."

"And that old superhero guy, Thalamus, wasn't really a superhuman at all, he was just like Lance. Real smart, only with him it was numbers?"

Danny wondered where all this was going. "That's it."

Duke said, "Son, when I was growing up there was a kid I heard of who had to be locked up for a while because he kept seeing things that weren't there. Always the same thing: floating blue lights. Now, I'm pretty sure he wasn't a superhuman because he never showed any other signs, but maybe he was like Thalamus or Lance. Not quite superhuman. His only gift was that he could see the lights."

"Could be," Danny said. "If so, I'd like to meet him. Take him up to the roof of a high building and see if he can spot one of the lights."

"I can't say for sure I know exactly where he is, but I know where he was before the war started. The same place he's been these past forty years. Living in Edillon, about an hour west of Sioux City. And I lied: he's not just some kid I'd heard about... He's Marvin Tansey. My cousin."

At dawn on the morning of their escape, Alia and Nathan had been hiding in the branches of a giant oak tree, looking toward the compound, when they saw two of the overseers' trucks roaring out through the gates. One headed north, the other south, and they stopped about every thirty meters to drop off a slave.

Alia had said, "It's a man-hunt. They're going to comb the area until they find us."

All they could do was sit and watch, until, hours later, one of the workers passed directly under the tree—and looked up.

The woman immediately lowered her head again and said, "They're going to kill you when they find you. That guard you hit? He's dead."

Nathan clapped a hand over his mouth. "Oh no!"

"It wasn't you. Viv had him shot because he fell asleep on duty."

Alia whispered down, "*You* should run—now! They can't catch all of you!"

"Yeah, they can." The woman briefly glanced up again. "I won't tell them I saw you. But you need to get out of here, find someone who can help us." The woman moved away, pretending to check the ground for clues.

The search went on for a lot longer than Alia had expected. She'd figured that the overseers would give up and recall the search-party after a few hours, but night fell and the slaves were given flashlights.

At some point before dawn the same woman passed underneath their tree again and said, "They're calling it off, finally. Go north, and move fast."

The sun was nudging the horizon when they finally climbed down from the tree.

Hungry, exhausted from lack of sleep, and muscles aching from sitting in the same positions for over a day, they began to move in what Alia hoped was a northerly direction.

They found a small house an hour later. It had been picked clean by looters but the water in its taps was cool, clean and the most delicious thing Alia had ever tasted.

"We should rest here," Nathan said as he sat on the kitchen counter and watched Alia splash water on her face.

There was nothing to dry herself with, so Alia used her sleeves to wipe her face. "No, they'll know about this place so they'll search here. We have to keep moving. Besides, we have to find something to eat!"

That afternoon, when Alia guessed they were about twelve miles from the compound, they found a man lying face-down on the side of an overgrown road. His black uniform was damp, but clean, suggesting that he hadn't been there long. As Alia cautiously approached him she felt something hard underfoot, and stepped back to see a large assault rifle. On the shoulder of his jacket was a symbol they didn't recognize—a blue eye inside a golden sun. The man had a pistol in his holster with a full clip of ammunition, and a backpack still strapped to one arm.

"You think he's dead?" Nathan whispered as he very slowly approached the man.

"Definitely. Look at the way his body's twisted."

Nathan found a long stick and used it to gently poke the man's arm. After a few seconds and several much harder pokes, he declared, "Yep, he's dead."

"Nathan, his eyes are open and the blood coming out of his mouth has already congealed. Take his guns and his backpack."

He reluctantly pulled off the man's backpack—the body was stiff and cold, and made unsettling cracking noises when he tried to bend its arms—and tossed it to Alia.

She opened it and began to remove its contents. "Liter of water, half-full. A two-way radio. And three, four... no, five of these foil-wrapped blocks."

"Emergency rations," Nathan explained, picking up one of the blocks. "For a while we all lived on this stuff in the glacier, until Evan was allowed to take the jet out and get more supplies."

"So who is he?" Alia asked.

Nathan pointed towards the man's neck. "He has dog-tags, but I'm not touching them. They're right next to his skin. Looks like he was hit by a car or a truck... Maybe it happened last night and whoever it was just didn't see him. And then didn't bother to check what it was they hit. Try the talkie-walkie thing."

"Walkie-talkie," Alia said.

"Oh, like *that's* a better name for it."

Alia had pressed the "Listen" button on the two-way radio and for a while there was nothing but static, then a voice came in: "Benton, you there?"

More static, then, "Benton. Come in."

"This guy must be Benton," Alia said. "If they come looking for him they'll find him and then they'll find *us*."

Nathan reached out for the radio, "Give it here. I've got an idea." He forced his voice deeper and whispered. "Benton here. Can't talk now. Maintain radio silence."

The voice on the other end said, "Acknowledged, Benton. Out."

"Well done," Alia said. "So now what?"

Nathan shrugged.

"I say we put some distance between us and this guy in case they do come looking. And we should leave the radio, too, in case they have some way of tracking it."

Nathan said, "Yeah... we *could* do that."

"Or?"

"Or we could go back to the compound. Alia, we're not going to find any more food out here—the overseers have already picked the area clean—and there's not much chance of finding someone who can help us free the other slaves. We have to do it ourselves. So we have this guy's rations and water, and we can get more water back at that house. That's enough to keep us going for a few more days. And we now have two rifles and a handgun."

She knew he was right, but she didn't want to admit that going back seemed more like defeat than the first part of a plan.

The sun had again set by the time they reached the hill overlooking the compound, and they climbed the giant oak tree in the dark. Once they had settled, Nathan took the radio and adopted his deep voice. "This is Benton. Come in."

A six-second burst of static, then a man's voice said, "Benton, state your position."

"Unclear. You got a lock on me?"

The radio said, "That's a roj, Benton. Status?"

"Tracking some looters to their base. Defenses are minimal. They've got a *lot* of supplies, not much firepower. Come get me and we can pick the place clean. Approach from the west, an hour after dawn." He had paused for a second, then added, "Gotta go. They're coming back."

Shortly after that, Nathan had crawled towards the compound and thrown the radio as close to it as possible. He'd explained to Alia, "The dead guys' friends are following the radio—we don't want them finding *us* instead."

"Think my powers are coming back," Nathan said to Alia Cord next morning. Alia knew she had slept a little, but not nearly enough. She was finding it hard to shake the feeling that they had never left the tree at all, that their trip to the house and the discovery of the dead soldier had been part of a dream.

"Seriously, I'm not really cold any more and I'm not hungry." He passed her one of the half-eaten ration blocks. "You have it. This is the raisin and walnut one."

As she reached to take the block from his hand, Alia glanced in the direction of the compound and saw something moving on the right. She pointed. "Look."

"You think that's them?"

"Has to be."

They watched for a few minutes as the dark shape cresting the low hill resolved itself into a wide line of fast-moving vehicles.

"OK... That's them," Nathan said, uncertainly. "But there's a lot more of them than I was expecting. I hope this works."

Alia held her breath as she counted the trucks and jeeps coming over the hill. "Twenty-four, I think. There's going to be a *massacre*."

Nathan said, "We can only hope."

"Don't say that—there's a lot of innocent people in there!" Alia chewed nervously on her lower lip. "Maybe we shouldn't have done it."

"It's too late to change things now."

The guards in the towers were the first to open fire. Nathan's superhuman eyesight was much better than Alia's so he provided her with narration.

"Guard on the west tower... he's the one with the hat that

has a bullet-hole in it? He's firing at the jeeps. There's no way he can hit anyone that far... Oh. Yeah, he can. Another one! He's a really good shot! He... And now he's dead."

Alia said, "Nathan, how do we know that the men in the black uniforms won't be even worse than the overseers?"

"Because they don't look like they're the settling-down kind. They won't want the slaves—ooh, the guys in that truck are loading a rocket-launcher!—they're going to just take the supplies and leave. But they'll kill the overseers first, to stop them taking revenge."

"What if they kill the slaves too?"

"They won't do that!"

Alia watched as the soldiers' vehicles narrowed the gap to the compound, racing for the western gates. Something flared from the back of the lead truck, streaked towards the compound and destroyed the gates before Alia had even registered what it was.

They saw the overseers come flooding, guns firing, and get picked off one-by-one. Alia didn't know whether to cheer or throw up. *We caused this. Those people are dying and it's our fault!*

As if he were reading her mind, Nathan said, "They asked for it. They took slaves. They deserve everything they get."

It was all over in minutes. The black-clad men had lost five or six people. All of the overseers were dead.

From their tree, Alia and Nathan continued to watch. Then she let out a breath she hadn't realized she'd been holding. "See that?"

"They're loading the trucks with the stuff the overseers were hoarding."

"Exactly. *They* are loading the trucks. Not the slaves. And look, there on the right—some of the slaves are talking to the soldiers. And that woman is *hugging* that one!"

Nathan said, "So we did right. We did a good thing. I knew that."

Within an hour, the black-dressed soldiers had loaded up their trucks and driven away, and Alia felt it was safe to return to the compound.

As they walked, Nathan asked, "So now how are we going to find Danny?"

"I don't think we *can* find him. It's been nearly two months. We have to come up with a new plan. If your powers *are* returning then maybe it's time we joined the front lines. It's time to fight."

At the shattered gates of the compound some of the former slaves were dragging the overseers' bodies into one pile while others were scavenging through the battleground. As Nathan and Alia passed through the gates they spotted a familiar face; the woman who had seen them hiding in the tree. She was crouched over one of the overseers, going through his pockets, and called them over to her. "You saw what just happened?"

Nathan smiled. "Oh yeah. In fact, it was our doing. We got the soldiers to come here."

The woman stood up, empty-handed, and returned Nathan's smile. "Then thanks to you, we're free now! We can rebuild this place, live and work here. Viv and Dex and all her savages are dead, and we're not. The soldiers didn't even take everything; they only took about three quarters. We've got more than enough food to last us through the winter! You'll stay with us, won't you?"

"For a while, yes," Alia said.

"Great. We're going to fix the gate, that's the first priority. And we'll finish digging the new trenches. That'll really slow down anyone who tries to take our stuff again." A man was passing, and the woman grabbed his arm. "Mathew! These kids are the two who escaped—and they're the ones who brought the Viper squadron in!"

Alia recognized the man as the same one she had worked alongside in the fields.

He grinned at her and doffed an imaginary hat. "Then you have our profound thanks, my friends!"

Nathan said, "Viper squadron? That's what they call themselves?"

"That's right. They're rebel-hunters, they said. The overseers here weren't the same kind of rebels, but I don't think the Vipers are too discerning. Their leader is a man called Krodin, apparently. I haven't heard of him before but I gotta say, I like the sound of him. I get the feeling he's the sort of guy who knows how to get the job done."

Alia shuddered, and hoped the others didn't notice. "Krodin?"

The woman said, "That's right. They didn't say if that's his first name or his last name, but whoever he is, he's got the right idea. He's going to save the country from the gangs. Bring back peace. You deal with the enemies at home first, the soldiers said. That's his motto. You sort out your own house, then you can go after the neighbors."

The man, Mathew, said, "Maybe he's only got *one* name. You know? Could be that the name Krodin is like Madonna or Prince or Bono or Elvis."

"Elvis *Presley*," the woman said, looking annoyed.

"Oh yeah, of course." Mathew said to Nathan, "Want to give me a hand? We're going to get some timber, try to find a way to block up the gateway until a new gate can be built."

"Sure," Nathan said. He gave Alia a very brief glance, then added, "I wonder if we'll ever get to meet this Krodin guy, then?"

Alia watched them walked across the compound, and thought, *We just helped the bad guys load up with supplies and weapons.*

Danny Cooper and Duke Tansey walked in silence along the edge of an overgrowing wheat field. There wasn't much for them to discuss. The town of Edillon was about three miles directly ahead and they had no way of knowing for certain whether Duke's cousin was still there, but they had to take the chance.

It wasn't the only chance Duke was taking, Danny knew. They didn't have any way to communicate with the riverside camp. A man called Cliff had been posted as a lookout and should have stopped Danny from approaching, but Cliff hadn't reported back, and the team sent out to find him had returned empty-handed.

Duke had chosen not to move the camp. That would be a huge task and greatly increased the risk of being spotted.

At the corner of the wheat field Duke crouched down behind the boundary fence and gestured for Danny to do the same. "Checkpoint ahead. Four of those soldiers in black."

"Can we go around them?"

"Not without being seen. Look."

Danny crept forward and peered through a narrow gap in the hedge. Forty meters away, on a narrow road, two of the soldiers stood on the roof of an old SUV, while another two were in the cab.

Duke said, "Sheer luck we got this close. They can see for miles up there. We can wait for night, but that's hours away. Or we double-back, but that's going to add at least three hours onto our journey."

"And we might run into other patrols," Danny said.

Duke said, "The one on the roof, on the left. Bare arms."

"What about him?"

"Those tattoos are gang markings. And I know for sure that some of these guys are military... So that's what they're doing. It's risky, but it's clearly working. You fight a gang, beat them, then give the survivors the opportunity to join up. Or die. That way your army gets bigger, and you never have to take care of your prisoners."

"So what do we do?" Danny asked.

"We bluff our way through. Leave your pack and everything else here, including your jacket." He pulled both handguns out of his holsters. "They need to be able to see instantly that your right arm is missing. Trust me, Danny. This is our best chance."

As Duke watched the soldiers, Danny dropped his backpack and removed his jacket.

"All right, they're not looking... Move out onto the road. Walk ahead of me. I've caught you and I'm turning you in, got that?"

"Just don't accidentally shoot me, OK?"

"The safeties are on—you'll be fine."

Danny climbed over the boundary fence and Duke immediately followed, then whispered "Go!"

With his one arm raised, and trying to look defeated, Danny walked along ahead of Duke. He glanced around to see Duke was aiming both handguns at his back.

"Here we go," Duke muttered. Then he shouted, "Hey! Hey, you guys! I caught one!"

The two soldiers on top of the vehicle immediately swung towards them, their weapons raised. "Don't move! Drop your gun!" The two inside the car jumped out, handguns ready.

"I can't!" Duke shouted back. "If I lower my gun, he'll run.

And he's *fast*. This is the kid that other patrol said they were looking for. Danny Cooper."

One of the soldiers on the roof said, "It *is* him! Messner, Dean, secure him. We've got you covered."

The two soldiers on the ground slowly approached Danny. The one called Messner said, "Don't move. Not a muscle. Don't even *breathe*. You, the cowboy... We've got him from here. Lower your gun."

"Not yet," Duke said. "I want my bounty. The other patrol promised us a half-ton of food for every member of the New Heroes we turned in."

"You'll get it. You have my word."

"Sorry, friend, but that's not good enough. I want to speak to the officer in charge." He nodded towards the SUV. "I figure that's him on the roof."

Without looking away from Danny, Messner called out, "Captain... need you down here."

As the other soldier jumped down from the roof and strode cautiously towards them, Danny thought, *I should have asked Duke exactly what he was planning. How is this going to get us past them?*

"I'm Captain Fontana. What's the problem?"

Duke said, "We were made certain promises. A half-ton of food. Now, I'm willing to compromise. We're fine for weapons and ammo and gas, but body-armor like yours... That we can use."

The captain said, "Then enlist."

"I'm thinking that maybe six sets of body armor might go missing from your stores. No one's going to notice because they'll be celebrating that you've caught one of the New Heroes. The *leader*, in fact. There's gonna be so many medals you'll have to get an intern to act as a surrogate chest."

The captain grinned at that. "I think we can come to an arrangement."

"Good to hear. Now, watch him. Kid's fast and with only one arm handcuffs aren't much use."

"I see that," the captain said.

"Also... The three of you are blocking your fourth man's aim."

"What?"

Danny felt something slam into the back of his legs, and as he collapsed the air above him was shattered by four deafening gunshots.

He rolled onto his side to see Duke lowering his guns. There was smoke wafting from the barrels.

All four of the soldiers were dead, each one shot in the head.

"Told you I was a good shot. Sorry I had to knock you down like that."

Danny jumped to his feet. "You said you were going to *bluff* your way through! You said that the guns' safeties were on!"

"I just shot four guys in the face. I think that's worse than lying." He put away his guns and started checking the soldiers' pockets and pouches. "Give me a hand here. We're taking everything they have. Their car will get us to Edillon in ten minutes."

"What you did... Duke, that's *murder*."

"This is *war*, kid. It's not meant to be nice."

Chapter 21

In a refurbished elementary school in Pueblo, Colorado, Colin Wagner didn't hold back his tears when he saw his father for the first time in months. Colin had been on the road with the other hostages from Sakkara when they learned that the refugees from the Substation had been shipped here.

After he had incapacitated Shadow, he had flown them two-at-a-time from the roof of Sakkara down to the ground. He'd led them west, through the devastation of Topeka, then cross-country in the direction of the only place he knew might be safe: The Cloister.

Shortly after they passed Wichita—skirting north of the city in a wide arc to avoid any patrols—Colin spotted a platoon of US Marines mopping up after a firefight with a group of mercenaries. The Marines' commanding officer managed to get word to Warren, and directed the refugees to the temporary base in Colorado.

Now, he stood back and used the back of his sleeve to wipe the tears from his cheeks as he watched his parents embrace. Abigail was almost squashed between them, but didn't seem to mind: she clung on to Warren's neck like she was never going to let go.

Warren and Caroline finally broke free, and Warren turned to Colin. He put his free arm around Colin's neck and pulled him close. There were tears in his own eyes. "I have never been more proud of you, son."

On the other side of the room, Niall Cooper was riding around on his father's shoulders while his mother fussed over him. No one had mentioned Danny yet.

A few hours later, when almost everyone else had retired to the school's makeshift bedrooms, Warren and Facade found a quiet room. It looked and felt like the principal's office, and as Colin sat down opposite the desk he realized that he was inexplicably feeling guilty.

Facade said, "First, I can't thank you enough for getting Niall out of there."

Colin said, "No, we can't thank *him* enough. He took care of Abigail all on his own for so long... He's the bravest kid I ever met."

"I appreciate that. Now... Second thing. The time for celebrations and joyous reunions is over. Krodin's shattered the country's infrastructure so we have no idea how much damage has been done. General Mendes is sending us some info from satellite feeds, but it's not enough. The war is still going on, and it's looking like Krodin's only getting started. So far, this place is safe because almost no one knows it's here."

Warren sat down on the other side of the desk, in what would have been the principal's chair, and said, "I know you've got a million questions..."

"Is there any news on Stephanie or Danny or Renata?"

"Nothing concrete. On *any* of them. And you're no doubt wondering why Cassandra's communications stopped... So are we. She and Lance are missing. Just vanished. We don't know how or why, but we're fairly sure that Krodin is still looking for them."

Colin said, "Which means he's not the one who made them vanish."

"That's what we're hoping."

Facade asked, "How much damage did you do to Shadow?"

"He'll live."

The two men exchanged a look, then Facade said, "Pity. Our intel suggests that Zeke and Eldon are regaining their powers. We need to take them out of the picture before they're fully recharged."

Warren said, "And you're the only one who can get to them."

"I just got out of Sakkara and now you want me to go *back*? Dad, I'm not fully recharged either. I won't stand a chance against two of them *and* Krodin."

"You won't be going without back-up. You'll have *us*. When we evacuated the Substation we brought the Paragon armor with us."

Colin looked from his father to Facade and back. "That's crazy."

"I used to be a test-pilot," Facade said. "I can fly anything."

Warren said, "And I was a superhuman, remember? I could fly under my own power. Plus I once flew using Paragon's actual jetpack. We're not without experience. We'll tackle the clones, you go after Krodin. Of course, that's a worst-case scenario. Ideally, we'll be able to get the clones first, one at a time."

Colin asked, "What about Nathan and Alex? Their powers should be returning too."

Warren shrugged. "If we knew where they *were*..."

Colin leaned back in his chair, and slowly shook his head. "It's insane for you two to go back into action. You're..." He tried to think of a polite way to express his thoughts, then gave up and said, "You're too old. Sorry, but that's the truth. Stephanie said it takes a hundred hours of practice in the Paragon armor to become even half-way competent, and you two want to take on superhumans whose power-levels you don't even know. That's suicide. There's no *way* I'm letting you do that!"

"*Letting*?" Warren said.

"I mean it, Dad. I'm not letting either of you go to Sakkara because I don't want you to die. And you *will* die, if you go there."

Warren sighed. "I remember what it was like being your age. You think that anyone over twenty-five is ancient and ought to go and lie down before he hurts himself."

"You know that's not what I'm saying, Dad." He stood up and moved to the window, staring out at the night sky over Pueblo. "We need a better plan than sending in the codgers' brigade. What are our assets?"

"You," Facade said.

"OK. Me and...?"

"Just you. Until we can find Cassandra or one of the other New Heroes, you're all we've got."

Colin turned back to face them. "But, what about weapons and stuff?"

"Aside from the Paragon armor, nothing we can get our hands on easily. One of the projects in the Substation was..." Facade paused, and it seemed to Colin that he wasn't sure whether he should carry on. Then he said, "It was a contained nuclear blast."

"Meaning?"

"OK, you remember the blackout bomb? It had a weak force-field that kept the smoke in one area, made it almost impossible to see through and the smoke didn't dissipate so quickly."

"I remember. We used them on Krodin when he attacked. They didn't work, because he adapted to the smoke."

"I see. Well, imagine a fifteen-megaton explosion that was confined in a similar way. We could wipe Sakkara and everything inside it off the map, and not contaminate anything else. Or, if we wanted to be even more precise, we could just obliterate one single room."

"Wow... So, why don't we do that?"

"Because it's only a theory. We can't actually *build*

something like that. There's no way to generate a force-field capable of withstanding the explosion."

Colin asked, "Then why did you bring it up in the first place?"

Facade said, "Because there is *something* we can do that's similar, but it's potentially very dangerous and could have unpredictable and catastrophic side-effects. Warren?"

Warren slid open the desk drawer and produced a sealed glass canister containing a small quantity of very fine gray powder. He slid he canister across the desk to Colin. "Do *not* open it."

"What is this stuff?"

Warren said, "It's a molecular powder. Imagine you took something solid and you separated each and every molecule. The molecules themselves are still intact, but they're just not connected to each other. That's what you get. It was found in Lyon, in France, three years ago. A young photographer was taking test-shots of the flowers in his parent's garden when he noticed the stream of powder appearing out of thin air. It just materialized, like magic. It only lasted a few seconds, and he didn't manage to catch any of the powder before it drifted away on the wind. Certain that he wasn't seeing things, he set up his camera and waited. A few minutes later, it happened again. He filmed it, and caught the powder on one of his spare camera lenses. The young man knew that this was not a natural phenomenon, so he contacted the local university. They didn't know what the powder was, and were suspicious of the camera footage, but they were curious enough to keep an open mind. Eventually, someone working for us heard about it, and that raised a few flags. Everyone had been focusing on exactly where the powder had materialized. Our technician realized that *when* was a much more important question."

Colin peered into the glass canister again. "So, what exactly is it?"

"It's a ball-point pen," Facade said, "Or *part* of one, to be precise. The molecules are mostly the components of three different plastics, a small amount of brass, some dried ink, and a few trace elements."

"What am I not getting?"

"The date and time it appeared match perfectly with something Renata witnessed in California... Victor Cross testing the null-field that protected his power-siphoning machine. He threw a pen at it, and the pen disappeared. Then he tested it further, by slowly pushing the tip of a second pen towards it."

Warren said, "Last year, in the same spot in that same garden in Lyon, water molecules appeared. About two liters, over a period of about an hour. That aligns with the battle you and the others had inside the glacier at Zaliv Kalinina. Cross had set up a null-field there, too. And in the Substation our techs managed to reverse-engineer Cross's machines and get them working. Same thing every time. Anything that goes through the field reappears in France, as powder, or liquid, or gas."

"So stuff passing through it isn't just disintegrated. It gets *teleported.*"

"Yep. Molecule by molecule," Facade said. "As near as we can figure, the exit-point is probably about one hundredth of a millimeter in diameter. Anything that goes through the null-field is squeezed out through a point so small you'd need a microscope to see it."

Colin passed the canister of powder back to his father. "Wow. Does Cross know this?"

Warren shrugged. "No idea. But we do know that his ultimate goal had always been to retrieve Krodin from Mars, so our guess is that the null-field comes from an attempt to create a teleportation machine. After that failed—or possibly in tandem with its development—he began his cloning experiments, hoping to breed a superhuman who could teleport long distances."

Facade added, "And that brings us back to the idea of the contained nuclear blast. The only technology we have that could contain the blast is the null-field, and until we can work out a way to make sure its output isn't anywhere close to a populated area, we can't use it."

"Because it would be bad?" Colin asked.

"Well, yeah! You turn on the tap and the water comes out at a steady speed, right? Now you put your thumb over the opening, leaving just a tiny gap, and the water squirts out much faster. The water's trying to move at the same rate, the same number of liters per minute. So now imagine that it's not just a trickle of water coming from the tap, it's the Niagara Falls and you're forcing it through an opening smaller than the point of a pin. It would come out with enough force to cut through a mountain. Multiply that force by a *billion,* and instead of water it's fire and radiation. It would incinerate everything in its path for a million miles. Hey, if the angles were right it could probably slice the *moon* in half." Facade shrugged. "So... we won't be doing *that.*"

Colin said, "If you could change the point where the stuff materializes, then you could set it in deep space, or the heart of the sun."

"I don't know the math or the physics myself, but every time our techs tried to change the output location, the whole thing stopped working. From what I'm told it'd take someone of the genius level of Victor Cross to sort that out."

"So where is he?"

"Yeah, well, that's one of the tricky ones," Warren said. "We left him in the Substation with a squadron of General Mendes's people guarding him. There was this whole thing that Lance set up to make Krodin believe he wasn't there, but Krodin eventually saw through it and found him. And then he left him there, chained up."

"That must be annoying for Victor."

"Yeah, I'd say so. He makes it his life's work to retrieve Krodin from Mars, and then Krodin dumps him."

Facade said, "Heh... When I was twenty I spent a fortune hiring an artist to do a portrait of this girl I liked just so that she'd fall in love with me. She ended up dating the artist for four years."

Colin laughed. "So, Victor's still in the Substation?"

His father said, "Remember when I said that was one of the tricky ones?"

"Yeah..."

He got out."

Victor wasn't sure that Krodin really had left him alone. The only way he could be certain would be to leave the metal room and check. And he wasn't in a position to do that.

He said there's a way to get free. But there's not. I'm smarter than him and I can't see a way out. Therefore, he was wrong.

Another part of Victor's brain said, *It's supreme arrogance to assume that there isn't a solution just because you can't see it. Absence of evidence is not evidence of absence.*

Clearly, if there is a solution, then it's something I've not yet considered. Or something that I have considered but dismissed as unworkable.

He got up from his stool and walked around the metal room in as large a circle as the chain would permit.

"What have I not considered?" He asked aloud.

Time-travel. In a few years I invent time-travel—real time-

travel, not just hopping a few seconds into the future—then I come back to this time and free myself. He looked towards the door, almost expecting it to be pulled open by his future self. Nothing.

Spontaneous disintegration of the chain caused by... caused by... the universe being nice to me for a change. Yeah, that's *not happening.*

Rescue by sudden shift in loyalty of my clones. That one actually might happen.

"What were his exact words...? He told me, 'There *is* a way for you to escape, Victor. But if you can't see it then you're not as clever or as courageous as you believe you are, and that means you're no good to me.'"

Why would I need to be any more courageous than I already am?

I certainly can't be any more clever.

Courage is... what? Standing tall when faced with certain death. Doing something that you know has a high chance of failure. Accepting unpleasant truths. It's biting the bullet and...

Victor swallowed. "No."

Yes, he told himself. *That's what it is. Biting the bullet. The story goes that in the days before reliable anesthetics soldiers on the battlefield who were about to undergo major surgery would be given a bullet on which to bite down, to help them ride out the pain.*

That's what he meant.

Victor reached up to the collar around his neck, and again tried to pull it off over his head. It was still too tight. A couple of centimeters larger and he'd have been able to squeeze it past his jaw.

He picked up the metal stool, holding it by the legs. It was heavy. But he wasn't sure whether it was heavy enough. And there was only one way to know for sure.

With all his strength, he slammed the seat of the stool into the side of his face. The pain was excruciating, so much that he let the stool fall from his grip and he almost collapsed to his knees.

When he'd recovered a little, he picked up the stool and did it again, crashing it into his face in the same spot.

Over and over.

Blinded by tears, blood and an agony that was a billion light-years beyond anything he had ever imagined, he cursed Krodin, and the universe, and a god he didn't believe in, until finally he was cursing only himself.

The part of his multi-level superhuman brain that monitored and controlled the rest—the core of his being—told him that he had no one else to blame. *How do you like being the smartest person in the universe now, Victor? You chose the paths that led you here. Only you. So you will bear this pain, this mutilation of your own flesh, this humiliation above humiliations. You will bear this because this is the price of your actions.*

An hour later, he could take no more and he let the stool crash to the floor. The lower half of his face was a mess of blood and torn flesh. Almost all of his teeth were now broken, bloody fragments scattered across the floor. He grabbed hold of the collar with his blood-slicked hands.

He felt—and heard—the fractured pieces of his jawbone grind together as he forced the collar up past it.

But his nose was in the way.

Please, no...

He almost couldn't do it. For a moment, death by starvation seemed preferable to enduring yet another surge of agony, but his mind's eye conjured up an image of Krodin. His flawless immortal, ageless face sneering and judging. Everything Victor had achieved had been to prepare the way for Krodin's return, and the immortal had all but spat at him.

I might not win this, but I'm damned if I let him be the one who beats me.

He smashed the stool into his face one more time, shattering his nasal bones and ripping through the cartilage.

And moments later, Victor Cross pushed open the door and staggered away from his metal cage.

Chapter 22

So far, the war had not fully reached Chicago. Working together, the army, National Guard and the police had managed to keep Krodin's forces away from the city.

Stephanie and Mina had passed through the north barricades at Evanston, along with thousands of others all traveling on foot. Drivers had to abandon their cars long before they reached the city.

It took them a further two days to reach Chicago's downtown area—they slept in doorways, taking turns to keep watch—and now Stephanie announced that they had reached their destination, the junction of North State Street and East Washington Street.

Mina looked up at the ornate building across the street. "It's a Macy's."

"That's right," Stephanie said. "It looked a lot better the last time I was here."

Several of the store's windows at the street level had been smashed, and inside they could see dozens of clusters of people huddled together on sleeping bags. Outside, guarding the windows, burly men scowled at passers-by and told them to, "Just keep *walkin'*, pal. Nothin' for you here."

"Come on," Stephanie said to Mina, leading her across the street. "We need to get inside."

At one of the broken windows, a huge, bearded man with a baseball bat glared out at them. "What do you want?"

"Access to the roof," Stephanie said.

"Yeah, *that's* not gonna happen. Not unless you've got two thousand bucks. That's a grand each, and that gets you a week. A minute over, and you get the bat. You got two thousand bucks? Pretty good price for downtown Chicago, let me tell you."

"We don't have that."

"Then maybe you've got the equivalent in food or ammo? Didn't think so. You want somewhere to sleep, the park's half a mile east. I heard there's no entry fee. Plus you're closer to the water for when the fishing boats come in."

Stephanie said, "We're looking for someone. I promise we're not going to try to stay without paying. We just need about ten minutes. Well, call it twenty because I'm assuming that the elevators aren't working. How about it?"

The bearded man considered that, and said, "Two hundred bucks for twenty minutes. One of my boys gets to accompany you the whole time, make sure you're not stealin' anything."

"We don't have two hundred dollars," Stephanie said, reaching into her backpack. "But we do have *this*." She pulled out Brendan's handgun and aimed it at the bearded man's chest. "*Now* do we have a deal?"

The man swung the bat at Stephanie, but she'd been expecting that and stepped back out of its reach.

He glared at her. "You're not gonna kill me, girl!"

"You're right. I'm not. I'm going to shoot you in the left knee. You'll never again be able to walk without pain. Think about that. The rest of your life, you won't even be able to stand upright for more than a few minutes. Let us up to the roof and that doesn't have to happen."

"How do I know the gun is even loaded?"

"There are two ways to find out. Want me to demonstrate the first one?"

"You ever even fired that thing?"

"This one? No. But I can shoot the fleas off a dog. I've been trained by the best in the world."

The man sneered. "Bull."

"You'll see that my hand isn't wavering. That I'm not sweating. I've faced much bigger guys than you and I've walked away. They haven't. So you have to understand that I'm not fooling around here. I'm as serious as serious gets. I've come half-way across the country to get here and there's no way I'm going to be stopped at the very last stage by a *bouncer*. Now, do we have an understanding?"

"You been practicing that speech? Because it sounds to me like you two girls just... oughta..." He looked around. "Where's the *other* one?"

"Oh, she'll be on the roof by now, probably."

The bearded man began to speak, but a high-pitched whine from above interrupted him. He turned to look upwards.

Stephanie stepped back too, watching as Mina drifted over the edge of the roof with a jetpack on her back and carrying silver armor in her arms.

Mina settled down in the middle of the street, and already they were surrounded by people. The bearded man said, "That's *Paragon's* armor!"

Stephanie started to pull on the armor. "It is. He hid this spare suit here a long time ago, inside a fake ventilation shaft on the roof. A lot of spare suits hidden in a lot of cities."

"How did you know?"

"He was my father." She took the jetpack from Mina and as she clipped it into place she said, "Hold on tight. There's another suit not too far away, and there should be plenty of fuel."

The bearded bouncer said, "You're the New Heroes, then? Thought you guys didn't use guns."

"Circumstances have changed," Mina said.

Stephanie started to turn away, then paused and turned back to face the bearded man. "You know what you are? A war-profiteer. In some countries they hang people like you from the lampposts."

"Hey, I'm just looking out for myself. 'S just self-preservation, that's all."

Stephanie pulled on the armor's titanium-plated gloves. "Self-preservation doesn't mean threatening and exploiting people weaker than you."

The man smirked, and said, "Yeah? Who gonna stop—"

Stephanie planted her right fist deep into the man's stomach, and as he double-over, she hit him in the chin with her left.

He collapsed backwards into the store, and as he hit the ground his jacket flew open, spilling hundreds of twenty- and fifty-dollar bills across the floor.

Mina started to grab for the money, but Stephanie held her back.

"Leave it." She nodded towards the other on-lookers on the street, many of them now cautiously making their way towards the store. "Let them have it. We're going."

Mina put her arm around Stephanie's shoulders and held on tight.

The turbines in Stephanie's jetpack roared into life once more, and as they rose into the air Mina smiled and waved down at the people below. "Bye!"

"He's alive," Zeke said. "His heart's beating about once every two minutes, but it seems to be steady."

Krodin crouched down on the ice, close to Shadow's face. The clone's eyes had frozen over.

Behind him, Zeke said, "His breathing's incredibly shallow, almost imperceptible."

"How long to thaw him out?" Krodin asked.

Zeke scratched at his pure-white beard. "A few hours. Maybe a day. Slower would be better if we want to avoid too much damage. After that, he'll need to recover. That'll be another couple of days at least. And that's not even taking into account all the damage he's *already* suffered."

Krodin stood up. "You have thirty minutes to get him free."

"That's not enough time!"

"Our enemies know that we no longer have the hostages. There's nothing now to stop them from obliterating this region."

"But they can't hurt you, can they?"

"It's doubtful, but they will try. Humans don't give up easily. Thirty minutes, Zeke. If Shadow is not free by then, we leave him behind."

When Krodin returned to the Operations room Eldon informed him, "We've had a sighting. Mina Duval and Stephanie Cord, in Chicago. Two hours ago."

"Two *hours*?"

"That's how long it took for the message to get to us. Our people destroyed the cellphone towers. Cord was wearing armor, and using a jetpack. It's older equipment, but functional. She carried Duval to Wooded Island in Jackson Park, then after that they were *both* seen leaving with armor and jetpacks."

"So Stephanie and Alia's father had hidden some equipment..." Krodin called up a map of Chicago on the computer. "Where was the last sighting?"

"Heading due east across Lake Michigan. On a direct course for Cleveland, Ohio."

"Do any of the other heroes have a connection with Cleveland?"

"Renata Soliz's family live there."

Krodin considered that. "Then it's a bluff. Renata would

never put her family in danger again, so she won't have taken refuge with them."

Eldon said, "OK... But we thought that too, so we never looked there for her. Maybe she *is* with them because she thinks we won't look."

"She's not there, and Stephanie knows that. Her true destination is elsewhere." Krodin looked around the room. "She *could* be coming here. We've not yet categorized everything in this building. Gather everything we need to maintain contact with our armies. We are abandoning this base. The explosives are in place?"

"They are, but they're not going to be powerful enough to destroy the whole building. The outer shell is designed to withstand anything but a direct nuclear strike. Once we trigger the detonator we'll have eight minutes to get clear."

Into his radio, Krodin said, "Zeke, what's your progress?"

The clone's voice said, "I'm cutting him free of the ice, but there's still a long way to go."

"Move faster."

"Then send Eldon down to help me."

Krodin looked toward Eldon. "Go. And take the detonator with you."

Eldon started to run from the room, but stopped in the doorway and looked back. "Krodin... we're not alone."

The immortal pushed past Eldon. Standing in the corridor was a silver-armored young woman.

"So you're the Fifth King. The Butcher of Uruk. The Devastator of Empires. You don't look like much to me."

"And you are Stephanie Cord, a human playing in a superhuman's world. Do you believe that your tricks and weapons are any match for my strength and endurance? To defeat you, girl, all I would have to do is stand here long enough for you to die of old age. Time means nothing to me." He looked toward Eldon. "Go to your brothers. Help Zeke to free Shadow. Then trigger the detonator."

As Eldon darted away, Krodin looked back at the armored young woman and said, "Walk with me a while. You are no threat to me so you can trust that I won't attack you."

"What would we have to talk about?"

"You will attempt to persuade me to relinquish my claim on humanity. And I will not. And *then* we will fight, and I will kill you. Or perhaps we will just talk."

"Why are you doing this? Why are you *like* this?"

"Your enemy Victor Cross believes that the universe is somehow sentient. It is aware, and intelligent. It created superhumans for a specific purpose. Cross believes that initially there was to be only me, but circumstances changed. The humans of this era stole me from my own time, forcing the universe to adopt an alternate plan. It created all the others in an attempt to fill the void caused by my apparent death. But the universe did not provide us with specifics of its intentions... All I know is that I was born to rule."

"*Or*... You're delusional."

"That *is* a possibility, yes. There can never be absolute proof that one is fully sane."

"So *why* did the universe create you to rule?"

"I do not yet know." He began to stride toward her. As he'd expected, the girl moved back out of his way. "I believe that I will learn that secret when the time is *right* for me to learn it. You can't beat me, Stephanie Cord. And you can't stop me. I've already shattered this nation beyond repair. The wheels are in motion and they cannot be stopped."

"Krodin, they destroyed a *city* trying to kill you. Doesn't that tell you that the humans don't want you? Why would you want to rule over people who hate and fear you? What do you *get* out of that?"

He smiled. "I met your father, briefly. We didn't have time to talk, but he was an impressive warrior. The others had powers, he did not, yet he fought without hesitation. I've read Sakkara's files on you and your sister. You are very much like him. He would be proud of you."

"If you *talk* to the world's presidents, explain that you want to unite all the nations..."

"Have you ever met a politician, Stephanie? In my time, as now, they were impossible to work with. Ask me a question. Anything. As simple or as complex as you like."

The girl shrugged. "What's your favorite color?"

Krodin said, "I *could* answer that, and thank you for asking, but the real question is not what is *my* favorite color, but which colors are best for the greatest number of people. Is there a fair distribution of colors? Is any one color intrinsically *better*? If I choose red, the supporters of yellow will accuse me of bias. And what about color-blind people? Or those who are *wholly* blind? *You* have to clarify where you stand on those issues before you judge *me* and accuse me of not knowing what my favorite color is."

Stephanie couldn't help smiling at that. "I see your point."

"I prefer to dispense with politics and actually make decisions and get things done." Into his radio, Krodin said, "Eldon. Report."

"We're getting there... Shadow's just about free."

"Trigger the detonator, then fly up here with him."

"I..."

"You're questioning me?"

"Krodin, it'd taken all of Zeke's energy to get Shadow out. He's too weak to fly on his own, and I can't carry both of them.

There isn't enough time to make two trips."

"Then consider Zeke a sacrifice. His premature aging would have killed him soon enough."

Stephanie Cord backed into a doorway as Krodin passed. He chose not to strike out at her. He made his way up through the levels, with the armored girl following, until he reached the roof.

Then he looked back at her. "You have about four minutes to gather any personal belongings you might have left behind. I know you humans can be sentimental about such things. The bomb is designed to shatter the central support pillars. The outer shell will probably survive, but the inner walls and floors are not so strong. Unless you want to be crushed, you should leave now." He tossed his radio to her, then stepped up onto the low wall encircling Sakkara's roof, and jumped.

Stephanie rushed to the wall and looked down. It hadn't been a particularly elegant jump: the immortal landed about half-way down the sloping wall, and from there he'd tumbled to the ground, rolled to his feet and started running.

Something rushed past her and she ducked in time to see one of the clones flying out, carrying what looked like the frozen body of another. They followed Krodin's path, swooping down to meet him.

Then the radio in Stephanie's hands beeped and a voice said, "Don't—you can't *leave* me!" It sounded like Colin, but a lot older.

She raised the radio to her mouth. "He's already gone. Who is that?"

"This is Zeke... I'm trapped down here. There's a bomb here. A *big* one."

Stephanie ran back down the stairs, back into the building.

"Can you defuse it?"

"I wouldn't know where to start!"

"Then where are you? I'm coming to get you out."

"The foundations, below the basement. The only way down is through the hollow core of the central pylon. Right now I don't have the energy to climb back up."

Stephanie raced down another flight of stairs. "Zeke, you have to focus on the bomb. Do you know how much time you have left?"

"Two minutes, fifty-four seconds."

"OK. That's plenty of time. What can you tell me about it?"

"I don't know *anything* about bombs! Krodin said the explosive is Penta-something. The thing is about the size of a fridge. But I can see a whole mess of wires and tubes. Wait, there's a small circuit board hidden behind the timer. I... Yeah, it's a tight squeeze but I think I can just about reach it."

"No! Zeke, don't touch *anyth—*"

The shockwave lifted Stephanie off her feet and slammed her into the ceiling. She barely had time to register what was happening before everything around her disintegrated into white-hot agony.

Chapter 23

Kenya turned over inside her sleeping bag, but was no more comfortable on her left side than she had been on her right. She turned back. *Bad move*, she told herself, and turned onto her left again.

Next to her, Renata whispered, "For someone who can move in complete silence, you sure do make a lot of noise when other people are trying to sleep. If you don't stop fidgeting, I *will* kill you."

"Sorry," Kenya said. She turned onto her back and stared up at the top of their tent. After a few seconds of silence, she added, "You're supposed to ask me what's on my mind and if I want to talk about it."

Renata sighed heavily. "Go on, then."

"These people are not superhuman and a lot of them are going to get killed because of us."

"We don't know that for sure."

"Renata, you know what it was like for me in Africa."

"You took it upon yourself to make amends for everything you did while you were under Yvonne Duval's control."

Kenya turned to face Renata, and propped her head up on her elbow. "Before that. While I *was* under Yvonne's control. My parents and my brother and I led our Trutopian community into war with everyone else. I didn't know I was superhuman at that point—I just kept fighting, and they kept following me. There were at least two hundred of us at the start. We picked up more along the way, but three weeks later I was the only one left of our original group. *I* led those people to their deaths. I don't want to do anything like that ever again. These soldiers here... I understand their reasons for fighting, and I'm happy to fight alongside them, but I can't lead them."

"We have to get back to the Substation, and we've still got over a hundred miles to cover. On foot, avoiding the Vipers, that's a week at least. With Gunderson's help we can be there this time tomorrow."

"It's almost a guarantee that some of them will die."

"They *know* that, Kenya. And they accept it."

"If we had a specific reason to go back, maybe I could accept it, too. But we're going back on a whim, just in case. We have no reason to believe that there's anything there now but corpses and cinders."

Renata asked, "What else can we do?"

"Stick with these people and *assist* them, not make them work for *us*. Having special abilities doesn't mean we're always right or always in charge."

"But Gunderson himself said it: they've just been attacking convoys and disappearing back into the woods. They're not inflicting any real, lasting damage on Krodin's armies. Especially not with all the mercs he's bringing in. For the sake of their morale, the soldiers here need to know that they've making an impact. Otherwise they're just throwing stones at the moon."

From outside the tent, a man's voice said, "If you two don't shut up right *now*..."

"Sorry!" Kenya said in a half-shout, half-whisper.

Renata whispered, "If you can't sleep, try counting backwards from one hundred. If you realize along the way that you've lost count, you start over."

"Does that work?"

"Yeah, usually. I think it just bores your brain so much it gives up and goes to sleep."

They were woken at dawn by Gunderson unzipping their tent-flap and walking in. "Time to go to work, ladies."

Renata and Kenya were both buried deep in their sleeping bags and barely moved. Renata said, "Don't you ever knock?"

Gunderson laughed. "Knock on a tent. Good one!" He nudged Kenya in the shoulder with his boot. "Up!"

"We're up, we're up!"

"Good! Get dressed. We eat in ten minutes, then we're going to war again. *This* time, we're going to win." He backed out through the tent-flaps.

"I *hate* that guy," Renata said, making sure she was loud enough for him to hear. "I hate morning people. *He's* a morning person and it lasts all day long."

Kenya nodded, but said nothing. Renata and Gunderson's friendship was strange to her. They seemed to be flirting, and at eighteen he was only a year older than her, but Kenya knew how Renata felt about Danny. Why would she flirt with another man, especially when she had no idea where Danny was, or if he was even still alive?

They had met Gunderson on their third day with the band of rebels who called themselves The Steadfast. They were a collection of locals, former police officers and soldiers from all aspects of the US military whose units had been withdrawn or destroyed.

When the war broke out Gars Gunderson had been neither a soldier nor a local: he had been hiking across the Great Salt Lake Desert the long way, from south to north, when his group was attacked by a small band of mercenaries. Gunderson was the only survivor. He didn't talk about it at all, but one of the others had told Kenya that he'd tracked the mercenaries one-by-one, slit their throats, and then cut out their hearts.

Kenya didn't believe a word of that. Gunderson was large and blond and bearded and always happy. It was hard to picture him taking on a bunch of trained mercenaries armed only with a knife and a thirst for revenge. He seemed the sort who'd be more at home putting a turf roof onto a log cabin than crawling through a building's ventilation shafts with a gun in each hand. The previous day she had seen him dive into a fast-moving river to rescue a drowning puppy that turned out to be a rather angry beaver.

In the camp's hierarchy, Gunderson was more of a trouble-shooter than a soldier. People constantly asked him for help, and he either helped them directly or he found someone else to do it.

She understood that this camp was only one of a number of outposts under The Steadfast's control, and that few people here were permitted to know the whereabouts of any of the other outposts, in case they were captured and Krodin's people interrogated them.

But sometimes she wondered if maybe that was all a crock of lies. Maybe this collection of five dozen people was all there was.

Two days ago Kenya and Renata had led the raid on a Viper communications post, and the members of The Steadfast had certainly done their share of the work, so there was no doubt that they knew how to fight, but she had never yet seen anything that might prove the existence of other outposts.

Beside her, Renata had finished dressing and was ready to go, while Kenya was still lacing up her boots.

"Are you all right?" Renata asked.

"Sure."

"You really don't like him, do you?"

"It's not him. It's everyone." She gave Renata a half-smile. "I liked it better when it was just you and me, and not sixty other people staring at me all day long. They call me Scarface."

"Who does? Gunderson?"

"No, but some of the others. That first one we met, the one who stopped the excavator for us?"

"Elijah Lehmann. He smells of garlic and stale sweat. Want me to sort him out for you?"

"I can fight my own battles, thanks. Anyway, it's better to ignore these things. If you confront people like that, they know they can get inside your head and then they never stop." Kenya smiled and stood up. "It's the time-tested best way to defeat bullies."

Renata said, "Not sure I agree with that. Let's go. What did we have for breakfast yesterday?"

"Two-day-old bread."

Renata made a face. "Oh yeah. That means today we're having *three*-day-old bread."

Outside, there was a sharp chill in the air, and everyone's breath formed misty plumes as they spoke. Kenya spotted Gunderson and eight others gathered outside the weapons tent—he was two meters tall, so always easy to pick out of the crowd—and made their way over to them, but her stomach lurched when she spotted Elijah Lehmann was with them.

When Gunderson saw them he grinned, as usual, and said, "Today's mission... comes to you courtesy of our superhuman friends Kenya and Renata."

Renata said, "Our destination is approximately one hundred and fifty kilometers to the north. The exact location is on a need-to-know basis, as are many of the details at this stage. I *can* tell you to prepare for a subterranean environment. We should reach the target destination at sunset, but instead we'll make camp five kilometers away and resume the mission tomorrow morning. This could be dangerous in the extreme. There's a strong chance that we'll be facing hostile enemy forces and could come under heavy fire." She looked around at the men and women in the group. "There is also the possibility of a hostile *superhuman* encounter. As things stand, I haven't yet recovered my extra-normal abilities so Kenya Cho is our most powerful member. Kenya?"

I hate it when she does this! Kenya thought, stepping forward and very much aware that everyone was looking at her. *What am I supposed to tell these people? Don't get killed?* Aloud, she said, "This is primarily a mission of exploration, but in truth we don't know exactly what we'll find. We'll be cutting straight through Viper territory so I want everyone to bring full body-armor and at least two handguns, eighty rounds each. We'll be taking three vehicles and moving fast, in tight formation."

One of the women said, "You're not telling us exactly where the target is... So what about our fail-safe extraction points?"

"There are none," Renata said. "We go in, we accomplish the mission, we come home."

Lehmann raised his hand, and said, "Gunderson, I don't understand why we'll have to wait out the night. If it's an underground location, then it doesn't matter whether it's night or day. It'll be dark anyway."

Gunderson shook his head, and said, "I told you, I'm not running this one. Direct your questions to Renata and Kenya."

Lehmann rolled his eyes. "Are you serious? They're *children!*"

Renata said, "We're young, yes, but each of us has more combat experience than all of you combined."

"Yeah, well, *one* of you ought to wear a mask or learn how to dodge a punch."

Everyone fell silent, and Lehmann shrugged and added, "No offense. I'm just saying."

On the edge of her vision Kenya saw Renata tense up, so she

put her hand on her arm and said, "Let me." She turned to Lehmann and asked, "What do you mean?"

"Just saying."

"Saying *what*, exactly?"

The man nervously wet his lips. "You know. You've got a lot of... scars. On your face."

"How many?" Kenya asked, stepping closer to him. "How many scars do I have?"

"I don't know. What sort of question is that?"

"You're the one who brought up the subject, so they must be important to you. The fact is my skin doesn't heal as well as a normal human's." She held up her hands. "The scars aren't just on my face. They're everywhere. I'm sorry if they bother you so much, but none of the people whose lives I've saved have complained. As far as I *know*, anyway. Perhaps, like you, they wait until they think I'm just out of range before they call me 'Scarface.' But back to the question. What was the purpose of you mentioning my facial scars? Does it make you feel big and strong to comment on someone else's physical features?"

Lehmann again looked towards Gunderson, but the big man just said, "If you've built a bridge of straw, it's better not to cross it with a burning torch."

"What does *that* mean?" Lehmann looked back at Kenya. "I'm sorry. OK? I won't mention it again, I swear."

Renata said, "You're promising *not* to bully a teenage girl about a physical attribute she can't change? Wow. Big man. I wonder if there's an award for that?"

Lehmann didn't respond to that, but Kenya noticed that the others had slightly moved away from him. She said, "We're traveling during the day because the Vipers' infra-red detectors will pick us up a lot easier at night. According to the intel we picked up on the raid the other day, there's a narrow window in their patrol schedules: if we hit that just right, we can avoid an encounter completely. In the event that we *do* engage them, and can't defeat them, then we call off the mission and make it look like just another hit-and-run."

Gunderson said, "So. If we're all done? You know the mission—or at least as much of it as you need to know at this stage—so we move out in twenty minutes. Eat, gather your equipment, and make any preparations you feel are necessary."

As the others moved away, Gunderson called Renata and Kenya aside. "Lehmann is a good soldier. If he were not, I wouldn't allow him on this mission."

"I know that," Kenya said.

"When we're done, I'll request that he be reassigned to another outpost."

"No, don't. He's been embarrassed among his friends. That'll keep him under control for a while. If you move him elsewhere, that'll be like pretending it never happened."

Gunderson nodded and smiled. "You are wise and compassionate, Kenya Cho. Now, there is news that might interest you both. Another outpost has made contact through various channels. I won't tell you which outpost or where they are, so please don't ask. But the word is that your friend Danny Cooper is alive and well, and working with them."

Renata clapped her hands to her mouth. "Are you sure?"

"They say they are positive that it's him, and I trust them. Danny is on a mission at the moment, but when he returns we'll arrange something. A call, perhaps a meeting. I can also pass on a message for him, if you like."

Renata said, "Tell him I'll meet him on a rooftop somewhere."

Gunderson said, "OK. Is that a code he'll recognize?"

"It's not a code. We just always seemed to spend a lot of

time on roofs."

"Makes sense. Now, I'd like to speak with Kenya alone, if that's all right with you both?"

Still smiling, Renata said, "Fine with me."

Kenya watched her leave, then turned back to face Gunderson.

He said, "Lehmann's comments were... thoughtless. Cruel, even. But I want you to know that if things were a little different, I would pursue you with romantic intentions."

Kenya didn't know how to react to that. It sounded like a compliment, but it hurt. "If I didn't have my scars. If I wasn't ugly."

"No, if we weren't in the middle of a *war*. Scars don't make the victims ugly, Kenya, only the perpetrators. And *you* are far from ugly. Believe me. You have the purest soul I've ever known, and you are *glorious*."

Chapter 24

"I keep thinking I've seen that kid before," Mathew said to Alia as they laid out the pieces for the Compound's new gate. They were inside the barn, which had been cleaned out and was now Mathew's workshop.

"Nathan? Maybe you *have* seen him before."

"Well, where are you two from?"

"Not anywhere near here. You?"

"Originally? You wouldn't know it. It's a tiny place, a town called Parity right on the border."

Alia didn't bother to ask "*Which* border?" because she was worried that he might tell her. Mathew was a hard worker but he seemed to be unable to do anything without it reminding him of a story that the urgently needed to relate.

"I left Parity when I was nineteen. Just hit the road and never looked back." He smiled to himself. "Found myself in the heart of Tennessee after that. You ever been to Tennessee? It's great. The people are so friendly. And they sure know how to run a bar. I've visited bars all over the south but I have never, *ever* been to a bar as awesome as the ones they have in Tennessee. Shalvey's bar was the best. You got a favorite bar, Alia?"

"I'm only seventeen, so no."

"Oh yeah." Mathew stepped back and looked down at their handiwork. "That's everything, right?"

"Looks like it," Alia said.

Mathew had designed the new gate, and enlisted Alia's help in shaping and sawing the wood. At first, he had wanted Nathan to help him, but the boy hadn't show much interest. Mathew had told Alia that he preferred students who asked questions: "I was a wood-shop teacher. There's nothing more satisfying than working with fresh timber, making something useful or beautiful out of raw materials. But that boy doesn't have the *bug* for it, you know? He told me that he didn't even realize there were different kinds of wood." When he'd said that, Mathew had looked as though he were about to cry.

He had taught her the different joints they would be using, and why those particular joints had been chosen. "These are not going to be fancy gates. They'll to be functional. Basic. That might not sound like fun, but trust me, when the work is done, you'll feel a swell of pride like you never imagined. The simplest forms can be the most satisfying when they're done right."

Alia counted the lengths of wood, checking that each piece had its mirror-image in the other gate. "That's definitely everything on the list. So we just need to put them together now, right?"

Mathew nodded. "Go on..."

"Each gate will be too heavy for even four people to lift, so we should assemble them where we need them, rather than in here?"

"That's one option. But in here we've got a nice flat floor. Out there, the ground is very uneven, plus we'd be getting in everyone's way. That's another lesson for you, Alia. Don't create obstacles for yourself: other people will be eager enough to make your work harder. So we assemble the pieces here. But in which order?"

"You're the teacher, you tell me."

"Ah... but if I tell you, you'll forget. If I make you do it for yourself, you'll either get it right—in which case, well done—or you'll mess it up and you'll never forget *that* lesson. So, it's up to you how you want to proceed."

She walked around the lengths of timber, staring down at them. "We've got all the pieces here, we know how they go together. We've got the tools over there, and the necessary screws, nails and glue over *there...*"

It took them a whole day to complete the assembly of the new gates, and Alia had done most of the work herself, only calling on Mathew's aid when a second pair of hands was needed to hold something steady.

The next morning, six strong adults were recruited to carry each gate out to the gateposts, and Alia was with them every step of the way. She crossed her fingers as they were lifted into place, held her breath as the hinges were bolted on, and said a tiny prayer when Mathew insisted that the gates be closed for the first time.

Alia couldn't take her eyes off the gates as Mathew applied grease to the hinges. *What if they don't close? If they're too wide, we can shave a little off each side. It won't look great, but it'll work. If they're too narrow, there'll be a gap. I guess we could add a lip to one side, but then that side would always have to be opened* first. *And if they're not hanging straight then the gap won't be the same width at the top as it is at the bottom. It's going to look awful!*

Mathew closed the lid on his can of grease and walked away, calling back over his shoulder, "Give them a go."

The heavy gates closed smoothly and silently, and seemed to fit together perfectly. Alia realized that she had actually been trembling with anticipation.

She walked up to the gates and failed to suppress a grin. There was a gap of one centimeter between the two, and it was perfectly even from top to bottom. Exactly as planned.

Alia turned around to point that out to Mathew, but the man wasn't there.

She found him back in the barn, sweeping up.

"They're perfect! I mean, absolutely perfect."

"They're just *gates*, Alia."

"But you didn't even stay to see if they closed properly!"

"That's true. But I knew that they would. I've made gates before. And how many times did we check the measurements? Ten? Twelve?" Mathew shrugged. "We knew exactly what we wanted to make and we made them with skill and care. How could they *not* work?"

"You're almost at full strength now, correct?" General Mendes asked Colin. They were in a field in Wyoming, sitting in the back of her armored personnel carrier, waiting for dawn. Rain lashed the windshield but the driver didn't bother using the wipers: there was nothing to see out there but drenched, miserable-looking soldiers.

"I think so," Colin said.

"Good. The reason I wanted to see you in person is that there is certain information that can't be trusted over standard communications channels. Bracken? Take a walk. Fifteen minutes."

The driver said, "Yes, sir!" then climbed out of the car and slammed the door shut.

Mendes said, "Colin... We're keeping this suppressed for now, but Sakkara has been devastated. It's looking like Krodin himself was behind it."

Colin felt the hairs stand up on the back of his neck. "When you say 'devastated'...?"

"An explosion somewhere deep inside the building. Sakkara was designed to survive almost any external attack—but Krodin's bomb was detonated in the heart of the building. It shattered the internal structure. All the inner floors and walls were pulverized in the blast. Krodin and two of the clones were spotted fleeing the area *after* the explosion, so we know they weren't caught in it."

"Why would he do that?"

"Hard to be certain, but our strategists are thinking that it's probably because without hostages there was nothing to stop *us* attempting to destroy it while he was inside. So he destroyed it himself."

Colin said, "Yeah, that's the part that I don't get. Why?"

"Because there was a lot of equipment in there that we might have been able to use against him. He couldn't take it all with him, so he destroyed the building. That crushes the equipment and also has a demoralizing effect on anyone who's ever lived there. Not to mention that it means Krodin now doesn't have a headquarters."

"But that's a good thing."

The general shook her head. "No, it's not. When he had a headquarters we knew his location at least some of the time. Now? He could be *anywhere*. It also suggests that he believes that he doesn't *need* a HQ any more because this phase of his work is done. He's sparked a civil war and now it's at the stage where it doesn't need him to oversee it. The factions will keep fighting until one of them is victorious. Then he just has to defeat the winners, and he's on top."

"How are we going to stop him?" Colin asked.

"You tell us: you're the superhuman."

"If there was a way to knock him out for a few hours... I was thinking we could fly him into space and throw him at the sun."

"You're not the first one to suggest that. We even have a team working on the calculations, but it would take us weeks to prepare a rocket or missile. Can *you* fly into space?"

"I don't know. Probably. I know my dad did, a few times."

"Then it's worth considering. But that's not the only reason I wanted to talk to you in private. Our comms division intercepted a series of code messages from one of the resistance cells to another. From what we can tell, Daniel Cooper, Kenya Cho and Renata Soliz are still alive. Kenya's abilities are recovering, but as yet there's no word on whether the same is true for Daniel or Renata."

Colin slumped in his seat. "They're alive."

"So it would seem. And they've not been idle. We don't have any solid intel on the others, but there are unconfirmed rumors that Mina Duval and Stephanie Cord have been seen in Chicago. According to the stories, Stephanie went there to retrieve one of her father's old Paragon suits. This correlates with other stories of a jet-powered human figure in flight over the city, but correlation isn't proof."

Colin nodded. "OK. That's still good news, though, right? What about the others? Anything on Lance McKendrick?"

"No. But he's an expert at disappearing. I doubt we'll see him again until he *wants* to be seen. We still believe that he's taken Cassandra Szalkowska with him: a telepath would be a very efficient early-warning system."

"So what's our plan to stop all this? To end the war?"

"I'm not sure that it can be stopped. I believe that the war has passed the point of no return, what my instructor used to call The Peace Event Horizon. Even if we take Krodin down, his armies are strong enough and dedicated enough to keep fighting. There's no evidence that he's been issuing instructions to them."

"So the only way to stop the war is to beat all of his armies individually?"

"That's what it looks like. And that's why we need the New Heroes back. Colin, I want you to find Renata and Danny. My people will give you all the information they have on the resistance cells."

*

The small town of Edillon was little more than rubble and ashes.

Duke Tansey and Danny Cooper walked slowly along what had once been the town's main street. They were wearing the armor they'd taken from the soldiers at the checkpoint, but Duke had sprayed it with white paint: "We don't want any of our own people taking shots at us."

As they climbed over the rubble of what had once been a store, Danny spotted a miraculously undamaged candy bar. He offered half to Duke, but the older man shook his head and they moved on.

"Used to be a general store right there," Duke said a few minutes later, pointing to the left. "Sold everything from mouse-traps to lottery tickets."

"Where's your cousin's house?"

"We're standing on it."

Danny looked down at his feet. "Oh man."

"We've not found any bodies, that's a good sign. Everyone here got out before Krodin's people moved in."

"Yeah, but where did they go?"

"Could be anywhere. But I reckon I know where my cousin is..." He nodded directly ahead. "Gwendolyn Higley's house. Inherited it from her great uncle who was always convinced that a nuclear apocalypse was on the way. The place has a fallout shelter in the back yard."

Duke started walking, and Danny followed. "Any particular reason your cousin would be there?"

"Gwen and Marvin are close. Can't say I approve of that."

"You mean, they're boyfriend and girlfriend?"

Duke grunted something that Danny guessed was probably "Yes."

"Nothing wrong with that," Danny said. "You can't help who

you fall in love with."

"Yes, you can. If you're in danger of falling in love with the wrong person, you just steer clear of them. Simple."

"What makes Gwendolyn the wrong person?"

"She's not the wrong person. *He* is."

Danny said, "Ah. OK, then."

Duke pointed ahead. "There's the hatch."

The entrance to the bunker was a square meter of metal set into the ground, and resembled an ordinary manhole cover. Duke walked over to it and pounded on it with his foot, then shouted, "Marvin, you in there?"

Danny and Duke looked at each other while they waited. Then Duke crouched down, picked up a half-brick, and started slamming it down on the hatch over and over.

"Is that Morse code?" Danny asked.

"No, it's Duke-code for 'Open the blasted door or I'll spend all day hitting it.'"

Something inside the hatch went *shunk!* and Duke stepped back. "Figured that would do it."

The hatch was pushed open and a forty-year-old man who looked like a slightly thinner version of Duke was looking up at them. "Duke."

"Marvin."

"What do you want?"

"You still seeing those blue lights?"

Marvin muttered something under his breath and climbed out of the hatch. He was followed by a woman of about the same age. Neither of them looked pleased to see Duke.

Marvin said, "You haven't said a word to me since Roberta's wedding and *this* is what you want to talk about?"

"Yes. Are you still seeing the blue lights?"

The woman—Danny assumed she was Gwendolyn—said,

"What's this about, Duke?"

To Marvin, Duke said, "Kid here's a superhuman. Says the blue lights are real. They're the energy the superhumans need. Now, it sounds like bull but I'm inclined to believe him. He's lost his powers and most people can't see the blue lights. So we need you to find one for us. He'll walk through it and his powers will come back. Then we'll leave and you can lock yourselves back into your sordid love-nest."

Marvin looked like he wanted to strangle Duke. "Seriously? We were doing fine hiding out down there and you come along and give away our location to anyone who might be watching." Then he stepped back and seemed to notice Duke and Danny's armor and weapons for the first time. "What's going on?"

"There's a war."

"I know that. You're fighting? *You*, the guy I had to protect every day when we were in high-school? Times sure have changed." He turned to Danny. "So you're a superhuman? Is that for real?"

Gwendolyn said, "He's Danny Cooper. Quantum's son. I recognize him from the news."

"Mister Tansey, we need your help," Danny said. "When was the last time you saw one of the blue lights?"

"Not since before the war started. When I was your age they were all over the place. I'd see maybe ten every day. They'd just be drifting about, passing through walls and people or floors. A couple of times I saw them hit a person and disappear, like it was soaking into them. So, those people were superhumans?"

"Probably, yes. Did *you* ever walk into one of the lights?"

"Sure. Well, I did after I got over being scared of them. I used to think that they might be ghosts."

Duke barked a short, sharp laugh, and Marvin fixed him with another glare. "I was thirteen and terrified, seeing things that no one else could see."

Gwendolyn said, "I'm sorry, but I'm not following this. Marv, we've known each other for twenty-one *years* and you've never mentioned this to me!"

"I didn't want you to think I was crazy. *I* thought I might be."

"Even if I did think you were crazy, that wouldn't change how I feel about you." Then, after a pause, she added, "Though I might have put a lock on the knife-drawer."

Duke said, "Marvin, can you help or not?"

Marvin turned in a very slow circle. "Not seeing anything right now... But they're a lot easier to spot at night."

Gwendolyn said, "You're welcome to wait. But inside, please, not out here!"

"It's a relief to think that all this time I was right." To Danny, Marvin said. "Obviously you can't see them, but others can." He resumed looking around. "This is one of the best days ever! It's like... like..."

Gwendolyn said, "Find the right word later, please! We should be inside!"

"I'm not searching for the right word, Gwen. I'm looking at one of the blue lights. Right now." He pointed straight ahead. "About three hundred yards that way."

Danny said, "Show me."

Gwendolyn stayed behind to guard the bunker, calling out, "Duke, if anything happens to him, you'll answer to me!"

Marvin clambered over scorched rubble that had once been a neighbor's house, with Danny and Duke following.

"It's not moving fast," Marvin said. "You see there where there's just the corner of the building still standing? About eight feet to the left."

Danny ran ahead, almost tripping over a heat-warped girder. "Where?"

"Forward," Marvin called. "Forward... one step to your right..."

Danny looked around. He still couldn't see even the slightest hint of a blue ball of light. He shouted back to Marvin, "Well?"

"It's gone. You've already absorbed it."

Danny picked up a small rock from the ground, tossed it gently into the air, and concentrated.

The rock stopped moving.

Danny Cooper grinned to himself. *Oh yeah. I'm back.*

Chapter 25

At sunset, five kilometers south of the Substation, the members of Renata's Steadfast cell surrounded the broken man as he staggered along the dirt-track road. They had been setting up camp when the lookouts had spotted him coming.

Now, eight separate guns were trained on him as he stood slightly wavering. The scabbed blood on his face cracked as he tried to speak, fresh blood spilled onto an already crimson-stained shirt.

"Who are you?" Lehmann demanded. "What's your business here?"

One of the others said, "Poor guy can barely *stand*..."

Lehmann said, "What faction are you with? Answer me, or that'll be the last question you ever hear!"

Renata rushed up to the group, and stepped between the stranger and Lehmann. "It's all right. Everything is OK. We're not going to hurt you."

The team's medic, Sabin, approached, shining a flashlight into the man's face. "Man, someone really did a number on you, didn't they?" She helped the man to sit down on the ground, and checked him over before taking Renata aside. "His jaw's been shattered. Nose broken, cheekbones too, I think. No other major injuries that I can see. No ID on him, no weapons. I figure he's in his early twenties. He's very dehydrated, probably starving, too: there's no way he can eat with his jaw in such a mess. That and the pain he must be suffering explains the disorientation. Whoever he is, he's been through the mill. We need to get him to a hospital. An aid station at the very least."

Renata considered that for a moment. "No. We can't spare anyone right now. The mission has priority."

Next to her, Lehmann said, "Then maybe it's time we *knew*

the mission."

"Not yet. Take Bosch and watch the perimeter."

As Lehmann left, Kenya approached Renata and Sabin. "I know who he is. Renata, this changes *everything*."

"Who is he?"

"Victor Cross. I gave him a pen and paper and he wrote down his name."

Renata felt her heart start to race. "I want to talk to him."

Sabin said, "He needs urgent treatment, Renata. The condition he's in I'm astonished he's not already dead."

Renata was already walking back towards Cross. "Everyone... strike the camp. We're aborting the mission. Heading back in ten minutes." She crouched in front of Victor. "You look like you've had a bad day. No less than you deserve, I think. But who did this to you, Victor?"

He pointed at himself.

"Huh. There's a long list of people who'd love to take a shot at you. I didn't realize that your *own* name was on that list too."

It was almost midnight when the team spotted a Viper patrol ahead. As they pulled off the road and into the trees, Renata said to Kenya, "Stay in the car, and keep an eye on him." She and the others got out and waited. If the Vipers spotted them, they'd have a better chance to fight back if they were on foot.

Victor was in the back seat beside Kenya. The medic, Sabin, had loosely wrapped thick bandages around his neck and jaw and had given him a strong pain-killer, but he was clearly still in discomfort.

Kenya hated traveling at night. Her weak night-vision meant that all she could see outside the car was different degrees of darkness. She unclipped her seat-belt then reached out her arm to check once again that the door was open: she didn't want to have to fumble in the dark for the handle.

Next to her, Victor groaned softly, and Kenya quietly shushed him.

She could picture Renata and the others crouched behind the cars, watching for the Vipers. She knew that many of them were mercenaries, but The Steadfast had encountered more than a few who had deserted from the military or police, or had been ordinary citizens recruited through threats or the promise of a better life.

She tried not to judge them: she had probably killed more people than any of the Vipers ever would.

Someone next to the car, on Victor's side, whispered. "I see them... Full squadron, on foot."

Kenya held her breath. If the Vipers attacked in daylight she'd have little trouble fighting back. But now, in almost total darkness, she didn't rate her chances very highly.

She could hear the slight irregular crunch of the Viper squadron's boots on the road. The sound was gradually getting louder, and louder.

Then, finally, it was clear that the footsteps were starting to fade. The squadron was passing by.

Victor moaned again, and this time the man on his side of the car peered in through the open door. It was Lehmann. "Kenya... keep him quiet!"

"I can't!" she whispered back.

"Put your hand over his mouth!"

"If I do, he'll scream with the pain."

Lehmann reached in with his free hand towards Victor's face, but hesitated, clearly unsure exactly what to do.

Victor made a grab for Lehmann's gun.

The young man reacted instinctively: he slammed the gun into the side of Victor's face. Victor screamed.

Kenya threw herself out of the car. Around her, the members of The Steadfast were already running, but she could see almost nothing.

Gunfire erupted from behind her, and she briefly glanced back to see trees and running silhouettes against flashes of light.

From somewhere to her left, she heard Renata shouting, "Kenya—this way!" but she couldn't tell exactly where.

She continued to run, almost blindly, and slipped into silent mode.

They can't hear me, and I can't see them...

There was a flashlight in her backpack, but she couldn't spare the time to stop and look for it.

Pounding footsteps behind her, someone chasing her—then Lehmann pushed past her, crashing through the undergrowth.

Another gunshot, and Lehmann collapsed, a red bloom on the back of his jacket.

Eighty miles south-west of Sakkara, Krodin and Eldon sat in an abandoned school bus and watched as Shadow's chest rose and fell, rose and fell. The injured clone was stretched out in the back seat and wrapped in a dozen blankets.

Eldon said, "He's definitely healing. That looks like normal sleep to me."

Krodin nodded. "He's the strongest of you all. Almost a match for Colin Wagner."

"*Almost?* We defeated Colin!"

"Yes, collectively. And using Victor Cross's device to strip Colin's power. One-on-one, and without such tricks, Colin is still more powerful than Shadow at his best." Krodin leaned back in his seat and closed his eyes. "I want a report on the status of our forces."

"OK... *How* do I get that? We don't have any communicators to talk to the mercenaries."

"Use your imagination, Eldon. If you have one. The nearest battlefront will be in Texas. Go there, find our people, then get them to communicate with the others. Then you come back here and tell me."

"All right," Eldon said. "But it'll take a few hours."

"I'm immortal."

The clone nodded. "Yeah, that's a point."

When he had left, Krodin watched Shadow for a while. The other clones meant nothing to him—they were cattle at best—but Shadow was different. Shadow had freed him from that cold, desert world.

They had spent four months together in the return capsule, with barely enough room to move. At first, Shadow had spoken only in an ancient Sumerian dialect, so the conversation was stilted, but Krodin had learned some English in his short time in America, and he was a master of languages.

Shadow's knowledge base had been very weak, and his senses of morality and honor seemed to be entirely absent, but Krodin had found him interesting. An artificial man. A construct grown from a tiny particle of another person.

The computers installed in the craft taught Krodin to read English, and they held countless stories and articles, more than an ordinary man could read in a hundred lifetimes.

Within a week, their roles had switched: Krodin began to teach Shadow. The boy was bright, and at times creative, but he was not even slightly interested in the politics and history that Krodin found fascinating.

On the last day of their journey, with the Earth filling the sky ahead of them, Shadow had instructed the craft's computers to talk to those on the planet.

This was how they learned the locations of Victor Cross and Shadow's brothers. Shadow had said, "Victor first. The place is called the Cloister. It's probably the most impregnable prison on the planet. But you're indestructible and I'm strong. We should be able to just walk in there and take him."

Krodin's response had been, "No. We do not need Cross now. Later, perhaps, but now he is safe in the impervious prison."

"He's not going to like that."

"That's of no concern to me. Our first action should be to free your brothers. We will go to the home of those you call the New Heroes."

"And kill them?" Shadow asked.

"Perhaps."

Now, Shadow groaned slightly in his sleep, and Krodin almost felt empathy towards him. Almost. In his already long life, before his misguided followers had stolen him from the past, he had lost many people. His final loss had been the hardest to take. Alexandria. The only person he had ever truly loved. And she had never returned that love. She had married him out of duty, or fear. Perhaps both. Alexandria had borne him seven offspring. Three daughters and four sons. He had liked some of them. By the time he was taken, he had been with Alexandria for thirty-five years. Some of his children had grandchildren of their own.

He wondered how far his bloodline extended. There was a possibility that after his disappearance all of his children and their own progeny had been put to the sword. Certainly, that was something he himself had done when he'd conquered a nation or an empire. But perhaps one or two had been missed. It could be that his blood still flowed in the modern man.

He smiled to himself, amused at his automatic use of terms

that were now considered archaic. *It's not blood. It's genetic material.*

Shadow groaned again, and Krodin's response was to move to the front of the bus where it was quieter. *Perhaps I don't have any empathy after all.*

If the Helotry hadn't taken me from the past... I would still be alive now, and I would have this whole world in my grip. And more besides: we would have established colonies on other worlds.

But these humans are so slow to make progress, and slower still to recognize its worth.

His knowledge of recent history had come from the computers in Victor's craft. *It took sixty-six years for the humans to advance from their first controlled powered flight to setting foot on another world. That is impressive, but of course they allowed politics and ennui to hamper them. In the half-century since, all they have done is send machines to the other worlds. They have not even returned to the moon.*

Under my rule, we will conquer the universe, as is our destiny.

It will take millions of years, perhaps billions. But I will see it come to pass. And then...

Krodin stared out through the school-bus's cracked windscreen. He didn't like to think about what would happen then.

The latest science said that at some point the universe will end.

What did that mean for an indestructible immortal?

When Eldon returned to the school-bus, he was hesitant to give Krodin his report. He remembered what had happened to Tuan, and Zeke. And to the traitor Roman.

Krodin said, "Tell me," and Eldon was briefly consumed by the urge to fly away and never return.

Again, Krodin said, "Tell me."

"Renata Soliz and Kenya Cho were working with a resistance group called The Steadfast. They were returning to the Substation for some reason and they found Victor. He managed to get out of the Substation and he's alive, just about. Then they ran into a Viper patrol and, well, it all went crazy and they caught Renata but Kenya escaped. She made her way back to their camp, but by the time she got there one of her own people had squealed. Our guys burnt the camp to the ground. Now Kenya's on the run again."

Krodin stood up, and stretched. "So. We have Renata."

"And Victor, too. Though he's in a *very* bad way. But..."

"But what?"

"Well... Kenya escaped."

"She is hardly the most powerful of our enemies."

Eldon relaxed. "I thought you might be angry!"

"Renata is a much greater prize than Kenya is a loss. But she is to be pursued. I want her caught. Alive if possible, but that's not necessary. How are the rest of our forces poised?"

"Some cities are holding out, and we've yet to find the president or any of the other bigwigs, but if you want it in numbers, then we currently occupy about seventy-two per cent of the country. The rest of the world is panicking in case they're next."

"They *are* next." Krodin smiled. "We are on the edge of victory, especially with Shadow recovering and Cross returned to us. When we have taken this land, the other nations will fall to their knees. They will cut each others' throats to be first in line to swear fealty to me. *That* is true power." He slapped Eldon on the shoulder. "You've done good work, Eldon. Now... I want you to bring me Victor and Renata. And I want Renata unharmed. If she is not, then all of those involved in her capture will die. As will *you*. Go."

Kenya Cho raced through the burning forest, her tears carving paths in the dirt and soot that covered her scarred face. She was almost thankful for the fires: the flames illuminated the thick clouds of smoke, throwing back enough light that it almost compensated for her poor night-vision.

The soldiers were close behind her. A whole Viper squadron. They were hunter-killers, given full authority to use any means necessary to stop the rebels. Somehow they had learned where Kenya's people were hiding, and rather than waste time tracking them down, the Vipers had chosen to burn them out.

I'm not going to make it, Kenya thought. *They're driving me this way because they have someone waiting at the other end!*

Ahead, the flickering light of the fires showed a small crevasse in her path. Kenya increased her speed and jumped. She somersaulted in the air, silently landed in a crouch in a small clearing, rolled onto her feet and kept going.

"Sarge, I see her!" A voice called out from her left.

"Don't move!" A second voice yelled. "You move, you die!"

A black-clad soldier threw himself at her, and Kenya dodged to the side then slammed her elbow into the back of his neck as he passed her. The soldier's gun flew from his hand: Kenya threw herself after it—and was within inches of grabbing it when a large, thick-soled boot kicked it away.

They were on her in seconds, grabbing her legs, dragging her back to the clearing.

"Get her on her feet!"

One of the soldiers grabbed hold of Kenya's hair and hauled her upright.

"Resisting arrest." A man with sergeant's stripes on his uniform stepped up to her, and Kenya flinched.

No, not him!

Sergeant Antonio Lashley grabbed Kenya's chin with a leather-gloved hand and roughly pushed her head back. "Now that's a nice find. Kenya Cho. Well, we got your pals. Every one of them. They're dead. We gave them a chance to surrender, but they figured resistance was the best option. When are you freaks gonna learn? You *don't* resist us. If you resist, you die."

"You can't do this! This is America!"

"Not any more. America was just an idea—and it's an idea that's gone now, wiped out just like half the planet." Sergeant Lashley pointed to the symbol on his shoulder; a blue eye inside a golden sun. "What's left of the Earth belongs to Krodin."

"We'll stop you!"

He planted his out-spread hand on her face and pushed her back—two of the soldiers caught her arms and dragged her forward again. "Pathetic," Lashley said. "There are so few of you punks left we could waste the lot of you with one clip!"

Kenya glared at him, her teeth gritted. "*Someone* will stop you."

The sergeant laughed. "Who? There are no more heroes. There's just us." To his men, he said, "Take her. Find out everything she knows before you kill her. She was working with Cooper's cell; hurt her until she talks. Then *keep* hurting her. Record everything. Cross is going to want to see it. Maybe she'll tell us what we need to get the rest of these rats out of their tunnels and into the open." He looked around. "The rest of you stay sharp. There could be more of them about."

The soldiers marched away, dragging her backwards over the rough, cinder-strewn ground. She looked up to see the sergeant smirking at her.

"Someone will stop us. Hah. Good one," Lashley yelled after her. "You so-called New Heroes are only making things worse for everyone. When are you going to accept that Krodin is the only power now?"

And then the soldiers dragging her suddenly stopped. The sergeant was staring at something beyond her.

With some effort, Kenya twisted her head around to look.

Fifteen yards away, the air was glowing. A sphere of orange light. It flared briefly, and disgorged a human figure onto the ground before it faded.

Lashley rushed over, stopped when he was next to Kenya. "What the...?"

The figure straightened up, silhouetted against the burning forest.

Kenya squinted, trying to make out the features. The flickering firelight showed a polished steel helmet, metal gauntlets, a glimpse of sweat beading on dark-brown skin.

The sergeant yelled, "Open fire!"

The soldiers let go of Kenya to use their guns. She ducked down, and ran.

The gunfire was quickly replaced with screams, then Lashley yelled, "You? That's not possible—you're *dead*!"

A final, brief scream, then silence.

Kenya knew she should run and keep running, but something drew her back to the clearing. She crept slowly, silently, through the smoldering forest, and saw the strange warrior crouched among the dead bodies of the Viper squadron.

On the ground, not more than a yard away from Kenya's feet, Sergeant Antonio Lashley stared at her through dead eyes. The rest of his body was quite a distance from his head.

The armored warrior straightened up, and slowly looked around.

Who is *that?* Kenya asked herself. The armor wasn't familiar—it seemed cruder, less advanced than the armor worn by the members of Team Paragon.

Every other superhero—powered or otherwise—was either dead, imprisoned, or a long way from here.

But I know them all... So that means... Kenya could hardly bring herself to even entertain the thought. *No. It's impossible.*

She moved closer. "Are you... Are you Paragon? But you were *killed.*"

The stranger turned toward her, and now Kenya could see a lot more clearly.

"No," the woman said. "I'm not Paragon." She looked around again. "What *is* this place? How did I get here? And these men... Why are they wearing Krodin's symbol?"

"I'll tell you everything I know. But... Who *are* you?"

The woman wiped the blood from her sword and returned it to the scabbard on her back. "My name is Abigail de Luyando."

Chapter 26

Brawn looked down at the soldier and for a moment he wondered whether he wanted to take orders from someone less than half his age.

Unperturbed by Brawn's scowl, the soldier—Corporal Borujerdi—repeated his instructions: "You are to accompany me aboard the transport immediately. Alone. I will not tell you your destination. You will take no electronic devices that can be tracked. You will submit to a full body search."

Brawn looked from the soldier to his helicopter and back. "Is that so? Let me show you something, kid." He grabbed hold of the soldiers arms, turned him around and lifted him up, then carried him to the edge of the shopping mall's roof, and turned in a slow circle. "See out there? I'm counting twenty-five, thirty columns of smoke... Some of those are whole *towns*. We've been asking for back-up since the war began and so far you're all we've been sent. Now you come here and you want to take me away?"

The soldier tried to struggle free, then looked down and saw that Brawn was holding him over the edge. "No! Look, I'm just obeying orders!"

"You were instructed to take me somewhere, right. I'm not one to boast, son, but I'm a pretty big player here in this town. Without me, people will die. So you tell whoever's pulling your strings that if they want me, they've got to give something in return."

"I was told you'd... Look, can you just put me down?"

Brawn set the corporal down on the roof. "I wasn't going to drop you."

As the young man quickly backed away from the edge he said, "We can send you food and ammunition. No personnel.

We're stretched thin as it is."

Behind them, Sergeant Irena Rosenblum said, "We don't *want* food or ammunition, or personnel. We want *evacuation*."

Corporal Borujerdi turned to face her. "I'm sorry, Officer, but we can't do that."

"There are sixty-one of us here," Brawn said. "Your copter can take twenty at a time. Three trips. Four if we take our supplies."

"I'm sorry, no." The soldier stepped closer to the sergeant. "Look, they don't want this widely known, but there's nowhere to evacuate *to*."

"Canada," Brawn said.

"The Canadians have shut their borders. And so have the Mexicans. No one will take our refugees because they know that'll just make them a target."

"They're *already* a target," Brawn said. "Krodin's not going to stop with America. He's going to bludgeon the world into submission."

Irena put her hand on Brawn's arm. "That's why you have to go. You know that."

"Yeah, I know."

The corporal gestured towards the copter. "And we have to go *now*, Brawn."

"Got it. Give us a minute." He glanced at the soldier. "Private conversation, son. Seriously, walk away."

"No, we don't have time—"

"You can walk away of your own accord or you can crawl away crying and whimpering. Your choice."

As they watched Corporal Borujerdi hurriedly climb into the copter, Sergeant Rosenblum said, "That was a bit unkind."

"I know. But I don't like people giving me orders."

"You *are* going to come back, right?"

"Sure plan to, yeah."

"You'd better. When all this is over I expect you to formally ask me out on a date."

Brawn smiled. "And I expect you to accept."

Sergeant Rosenblum nodded. "Well then. Have fun fighting the bad guys."

Danny moved, and time around him stood still. At a waterfall, he watched suspended raindrops glisten in the sunlight. The rippled lake below was a frozen, warped mirror.

Ahead of him, a bullet slowly emerged from the handgun held by a black-uniformed woman. From Danny's perspective, the bullet would take eight or nine minutes to reach its target: a cowering old man.

Danny pushed the bullet off-course and removed the gun from the woman's hand, then tossed it into the lake. Once the weapon left his field of influence, it slowed to a stop in mid-air. He took a set of handcuffs from the woman's belt and placed them around her wrists, taking care not to move her arms together too quickly or he'd snap the bones. The woman was going to suddenly find herself weaponless, handcuffed and with inexplicable bruises on her arms.

He moved on to the next soldier, another woman, this one about to fire a rifle past the cowering man and towards a fleeing resistance soldier. Danny removed the rifle's cartridge before throwing both into the lake. He handcuffed the second woman, too.

There were fifteen of Krodin's soldiers in this squadron that was currently raiding a refugee camp. Within a second of real-time, every one of the soldiers was disarmed, handcuffed and—thanks to a roll of duct-tape he'd found in one of their cars—gagged.

He resisted the temptation to slip back to normal time and watch their reactions: there was a lot more work to be done.

After passing through the blue light in Edillon he had returned to Duke, Marvin and Gwendolyn, and made Duke promise to protect Marvin: "I'll be back soon, I promise. I need to find some of the others, bring them here."

He wasn't sure where to start looking, but as long as he stayed in fast-mode, he had all the time in the world.

He left the refugee camp and returned to the road, moving at what seemed to him to be a leisurely jog, heading west towards Sioux City.

As he passed through the town of Lawton, he saw one of the Vipers' trucks in pursuit of an ordinary-looking car. He reached into the truck and removed the keys from the steering column, then took the soldiers' guns. He walked up to the other car and dropped the guns onto the back seat.

Sioux City was under siege from Krodin's army, marching from the north and west. When Danny realized just how many of them there were, he almost gave up. *No, keep going. You can get them all, one at a time if you have to.*

Less than an hour later, in real-time, there wasn't a single weapon to be found among Krodin's forces. Every soldier had been gagged, blindfolded and handcuffed. Every vehicle had been disabled. From Danny's perspective, it had taken about a week.

He knew that he'd have to rest sometime, but not yet. Judging by the maps he'd taken from the soldiers, the Substation was over eight hundred miles to the west.

If I stay in fast-mode and don't keep stopping to help other people, I can get there by tomorrow morning.

Danny toyed with the idea of finding a bicycle and using that to make the journey a little easier, but his sole experimental test-run with a bike in fast-time had resulted in a large collection of warped and broken bicycle parts.

He kept walking, and vowed to not help anyone else until after he'd checked out the Substation.

He broke that vow four times before he reached the end of the street.

It was midnight in Kansas, the center of the United States of America. Colin Wagner floated in place above the ruins of the city at a height of almost two thousand kilometers. High enough that he could see the entirety of the nation.

He had never flown this high before, and now he couldn't understand why he hadn't tried it. Up here, he could see everything. Almost all of the northern states were dark, with only those on the east coast showing any light. The southern states, Texas in particular, looked almost like everything was business as usual, but anyone familiar with the geography would see that certain cities that should have been bright were now barely visible, and one or two others were much brighter than they should be. They were burning.

How many have died? Colin wondered.

Quantum's prophecy told of a war in which billions would die. We all thought he was referring to the Trutopian war, but only a million died. So was it this? Did Quantum see Krodin's war instead?

He looked towards the east again. Europe was an hour's flight away. He hadn't been back home since his identity was exposed and they had all fled to Sakkara.

And now there is no Sakkara. There's no Topeka. A whole city just wiped out.

He wanted to be able to go home, to go back to that moment before his and Danny's powers had kicked in. *If there was a way to go back and prevent that from happening...* He shook his head. Wishing for a better past was not going to fix anything.

I wonder what Brian's doing these days? He felt a twinge of guilt that he hadn't spoken to his old friend in two years, and a further twinge when he realized that he'd barely *thought* about Brian in all that time.

I could go there now, see how they're all doing. Just spend a few hours with the neighbors and everyone from school.

There were relatives, too. Cousins, aunts, uncles. Colin knew that his parents had kept in touch with them, but he hadn't bothered. He could have argued that he was always too busy saving the world, but that would have been a lie.

But now we really do *have to save the world. We've got to save it from an indestructible man who's more powerful than all of us combined... And, let's be honest, a man who believes that he's destined to rule the world and for all we know, he's right.*

He allowed himself to drop down, heading straight toward the craters that had once been Topeka, hoping to see some familiar landmark. But at a height of fifty kilometers he caught sight of Sakkara, and changed his mind: the building seemed intact, but all of its windows had been destroyed, with debris scattered in every direction. He flew north instead.

The first major city ahead was Omaha, and after that, Sioux City.

Kenya followed the woman through the burning forest, unsure what to think, or what to believe. She hadn't spoken since telling Kenya her name, and Kenya wondered if maybe that was because she was just as confused and was trying not to show it.

The forest ended at a wide, shallow stream, and the woman splashed across it, so Kenya followed. She called out, "Slow down, please! I don't see very well in the dark!"

The woman stopped, and turned back, looking past Kenya toward the burning forest. "I recognize one of those men back there. Antonio Lashley. Lash, we use to call him. He used to be a Ranger... I killed him. I... I was disoriented, and I reacted without thinking. I killed them all."

"I'm glad you did. They were trying to kill *me*."

"Tell me where I am, exactly?"

"Somewhere along the border between Idaho and Wyoming."

"OK... And you are?"

"Kenya Cho. I'm with the New Heroes."

"I have no idea who that is."

"We're superhumans. Me, Renata Soliz, Colin Wagner, Danny Cooper, Mina... Those names don't mean anything to you, do they?"

Abigail de Luyando said, "No. And I don't know how I *got* here. I was talking to Brawn. Casey Duval said that his software bomb was a bluff... I tried to tell the others, but Slaughter came after me. She took my own ax and was about to..." She shook her head. "I can't be here. This isn't real. Slaughter hit me with my ax hard enough to kill even me. There was a flash of light. Then it was night, I was in the forest with those soldiers trying to shoot me."

Kenya said, "Abigail, this *is* real."

"Call me Abby, please."

"Abby, then. I *think* this is real. I mean, weird stuff happens to us all the time. Time-travel is to be expected."

"Time-travel?"

Kenya nodded. "Yeah. It must be. Casey Duval was Mina and Yvonne's father, and he died thirteen years ago. And I think Slaughter's dead too. Or is she? I can't remember. But she's not been around since all the superhumans lost their powers that time."

"OK... *What's* going on?"

"You knew the name Krodin, so you know who he is. Well, he's back, and he's waging a war throughout the entire country. My friend Renata and I were with a resistance group. We'd picked up a man called Victor Cross, one of Krodin's chief allies, but we were attacked. I couldn't fight back—my night-vision is very weak. I don't know what happened to the others but I was running for hours. One of the patrols spotted me shortly before you appeared: they couldn't catch me so they set fire to the forest."

The woman said, "Wow. OK. So, how did I get here?"

"I don't know, but you've traveled from the past. Must be from before all that stuff with Casey Duval and his giant battle-tank. That was when every superhuman on the planet lost their powers at the same time. Most of them went back to their normal lives. Energy and Titan got married and had a son. Or, no, they'd already been married for a few years at that stage. Same with Solomon Cord. He stopped being Paragon because even though he'd never had any powers to lose, there was no one else to fight. So he and Vienna moved to Virginia to raise the twins."

Abby sat down on the ground. Kenya crouched opposite her and asked, "Are you all right? I can't see your face properly in this light."

"This is a lot to take in. What about my other friends? Are they still around? Thunder and Roz Dalton. Max, too, I guess. And Brawn. What happened to him when the powers went away? The only thing he ever wanted was to return to normal."

"No, Brawn never changed back. He's one of us now, though. There was a whole prison thing going on and... Too long to get into now. He's still much stronger than a human, but he's not a superhuman any more. I don't know much about the others. I've only been with the New Heroes for year. Which one are you. Abby? I mean, what's your *superhero* name?"

"I'm Hesperus."

Kenya clapped her hands to her mouth. "Oh no!"

"What? What is it? You... Ah. I see." Abigail de Luyando put on a brave smile that didn't fool either of them. "I'm dead."

Chapter 27

Alia and Nathan sat in the Compound's dining hall with maps spread over the largest of the tables as they plotted a route back to the Substation.

"I could just *fly* us there," Nathan offered, for about the eighth time. "My powers are getting stronger every day."

"I know," Alia said. "But if we fly we'll be seen and Krodin's people will attack us. *You* might be bullet-proof but I'm not."

"If they come for us, I'll fight back."

"What if it's Shadow? What if it's *all* of them? No. We're going on foot—or in a car, if someone will give us a ride—and we'll keep our heads down. All I want to do is go to the Substation just in case Danny returned there. We're not even going to go in: when we get there, you listen out for Danny's voice."

Nathan said, "Yeah... I don't really *have* super-hearing, Alia. That's Colin you're thinking of. You think we're all identical because we're clones?"

"Em... yes, I do."

"Well, you and Stephanie are twins: you're just as identical to each other as us clones are to Colin."

"I'm not getting into that argument now! So you wouldn't be able to hear Danny if he was inside the Substation and you were on the surface?"

Nathan shook his head.

"All right, then. Well... What do we do? Stay here or go looking for Danny or the others? Krodin's people know this place exists now, so they might come back if they run out of supplies. Should we stay and defend it? Or go out there and find *them*, bring the fight to them? They won't see it coming and then we could take all their supplies and bring them back here.

If we win, that is. We probably will because you're superhuman. And you could even pretend to be Shadow and give them orders. Or you could pretend to be Colin and lead them away while I sabotage their base. Or we could not do any of that and instead you know where we could go? Greenville. It stands to reason that some of the others might go there, because if they can't go back to Sakkara or to the Substation then it's the only place we all have in common."

"Call it a wild hunch, Alia, but I've got the feeling that you've been thinking about this a lot,"

"I miss my sister and my mother."

"I know." Nathan looked down at the maps again. "Greenville. That's not the worst idea I've ever heard. We have supplies there, too. But it's about fifteen hundred kilometers away, in a straight line. By road it'll be a *lot* longer. It'll take us weeks... Unless we fly. So we're back to that again. If we fly, someone will see us."

"What if we fly at *night*?"

"Krodin's people are very well equipped, Alia. They'll have thermal sensors."

"Right. But those sensors aren't going to be aimed at the sky."

Nathan looked at her for second, pursing his lips and rapidly tapping on the table with his fingertips. "It'll be *cold* up there."

"I'll wear a jacket."

"All right. Let's do it."

Victor Cross woke to find Krodin looking down at him, smiling.

For the first time since his escape from the Substation, Victor wasn't in pain. *They fixed me. They...* He realized that he couldn't move his jaw. *They haven't fixed me. There's no pain because I've been given massive doses of painkillers.*

Krodin said, "The medics have wired your jaw shut, to help it to heal. You look... terrible. But you'll recover, in time. Don't try to speak: your lips and mouth have more stitches than skin at this stage. One of the medics was an orthodontist before the war. Apparently she had to remove your remaining teeth... They were too badly damaged to save. You had..." Krodin looked to the left. "What was the infection?"

Out of Victor's view, one of the clones said, "Septicemia."

"Yes, septicemia," Krodin said. "An infection of the blood. But I suppose you know what it is, with your vast, unparalleled knowledge." He reached out to Victor and helped him to sit up.

We're inside a bus, Victor thought. *A school-bus. It's not moving. No scent of gasoline in the air... but there's mildew. This is an abandoned school-bus. He's the most powerful man who ever lived: why don't we have a proper base of operations?* He looked towards Krodin, and made a writing motion with his hand.

Krodin shook his head. "No need. I can anticipate all your questions. Our forces are winning the war, but the New Heroes are regaining their powers. And there is a new player in the game, a new enemy who might well be superhuman. We don't as yet know who, but they left a squadron decapitated and sliced into pieces in Wyoming. I brought you here because you know more about the superhuman energies than anyone else. You will help Shadow to recover, and Eldon to come to full power. You will also reconstruct your device that removes the others' abilities. Our immediate assets are everything you see in this vehicle. And we are here because a headquarters would give our enemies a specific target. I had to destroy Sakkara for that same reason. We have Renata Soliz here. She's unconscious right now. Her powers have yet to return, but they could at any moment."

Moving carefully, Victor grabbed the bar running across the back of the seat and pulled himself up.

"You want a mirror, so you can see your face," Krodin said. "I advise against that, Victor. Believe me, you don't want to see it. Wait a few weeks at least until the swelling has subsided. Or better still, give it half a year. By then, the framework will have been removed."

Framework? Victor carefully raised his hands towards his face. His entire jaw was encased in a complex metal cage. Thin, strong spars pierced his jaw in twenty different places, and the lower half of the framework seemed to be welded to his skin.

Krodin said, "It's a medical adhesive. We have a solvent to remove it, but we won't be using that. If we do, you'll never recover. And no more solid food for at least a month. As I said, you'll get the framework removed in about six months—that's a big operation itself—but there will still be a long way to go before you get your new teeth and everything has healed. In total, you should be back to normal in two years. Except for the scarring. Your looks have been ruined forever."

Victor thought, *This is your fault! You could have freed me! You could have come for me at any time.*

"And now you're blaming me. Victor, *you're* the one who shattered your jaw, not me. You could have found another way to free yourself."

Victor carefully shook his head.

"You didn't see another way out?" Krodin asked. "That's disappointing. I mean, *I* didn't see any other way either, but then I'm not the one who repeatedly claims to be the smartest person who ever lived. Maybe breaking your own jaw *was* the only way. Now, you're wondering why I left you there. It's very simple, Victor. So simple that even Eldon would be able to tell you." He glanced back at the clone. "Eldon?"

"It's because despite your massive ego, this is not *your* show, Victor. You're not the boss. You're not the master, you're just one of the puppets, like me and Shadow. Krodin is the master. Everything that happens, happens for him."

Krodin said, "Because of."

Eldon corrected himself: "Happens *because of* him. Krodin is the one true leader of the human race."

Krodin turned back to Victor. "There you have it, with almost no coaching by me. Now, time to get to work, Victor. See what you can do to help restore Eldon's powers. And then you can have one of your protein shakes. They taste like strawberry-flavored paper, but they're all you'll be able to eat for a long time."

Krodin moved towards the bus's door, and looked back. "Oh, and just in case you were wondering, no, this is not punishment for the disrespect you showed me when you were in your metal cage. That comes later."

Eldon followed Krodin out of the bus, and Victor carefully walked up to the front, holding onto the backs of the seats to steady himself. The windows were filthy: just about all he could see through them was that it was daytime outside.

He turned around awkwardly, and made his way to the back, where Shadow was stretched out. As Victor approached him, Shadow opened his eyes.

"Don't tell them that I'm conscious. If they know that, they'll send me out there to fight Colin. I..." The clone looked away. "I can't face him yet. I'm not strong enough. He almost killed me, Victor. He hit me over and over. A hundred times, maybe more. Then he left me frozen in Sakkara's basement. He let me live because a dead man isn't scared of anything. He wanted me dead, but he wanted me afraid even more. The New Heroes think I'm a monster because of the things I've done, but Colin is worse."

Victor shrugged, carefully.

Shadow said, "He killed Tuan. Krodin did, I mean. Tuan said something disrespectful and Krodin crushed his throat. He killed Roman, too, but Roman had betrayed us so he deserved it. And now he's killed Zeke." Shadow quickly glanced back towards the doors. "Oscar died of old age, did he tell you? The accelerated aging process was flawed. I'm still aging faster than I should, but only at about twice the normal rate. From the time you sent me to Mars to the time I came back, Oscar had aged about eighty years. Zeke looked like he was sixty when he died. It's your fault, Victor. Everything is your fault. You wanted the end of the world, and now here it is. Are you happy?"

Victor turned away. *It's true. He's aging rapidly. Some sort of cellular degeneration that I hadn't foreseen. But all of the clones came from the same source, so they should be identical.*

Maybe it's the energy that's causing the decay? If so, why doesn't it affect the natural superhumans. It's not like they're any different. Whatever happens to Colin should happen to the clones, and vice versa.

Unless there's more to it than that. Krodin believes that the universe created the superhumans to replace him. Maybe the universe doesn't like someone else copying its ideas and playing in its sandbox.

He tried to smile at that idea, but his face was so numb from the painkillers that he had no idea whether his lips were working.

Chapter 28

In the heart of Sioux City a silent crowd—Colin estimated maybe two hundred people—had formed among the shattered buildings and ruined streets. He landed at the edge of the crowd and a half-brick bounced off his head. "What was *that* for?"

"Murderer!" A woman screamed. "Child-killer!"

A man shouted, "You started this war and now the blood of millions is on your hands!"

Colin said, "I did *not* start this war! I... Oh. Right. See, there's this bad guy who stole my DNA and made, like, nine clones of me. *They* started the war. We're trying to stop it. Only, we all lost our powers for a while and... You don't believe a word of this, do you?"

Another brick hit him in the face and bounced away. He caught it before it reached the ground, then crushed it into powder in his fist. "What's going on, anyway? What are you all gathered for?"

A wide circle had formed around him, and Colin had to resist the urge to fly away. "I promise, I'm not responsible for the war... Will someone please tell me what happened here?"

An old woman said, "Those soldiers. They were coming for us. We'd barricaded the streets but there was hundreds of them. They overran the police and the armies and... And then... it might have been one of *your* people, because suddenly the soldiers were all tied up and their guns were gone. So we took their supplies and now..." She stopped, and looked away.

"What?" Colin asked.

A man nearby said, "The soldiers..." and pointed toward the center of the crowd.

Colin couldn't see past everyone, so he floated up to get a better view.

A platform had been constructed from wooden planks and scaffolding poles, and standing in a line, with their arms tied behind their backs, and hoods covering their heads, were three of the black-clad soldiers.

Beside each soldier, suspended from an overhead gantry, was a rope with a noose at the end.

Colin darted forward, quickly disintegrating each of the ropes with a plasma bolt. He landed on the stage in front of the men, and turned to face the crowd.

They had surged forward, angry, and were chanting. "Justice! Justice!"

A tall, wiry man at the side of the platform strode towards Colin. "You... You shouldn't have done that! Your kind doesn't get to interfere any more! You superhumans *brought* this war on us!" The man had a camouflage jacket tied around his waist, and a semi-automatic rifle slung over his shoulder.

"Who are you?"

"Steve Lacey. And what's it to *you*, freak? We've had enough of you pushing us around. We're takin' our city *back*."

"And you're going to do that by murdering your prisoners?"

"We're sending a *message*!"

"Is the message, 'We're a bunch of bloodthirsty savages who are no better than the people who attacked us'? Because that's what it looks like to me."

Lacey snarled at Colin, and jabbed his index finger at the nearest prisoner. "This one was caught setting mines in a playground! And you want us to let them *go*? They attacked us for no reason, butchered our families. Treated us like vermin... They killed *thousands* of us! Where were you New Heroes when we needed you the most? You're supposed to protect us— instead, now you're protecting *them*!" He removed the gun from his shoulder, and held it in one hand, its muzzle pressed against the middle prisoner's head. "Give me one reason why I shouldn't blow this jerk's head right off!"

"Because that would be a war-crime."

Lacey lowered his gun a little. "No. No, this is *justice.*" He pulled the hood from the condemned man's head.

The man flinched when he saw Colin. He looked about sixty years old. He had a patch over his left eye and tattoos on his arms. There was a strip of tape across his mouth.

Lacey said, "This... *animal...* calls himself Douglas Albano. While our cops were manning the barricades Albano and his friends came begging to be let in, claiming that they were fleeing the soldiers. They said that in return they'd help defend the city. They were convincing enough that the Chief recruited them, gave them weapons... then Albano and his men turned on the police. They butchered an entire division, then opened the barricades and allowed the soldiers in. Then they targeted the hospitals and the shelters. *Hundreds* died because of him!" He pushed the gun into Albano's face. "But that'll stop when *he's* dead."

"If you squeeze that trigger I'll break every bone in your arm. I'm told that someone saved you all, probably one of my friends. Did he save your lives just so that *you* could become the murderers?"

Lacey let the gun fall to his side. "It's justice."

"No, it's revenge. It's mob law. Things *will* be better, one day. And when that day comes, you will want to be able to look at yourself in the mirror and know that you did the right thing. Not that you acted from anger, and hate, and fear." He walked closer to Lacey. "You know I'm right. I'm not saying that you should let them go. Put them on a chain-gang and make them clean up their mess, get them repairing the roads and buildings. You have to treat them like human beings precisely because they did *not* treat you that way."

A woman at the front of the crowd said, "We can't feed them *and* ourselves!"

"You have to try. You don't fight hate with more hate. You beat it with compassion."

Lacey said, "These people chose me to lead them. You don't get a say in this. You're not *from* here."

"*That's* how we're playing it? Because I'm a foreigner, my opinion is worth less than yours? That way of thinking is what *causes* wars, not solves them." He turned his back on Lacey and called out to the crowd, "There has to be *one* among you who agrees with me!"

From off to the left, a man's voice said, "I agree with you. Dostoyevsky said that the degree of civilization in a society can be judged by entering its prisons."

Someone else shouted, "Dostoyevsky was a commie!"

The first man shouted back, "How could he have been a communist? He died thirty-seven years *before* the Russians adopted communism!"

Colin thought, *Great. History lessons.* He looked over towards the first man. He was stocky, a little taller than Colin, and had a thick brown mustache.

The crowd parted to let the man through. He stopped in front of the platform and said, "I just got here, so I missed the start of this circus. Name's Duke Tansey. I grew up on Douglas Street. Some of you know me. Mister Wagner... You and I have a mutual friend: Danny Cooper. He freed this city, pretty much on his own. We all owe him for that. And we'll honor your intentions." He pointed to Steve Lacey. "You. You're going to jail." He climbed up onto the platform.

Colin began, "Why is he...?"

Duke nodded toward the prisoners. "They're not the first

271

three. There's a *pit*. Passed it on the way in. At least fifteen bodies, all with their hands tied and their necks broken."

Lacey started to back away. "It had to be done. We had to *show* them."

"Show who?" Colin asked. "Do you think that Krodin's forces have spies reporting back? Do you imagine that the rest of his armies will hear about you executing their colleagues and think, 'Those people in Sioux City are right. We're the bad guys here. Let's change our ways.'?"

Duke stepped to the edge of the platform and shouted, "This war is not over. Not by a long way. Instead of forming lynch mobs and crowing about how we're all so much better than the enemy, we should be shoring up the defenses and stockpiling our food and ammunition because the enemy *will* come again, and we need to be ready for them!"

This drew cheers from the crowd, and Duke said to Colin. "I've got this. You go. There are other places that need your help."

Colin said, "Thanks. Did Danny say where he was going?"

"Just that he had to find the others."

"OK. Thanks."

Duke nodded, and said, "Before you go..." He pointed into the crowd, off to the left. "Fellow there looks like a skinny version of me?"

"I see him."

"He's my cousin, Marvin. He's not a superhuman but he can see the blue lights. You might want to talk to him."

For over a day, Krodin had left Renata lying on her side, hands behind her back with her wrists tied to her ankles, in the middle of an overgrown field.

When the clone had first dropped her here, Krodin had

walked over to her and spent some time just staring at her before walking away.

Now, he had returned.

"Come to stand and gloat?" Renata asked.

"No. Trying to understand. I know a piece of the puzzle, but not all of it. Something tells me that you are important. Vital."

"Well, great. Does that mean that you won't kill me, or that you will?"

"I don't kill for pleasure, Renata. On a whim, perhaps, but never for pleasure." He began to walk around her. "I've read Victor's files. Unlike most superhumans, your ability is designed for defense, not attack. That fascinates me. You can, of course, use your power to hurt another person, but that's incidental, I suspect. Your gift is unique. *Why* do you have that power?"

"The powers just come," Renata said. "There is no why, no reason. Look, if you're not going to kill me, please prop me up on my knees or something. Half of my body is going numb."

Krodin reached down with one hand, grabbed Renata's arm and effortlessly lifted her up. He snapped the ropes around her ankles with his free hand and set her down. "Don't run. There's nowhere to run to and I will catch you."

She nodded. "I understand."

"Renata, you're wrong. There is a reason we have abilities, and it is because of the Chasm."

"And what's that?"

"I don't know. Victor Cross knows more than I do, but at this time his injuries prevent him from speaking much—though he is recovering. I know of your history, so I'm sure it will interest you to know that Victor received those injuries at his own hand. He was chained, an unbreakable collar around his neck, and I refused to free him. So Victor willingly broke his own jaw so that he could remove the collar. He said it took more than thirty blows to shatter his jawbone."

"He told me that he did it himself, but..." Renata shuddered.

"I *know*," Krodin said. "It's inhuman that someone could inflict so much pain on themselves. But Victor is not human. Nor are you and I." Then Krodin leaned closer to her and, in a fake whisper, added, "You owe me. It's because of me that Victor can't talk. If he were here, well, you've *met* him. The files—and his children, the clones—tell me that he talks even when he has nothing to say." He pulled back, smiling. "But no matter. You are a piece of the puzzle, Renata, but there are other pieces, some more important than you, some less so. Together, you and I are going to start mapping that puzzle. We will find the missing pieces and we will find the solution."

He stared at her face for a few seconds.

"And *then* I will kill you."

Chapter 29

Kenya Cho had flown many times, but never like this. Never while holding onto the hand of a superhuman woman armed with a razor-sharp sword who didn't seem to understand the concept of "No! That's too fast!"

They flew east, almost three hundred miles in less than an hour, and when Hesperus set her down on muddy, rain-soaked ground, Kenya's knees were trembling and her head was spinning.

"If you need to throw up, go ahead," Hesperus said.

"I'll be OK. Just give me a second. Maybe I'll feel better after a short rest..."

"Kenya, do you know where we are?"

"Couldn't see a thing with all the rain. I was mainly concentrating on not dying."

"Well, look around."

Kenya raised her head. They were in an army camp, and the hundreds of drenched soldiers now aiming their weapons at them were wearing black uniforms with a familiar symbol on the shoulder: a blue eye in a golden sun. "Abby, I think we took a wrong turn somewhere."

"No. *They* did." Abby called out, "I want to speak to whoever's in charge."

A man said, "You can speak to me. Captain John Reiser." He took a single step out from among his men, and stood watching Abby with his hands casually resting by his side.

Kenya guessed that he was fifty years old. He had a strong build, a weather-beaten face, and the way he carried himself told her that he knew how to fight.

He looked at Kenya for a moment, then said to Abby, "Don't know who you are, but we've got a Viper squad out searching for her. Hand her over."

"Every member of that squad is dead, including Antonio Lashley. You're mercenaries waging war against the American people. That ends now. Do you value your life, Captain Reiser?"

"What do *you* think?"

"I think that if you do value it, you'll order your men to drop their weapons."

"And *why* would I do that?"

"You work for Krodin?"

He nodded. "He pays well."

"Then your options are to surrender to me, or die."

Reiser grinned. "*You* are gonna take us all on? I have one hundred eighty men and women under my command. Each one of them would give their *life* to save me." He tilted to the side a little and peered at Kenya. "And the only back-up *you* have is Cho. She's good, I'll grant you that, but she's not *that* good."

Abby said, "She doesn't need to be that good. *I* am. Surrender."

He smirked. "Not a chance. We'll cut you down before you could even—"

Abby's sword was at his throat. A moment ago, it had been in its scabbard on her back.

"I... OK, yeah, *that* was fast."

"So. About surrendering. Had any further thoughts on that?"

Reiser swallowed hard, and his Adam's Apple scraped against the tip of Abby's sword. "He'll kill me."

"Perhaps. But he'd have to get to you first. You might be able to run and hide. Change your identity. But if you don't surrender, I *will* kill you here and now. In weather like this, up to our ankles in mud, I'm probably only about eighty per cent efficient. But I wouldn't risk it if I were you."

For a long moment, Reiser just stared at Abby, and Kenya

was sure that the pounding rain was the only reason she couldn't see tears in his eyes. "He'll kill *all* of us. You know what he did at Sakkara."

"Stop thinking about Krodin," Abby said. "He is *not* the most immediate danger to your life. Order your men to drop their weapons. You saw how fast I was able to draw my sword and put it at your throat. Do you have *any* doubt that I could slice through the uniform of the man standing next to you—with such accuracy that I don't break the skin—and have the sword again at your throat without either of you noticing that I'd moved?"

"That's bull. For Daniel Cooper, maybe, that sort of speed is possible, but I'd still notice. I'd be able to sense—"

The soldier on his left said, "Captain..."

Reiser turned to look. The man's soaked uniform had been slashed open from his left shoulder to his right hip.

"Now, Captain John Reiser, soldier for hire," Abby said, "are we any closer to a decision on that weapon-dropping thing we discussed earlier?"

Reiser looked away from Abby, and said, "Drop your weapons."

The man on his left said, "Sir?"

Louder, Reiser said, "That's an *order*. You will *all* drop your weapons!"

There was confusion, at first, but then he snapped at the soldiers closest to him: "Do it!" They let go of their guns. The soldiers behind them did the same, then those around them. The effect quickly rippled through the entire camp.

Reiser asked Abby, "Now what?"

"Now your men march north. One mile. Any attempt to turn back, or shoot at me, and they will need a new captain. But not for long, because I'll come for them next. One hundred and eighty, you said? That's a lot of blood to wash away, even for rain as heavy as this."

Captain Reiser issued his orders, and his men began to march away.

Kenya was finding it hard not to smile as the soldiers stomped their fallen handguns and rifles into the mud.

When the last of the soldiers was out of sight, Abby slipped her sword back into its scabbard and said to Reiser, "You know, I wouldn't really have killed you. I've killed a number of people, true, but never in cold blood. I'm just not that kind of person."

Through clenched teeth, Reiser said, "Krodin's gonna have your *head* for this!"

"I think I'm probably already on his naughty list. But send him a message, please. Tell him that the girl with the sword is coming for him. He *might* remember me. It was twenty-five years ago, immediately before his trip to Mars."

"Does the girl with the sword have a name?"

"He didn't know my name then. It wouldn't mean anything to him now."

"I think I know *what* you are, if not who."

"And what's that?"

"Dead meat." In one fast, smooth and practiced movement, Reiser reached behind his back, drew twin handguns from the back of his belt, and swung them up and forward, aiming them at Abby's face.

Her sword flashed, and Reiser was watching his own hands— still holding onto the guns—drop to the ground.

She stepped back to dodge the blood spraying from his wrists as, shuddering, Reiser collapsed to his knees.

"You need to slow the blood-loss," Abby said. "Put your wrists into your armpits like you're folding your arms. Do it *now*, Reiser. Hold them there and squeeze as hard as you can."

The man did as he was instructed, and Kenya said, "Abby, we can't leave him like this!"

"I know. Find something to tie off his wounds."

Still shuddering, Reiser groaned, trying to protest.

Abby leaned close and said, "Stop complaining, Captain. This is a war that you *willingly* signed up for. Well, you've got it. And think of all the money you're going to save on gloves, rings, manicures and piano lessons."

"I'm going to kill you! I'm going to kill you slowly. It's going to take *weeks* for you to die! You'll be *begging* for death!"

Abby's sword was at his throat again. "Do you want me to have to put a tourniquet on your neck?"

The man flinched and looked away. "Please don't kill me!"

"Then tell me what your people did with Renata Soliz and Victor Cross."

Alia Cord kicked a small stone ahead of her as she and Nathan walked side-by-side through the silent ghost-town of Greenville, Kansas. "Looks like there's no one here. I'm starting to think that this might not have been the best idea."

"No, I think it was. Someone will turn up eventually." He pointed off to the left. "The building we were using is over that way, isn't it?"

"Yeah. At the corner of dust and tumbleweed."

A voice from the distance called out, "Helloooo!"

Alia grabbed Nathan's arm. "That's Mina!" She shouted, "Helloooo to you too! Where are you?"

"I'm two blocks north of you. Hold on, I'm coming!"

A minute later, Mina came around the corner on a bicycle. "Hi guys... So, where's Danny?"

Nathan asked, "Wait, how did you know we were here?"

Alia said, "Mina can see people's auras. Your powers are

back, Mina?"

"Not yet. I *saw* you flying in. I..." She looked at Nathan, and her grin faded. "We should talk. Stephanie left me here: she went to Sakkara to see what was happening. Did you hear about Topeka? No? Well, it's *gone*. It's just rubble now. Sakkara survived. Steph should have been back by now, but we've only got your dad's old armor and I'm not good enough with it. *And most of it's too big for me.*"

"Where's Alex?" Nathan asked.

"He died. We had to leave him for a few hours because you all look like Colin and he was drawing too much attention. We went to a thrift store to see if we could find some kind of disguise. And then the soldiers came and... We had to hide out in an old man's house. By the time we got back to Alex, he was dead. It looked like someone raided the camp, and he tried to stop them."

To Alia, it seemed as though Mina was wondering how long she was supposed to look sad. She glanced at Nathan, standing next to her. He had gone very still, and was staring at the ground.

After a minute, Mina asked, "What about Danny? Wasn't he with you?"

"We got separated," Alia said. "We decided to come back here in the hope that someone else would do the same."

"Well, you were right. Now we just wait for the others to make contact. Or maybe we should go after Steph."

Alia said, "We should try to contact her first. I heard that when you're lost and someone's looking for you, the best thing to do is stay put."

"That's why I didn't go looking for Steph. But then I couldn't remember if that was when you wanted to be found, or if you *didn't* want to be found."

Nathan said, "It's if you want to be found." He moved on, walking past Mina without looking at her. "This is far from over. Either we're taking the fight to Krodin's people, or they're going to come here. We need to prepare."

Renata woke to again feel bugs from the field crawling across her face. She shook her head briskly, but one of them seemed more determined to hang on as it made its way from one side of her forehead to the other.

Then a hand came into view, far too close for comfort. She turned to see Victor Cross reaching out towards her with his middle finger tucked behind his thumb.

With his ruined lips barely moving, he said, "Stay still..." He flicked his middle finger at the bug. "It's gone."

"Thanks," Renata said. "Help me sit up?"

Cross grabbed her arm and pulled, and Renata could see that the effort was causing him considerable discomfort.

"Again, thanks. But you don't *deserve* thanks, Victor. You're the worst human being who ever lived. Krodin can't help what he is. But you're aware of how bad you are and you don't care."

Victor sat down in front of her. Past him, she could see the old school bus, with its tire-free wheels and grime-covered windows.

"He's going to kill me, isn't he?"

"I think so, yes," Victor said.

"He'll kill you, too, when he no longer needs you. That might even be before he kills me. So now that you can talk again, tell me, Victor... Why are you doing this?"

"You don't have the mental capacity to understand the answer to that."

"Don't you care that millions of people have died because of you? That *tens* of millions have suffered? There are people dying right now because of what you've done."

"Try to put things in perspective, Renata. Imagine that the lifetime of the planet Earth, from the moment it was formed up to this very second, is scaled down to a single twenty-four-hour day, OK? Human beings as we know them show up in the last two seconds. That's about as long as a sneeze."

"And why is that important?"

"The earliest ancestors we recognize as human appeared about two hundred thousand years ago. Spiders have been around for at least three hundred *million* years. Imagine a powerful alien race, five billion years from now, using their advanced technology to look back through the entire history of the long-dead planet Earth. Would they even notice us, and our great achievements? We..." Victor put his hands on his chest and then spread his arms wide. "We are not significant. So far, our self-absorbed species is just a blip."

"So you want to kill us all, is that it?"

"Of course not. I want to make sure that we don't remain a blip. The end is coming and I want to avoid it."

"What do you mean, the end is coming? I thought that was billions of years away."

Victor shook his head and waggled his index finger at her. "No no no no no! The end of the *Earth* is billions of years away. I'm talking about the end of *life* on Earth."

"And when is *that* going to be?" Renata asked.

"Sooner than you might think." With some difficulty, Victor pushed himself to his feet, then walked over to the school bus's door. He opened it and leaned in. "Krodin, it's time to move on."

Krodin shouted back, "We stay here. Let the war play itself out."

"Plans change." A little louder, he said, "Shadow? Can you

come out here?"

Shadow came to the door, and Victor said, "Magnanimous transmigration."

The clone immediately straightened up, becoming more focused and alert.

Victor turned to Renata and winked. "I programmed their brains. Got a *lot* of trigger-phrases buried in there." To Shadow, he said, "Go to Site B. Bring the crates marked with an X. Be careful with them, but hurry."

Shadow said, "Yes, master," then immediately darted up into the air. In seconds, he was gone.

Renata looked at Victor. "You programmed him to respond with, 'Yes, master'?"

"We'd been watching an old horror movie the night before."

"So what's in the crates?"

Victor glanced at the bus. "Some items that I need to help readjust the power hierarchy around here."

Chapter 30

In a stone-walled windowless room Cassandra Szalkowska said, "It's almost here."

The man sitting by her bedside lowered his book. "What's almost here?"

She didn't respond. Images ran through her head that were not her own memories, or her imagination. She swung her legs off the bed and followed the man out into the corridor and into another identical room where a younger man was staring at a complex chart made up of dozens of photographs, drawings, notes and diagrams.

"Lance... I can see it. It's almost here."

Without turning around, Lance McKendrick said, "OK. But do we know what it *is*, yet?"

"No But it's coming. It's... I don't know the words. I don't think that there *are* words for it."

"That's good enough for me." To the older man, he said, "Gather the others, Max."

Five minutes later, they were all assembled in the only room large enough to take them all: the former staff's mess-hall.

Lance looked at them all in turn, as though memorizing their faces. Then he said, "One way or another, this is all over soon. Krodin's armies have swarmed over the country but their progress has been hampered by the New Heroes. They're not strong enough on their own, because if we're right, Krodin is about to get much, much more powerful. We have a tiny window of opportunity to stop him—to stop *everything*—before it's too late. When that window closes, we are dead. All of us. Every living thing on this planet will die. So it's up to us to save them."

A young man said, "Laying it on a bit heavy, aren't you?"

Crouched beside him, the blue giant said, "*Let* him, Razor. He loves doing his speeches."

"Enough," Lance said. "We need to move on this, and none of us knows exactly what we're facing. We are running through a dark, trap-filled room we don't know, trying to find a light-switch that might not be there. Cassandra? I think it's time for a chat with our friend at the end of the corridor. Max, you go with her."

Cassandra hated this. Three times before she'd had to talk to Yvonne Duval, and each time she'd felt sick for days afterwards.

As she walked alongside Max, Cassandra tried to clear her own mind, to center herself in preparation for the assault into Yvonne's poisonous mind, a nest of schemes and thoughts and hatred that twisted and coiled and never stopped squirming..

Focus, she told herself. *Clarity. She's not in charge. I am. My mind, my rules.*

"How did you do it?" She asked Max.

"Squibs. You know how in a movie when they need to make it look like someone's been shot? Squibs are little packs of fake blood with a tiny amount of explosive to make them burst at the right time. Before I went into hiding Lance and I agreed that if anyone came for me—"

"I meant, how did you cope with having to read people's minds all the time?"

"Oh, I see. That's just a matter of training and experience. I wasn't much good at it when I was your age. Took me *years* to be able to read someone's mind without getting lost in there. My sister once said that the way I did it reminded her of a psychologist or a social worker assigned to a tragic case: you do the best job you can and then, at the end of the day, you have to set it aside. You don't forget about it, but you compartmentalize it, tuck it away so that it doesn't interfere too much with your own life. Cassandra, I've looked inside the minds of the worst people imaginable. I mean, people who have committed crimes so unspeakably evil that a couple of times I wanted to attack my own brain with an ice-cream scoop to get rid of their memories. But bad memories fade, even other people's."

They stopped outside the door to Yvonne's cell. She was the last prisoner in the Cloister. General Mendes had wanted to move her along with the others, but Lance had insisted: "She used to be one of ours. She's our responsibility."

Max said, "Are you ready?"

"No. I keep thinking about where it went wrong for her."

"Ah, *that* is a treacherous road for a telepath, young lady. It leads to empathy. If you start seeing things from her point of view, you might as well quit."

"She never had a normal childhood. She was poked and prodded and tested and—"

"Wait, are you talking about Mina or Yvonne?"

Cassandra smiled. "OK, you've got me there. Mina had the same childhood and she turned out fine. Well, a bit flaky, but she's not evil."

"It's the same with Colin's clones," Max said. "No one is born good or evil. It's a choice we make that's guided by our experiences. And it also depends on your point of view. Most of your friends see *me* as evil. I've done some questionable things, certainly, but for good reasons. It's all a matter of scale. Ask Lance. He despises me—well, you already know that; you're a telepath—but he knows I'm not the bad guy."

"Ah, so *that* was why Lance brought Danny with him when they thought Shadow was coming for you: Danny knew that Lance doesn't like you so he was more inclined to believe that Lance really *did* kill you. Danny's reaction was enough to convince Shadow that it was real. That way he didn't check."

"Correct. Krodin had to believe that I was dead." Max shrugged. "It's actually quite liberating, being officially dead. Now... shall we go and face the monster?"

Cassandra nodded. "Let's do this."

Colin darted down through the rainstorm and kept low as he zoomed across the mist-shrouded fields, never more than a meter above the ground. He banked left around a cluster of trees then zig-zagged through a herd of disinterested cows, then spotted his target directly ahead.

He dropped his speed to a walking pace, and then, ten meters away, he hovered.

The blue light was slowly pulsing, drifting as though caught on a gentle breeze that affected nothing else. As he watched, it passed through the upright pillar of a wooden fence.

He'd seen them before, several times, but had never had the chance to actually examine one.

Marvin Tansey had told him, "Thing is, the way they move is not actually random. I used to keep charts. This was back in the day when there was a lot more of them. They *look* like they're moving randomly, but I worked out their pattern. When I told my doctor about that, she said I was just applying logic to my delusion to make it seem more real. Or something like that."

Colin circled around the blue light. It seemed to be about half a meter in diameter, spherical, but not solid.

If this is the energy that we're using when we fly or whatever... Where does it come from?

Marvin's charts had been lost long ago, but he had done his best to recall everything he'd noted about the lights. "They drift about, back and forth, moving slowly, but if you actually *plot* their paths, you know, follow them and note their positions every few hours, you'll see that they're moving east. Guaranteed. You see one in the morning, follow it around all day, and by evening you're going to be a couple of miles east of where you started. But the thing is, back when I was a student, I was in Japan and I saw a few there. They were moving *west*. I often thought about taking a trip to Australia or South Africa, see which way the lights there were heading."

East, Colin thought. *So I could follow this one, but at the speed it's moving an entire civilization could rise and fall before it gets anywhere near its destination.*

Marvin had said, "I saw them pass through people and walls and cars and once, at the zoo, through an elephant, but sometimes they'd hit someone and disappear, like they're being absorbed. Your friend Danny said those people were probably superhumans."

There's no way of knowing what powers a superhuman will get, Colin thought. *Could be plenty of superhumans out there whose power is invisibility or flight or control over teacups, but they've just never had a reason to find out.*

He was uncertain what his next move should be. The war was still raging, but this felt important.

Should I fly to Japan and see if I can find a blue light that's drifting to the east?

Or use Marvin's idea: go to the southern hemisphere and see what the lights do down there?

Are the lights going to *somewhere, or* from *somewhere?*

If they are going somewhere, then where, and why? What's east of here that's drawing them?

He followed the light for another few minutes, then rose up through the mist and into the early-evening sky, thinking that if Marvin had been telling the truth that there used to be a lot more of the lights, then at one time it must have been a fascinating sight: hundreds of them drifting lazily over the landscape, passing through solid objects, always moving east.

East, he thought again. *What's to the east? I've been east of here. Lieberstan is east. So is Romania.*

Where are they going? And why? What's...

Colin remembered talking to Victor Cross in Cross's headquarters in Zaliv Kalinina. He had allowed himself to be captured because his father and Lance had hidden a tracking device under his skin. *Cross was interrogating me... Actually, no, he was showing off.*

Cross had said, "I have lots of questions for you. I'll give you a taster so you'll have enough time to come up with clever lies that won't fool me for a second because I'm too smart for you. First one... What were you doing in Romania when my people picked you up? You were going somewhere. Where and why?"

Where was I going? Colin asked himself.

He had left Sakkara, run away from home because his parents had been OK with bringing Max Dalton on board and they'd just refused to listen to Colin's arguments against that.

He had made his way across the United States, covering most of the journey by hanging onto the undersides of trucks. In Jersey he'd stowed away on a huge cargo ship that docked nine days later in Lisbon, Portugal.

From there he had traveled across Spain, France, Italy, Slovenia, Hungary and finally into Romania, where Cross's people had picked him up.

Always east, Colin thought. *I thought I was just drifting, but I was following the same pattern as the blue lights.*

Why east? Where was I going? Was I subconsciously looking for something?

Or was something drawing me there?

*

Danny Cooper stopped at a half-destroyed hardware store in Nebraska and gathered up all the foot-long plastic cable-ties he could find among the debris. He came away with seventeen. Last time, the haul had been a lot better: eleven packs, each containing one hundred ties. He still had one of those packs left.

Three ties were required for each of Krodin's soldiers he encountered: one for the wrists, and two joined together for their ankles.

Ideally, he'd also have some rolls of good quality duct tape with him to cover the soldiers' eyes and mouths, but duct tape was awkward at the best of times and even more tricky for the one-armed.

Back on the ruined street, he saw two young boys helping their mother to pick through the rubble of a grocery store. One of the boys found a half-crushed box of cereal and his mother almost cried with relief.

He approached them slowly, making sure that they could see him coming. "Hello?"

"Keep away!" the woman said.

"I'm not with the soldiers, I promise! My name is Danny Cooper. I'm with the New Heroes. I can help you."

The woman grabbed hold of the smaller of the two boys and hissed at the other, "Oliver! Come here!"

Danny said, "Please. I need your help. You might have seen the soldiers tied up with these?" He held up the cable-ties. "That's me. But with only one arm I need to partly close them in advance. If you'll help me do that, I'll find you enough food for a month."

The woman said, "We're not getting involved! If we help you, then we're collaborators! So no. Please, just go."

"I understand." Danny slipped into fast-mode and spent some time scouring the area. From the woman's perspective, he was gone for less than a second before he reappeared with a battered shopping cart filled with bottles of water, canned food and preserved meats. "This is yours. And there are no soldiers within twenty miles. Find some shelter."

The woman asked, "Is anyone coming to save us?"

Danny was tempted to stand tall with his shoulders back and say, "We're already here," but decided against it. Instead, he said, "They're on the way. Things will get better, soon."

He wished he could believe that.

Chapter 31

Alia Cord handed the warped, three-meter-long steel bar to Nathan, and he wedged one end under the edge of the slab of reinforced concrete, then all three of them took hold of the other end and forced it upwards.

Alia knew that Nathan was doing almost all of the work: she and Mina were probably slowing him down by getting in the way.

He's exhausted—he'll collapse if he goes on much longer.

But she didn't want to stop. None of them did.

It had been five hours since Nathan had carried Mina and Alia to Sakkara.

Still under the belief that Krodin held Sakkara, Nathan had decided that a high-altitude fly-by would give them a better idea of what was happening. The scale of the devastation of Topeka had shocked him, but seeing the outer shell of Sakkara mostly intact, still standing over the scattered debris of its interior, had been somehow worse.

They had come in search of something—anything—that they might be able to use as a weapon. Nathan had set them down outside, on the debris that had been ejected through Sakkara's windows. The building's interior floors and walls were now just piles of rubble filling the basement.

As they'd carefully clambered over the rubble, Nathan had said, "Stop! Quiet!" A few second later. "There's a noise. Rhythmic... It's Morse code. Three short, three long, three short. S.O.S."

Mina had said, "Someone's trapped."

Nathan held up his hands. "Quiet!" He rose into the air, and drifted slowly to one side, then back, trying to pin-point the source of the noise. "It's coming from inside."

Alia was certain that it was Stephanie. *She must have been here when it collapsed!*

Now, they had shifted several tons of rubble, but they still had no idea exactly where to look or how deeply she was buried. If Mina's powers had returned she would have been able to instantly pin-point Stephanie's location, but without that they were reduced to stopping every few minutes so that Nathan could listen. His enhanced hearing wasn't nearly as sharp as Colin's, nor was his ability to detect and manipulate energy, but between the two skills they had determined that Stephanie—if it really *was* her—was trapped close to the north-east corner of the building.

The slab of concrete shifted to the side, and Alia wondered, *How long ago did this happen? How long has she been trapped?*

By hand, they cleared away the smaller pieces of debris, Alia and Mina working together, and Nathan—being considerably stronger—worked alone on the opposite side of the pile.

Alia's hands were raw, her arms, back and shoulders aching. But she wasn't going to stop. If things had been the other way around, Steph would never have quit. You don't quit when it's family.

Nathan hauled a slab larger than himself away from the pile, and tossed it to the side. It shattered on impact, and when the fragments settled he stood there panting heavily for a moment, then said, "OK. Sound check!"

Alia and Mina froze, watching him.

Nathan looked at Alia, and shook his head. "Nothing. The heat signature is still there. Whoever it is, they're only about two meters down."

Mina said, "She could be asleep."

"Sure," Alia said. "We'll keep going."

Nathan pulled off his shirt and used it to wipe the sweat

from his face, then reached down to grab hold of a girder that Alia knew was too heavy for him.

As he grunted and strained to shift it Alia clambered over the rubble towards him. "Let me help."

"I... can... *do*... it!" The girder shifted a few centimeters, and Nathan grinned. "See?"

"Take a break, please. You're exhausted."

"I can keep going."

"Take a break. That's an order. You too, Mina."

She found the steel bar again, and used it to clear a couple of the smaller pieces. *We have to keep going. We can't stop. Steph would never give up on anyone. And we have to get to her soon, because if we don't then this stops being a rescue and starts being a recovery.*

She thought of their mother, waiting for them somewhere, and made a vow: *I'm not bringing my sister home in a body-bag!*

Another breeze-block. A lump of drywall. A smashed length of timber. The shattered remains of a workbench from the machine room.

OK, that's been forever—the others have had their break and now they have to start again. Alia glanced over at Nathan and Mina, and realized that her friends hadn't yet sat down: they had just continued working on the other side of the pile.

She looked down again and saw that the girder had to be next: she had cleared away the larger pieces of rubble around it. "Nathan... can you help me with this?"

A woman's voice from behind her said, "Let *me* do it."

She turned around. A silver-armored woman was climbing in through a window, and there was someone else behind her.

Mina shouted, "Kenya!" and ran to greet her friend.

The armored woman glanced at each of them for a moment, but stopped when she saw Alia. "Wow... All right. Step aside, please."

She moved in front of Alia and took hold of the massive girder. She lifted it as though it were made of paper and set it aside, then began to dig through the rubble, shifting it faster even than Nathan at his best.

Kenya joined her, and Alia watched with relief and fascination as the pile of debris was reduced further and further.

Then the woman slowed. "Kenya, step back... We're almost through. I can see, now." She looked over towards Alia. "Come here."

As Alia approached, she could see that there was a hole in the debris at the armored woman's feet. The woman said, "She's pinned under a workbench. I'm going to raise it up—you grab her arm and pull her out."

Alia reached into the dark hole, and touched something round and metal. It moved a little, and she was touching a hand. Stephanie's hand. She grabbed hold, and Stephanie's fingers closed around hers. "I've got her!"

The armored woman rose into the air over the workbench. She grabbed both sides of it and pulled as she rose higher.

A cloud of dust and grit drifted down over Alia as she dragged Stephanie clear.

And seconds later, she was out. "She's unconscious," Alia said. "Mina, bring the water."

Kenya said, "Her armor saved her from being crushed."

Grinning, Alia said, "Yeah, our dad sure knew how to make armor."

The older woman said, "This is true. He made mine, too."

Alia stood up to face her. "Thank you! I don't know who you are, but that was amazing. The girder... How did you lift that so easily? It was clearly heavier than the bench!"

"I'm stronger with metal than anything else." The woman smiled and shrugged. "I have no idea why that is, but sometimes it comes in handy." She paused for a moment, then said, "So you're Alia, and this is Stephanie."

"Right. So, who are you? You do look sort of familiar..."

"I'm sure you've seen photos. I'm your aunt." She extended her hand. "Abigail de Luyando. Pleased to meet you. Call me Abby."

Alia stared at her. "But... We were told that you *died*. Slaughter killed you in battle."

"So I've heard. But somehow I'm here. Alia, are you going to shake my hand or not?"

Alia opted for a tearful hug instead.

Kenya said, "If there's nothing else here, we should go. For all we know, the rest of the building is about to collapse on us."

Nathan said, "I can take Steph." He crouched next to her and gently lifted her in his arms, then rose up toward the nearest window.

"What about the rest of us?" Mina asked.

Abby said, "I can take you." As they moved towards the window, she asked Alia, "How *is* your mother? To me, it's only been a few days since I saw her."

"We don't know where she is—where any of them are—but I'm sure they're safe. Lance was taking care of the civilians. He's good at that sort of thing."

"Not Lance McKendrick? Constantly gets into trouble and talks his way out of it?"

"Yeah, that sure sounds like him. He said once that he'd had a crush on you."

Abby laughed. "Yeah, *that's* true. So, did he ever get married?"

"Not that I know of. What about you? Mom never said much

about you. Neither did your brothers. Dad once said they were just too hurt. They didn't want to believe that you were gone. They're all still around, though. They're all going to freak out when they learn you're alive again!"

"I imagine they will, especially since they didn't know I was a superhuman. And they're older than me now. That's weird."

"Same thing happened to Renata. She was frozen in time for ten years, so now her younger brother and sister are older than her. How long were you gone?"

Abby waited until Alia climbed out ahead of her, then followed. She floated down alongside Alia, Mina and Kenya.

"Sixteen years, according to Kenya. I'm twenty-four, but I'd be forty now, if I'd lived."

Mina said, "That must be strange."

"You have no idea. It's good not to be dead, but..." She looked around the devastated landscape. "This was Topeka. I loved this city. And now... The whole world has changed." She turned to Alia again. "Kenya told me about your dad. I'm so sorry to hear that. I loved him. Everyone did."

Alia nodded. "Thanks."

"I was fourteen when I met him, and I knew instantly that I could trust him. That's the kind of man he was." She smiled again. "You know, he was the first person I ever told... I'd been *terrified* of how people would react, but Sol just listened to me crying my heart out and when I was done he said, 'OK, then. I'm cool with it. Anyone who isn't cool with it is a jerk.' And then he thanked me for confiding in him. That made such a difference. When I told Lance, he made a big deal about how it *wasn't* a big deal, but I could see that he was upset. Maybe he really did love me." She looked around at the confused teenage faces staring back at her. "And... you don't know what I'm talking about, do you?"

Alia shrugged. "Nope. What was it?" Then she said, "Wait, is this about you preferring girls to boys?"

Abby said, "Well... yes. You're not shocked?"

"No. Lots of people are gay. When we were kids there was a guy on our street and some of the neighbors gave him a hard time about it. When I told Dad, he said, 'Alia, his life is more important than anyone's opinion of it. Being gay isn't a choice. Being a bigot *is*.' And Mom always said that hating something that you don't understand means *you're* wrong, not the thing you don't understand."

Abby was silent for a long while, then she smiled at Alia and said, "I am *so* proud to be your aunt." She spread out her arms. "OK. Don't think I've ever carried three people before, so hold on tight. One in each arm, one on my back. And someone probably ought to tell me where we're going."

"You were a pawn," Cassandra told Yvonne Duval. "Victor Cross is alive. He used you. You danced to his tune like an obedient puppy."

I guessed that, Yvonne thought. *He set me up and then skipped away. But you're not the sort of person to gloat, Cassandra. Why are you here? And why are you with this jerk?*

Cassandra glanced back at Max Dalton leaning against the doorjamb with his arms folded. "You don't like him?"

I've read more than enough about him to know that he's not to be trusted.

"Now, *there's* a dilemma. Should I trust the person I don't trust doesn't trust?"

Yvonne thought, *Go through that again?*

"The enemy of my enemy is my friend. You've heard that? If you don't trust Max and I don't trust you, does that mean that *I* can trust Max?"

Not even slightly. Once you know that someone has lied to you about something important, you can never go back to the way things were. Never. *It'd be like trying to unburn a candle. So what brings you back to the Cloister today?*

"Actually, we've been living here for weeks. We're hiding out. Victor brought Krodin back from Mars and he's triggered a civil war."

I figured there was something going on. The guards were late with my meals three times in the past ten days. They're usually never late. Plus we normally get one or two helicopters every day. There hasn't been one in over a week. So, stop avoiding the question, Cassandra. What do you want?

"I'm not avoiding the question. I'm avoiding the answer."

What's got everyone so scared that they have to come to me for help?

"I told you. Krodin is back. He's stronger than all of us combined. How do we stop him?"

Yvonne shrugged. *Television. Internet access. More books. I don't deliver if you don't.*

"The internet and television don't much work these days. Books... I can't make promises. But I do know that the people in charge here will be much more lenient if you help us. You've been in here for nearly two years now. But did you know that for the *past* year Victor was here too?"

No. I did not know that.

"He was outside, in a cell made of this stuff." Cassandra tapped on the eighteen-inch-thick transparent aluminum wall between them. "He didn't like it much. Give me something, Yvonne. I'm sure you studied all the reports when you were in Sakkara. Krodin must have a weak spot. What's his Achilles heel?"

Why must Krodin have a weak spot? Do you think that

there's some sort of cosmic scales and that everyone's attributes all balance out? Because that is clearly an insane rationale. The belief that the life is ultimately fair. An ugly person has a kind nature. A beautiful person is vain. A stupid person is skilled with her hands. A person unable to walk must have a saintly disposition. Yvonne shook her head. *Finding the good in everything is a childish, blinkered, and frankly dangerous view of the world. Sometimes there is no silver lining. Wanting something to be true doesn't make it true.*

You have to consider the possibility that Krodin is not only faster, stronger, more durable and more intelligent than you, there's also always the chance that he is right. One world, one leader. It makes a lot of sense to me. No border conflicts, no wars, no need for passports or immigration control. No nation is richer or poorer than the others because there are no others. Go ahead, Cassandra. Name a single downside to a united Earth.

"People's cultures would disappear. Their heritage."

So what? That happens anyway, over time. Your name, Szalkowska, is Polish in origin, so that's your heritage. But you've never been to Poland, have you? Your heritage can't mean that much to you if you've never been there.

"I was in a prison camp until a couple of years ago. I have an excuse."

People are so dumb about the past. They cling on to what they decide are their ancestors' triumphs and conveniently forget all about the horrible things those ancestors have done. The wars waged, countries pillages, sub-cultures wiped out. Did you know that there is not one nation on this planet that doesn't have a history of butchering another nation's people? Not one.

Under Krodin's rule people wouldn't be expected to forget the past, but they also wouldn't be allowed to use it as an excuse to murder other people who are marginally different. The old "I will kill you because your ancestor killed my ancestor" approach would be gone forever.

So if that's what Krodin's trying to do, then why not let him? Give him the reins and see how well he guides us into the future.

Cassandra started to turn away. "You're not going to help. Fine."

Yvonne thought, *This is me helping! You could approach Krodin and say, OK, we'll try it your way.*

"That's not how things work."

Maybe it should be. See, there you are, stuck in your traditions again. 'We've never done it that way before, therefore we won't even consider doing it that way now.' That attitude is why we have poverty and wars and cruelty and hate.

"You, talking about cruelty and hate... Yvonne, you're a psychopath. The war you started killed over a million people!"

That doesn't automatically mean I'm wrong about everything. You have to open your mind, Cassandra. That's the only way you'll be able to put new things into it.

Renata had been a little surprised to find that Krodin was allowing Victor to assemble his machines. Over the past day, Shadow and Eldon had retrieved fifteen large crates from wherever Victor had stowed them. Most of the crates contained electronic equipment that looked like it had been built by hand, and Victor wasted no time in connecting them together, though he'd refused to explain what they were for, answering even Krodin's questions with, "Wait and see."

He had worked through the night, and this morning Renata had woken to find that she was looking up at the underside of something dark and metallic hovering a few centimeters above her.

As she'd tried to squirm out from under it, it rose up a little and moved away, then she could see that it was a hovering vehicle that resembled the New Heroes' former transport, the ChampionShip. A hatch in the side opened, and Eldon climbed out. "It started raining last night so we parked it over you so you wouldn't get wet and catch pneumonia and die."

"You could have brought me *inside* it," Renata told him.

"Oh, yeah. Never thought of that."

The clones had loaded all of Victor's equipment into the vehicle, and then cut the ropes around Renata's legs. Her hands were still tied, but she was able to climb into the craft unaided.

Now, as the craft began to rise up, leaving the old school bus and the field far behind, Victor was trying to explain a complex concept to his colleagues. "Think of the universe as a single crystal. Not just the three-dimensional aspect of the universe, but the fourth dimension too. Time. So it's all one crystal, OK?" Victor used his hands to roughly describe something the size and shape of a football. "But there's a crack in it. Not a big one. Tiny. An imperfection. Luckily, this crystal has the ability to *repair* cracks. So—"

Eldon interrupted him. "You've lost me. Victor, you need to simplify this! We're not all geniuses!"

"Well, *that's* true," Victor said.

Shadow pointed toward Renata, who was sitting on her own closer to the rear of the craft. "And why is *she* here? What do we even need her for?"

Victor said, "I'll explain Renata's presence soon." He thought for a moment, then said, "Here's a simpler model. You know that liquid you can put in your car's tires that turns solid when it gets exposed to air? It automatically repairs minor punctures."

"No," Eldon said, "but I can picture that. Go on."

"The universe is the tire. Superhumans are the liquid. The Chasm is the puncture."

Krodin nodded. "I understand. We were created to fix a flaw."

"Close. To be precise, *you* were created to fix a flaw. The universe is sentient. Possibly not self-aware in the way *we* are, but it knows when something is wrong. It knew that the Chasm was coming, and it created you as a solution."

Renata said, "And what *is* the Chasm?"

"It's a glitch. A puncture in reality. For those without the most basic understanding of astronomy—that's you, boys—the Earth spins, the planets revolve around the sun, the sun revolves around the center of the galaxy, the galaxy revolves around the galactic cluster, and so on. And all the while everything is expanding... With me so far? We're moving all the time. And this little corner of the galaxy is about to pass through the Chasm. It'll be brief. A few seconds. A minute at most."

Shadow said, "And...?"

"And I don't know. Obviously, it'll be bad. But I'm thinking that the planet might survive. Lower forms of animal life, possibly. Humans? Not a chance. Brains wiped, nervous system zapped."

Renata said, "So... everything in the universe is expanding all the time but the Chasm is in the same place?"

"Yes. Because it's not *part* of the universe. It's the glitch. The crack." He sighed when the light failed to dawn in their eyes. "If I drill a hole in the wall, is the hole *part* of the wall? No."

"Well, yes, it is," Shadow said. "The hole can't exist if the wall isn't there. It wouldn't be a hole. It'd be... I don't know. Nothing."

"And what *is* a hole, Shadow? It's nothing where we expect something. The wall defines the hole, but the hole is not part of the wall."

Renata said, "I think I preferred it when I was tied up

outside."

Victor turned to her and smiled. "Ah, the lovely Ms Soliz. Now you get to hear *your* part in all this. Do you know, I almost told Lance McKendrick when I was his prisoner in the Substation? That didn't happen because he was being a jerk, as usual."

"So what *is* my part, Victor? Why am I here?"

"*You* were the universe's last-minute emergency get-out-of-trouble back-up plan. And you blew it. Spectacularly. You might very well have doomed the entire human race."

Chapter 32

There are so few of them now, Colin thought. *Even a couple of years ago there was a lot more.*

On his flight across the Atlantic ocean, he had seen one of the blue lights, and one more in Spain. Both had been moving east.

Now, over the coast of Albania, he saw another.

There has to be a better way than this. He tried to picture the Earth. *If the lights in America and Europe are moving east, and Marvin said those in Japan were going west, then they're all heading for a point somewhere in the middle. But that could be anywhere between here and Japan. I should do what Marvin said, and go south. If I can find another down there, it'd be easier to see from their paths which way they're heading.*

And then maybe I can figure out what to do when I get there.

He turned south, crossed the Ionian Sea and the Mediterranean and toward Libya.

The Libyan coast was in sight when a voice inside his head said, "Hey, Colin."

He slowed to a stop. *Cassandra?*

"Yes, it's me. So... how are things?"

Um. You tell me. Where did everyone disappear to?

"Can't tell you the location, but we're safe. We had to go dark because Krodin was looking for us. He probably still is, but time is short and we no longer have the luxury of safety. Krodin's about to play his final hand. We have to stop him."

OK, but I'm on to something here. It could be big.

"The blue lights... I can see them in your mind. But we need you to stop Krodin."

What can I do? That guy fought Brawn and Thunder and the others to a stand-still!

"He's never fought *you*."

Give me two days. One day, even.

"Colin, Stephanie's been hurt. She was inside Sakkara when Krodin destroyed it. She was trapped for *days*. They got her out but she hasn't regained consciousness yet."

How serious is it? Is her life in danger?

"Not right now. But she's in a pretty bad way."

Then I'm not going back yet. I'm trying to find the destination of the blue lights because it's important. I don't know how I know that, but I've got the feeling that things are coming to a head and I need to do this. I'm meant to do this.

"I get that," Cassandra said. "Lance will be furious, but I'll try to make him understand. I... I spoke to Yvonne again. Yes, *that's* where we are. She told me that I have to open my mind because that's the only way to put new things into it. Colin, I did open my mind. Last night, I relaxed all the barriers I've built up over the years and I let everything in. I saw something. No, I *felt* something. A void. An emptiness. It's coming for us. I tried to explain it to Lance, but he dismissed it. You can't fool a telepath like that, though. I could see his thoughts and memories. It's called the Chasm."

That thing again. Victor Cross is obsessed with it. Some ancient prediction or something. You're saying that it might be real?

"I'm saying that it *is* real. You do what you have to, Colin. I've got a feeling it's all connected."

Cassandra walked into the cell that Lance was using as his office and said, "I made contact with Colin."

Lance looked up from the notes he'd been examining. "OK. He acted as we guessed?"

"Pretty much."

"Good." He stood up, and gestured towards the door. "It's important that he understands the stakes. Cassie, there's something I need you to do but I don't want you peeking inside my head until I've got it all worked out, OK?"

"Sure."

They walked side-by-side along the corridor. Lance said, "You know the puzzle about the three blind men and the map? No? They're lost in the wilderness, but they do have a map. Let's say that their sighted guide was eaten by a bear, because he was evil and not pertinent to the story. So they don't know where they are, or what the surrounding area looks like, or what the scale of their map is. Or even which side of the paper their map is printed on. So. Using the map, how do they survive? And no peeking!"

Cassandra said, "They don't survive. It's a trick question."

"No, they do survive. But how?"

"They hear an airplane approaching so they wave the map around like a flag to attract its attention."

They had reached a sealed elevator door, and Lance keyed in a code to release the lock. "Good one. But that's not it."

Cassandra frowned as they stepped into the elevator car. "They... set fire to the map and someone sees the smoke?"

"Not that." Lance placed his left hand on the elevator's palm-scanner. The doors closed and the car began to rise.

"It's really, *really* hard not to cheat and read your mind for the answer!"

"I know. Go on, see if you can work it out."

"What else do they have with them?" Cassandra asked.

"Just the map. And let's say that they have enough food and water to last them until they're rescued or they find their own way out. They're not going to die of thirst or starvation. And they have clothes, obviously, so they won't freeze."

The elevator stopped with a slight bump, and the doors opened. "Oh, I've got it. They *shout* for help."

"But that's not using the map, is it? They have to use the map to get to safety. That's the rule." At the exterior door, they showed their key-cards to the guards, who scanned them and then unlocked the door.

As Cassandra walked outside into the Cloister's courtyard she said, "They roll the map into a cone, like one of those old loudhailers, and *then* they shout for help."

"That's a good one. But still wrong."

"Then I give up. Tell me."

"Sure?"

Cassandra nodded.

"OK. But contact Danny first and tell him where we are. He's to come here ASAP."

A few seconds later, she said, "Done. He's on the way."

"Great. OK, so back to the three blind guys and the map. This is how they got to safety... They said to their horses, 'Home, boy!' or 'Home, girl!' and the horses—who knew the way home, because horses are smart—brought them back to the ranger's hut. Or whatever. The end."

"You never said they had horses!"

"Ah, but I was picturing them in my head. If you'd looked, you would have seen them."

"But you told me *not* to look!"

"And you didn't. Now I know that I can trust you."

Cassandra shook her head. "But... the *map*! You said they had to use the map to escape!"

Lance reached into his pocket and pulled out a dog-eared map of Apache-Sitgreaves National Forest. "They did. See? They gave me their map, and I gave them horses that knew the way home."

She laughed. "But that's so stupid!"

"Hey! Show a little respect, please. I just saved the lives of three lost blind men." Lance looked to the side. "Hi, Danny."

Cassandra hadn't seen Danny since he and the others had fled the Substation. He looked thin, exhausted. His clothing was filthy and ragged, his beard and hair a lot longer than last time.

As Cassandra wrapped her arms around him, Danny gave Lance a serious glare. "Where are the others?"

Lance said, "Alex didn't make it. The others are alive. Renata's in Krodin's custody, but she's unharmed and surprisingly upbeat. Steph is injured, but it's not serious. She's hiding out in Greenville, with Kenya, Alia, Mina and Nathan. And... someone else."

"Colin?"

"He's on a different path."

Danny nodded. "All right. Out there... It's still bad. I've been helping where I can, but there's just too much for me. I've been tying up the Vipers whenever I find them, but that doesn't always hold them long enough for the real army to arrest them."

Lance said, "Don't beat yourself up. You've done an amazing job. If it hadn't been for you, Krodin's people would already have won."

"Don't patronize me, Lance."

"I'm not. Cassandra? Tell him."

Cassandra said, "What, *everything*?"

"Well, I meant tell him that I'm not patronizing him, but..." Lance shrugged. "Sure. Go ahead. The time for secrets is probably over anyway."

She said to Danny, "Max Dalton isn't dead. It was a con. He and Lance set it up so that Shadow would think he was, and then Krodin wouldn't look for him. It's true, Danny." She pointed to the prison behind her. "He's inside. Alive and well and... right this very second he's taking the last of the coffee and not making a fresh pot."

"I *knew* it was him who keeps doing that!" Lance said. "Danny, I'm no murderer, but we had to have *you* believe I could be. You believed it, so Shadow did too."

Danny said, "I need to sit down. And I need to eat."

They brought him inside, and in the guards' mess-hall—after he'd demolished an entire double-sized package of mint Oreos and downed three glasses of milk in the space of about ten seconds—Danny said, "Lance, I don't like being used."

"I know. I'm sorry, I truly am. But it was necessary. Sometimes you have to be the guy who takes that step."

Danny licked his index finger and mashed it around the cookie packaging to gather up all the crumbs. "I told you about the visions I had after the Trutopian war, back in Topeka?"

"You did. As I recall, you saw three things. Colin dead at the center of a crater. You saw another version of yourself, about the age you are now, but with both arms intact. And you saw yourself crouched over the dead body of a man you didn't recognize."

"In that last one, I heard someone say, 'You didn't have to kill him.'"

"That's what your dad said to me after I shot Max. Is *that* what you saw in the vision?"

Danny nodded. "The future is a dangerous land."

Cassandra said, "Right. We think we know what it's going to be like, all safe and secure. But it can be a *minefield*."

Lance said, "Yeah, let's *not* talk about minefields, please." He tapped his artificial leg. "Danny, did I ever tell you that I met your real father?"

"You did. The plague, and all that."

"I sometimes think..." Lance paused. "Cassandra, how much of this do you know?"

"Depends on what 'this' is," she said.

"Right. Well, you can pick the details out of my memory sometime, or I'll give you the reports. The short version is that there was a world-wide plague, very infectious, everyone dying. I had the cure inside me, a sort of negative version of the virus. I went to Quantum and touched his skin, and like *that*—" Lance snapped his fingers "—he was cured. Fast metabolism and all that. I told him what was going on, and then he... Well, he ran around the world and touched everyone. Every single person on the planet. In about a *day*. But that's a day of real time. For him, it was a lot longer."

Danny said, "So you saved everyone."

"No, he did. I just saved him. And it was *Max's* idea. But this is the hard part. All that time he'd spent on the road, house-to-house, village to village, town to town... Every person in every country in every continent. Caroline Wagner worked it out. She figured he was on the road for the equivalent of one thousand, seven hundred years. And he spent all of that time alone, unable to communicate with anyone, unwilling to stop."

Danny said, "I know all this. He was... Well, it broke his mind. He was never normal after that."

"Danny, I was the last person he spoke to before he started on his journey. I was the last one to see him in his prime. And I keep thinking that if I could go back in time and tell him to slow down, or take a break every now and then, things might have turned out very differently."

"I guess. But you *can't* go back in time, so regrets are useless. The past is the past and there's no way to change what's happened. The best you can do is learn from it."

Lance smiled. "Exactly. That's the best I can do. But it's not the best *you* can do. Remind me what Victor Cross called you?"

"He said I was the god of time."

"Yes, he did," Lance said. He looked from Danny to Cassandra and back. "Now... that brings us to the subject of why I wanted you both here today."

In Victor's flying craft, Renata could see that Cross was enjoying himself immensely as he held court. The only thing hampering him was the occasional flare of pain in his jaw when he spoke. Every few minutes the craft wavered slightly and he had to grab onto something to steady himself.

Victor said, "Krodin couldn't save the world because his worshipers, the Helotry, stole him out of the past. And, incidentally, created a paradox that could drive a normal person crazy trying to figure out. But that's not relevant. What *is* relevant is that the universe needed to fill the void left behind by Krodin's absence."

Shadow said, "Wait... *how* was Krodin supposed to save everyone from the Chasm?"

Victor looked at the clone as though he'd asked whether blue things are blue. "He's *immortal.*"

"So?"

"He would still be alive today. Keep up, Shadow. Four and a half thousand years ago Krodin began his conquest of the known world. Correct, Krodin?"

The immortal nodded. "That is correct. I was spectacular."

"You were indeed." Victor turned back to Renata and gave her a sly wink. "By conquering the world, he united it. Obviously there were still parts of the world that were unknown to him at the time and were therefore not yet part of his nation, but they would have soon enough been discovered and conquered. Only three hundred years ago we thought steam-power was the apex of technology. Look how far we've come since. Now imagine how far along we're going to be in another four *thousand* years. That's what was lost when Krodin was taken from his time. The human race would have spread to the stars by now. We would have colonized the galaxy."

Renata said, "So no matter what happened here on Earth, there would be other humans safe on other worlds."

Victor said, "Ms Soliz gets a gold star. But then we have to take that star away, because of what she did."

"Here it comes, then," Renata said. "Go ahead, Victor. *What* did I do?"

"You burned out. You used up all your reserves of energy by changing the entire world to crystal, and then changing it back. You can never do that again. That was our last hope."

Eldon said, "She was supposed to use that trick when the Chasm came! That way there wouldn't be anyone really alive for it to kill. Renata would wait until it passed, and then turn everyone back."

Victor grinned, grabbed Eldon's hand and shook it. "You're *not* an idiot after all. Well done. You're my new favorite. Not that there are many of you left." He turned back to Renata. "So we're all doomed and it's *your* fault. This region of space will pass through the Chasm and we have no way to protect ourselves. Renata Soliz, murderer of *billions*. You win the Most People Killed Ever award."

Renata shrugged. "You and Yvonne started that war. I just ended it."

Krodin said, "You used an elephant to carry a twig. Your solution was more drastic than the situation required."

"Even if any of this is true, how was I to know? I'm not taking the blame. All four of you can rot in hell for all I care, you bunch of twisted, deluded, hypocritical *psychopaths*."

She saw Shadow and Eldon both flinch at that, then glance at Krodin.

The immortal superhuman regarded Renata for a moment. "I am your captor. You should respect my strength. You should fear my wrath. And you will, when I no longer have need of you. But for now your life will be spared." Without turning around, he said, "Shadow... Have you fully recovered from your injuries?"

"I have."

"I would like you to hurt Renata."

Shadow stood up and moved towards her.

Renata started to back away. "No, wait... Come on, Krodin! You're indestructible and immortal—surely you can take an insult without resorting to violence!"

Krodin said, "I can. But I choose not to. Shadow, break her ankles."

Shadow grabbed hold of her right foot and right calf, and in the half-second before he twisted, Renata promised herself that she wouldn't give them the satisfaction of hearing her scream.

She was wrong.

Chapter 33

In a long-abandoned, rubble-filled room in the Cloister, Lance told Cassandra to lie on the bunk that he and Max had carried in. "This is just in case you collapse."

She lowered herself onto the low bunk as Max set down an old wooden chair beside it.

Lance said, "Cassie, you need to create a link to Krodin's mind."

"I've already tried. He's too different."

Max said, "It's tough, but you can do it. You're a stronger telepath than I was, and I managed it when he first showed up. Close your mind to everything else, OK?" He sat down in the chair. "Picture Krodin... Where is he?"

"A metal room... No, it's a vehicle of some kind. Flying... somewhere. I can't see. Victor is there, too. Shadow and Eldon. Renata's there, she's crying. She's in pain, scared..."

Danny asked, "Where are they? I should be there. I can free her and—"

Max said, "No. You stay here. Cassandra, forget Renata for now. Put her aside. Focus on Krodin. There is only Krodin. He believes himself to be the most important person in the history of the world. So pretend that he's right. Everything is about him. It's hard *not* to focus on him..."

Cassandra closed her eyes. She pictured a strongly-built man with shaggy, shoulder-length hair and an unkempt beard. She had never seen him, but this was always how she'd imagined him. A powerful, bronzed warrior standing in blood-splattered armor, the desert behind him littered with the countless dead.

Is this my imagination, or his memory? She wondered. *Or maybe it's his imagination. Yes... this is how he sees himself, his idealized version of how he is.*

Aloud, she said, "I'm in."

She was a ghost drifting through Krodin's memories. They stretched on further than she could see. Krodin had already been hundreds of years old when he was taken from the past, and every moment of those centuries was there.

Every meal he's had, every conversation, every quiet moment. Even his dreams. He's never forgotten anything!

She saw a thousand warriors fleeing from Krodin's army, a thousand more attempting to fight him man-to-man. She saw him standing on a balcony as his body was consumed in a pillar of fire.

She saw a stunning African woman carrying a baby in her arms, and felt Krodin's joy at seeing his first child. Yet she also sensed the woman's overwhelming sadness.

Cassandra pulled herself back. *No. I could get lost in there! Stay outside his memories. Observe them, but don't get caught up in them.*

From a great distance, she heard Lance's voice say, "Cassandra... Stay where you are... but link to Max's mind too. Can you do that? Two minds at the one time?"

"I can do it, but it's dangerous."

"He's willing to risk it."

She sensed Max's mind near her, and opened it.

She pictured him floating next to her, and he was.

This ghostly version of Max Dalton smiled as he looked around. "It's been a long, long time since I saw inside another mind. And even longer since I visited Krodin's... This is how *you* visualize it? A vast green landscape with the memories spread out like individual houses, connected by roads and paths and... are those *zip-lines?*"

Cassandra nodded. "Yep. That's how remembering something can sometimes suddenly take you to another memory even though you can't see the connection. You know? Like, the smell of moss always makes me think of an old four-pane window with peeling red paint on the frame. I've no idea why, because I don't think I've never even seen a window like that. This is how I picture some people's minds, though they're usually a lot smaller. What did *you* see when you looked inside someone's mind?"

"Usually clusters of bubbles floating in space, with each bubble connected to others by thin threads. Sometimes there are bubbles that have *no* threads."

"Forgotten memories?" Cassandra asked.

"Right. And I was able to create new threads, or sever old ones. So I could restore people's memories, or make them forget things. I once made a man forget where he'd parked his car while he was still sitting in it. With some minds I was even able to create new bubbles by copying old ones and modifying them."

"I can't do that. I can only *look* at their memories. And talk to their minds too, of course."

Max turned around in a slow circle. "I do like your zip-lines analogy. That's smart. What about *hidden* memories? They're quite a bit different to forgotten memories."

"Some of the houses have basements."

"I like that." He turned back to her. "Now... I don't have my powers any more, so I can only guide you, not help you. You need to stretch out and touch Victor's mind too."

"That's not going to be easy. Victor is *very* different. He's not like anyone I've ever read."

"I know."

"He's more like a city than a person."

Max said, "Lance believes that Victor's brain is the only engine that can process the information that Krodin doesn't know he possesses. First step... see if you can locate his mind. We can worry about the rest once that's done."

Cassandra reached out. Victor's mind was hard to miss. "I have him. He's... Max, until now his mind was always brighter than anyone else's, but now it's *glowing*. He's working at close to full speed."

She dropped into Victor Cross's mind and was almost swamped by the flood of images. A thousand pictures, sounds, ideas, memories and equations unfolded in front of her. A vast array that rippled as the elements rearranged themselves, seven, eight, nine times. The array split down the middle, a new element zipped into the gap, and the array closed in on it, absorbing it. Some elements swapped places, others were flipped or inverted, or merged. Some vanished, others were duplicated. Some grew while others shrank. Then the whole array folded in on itself, closing up, sealed away as though completed, and Cassandra felt herself zooming back... To see that the complex array was itself only one element in a much larger, constantly shifting plane of thoughts and memories.

Then she realized that Max was still with her, seeing Victor's thoughts through her eyes.

"Oh my..." Max said. "This is incredible. This is too much. It's too big!"

The plane stretched out ahead of them like a garden of flagstones that each featured rapidly moving animated images, and the flagstones themselves were moving and twisting and switching with each other.

Max said, "Just *one* of these is faster and more complex than the average human mind, and there are thousands of them spread out across this plane."

She remembered Yvonne's words: "You have to open your mind, Cassandra. That's the only way you'll be able to put new things into it."

Yvonne looked into Victor's mind before. I see now why she followed him. A mind like this...

Max said, "I know. How could all of this fit inside a human brain? This is beyond the limit!"

And then she realized that she was a mind inside another mind, linked to two more. It should be no surprise that Max was able to read her innermost thoughts.

He said, "Right. There are no limits. Everything we're seeing is your mind's interpretation of *his* mind. Victor has no limits, so you must set *yours* aside. Cassandra... look up."

She looked up. Above them was another plane of flagstones just like the one spread out below them. And above that, another, and another.

They stretched on, layer after layer, and Cassandra felt herself zooming backwards again, taking in a larger picture. The plane of flagstones was only one layer in a vast cube.

And there were thousands of cubes.

Colin had spotted another of the blue lights over the Central African Republic. It drifted lazily through a dense forest and he'd had to watch it for over an hour before he was certain that it was favoring one direction over any other.

It had been moving roughly north-east, and he figured that if it had the same destination as the lights in America and Japan, then that convergence point would lie somewhere in Asia.

Another light on the border of Iran and Turkmenistan showed that he was moving in the right direction.

And now he knew the lights' destination. The Khangai Mountains in the heart of Mongolia.

Hovering a hundred meters above the convergence point, Colin could see dozens of the blue lights slowly meandering over the mountains. Some appeared from beneath the surface, others drifted down from the sky.

He watched, and waited, until one of the lights below began to accelerate. Its path straightened out, as though it were being pulled towards the convergence point.

Then it disappeared, a meter above the ground.

Colin dropped down to ten meters, and slowly circled the point. He could see nothing out of the ordinary.

What is this?

He resisted the urge to reach out and touch the point.

So the lights come here, and then they disappear... But where does that energy go to?

Quantum said that the lights come from the Chasm, so... does that mean that somewhere in the world there's a place like this but the lights emerge from it?

He closed his eyes and tried to get a sense of the area, but there were no unusual heat signatures, there was no machinery or electronics in the area.

The closest human was at least fifty miles away, and there wasn't much wildlife in the region.

He thought, *Cassandra, can you hear me? I've found where the lights go, but I don't know what to do next! Hello?*

There was no response. He tried again a few minutes later, but still nothing.

Another of the lights came into view, and he watched as it seemed to be sucked into the convergence point.

I could touch it, see what happens... But maybe it'll siphon the superhuman energy out of me.

He realized that he was stretching his hand out toward the point, then snapped it back. *OK, I am so not doing that!*

But he wanted to. He wanted to see what would happen.

It would be a good thing to do. There had never been

anything like this in the history of the world and he could touch it and...

Colin darted backwards, eyes wide and breath coming in gasps. *What is* wrong *with me? I have no idea what that is—I'd have to be an idiot to put my hand on it!*

The urge was weaker now, but as he drifted closer again, it grew.

He retreated to what he hoped was a safe distance, and tried to contact Cassandra again.

"There are voices calling me," Cassandra said.

Next to her, Max said, "You have to ignore them. This is more important than *anything*. We're inside Victor Cross's mind, and you're still linked to mine and to Krodin's. That's all there is. Nothing else. Focus on that, Cassandra. Keep track of everything. Keep those plates spinning."

"I can do that."

"Good... because now it's going to get a bit tricky."

"What? This isn't the *hard* part?"

"This is a walk in the park. We have two more minds to connect."

In the rubble-filled room, Danny looked down at Cassandra on her bunk, and at Max slumped forward in the chair next to her. "Lance, how long is this going to take?"

"I have no idea. This is totally unexplored territory. We're pioneers. Could be minutes, could be hours." He shrugged. "Could be weeks."

"So we just wait and see?"

"*You* do. I have other stuff to attend to. For a start, we need to get Mina's powers back on-line. That doesn't seem to be happening by itself. I'd like to do the same for Renata, but we can't get close to her. Luckily, we still have two flyers. Nathan and Abby."

Danny started to nod, then said, "Abby? Lance, she's two years old!"

"Not that one. The *other* one." Lance walked towards the door. "Hold on a second." He came back a moment later carrying another chair. In his free hand, he was holding his walkie-talkie. "Alia, it's Lance. You remember the plan? Well, tell them it's time."

Danny asked, "Time for what?"

"Never mind that." Lance set the chair down next to Max's. "Where were we?"

"You're talking about the Abigail that Colin's sister is named after. But she died fifteen years ago."

"Sixteen years ago. But, yeah, *about* that... She got better. Sit down, Danny."

"I'm fine. What do you mean, she got better?"

Lance said, "Last year when Cross and his little pals had you captured, he tried to force you to change the past so that Krodin was never snatched out of time. You resisted, of course, and then he zapped you and took away your power. But at the last second you reached into the past... From what you told me later, it's pretty clear that you didn't have a plan. You were just flailing around like a drowning man."

"Yeah, well..." Danny shrugged. "I was under pressure."

"I know. Danny, sit down. Please."

"OK, OK!" Danny sat. "Happy?"

"Ecstatic. You made three changes to the time-line, as far as I can see, but I don't think you were conscious of any of them. First, you made it so that Cross had never turned on the null-field that protected him. That saved Brawn's life, so well done. Then you pulled Abigail de Luyando out of the past, from the moment before she was about to be killed by Slaughter. I *remember* that. There was a flash of light just as the ax struck. That was you, pulling Abby to safety. Some part of you *knew* that we would need her."

"So what was the third change?

"My favorite one! Back in the Substation Victor was trying to gloat about this, but I'd already worked it out for myself so I didn't give him the satisfaction. After Renata froze the world and then unfroze it, she'd lost her powers. She'd burned herself out. There's a tiny part of the brain that only superhumans possess. When Ragnarök used his power-siphoning machine it destroyed that part in all the developed superhuman brains. This is why someone like your father could never regain his powers. That's the part of the brain that Renata overloaded."

Danny said, "I remember Mina saying that Ren was normal, that she wasn't superhuman any more."

"And Mina was right. And then Renata *did* get her powers back—for a while, anyway—because that was the third change you made. You altered the past so that Renata never lost that brain-node."

"But... how would I even know how to do that? Until now, I didn't know that there *was* a special part of the brain for superhumans!"

Lance shrugged. "You know now. Maybe the you from one year ago remembered it from now? Time doesn't work in a straight line for you. Or, it doesn't *have* to."

"So all this... Isn't changing the past what got us into all this trouble in the first place?"

"Yeah, it is. But this time I *don't* want you to change the past. I want you to *visit* the past."

Chapter 34

Abby sat in the co-pilot's seat of the StratoTruck and didn't know whether to look through the cockpit glass at the rapidly-approaching mountains or at her niece, Stephanie, who was flying the craft.

Earlier, when the StratoTruck had landed in Greenville, Nathan and Mina had loudly argued over whether the best way to get to Mongolia from Kansas was to travel east or west. Kenya had solved the argument by using the craft's computer to prove that the shortest route was north through Canada, across the Beaufort Sea then south into Russia.

"You and Alia were eleven months old last time I met you," Abby said.

"Yeah, you owe us for sixteen years of missed presents," Stephanie said, smiling.

"Well, I would have bought those presents with the cash your mom and dad gave me for baby-sitting you, so we're probably even."

"Alia said Kenya told you about Dad."

Abby nodded. "She did. I'm so sorry to hear that. Vienna must have taken it hard."

"We *all* did."

"Of course. I didn't mean..."

Stephanie said, "No, my fault." She glanced at Abby. "Did Kenya tell you *how* he died?"

"No."

"Victor Cross kidnapped him, and Renata's family. He contacted Colin and told him that he had to choose: either Dad would die, or Renata's family. Colin... he chose Dad."

"I am going to kill Cross."

"Take a number," Steph said.

After a few minutes, Abby said, "So Colin is Energy and Titan's son? And you and he are... an item, right? Do you kids even say that these days? Or is it something more politically correct like, 'We're a pair bonded by consensual agreement and mutual attraction'?"

Steph laughed. "It's kinda complicated."

Abby couldn't help smiling. "So... Kissed him yet?" When the twins were born, she'd pictured conversations like this. She had loved the idea of being the cool aunt that they turned to when they felt unable to confide in their parents.

"None of your business!" Stephanie blushed. Then she added, "Not yet. Nearly held hands, once."

"Wow. Slow down, there, missy! You don't want to rush into things. Anyway, I forbid you to date anyone until I get a chance to embarrass you in front of him. That's the aunt's job." Abby turned around, still smiling. In the StratoTruck's main compartment Kenya and Mina were sitting together in one row, while Alia and Nathan were side-by-side behind them. All four of them were wearing the Team Paragon armor, as was Stephanie.

"When we fought Krodin..." Abby said, turning back, "it was tough. He adapts quickly. You hit him with something, it might hurt him, weaken him for a while. But next time, it won't have any effect. If I was him, I'd spend my free time trying to hurt myself in any way I could think of so that I wouldn't even have the temporary weakness in my next fight."

Stephanie said, "I know. We're going to have to come up with something he's never experienced or even imagined."

A light blinked on the console, and Stephanie said, "We've got company!"

"Krodin?"

"No. It's one of *ours*." She moved to the communications

console, and opened a radio link. "ST1 to ST2, come in."

A voice came back, "Hey, Steph. So, we're your emergency back-up crew. We're the *New* New Heroes. Or the Newer Heroes, if you prefer. Though to be blunt, a more accurate name would be The Cannon Fodder. The plan is that we attack Krodin and he's so busy laughing at us that you sneak up behind him."

"Razor... Seriously, they sent you? You're not a fighter!"

"I know. Mad, isn't it? But I'm not here to fight. I've been making some upgrades to Grant's armor and they're not done yet. Plus there's some other specialist equipment I can't talk about in case Victor's listening. If you are, Victor, then hi. We're about to kick your butt."

Alia rushed up to the comms console. *"Grant's* there?"

Grant Paramjeet's voice said, "Hi, Ali. So... I'm going to be grounded *forever*, aren't I?"

Stephanie asked, "Who else have you got?"

"Oh, wait and see," Razor said. "Our ETA is one hour, four minutes. That's nine minutes ahead of you. Unfortunately, it's about seven minutes behind the other unidentified craft the military satellites have spotted heading to the exact same location. So either Colin's fan-club have pooled their pocket-money, or Victor and Krodin are on the way."

"That's not good," Stephanie said. "And we're pushing the red line here. This is as fast as we can go."

"Same here. But Colin's strong, Steph. And despite that sweet little goody-two-shoes attitude he puts on, he can fight dirty when he needs to. He'll hold them back until we get there."

"Do we know what he'll be holding them back *from*?" Alia asked.

Razor replied, "Not a clue. Prepare yourselves, kids. This is going to be rough. If any of you want to back out, well, you should have done it before you left Kansas because it's too late now."

Stephanie said, "OK. Good luck, Razor."

"Yeah. You too, kid."

The sun was setting over the Khangai Mountains when Colin sensed an incoming craft. It wasn't anything with a heat-signature he recognized, but it was moving fast and on a direct path to him, coming from the west.

He didn't know what to do. The last communication he'd had with Lance, via Cassandra's telepathy, was, "Stay put. Help is coming."

So he had waited. More of the blue lights drifted toward the convergence point, then disappeared, and he was finding it more and more difficult to withstand the urge to poke at the point where they vanished.

Would I vanish too? Would anything vanish? If I throw a stone at that point, what'll happen to it?

He had managed to resist doing anything so far, and he was pleased with himself for that great achievement. So pleased that he felt he was due a reward. He could move a little closer to the convergence point.

Not going to do anything. Just moving nearer.

He stopped himself, and aloud he asked, "What *is* this thing?"

The unknown aircraft was much closer now, and slowing a little.

It was now close enough for him to make out its silhouette against the sunset: it appeared to be round, lacking any wings or obvious methods of lift or propulsion. The craft slowed to a stop a kilometer away, and in the fading light he saw something dart away from its side. Then a second object followed it.

They arced towards him, and he knew that the fight was on.

Shadow came first, and Colin knew that the clone was expecting him to counter-attack. Instead, he darted off to the side, leading them away from the convergence point.

Shadow crashed into Colin and they slammed into the ground in a tangle of fists and feet. Colin lashed out with a fast, hard jab at Shadow's face, hoping that the wounds he'd inflicted in Sakkara hadn't healed yet. Shadow saw the punch coming and ducked down, straight into Colin's fast-rising knee. The impact knocked Shadow back, but Colin had grabbed hold of the clone's arm and pulled him back in, smashed his fist into his face.

Didn't think that would work twice, Colin thought. But as he pulled his arm back to strike again, he was hit from behind, a powerful blow to the back of his neck that sent him crashing face-first into the ground.

Before he could recover, the other clone kicked out at him, again hitting the back of his neck.

He rolled to the side before the third blow could connect, but then Shadow was leaping at him, fists flailing.

"I *owe* you!" Shadow screamed. "You nearly killed me! When this is done, I'm gonna rip off your head and deliver it personally to your parents. And then I'm gonna tear your sister limb-from-limb, right in front of them!"

Colin allowed one of Shadow's punches to strike him in the shoulder, then grabbed his arm and spun, twisting around so that he was now behind Shadow. He locked his left arm around Shadow's neck, and placed the heel of his hand on the back of the clone's head. And pushed.

Shadow immediately began to twitch, and flail, and Colin rose up into the air so that Shadow couldn't use the ground for leverage.

The other clone—Colin now saw that it was Eldon—was hovering nearby, watching.

"Back off," Colin said. "I don't know if I have the strength to snap his neck, but I'm pretty sure I can choke him."

"You won't," Eldon said. "You do that, and your friend Renata dies. She's on our ship. You think we're dumb enough to come all this way without a hostage? Think of her parents, Colin. Her poor mom and dad, at home in their crappy Cleveland house. They already lost her once before."

Colin squeezed tighter on Shadow's neck, and hissed, "Is this true?"

Shadow did his best to nod, and Colin relaxed his grip a little. But not enough for Shadow to escape, or even to breathe properly.

Eldon asked, "Is killing Shadow more important than saving your friend?"

Colin didn't answer. He knew that they had to be stopped, but not at any cost. Not like this.

If they *did* kill Renata, then they had nothing to hold over him. And they knew that. This was their only shot. They were trying to persuade him that they had the power here, but in truth the upper hand belonged to him.

Victor Cross is behind this, and he's smart enough to out-think any plan I can come up with.

And Eldon might not be as strong as me or Shadow, but he's still very powerful and he's not a complete idiot.

Colin let go of Shadow, and at the same time he slammed his right fist into the small of the clone's back. Shadow bellowed with pain as he fell, and Colin rose up, put himself on a path for their aircraft.

Eldon immediately raced after him, and without slowing

down or changing path, Colin flipped over so that he was flying backwards and upside-down. He had a half-second to appreciate the look of confusion on Eldon's face, then he abruptly dropped his speed to zero and pulled back his arm.

He struck out at Eldon just as the clone was about to crash into him. The impact of the blow sent them both reeling, tumbling through the air, but Eldon received the greater portion of the damage.

Colin recovered first, and resumed his attack on their craft.

Chapter 35

Danny fidgeted nervously as he sat between Max Dalton's chair and Cassandra's bunk. He knew that he should be out there in the world, helping to fight Krodin's armies. Or finding a way to get to Renata. Or just doing *something*.

Instead, he had been instructed to sit here and wait until Max told him what to do.

He didn't like Max, but he trusted Lance, so he sat and waited.

They had been here for hours, and he couldn't help but think about what he could achieve in that amount of time. *I could disarm and tie up ten thousand enemy soldiers. Or clear a minefield. Or help a city full of people scavenge for food.*

What does Lance want me to do? He said visit the past but why, and when? How am I supposed to do that? I have no control over the visions.

Then Max raised his head, and looked at him. "Danny... It's time. Close your eyes and let Cassandra into your mind."

Danny closed his eyes and suddenly he was looking at himself, sitting in the chair with his eyes closed.

"You're seeing through my eyes," Max told him.

Danny blinked, and now he was looking up at the room's ceiling. He turned his head and saw Max and himself sitting in chairs next to the bed.

"My eyes now," Cassandra told him.

Then everything faded, and he was drifting through a misty darkness. "Where am I now?"

Cassandra was floating next to him, a transparent, ghostly figure, indistinct around the edges. "You're now inside your own mind."

"OK... I'm *usually* inside my own mind, but this doesn't feel the same."

Cassandra smiled. "Not like this. Watch."

Ahead of them the mist parted and Danny was looking at a large, modern-day library, or perhaps an art gallery. It reminded him of the museum of printing in the Kulturforum in Berlin.

Cassandra said, "That's because you were there recently... Watch." She plucked a book from a shelf that he hadn't noticed was there, and opened it to a page that showed a photograph of himself in the museum a year earlier. But the photograph was moving, animated: he saw himself moving in fast-mode as he disarmed and tied up four Trutopian soldiers.

Cassandra closed the book and let go. It floated back into its slot in the shelf and the shelf drifted away. "This is your memory. Each book is a moment, or an emotion, or an event, or a topic. If you spend enough time here you'll see that almost every page belongs to more than one book."

Alongside the neat rows of bookcases he noticed random vertical stacks of books—some even had gravity-defying gaps—and volumes that didn't fit in their shelves. Loose pages drifted around the floor as if caught in a gentle breeze. "Sorry this is such a mess," Danny said.

"Are you kidding? This is one of the best-organized minds I've seen. You should see inside *Mina's* head. Picture this after an earthquake and a hurricane, but with everything covered in something sticky."

"So... we're visiting my own memory. Does this mean that I can see things I've forgotten about?"

"That's why we're here. Lance needs you to remember how to access the time-line, like you did when Victor held you captive last year."

"It's not that I can't *remember* how to do it, Cassie, it's that I don't *know* how I did it!"

"Isn't that the same thing? Look, recall *one* element of that day. Something specific."

"I don't know..." Danny shrugged, and then realized that he had both of his arms. "Oh wow...!" He stared down at his hands as he opened and closed his fists.

Cassandra said, "Oh, I should have said. This is your mental image of yourself. Most people's self-images are very different to the real thing. Even mine. The me you're seeing now is how you normally see me. My own mental image of myself is taller and prettier. Look."

A second Cassandra appeared beside the first, and said, "See? Taller, prettier, no acne, better hair. That's my idealized version. But how we see ourselves changes depending on our moods. Trust me, you don't want to see how I view myself on the *bad* days. When I'm angry or having my period or just feeling down or when someone I like doesn't even notice me."

Danny said, "I'm sorry that my mental image of you isn't flattering."

"That just means you aren't physically attracted to me. I'm fine with that. And I knew it already."

He shrugged again. "Sorry."

The second Cassandra faded out, and was replaced by an image of Danny with both arms intact. The first Cassandra said, "This is how you want to be. You're definitely not ego-driven because aside from your arm, this is pretty close to who you really are." The two-armed version of Danny suddenly scowled with rage, a look of pure anger. "And *this* is who you're afraid you might become." The image faded out. "You're afraid to lose control because deep down you really *do* know how powerful you are. Your self-control is probably the most important thing in your life. More important than your family, than Renata, than your friends. Your father lost control of his own mind, and you're terrified that will happen to you."

"Suppose I went crazy? I could kill every person on the planet."

"You won't go crazy. Your very fear of that will always keep you in check. But we do need to explore what you can do... Recall something about that day, when Victor tried to make you change the past. Anything at all will work, but something specific would be best."

Danny said, "It was freezing?"

A book appeared in Cassandra's hands. She opened it in the middle and started to rapidly flip through the pages. After a few seconds, Danny realized that the amount of pages on either side didn't change.

"It's not a *real* book. It's metaphorical," Cassandra said. "You've been cold too many times in your life... Let's narrow it down. Victor was there, obviously. Show me that."

The book was replaced by another, and this time Cassandra found the memory almost instantly. "Here we are... OK. Wow. Those clones *really* did a number on you, didn't they? Most people would have passed out long ago."

The scene around them changed, and Danny and Cassandra were now watching Danny crawling across an icy floor. His face was covered in blood, his jaw slack, his Paragon armor battered and scratched. Standing in front of him was Victor Cross.

Cassandra said, "This is where you get a rush of memories, many of them not your own, and some of them are from the future. We can watch them, if you like. I know you can't usually recall your visions in great detail, but they're all here, intact, stored in your mental library."

"Unless it's necessary, no thanks. They're unsettling." He looked around. "So this is my memory of the event, right? We're not actually back in time?"

"Just your memory of it." She pointed to the right. "See how it's kind of indistinct over that side of the cavern? You never consciously took note of what was over there, so when you recall the event your brain automatically makes up stuff to fill in the gaps. But only stuff that's appropriate. It doesn't fill every gap with pink teddy bears."

"*Can* we go back to this time?"

"That's exactly what we're here to learn... Now, this is going to be a little tricky. See, we have your memories of this event, and right now I've also got a link to Victor Cross's mind. I've seen enough here to find *his* memory of the same event. That should give us a much better insight into how you managed to affect the past."

"You're quite something, Renata," Victor Cross said.

She froze, and looked toward the craft's cockpit. She had been working the ropes around her wrists against the edge of her seat and thought she hadn't been noticed.

Victor, at the controls, hadn't even looked around. "You've got two broken ankles and you're *still* trying to get free. The pain must be excruciating as it is. But what are you going to do if you get through the ropes? *Crawl* away?"

Krodin stood at the open hatchway, looking out. "The boy is withstanding Shadow's attack, Victor. You said that they would be able to defeat him."

"Yeah, I say a *lot* of things."

Krodin turned back, glaring. "You wish to die?"

"Oh, give it a *rest*," Victor said. "You need me alive more than you need your ego massaged. The Chasm is coming and..." He shook his head. "Huh. *That* was weird. Just remembered something about my mother that I hadn't realized I'd forgotten. Anyway. The Chasm is on the verge of wiping out all life on

Earth so let's not get hung up on who insulted whom."

Krodin said, "If you were any other man..."

"You'd kill me instantly. I know."

Renata resumed trying to cut through her ropes. If Krodin and Victor got into a physical fight then Victor would lose and this craft was going down. Victor had been right about the pain in her ankles, but she wasn't going to quit. If she had to, she *would* crawl away.

Krodin demanded, "Why are we *here*, Cross?"

"Look outside. What can you see, aside from a barren mountainous landscape and Colin Wagner fighting two of his clones?"

"I see a darkening sky. Stars emerging. A blue light drifting over the landscape. A second light moving in another direction."

"Not many people can see them... They're moving toward the nexus."

"And what is that?"

"Until Colin came here, I wasn't certain that it was more than a theory. The blue lights, as you see them, is energy that was ejected from the nexus roughly eighty years ago. Since then, it's been drawn back. There's very little of it left. Most has been reabsorbed into the nexus, some of it has been used by superhumans."

Renata said, "That doesn't explain what this nexus *is*."

"It's a kind of hole in the universe. Not like the Chasm, though. This one was created deliberately."

"By the universe?" Krodin asked.

"No. By me. About thirty-four minutes from now." He turned around and grinned at Krodin and Renata. "We're setting down. Hold onto your hats, kids, because things are about to get *really* freaky."

Chapter 36

Colin knew that he was losing this fight. Shadow and Eldon had finally realized that they needed to work together to stop him. Now, Shadow had Colin's arms behind his back while Eldon repeatedly hit him in the face and stomach.

Eldon was screaming, "Had enough yet? Have you? You think you can take a little *more*? All right then!"

Colin's body rocked from another fist to the face, then another. Shadow's powerful fingers were digging into his arms, while at the same time he had his knee against Colin's spine.

"Finish him!" Shadow yelled. "He's trying to break free!"

Colin flipped himself up and over, but Shadow came with him, now pulling so hard on his arms that Colin felt that his elbows were about to snap. Each blow brought fresh waves of agony surging through his entire body.

Then something was rushing at Eldon: a flying woman wearing unfamiliar armor and wielding a heavy sword. She crashed into the clone, knocking him aside, then darted at Shadow, stopping with the point of her sword only millimeters from his face.

"Let him go," the woman said. "I don't know which of you is which, so I'm just keeping you all alive until the others get here."

Shadow snarled, "A sword? We're bullet-proof! That's not even going to *scratch* us!"

"Want to take that chance?"

"We don't have to. The boss is here."

Colin twisted free of Shadow's grip and saw that the strange aircraft was setting down to land, thirty meters away from the convergence point.

Krodin jumped down from its hatchway before it landed. He

looked up at them and bellowed, "You—armored woman! I remember you! Fight me!"

The woman rushed down toward Krodin, and Colin took advantage of the distraction to lash out at Eldon with a powerful kick, sending him tumbling to the ground.

Shadow made another grab for him, and Colin darted away, zipping low over the landscape with the clone in pursuit.

He glanced back. Shadow was gaining on him. At the last second, something huge and metallic crashed down from above, colliding with Shadow, knocking him into the hard rock-face of the mountain.

The blue giant took hold of Shadow's head in his massive, metal-clad hand and slammed it over and over into the ground. "Feels good to be back in the armor," Brawn said, grinning at Colin.

"Good to see you... But how did you know it was him and not me?"

"Because *you* never look like you're enjoying a fight. Go, get the other one. This one's not going anywhere for a while."

Colin nodded, and darted back towards the convergence point.

Krodin was there, grappling with the stranger, and beyond them the members of Team Paragon were approaching fast.

Stephanie Cord cut the power on her jetpack and allowed herself to drop towards the other craft. Over her radio, she said, "Nathan—help Brawn subdue Shadow. Mina, you're with me. The rest of you keep Krodin busy. You can't hurt him, but you can distract him. We don't think he can fly, so stay out of his reach."

She reactivated her jetpack ten meters above the ground, and landed on the aircraft's ramp. Inside, Victor Cross was standing among a collection of odd-looking pieces of electronic equipment, typing one-handed on a small computer.

Renata was on the far side of him, hands and feet tied, lying on the floor.

Cross said, "Ms Cord, isn't it? Which one are... Forget it, I don't care. Try anything, blah blah blah, booby trap, big explosion, and so on. The usual. This is too important for you kids to screw up, so please go away."

"Letting you live was the biggest mistake we ever made."

"No, getting in my way now will be the biggest mistake *anyone* has ever made. This is end-of-the-world stuff."

Stephanie reached out to the nearest piece of equipment. "Suppose I remove these cables, then?"

"Suppose you notice that there are explosive charges packed around Renata's body? Seriously, kid, go away." Cross still hadn't looked up from his computer.

Renata said, "He's not lying about that. Steph, go! We can't stop this."

To Cross, Stephanie said, "Krodin will kill you, when he no longer needs you. Why are you doing this?"

"The simple truth, Stephanie, is that I don't want to die."

"Neither do I."

"No, I don't want to die *ever*."

"You want to be immortal, like everyone says Krodin is."

Still typing, Victor said, "In a way, I suppose... But not *quite.* Think of it like this... Who was the most famous person of the twelfth century? Any idea? Renata, how about you?"

Renata shrugged as well as her bound arms allowed. "I haven't got the slightest clue."

"Exactly. Everyone dies, and only a tiny few are remembered. Suppose I do something truly spectacular that's of great benefit to the human race: I might be remembered for a thousand years. Or ten thousand. Or even a *hundred* thousand. Picture that: one hundred thousand years from now, people still remembering your name, knowing what you accomplished."

"And that's what you want?" Stephanie asked. "You're willing to kill countless people just so that you won't be forgotten?"

"Oh, you live in such a narrow world. A hundred thousand years is just the *start*. I could become the most famous human being who ever existed. I could accomplish miracles. I could destroy a *galaxy*... But everything ends. One day, the universe itself will die. It will dissipate into nothing, or collapse back on itself, shrink all matter and energy into a singularity... And bang. It's gone. All of our achievements, no matter how great, will be wiped out as though they never existed."

Stephanie said, "True. But in the meantime, we have ice cream."

Victor stopped typing and stared at her. "What?"

"Don't sweat over things you can't change. Enjoy what you have instead of pining about stuff you *can't* have. The universe is going to end in eleventy billion trillion years or whatever. So what's the big deal?"

He hesitated. "I... I just... That *is* a big deal. It's the biggest deal ever."

Stephanie made a "so what?" face and shrugged. "Doesn't affect me. I'll be dead by then."

Renata said, "Victor, I had a conversation along these lines with your psycho protege Yvonne a couple of years ago. Remember when I froze the world? Of course you do. That was one of those things that people are going to remember for a long time." Renata gave him a playful wink. "So I unfroze Yvonne first, and told her that if she didn't call off the Trutopian war, I would freeze her again and leave her like that forever.

Our sun will burn out in five billion years, and she'd be still alive but frozen. Then at some point the universe itself would come to an end, and after that, who knows?"

Victor said, "*I* know."

"Yeah, but there *is* no after," Stephanie said. "If the universe is gone, then it's gone."

"No, Ms Cord. Then a *new* universe is created. This is not the *first* one. It also won't be the last. A new universe will form and it will be different. Anything we take for granted might not be there. It could be a universe where cause does not have to precede effect. Where there is no light. Or where gravity doesn't exist. It could be a universe where time runs backwards or where all time is simultaneous. It could be empty. Or a solid universe where nothing can move. Or it could be exactly like this one but a single blade of grass in a park in Bucharest is a millimeter taller. That one is not likely, but it illustrates the point. The next universe will be different. And I intend to live to see it. And the one after that, and so on."

Stephanie glanced at Renata, then back to Victor. "Where are you *getting* this from?"

"Some things you just instinctively know."

Renata said, "Now you sound like Krodin and his unshakable belief that he was born to rule the world."

Victor put down the computer and picked up another, almost identical one. "Let's say he was. Krodin was created to rule us and that all got screwed up when The Helotry stole him out of the past. So the universe created more superhumans to fill Krodin's role. And that's us. Each of us was created for a reason. No one person can handle everything. We were each given different parts of the puzzle. Quantum had the power to alter time: his job was to correct the time-line, make it so that Krodin was never taken from the past. But that failed because

Quantum started to remember the future, and not just his own: he was remembering *everyone's* future. So he went crazy, and then the universe created Danny. Same basic powers, but toned down a little and more stable. Plus the universe created me, with my incredible brain, to help guide Danny."

Renata asked, "Is this what you really believe, or just something you're making up?"

"I honestly don't know." He tapped the side of his head. "At any given moment there are hundreds of things going on in there. Sometimes I'm not sure which part of my mind is the real me."

Stephanie said, "What are you building, Cross? What *is* all this?"

He looked up at her. "This? Well, I've planted a lot of seeds ever since I hacked into Max Dalton's computers and found the Quantum prophecies, and spent a lot of time nurturing those seeds. This machine is where I reap the harvest."

Krodin didn't want to admit that he was enjoying himself. The woman with the sword had grown in strength and skill since he'd last seen her, though she was still unable to inflict any damage on him.

The blue giant was weaker, though. He remembered from the files in Sakkara that Brawn's superhuman abilities had been stripped by Ragnarök's machine. Now, his strength was augmented by machinery, but he was still not half the fighter he had once been.

The others were little more than nuisances, flitting about in their armored costumes and pointlessly shooting at him with ineffective rockets and items that make so little impact on him that he barely noticed their presence.

He knew that soon enough he would tire of this and simply

just kill them all. And then... He wasn't certain.

Cross had told him that the energy that created superhumans disappeared at this point, what he called the nexus. And after the effects of the Chasm had passed, there would be no more new superhumans. No more challenges.

Is that how it is to be for me? An eternity of uneventful peace?

But Cross hadn't yet told him *how* they would survive the Chasm.

For all of his long life, Krodin had relied on his instincts to tell him when something was wrong. Perhaps, as Victor said, that was indeed the universe itself guiding him. If so, it seemed that the universe was now telling him that he'd been wrong to allow Cross so much freedom.

Chapter 37

Danny found himself being guided through the void again, and this time he and Cassandra emerged hovering over a lush green landscape populated with houses of different designs.

"Krodin's mind," Cassandra said. They suddenly zoomed back—or Danny's image of Krodin's mind shrank; it was hard to tell which—and there was another mind next to it, a constantly shifting universe of incredible complexity. "And that's a glimpse of Victor's mind. *Just* a glimpse. This is like looking in through the keyhole of the Taj Mahal."

"Wow..." Danny said. "It's unreal. Victor's mind goes on *forever*!"

"Yeah, it's kind of scary, isn't it? And don't forget that *Krodin's* mind is still much bigger than a normal person's. He has hundreds of years worth of memories. Now... Danny... There are already five of us linked. You, me, Max, Krodin and Victor. Except that the last two don't know that we're peeking inside their heads. We have one more to join, and this is why we need *you*."

"OK... I've already gone far beyond anything I've ever imagined, so I can cope with this. I think."

"You need to cast your mind back... I don't mean remember things. Actually send your mind back. Do you understand?"

"You want me to send my mind back in time."

"Yes. The knowledge that Victor needs to process is shared between Krodin, and Max, and this last person. So you cast your mind back and make contact with him, and through me all of their minds will be linked."

Another voice beside Danny said, "I will guide you." He turned to see a transparent image of Max watching him.

"Come with me, Danny. We're going back. Let me show

you..." Max reached out his hand and touched Danny's forehead.

Everything changed.

Danny drifted through the smoke-filled battlefield, with Max by his side. Suspended in the air ahead of them, a man in a blue costume and wearing a jetpack was staring in shock at the large man below him who had been frozen in mid-fall.

Max said, "Titan and Ragnarök, thirteen years ago."

Danny drifted closer to Titan. Even beneath his mask, the resemblance to Colin was clear.

"This is shortly after Ragnarök's power-damper was used, stripping all the superhumans of their abilities."

Danny said, "*You* helped him design it."

"This is true. But we're not here to apportion blame. We need to get inside Ragnarök's mind. They're not stopped, just moving at a thousandth of normal speed. Ragnarök will hit the ground in about two seconds of real time, and he'll die. But that should be enough time."

"How *do* we get inside his mind?"

Cassandra's voice said, "Just hold him there, Danny, and let me do the work. The mind can move a lot faster than you realize."

Razor had landed the StratoTruck a hundred meters from Cross's vehicle, and now Lance was helping him to carry out the equipment.

Into his headset, Lance said, "Cassie... Give me the situation."

"We're in, Lance. I'm inside Ragnarök's head... It's a lot more like Max's than Krodin's or Victor's. I'm looking through his memories, but I can't see anything that will help. There's so much other stuff in here... I take it back. He's not like Max at all.

Beneath the surface it's like a *snowstorm*, millions of ideas and thoughts billowing about. I'm sorry, there's no way to determine what's going to be useful."

"Then you're going to have to *ask* him. Make contact with his mind, not just his memories."

"Lance, he's falling to his death! And it's his own fault—he forced Colin's dad to drop him!"

"I know. But make contact anyway."

The ground raced up towards Casey Duval and he found himself on the edge of panic, then decided that no, this *was* the right thing to do. Everything he had worked for was gone. After all these years, Max Dalton had won.

If he'd allowed himself to be captured they would pick apart his brain. Or force him to work for them. This was the right way.

If I can't win, then I don't want to face what's coming next.

A tiny part of his brain wondered why he hadn't yet hit the ground, then a voice inside his head said, "Hello?"

What? Is that real?

"I'm real. My name is Daniel Cooper... we need to know about the Chasm."

...What?

"I know this is a bad time," the voice said, "but I'm told that you're the last piece of the puzzle. We're from the future, thirteen years ahead of you. The Chasm is upon us and we can't defeat it without you."

The Chasm can't *be defeated. That's like trying to out-swim water. The Chasm is coming and I failed to fulfill my destiny.*

"You wanted to conquer the world, to unite it to defeat the Chasm."

That's right.

"Exactly *how* would uniting all the people of the world have helped?"

I don't know. I assumed that when the time came, it would become clear to me.

"Well, the time has come for *us*, thirteen years in your future, and you're not around to help... for obvious reasons. We need access to your knowledge."

You said I'm the last piece of the puzzle... Who are the other pieces? Casey asked.

"A man called Victor Cross. He was only a boy in your time. Max Dalton. And Krodin."

Dalton... that rat. I won't do anything that will help him!

"Even if it means condemning the human race?"

What do I care? I'll be dead in seconds.

"Not necessarily. I'm Quantum's son. I have his powers, but not his... difficulties. I can alter time. That's how I'm speaking to you. Help us, and I can adjust the time-line. You can die there in your time, and still be alive here in my time. I've already done that with Abigail de Luyando. She died sixteen years ago, but she's here now, alive. And so is Mina."

Who's Mina?

"One of your daughters. The twin baby girls you're about to leave behind. The people who found them named the blonde one Mina, and the dark-haired one Yvonne. They... they grew up into fine young women. Casey, I'm not a telepath, but I have a friend who is. I'm providing a bridge across time, and she provides the link between our minds. We want to also link you to Krodin, Max and Cross."

How will that help?

"One of our people believes that Victor Cross is the only one who has a mind capable of processing all the necessary data that the rest of you have been provided with."

He can really avoid the Chasm?

"Victor doesn't know we're using him. He's got his own thing going on."

Promise me that you'll let me see my girls again, and you have a deal.

Colin knew that he could defeat Eldon and Shadow one-on-one, but they were not letting that happen. Any time he got the upper hand with one of them, the other would dart away towards the New Heroes and Colin would have to chase after them.

We need Danny, Colin thought. *And Renata, too.*

Right now, Nathan and the swordswoman were attacking Krodin, while Eldon was grappling with Kenya and Mina. He grabbed Mina's arm and spun her about, throwing her into Kenya with enough force to knock both of them hundreds of meters away.

Shadow had been slammed to the ground and was now rushing back at Colin, enraged. He shouted, "Eldon! Either finish those two or help me out here!"

On the edge of Colin's vision another blue light was approaching, being drawn towards the convergence point. And then he knew what to do.

He waited until Shadow attacked again, then faked a move to the left. Shadow shifted direction long enough for Colin to again get his arm around the clone's neck.

"Back away," Colin roared at Eldon. "I'm not fighting you both at once. Eldon, drop to the ground and I'll let Shadow go. OK? That's how we'll do this. We can talk this out. You'll tell me what you want, I'll tell you what I want, and we'll hammer out a deal." To himself, he said, *Don't turn around! Don't see the blue light!*

Eldon shook his head. "We're just the muscle, Colin. It's

Victor and Krodin who make the decisions."

"Just drop to the ground, Eldon!"

Eldon looked down. "Why? You've booby-trapped the ground?"

"How would I do *that*? Of course not. Just set down and we can talk."

"Right. And... What, we're going to plan... out..." Eldon was looking towards the convergence point. "Plan out a way... to... work togeth... What *is* that?"

"What's what?" Colin asked.

"No, there's something there. Right there." He pointed. "I can't *see* anything but... I think that I should go to it. Just for a second. See what it feels like. Yeah, I'm gonna do it." Eldon reached out with his index finger and touched the invisible convergence point.

The explosion was instant, and devastating.

Eldon was obliterated.

Colin had been behind Shadow, with his left arm around the clone's neck. He was mostly shielded from the blast, but a wave of pure agony washed over his left arm. He flinched, letting go of Shadow.

He watched the still-burning clone fall toward the newly-formed crater. Shadow hit the side head-first, collapsed like a rag doll, tumbled down into the center of the crater.

Ignoring the pain in his arm, Colin dropped down next to him.

Shadow's entire body was blackened and scorched. He wasn't moving. He wasn't breathing.

Chapter 38

Inside the StratoTruck Razor and Lance knew that they could do no more. They stood side-by-side and watched the battle rage under the darkening sky.

"So what was that?" Lance asked. "Energy flare... But from what?"

"Looks to me like we're down to one clone now, and he's on our side. Just Krodin and Victor to beat," Razor said. "But they *can't* defeat Krodin."

"And they can't attack Victor because we need him."

Ahead of them, Krodin leaped at Brawn but the giant side-stepped and planted a power-assisted elbow into the small of Krodin's back.

"Nice," Razor and Lance both said at the same time.

Lance said, "He's holding back, obviously. Drawing it out. He could have killed them all a hundred times over by now."

"So what's stopping him?"

Lance shrugged. "Ah, who knows the mind of an immortal?"

"Cassandra does. We should ask her."

"Good thinking, son." Lance activated his radio. "How are we doing, Cassandra?"

The young telepath's voice came back, "Lance, I think that Victor is becoming aware of us. It could be that he's set up an early-warning system for someone tampering with his brain. Yvonne told me that he was very hard to read. I've channeled all of Krodin's memories into an empty part of Victor's mind, and Max and Ragnarök are feeding their memories in now, so if you're right, the process should start working automatically."

"Good work," Lance said. "Keep me posted."

Razor asked, "How do you know it'll work?"

Lance said, "Hah, long story! When all this is done, I'll tell you. If we live, that is."

"No. Tell me now."

"OK, what's this? You don't trust your old man all of a sudden?"

"Lance, how did you *know* that all of those minds have to be linked? Where did that information come from?"

"You know me... I'm good at understanding people. That's *my* gift. You must have got your mechanical expertise from your mother." Lance resumed watching the battle, where Colin and Nathan were attacking Krodin at the same time. "How *is* she, by the way?"

"Still furious with you."

"Still? It's been two decades, and I didn't even know about you. She has to forgive me sometime."

Razor said, "No, she's furious because I told her I'd met you, but you never called her."

Lance smiled. "Aw, she still loves me!"

"She told me that the reason you guys never really got together was because you were hung up on a girl called Abby. You'd been obsessed with her for years."

Lance didn't respond to that.

"Then you realized that was Max's fault. He'd manipulated your mind, made you fall for Abby so that you wouldn't go after his sister. And once you'd realized it, that broke the spell. But it was too late. You were leaving the next day."

"That's about right, yeah," Lance said, still watching the battle.

"She doesn't blame you for that. She never did. Neither do I."

"It would have been nice if... But things are the way they are." He slapped Razor on the shoulder. "I've been a lousy father—through no fault of my own, as agreed by all parties involved—but you turned out all right so I'm going to take credit for that. Well done me."

Lance's headset radio beeped, and he answered the call. "Go ahead, Cassandra."

"We... we're not done, but we have new information."

On the edge of Victor Cross's mind, Danny saw himself floating next to the images of Ragnarök, Cassandra and Max Dalton.

Cassandra said to Ragnarök, "Explain that in a way that I can relate to Lance."

"Who's Lance?" Ragnarök asked. "Wait, not Lance *McKendrick*? That guy gave me so much trouble..."

"Please," Cassandra said. "Time is stopped for you, but not for us. What did you mean?"

"The Chasm isn't what Victor Cross thinks it is. Like the rest of us, he only has part of the story. I can see it now, it's clear to me. It's not the end of all life wherever it touches: it just destroys the higher brain functions. Anyone caught in its path will be reduced to the intelligence level of, say, a household pet. There'll be no physical damage, but the personality and memories will be wiped out."

Max said, "And Victor doesn't know this?"

"No. He's certain that he can protect himself and come out through the other side with all of his functions intact."

Danny asked, "Why would he want to be the only living being left on the planet?"

Ragnarök said, "He wouldn't. He's got something else planned, but I can't see what it is."

"In a few minutes, this part of our galaxy will pass through the Chasm. All life will end."

Renata said, "You can stop it, can't you? You're the smartest person who ever lived! If there's any truth to what you said about the universe creating superhumans to avoid the Chasm, then that means it's your duty—your *destiny*—to save everyone!"

"I don't believe in destiny, Ms Soliz. I believe in opportunity. I..." Victor shook his head briskly. "OK, there's *something* going on in my head without my permission! I keep getting memory flashes that I didn't ask for."

Stephanie said, "Maybe it's your conscience."

"Funny. Or it's a surge of energy from the nexus," Victor said. "Which I'm about to create. It's a wormhole, sort of. The Chasm comes, rippling its way through this sector of the galaxy, absorbing all life. That's a *huge* amount of energy, as you can imagine. It'd be a shame for all that energy to go to waste, so my little apparatus here..." Victor tapped one of the machines in front of him. "It generates a tachyon well. Tachyons are subatomic particles that travel faster than light—with the right guidance they can breach time. Kind of like the machine that the Helotry used to pull Krodin out of the past. Theirs was powered by a nuclear reactor and guided by Pyrokine. Mine is powered by the energy the Chasm is about to steal. It will send some of that energy back in time, about eighty years. Then it'll be slowly drawn to this point in time. The nexus."

"That's impossible," Stephanie said. "You're saying that *you* created the superhumans?"

Victor nodded. "I'm about to, yes. Except for Krodin, and the handful of others who appeared prior to eighty years ago. But that's only a side-effect of the tachyon well generator. Its true purpose is to send *me* into the future."

Renata asked, "How far will you go?"

"Fifty seconds. It really only needs to be about *eleven* seconds because that's how long it's going to take for this planet to pass through the Chasm, but better to be on the safe side, right?"

"So everyone will be dead but you?"

Victor smiled. "Yes. And then, of course, I move on to phase *two*."

Cassandra said, "He's learning. He'll figure out what we're doing soon."

Max said, "It's too late, anyway. Either something got messed up along the way, or Lance's whole theory is wrong. All the information has been loaded into Victor's mind and no answer has appeared. Even if it did, even if there *was* something we could do to avoid the Chasm, we don't have enough time to implement it!"

"No," Ragnarök said, "there *are* answers... I can see them. Krodin would have spread the human race to other, safer parts of the galaxy. That failed. Renata Soliz could have frozen the world until the Chasm had passed. Again, that failed. But there were others... Leonard Franklin. Terrain, to everyone else." The ghostly image of Ragnarök closed his eyes. "I knew him. A telekinetic with control over inanimate objects. He was infinitely more powerful than he knew: his purpose was to relocate our solar system, to move it to a part of the galaxy that would be untouched by the Chasm."

Danny said, "Whoa... seriously? He could *do* that?"

"He had that power." Ragnarök looked around Victor Cross's mind. "Cassandra... Mina is my daughter. I would very much like to speak to her before I die."

"Hold on..."

A transparent image of Mina Duval appeared in front of everyone. She looked around, frowning. "OK... *This* is weird."

Cassandra said, "Mina... you're telepathically linked to us.

This man is—"

"I know who he is," Mina said. She drifted closer to Ragnarök. "You made me, and Yvonne."

He nodded. "I'm your father, and your mother too, I guess. Things were never meant to go the way they did, Mina. I'm sorry."

"How is this possible?"

"Danny has sent his mind back to the day I die. I only have seconds left, of real time... We're all linked to Krodin and Victor Cross's minds. We're trying to find a way to resist the Chasm. Max, Krodin and I all have part of the information we need, and Cross's brain is where it must come together. That's why they need me, it's the *only* reason they brought me here. But I'm glad that they did, because now I get to see you as a young woman. Mina, you and your sister are my single greatest achievement. And my greatest failure is that I never got to hold you in my arms."

Mina said, "I... wish I could..." She looked away. "Those are my friends out there, and they need me. I'm glad I got to talk to you. But you're already dead. You died thirteen years ago. Good-bye, father."

Mina faded away.

For a long moment, no one said anything, then Ragnarök again looked around Victor Cross's mind. "The universe kept giving us chances to save ourselves, and we screwed it up time and time again. I'm to blame as much as anyone."

Max said, "I think I am too." He laughed briefly. "Who'd have thought that you and I would ever agree on anything? Years of fighting, of scrabbling for power. We should have just sat down and talked."

Ragnarök nodded. "But we both refused to believe that we could be wrong. A long time ago I remember telling Lance

McKendrick that he should never assume he's smarter than someone else. 'That kind of cocksure attitude is nothing more than arrogance borrowed from the future.'"

"Yeah, that sounds like *both* of us. And Lance, too. The guy drives me *crazy* but..."

Max Dalton and Ragnarök stared at each other.

Then, simultaneously, they both said, "Lance is the missing piece."

Chapter 39

Lance said, "I didn't *want* it to be true, but I think they're right."

"It makes sense," Razor said. "There's no other explanation for how you could know all of this. You're the guide they need to put everything into place."

"Looks like it. There is one teeny problem, though..."

"What is it?"

"When we're all linked and Victor's brain starts to process the information, Victor will definitely figure out that something's wrong. It's going to get... messy. We'll be locked into his brain. The mind can survive the transfer into another body without any side-effects. But it takes a *superhuman* mind to survive the processing that Victor's brain is going to subject it to. Anyone else, it'd be like pushing boiled eggs through a sieve. From the way Cassandra describes it, it's amazing that Victor doesn't get lost in there himself. But I guess he's occupied with other things right now, so we *might* have enough time." Lance sighed. "OK, Cassie. I'm ready when you need me."

Victor carried a small padded stool over to the center of his ring of equipment and sat down. "Phase two is the big one. Renata, I told you about the life-and-death cycle of the universe. Eventually everything ends. The universe will be destroyed, taking everything with it. It crashes back into a singularity and then the cycle starts again. A new universe. Different laws, different realities... It's happened before, and it'll happen again. Except that 'before' and 'again' don't apply because time is an aspect of *this* universe, so time ceases to exist when the universe does." He scooted his stool over to a piece of equipment, connected one of his small computers to it, and began typing. "I'll be safe while the Chasm steals all of the life-energy on this planet. Then my machinery here will steal that life-energy *back* from the Chasm, and download it into me."

Wearing a wide grin, Victor looked from Renata to Stephanie.

Stephanie asked, "What, are you expecting *applause*?"

"Well, yes. Stephanie, the energy I'm about to absorb will give me the abilities greater than you could imagine. What I'm about to undergo is called apotheosis. I will become a *god*."

"A god ruling over an empty universe. Doesn't sound like fun."

"*This* part will be empty, but the universe is infinite. And it will all be mine."

Renata said, "And then one day, the universe will come to an end and even *you* will die."

"No. When the end comes I'll have the power to step outside the universe and reappear in the next one. I will be hyper-immortal." He disconnected the computer and tossed it aside. "OK. Done. Now I just wait."

"For the Chasm," Stephanie said. "Which is going to kill all life on the planet."

"Wrong. It's actually an energy wave that will destroy the minds and memories of all higher primates. It won't actually do any other harm."

"That's not what you said a minute ago."

"Renata's right," Stephanie said. "You've changed your story."

"No, I think you'll find... that the..." Victor jumped to his feet. "The *telepath*! She's inside my head!" He grabbed one of the computers and began to type frantically.

Krodin slammed his fist into the swordswoman's stomach, sent her flying back to crash into one of the armored children.

Something had to be done, he knew. Unite the human race, that was clear. That had been his goal all along. *Unite them, because...*

The thought slipped away again, like the fragments of a dream, and he mentally scrambled after it even as he fought the superhumans.

They could do him no harm. They were actually a welcome distraction. He could kill them with ease, but in truth he was enjoying himself. And the fight kept them busy while Victor Cross prepared his devices to avoid the devastation of the Chasm.

The unification of the human race is not *the ultimate goal,* Krodin realized. *It's the method to* achieve *the goal. I was meant to create one global nation because... because...*

Krodin had always instinctively known his purpose, his mission, his reason for existence. And now his instincts told him that he had been correct about his role, but he had greatly misunderstood his own importance.

I... I believed that I was the king, the emperor of the human race. But I'm not. I'm just a shepherd whose job is to safely guide the people to their destination.

He thought of Sakkara, and Topeka, and the thousands upon thousands of people whose lives had already been taken. He had been so cavalier, so flippant about death, but every life—no matter how wretched it might seem, no matter how sordid or corrupt or pathetic its past—had the potential to be glorious.

I believed I was strengthening myself with every life I ended, taking me closer to my goal. But I was not. Every death pushed me further away.

The New Heroes were staring at him now, and he realized that he was crying. He didn't care. *Let them think what they may.* He was immortal, and if he spent an eternity shedding tears for the dead, it would still not be enough.

One of the children, the girl called Mina, hovered in front of him. "He's broken."

Krodin laughed through his tears. "No, Mina Duval. I have finally been *repaired*. All of this was not meant to be. I was created to *save* the human race, not rule it as I believed. But it's not too late. Victor is working on a solution. If you had beaten me, somehow, and stopped him, the Chasm would have ended all intelligent life on this world."

Mina said, "Victor's *not* working on a solution. We've been listening to him bragging to Steph and Renata. Steph kept her radio on. Victor's got a time-machine and he's going to jump into the future to avoid the Chasm."

Krodin slowly turned and looked towards Victor's aircraft.

Lance McKendrick screamed, "No! Cassie—get me in there, fast as you can!"

"A few seconds, Lance—prepare yourself...!"

Lance looked out, and for an instant his eyes locked with Abby's. He wanted to reach out to her, to speak with her, and he could see that she wanted the same. But the moment passed and she was again entangled in the fight.

He turned to Razor. "I'm sorry, son. I wish—"

Then Lance was inside a shifting, complex, whirling mass of pictures and sounds and numbers.

He felt something pulling him through, and saw Cassandra, Max, Danny and Ragnarök before him.

"Krodin knows Victor's about to betray him—he'll kill him! Cassie, do this *now*."

He felt something rip away from the inside of his mind and dive into the maelstrom of Victor Cross's thoughts.

Ahead of them, an array of images was moving, twisting,

unfolding and rearranging itself, and then a piece vanished, but wasn't replaced. Another piece disappeared. And a third, a fourth.

"It's *collapsing*," Max said. "Where's our solution? Where's our *answer*?"

A column of arrays rippled and shattered, its pieces colliding with other arrays, breaking them, spreading the damage like a replicating virus.

Ragnarök looked down at his hands. "We're fading... Does that mean we're done?"

Lance knew, then. He knew everything. He turned to Cassandra and said, "Looks like *you're* driving. Do you know what you have to do?"

She nodded. "I know."

"You'll *tell* them, won't you?"

Cassandra's eyes filled with tears. "I'll tell them everything. Good-bye, Lance."

Inside his aircraft, Victor Cross staggered from one side to the other, clutching his head. "Not yet! Not yet!" He dropped to his knees and screamed. "My mind is dying!"

Stephanie Cord and Renata Soliz could do nothing but watch.

Colin darted after Krodin, but the immortal superhuman just swatted him away as though he were a bothersome fly.

Then Colin heard Cassandra inside his head. "Don't let him get to Victor! Stop him!"

He rushed forward again, but this time he was ready for Krodin's powerful fist: he dodged to the side, grabbed hold of his wrist and hauled him into the air.

Krodin twisted around, slammed his other fist into Colin's stomach as he screamed, "Enough!"

Colin felt something tear inside him. He lost his grip on Krodin's arm, but ignored the pain. He raced after him again.

Renata Soliz watched Victor Cross writhing on the floor, and looked over towards Stephanie. "What do we do?"

"Do *nothing!*" Cassandra's voice said.

Then Stephanie collapsed, and before Renata could react, everything went dark.

She opened her eyes, and was floating in a gray void. There were others here. Her parents, her sister, her niece. Danny was here, too. And Stephanie.

She realized that the gray void was something out of focus, and at that thought it seemed to sharpen. Blurred lines became distinct.

It had seemed gray because whatever this place was, it was filled with people.

Hundreds of people... or, rather, their souls, or their minds, Renata couldn't tell the difference and wasn't sure that it mattered.

But as she grew accustomed to this strange realm, she realized that her initial guess had been wrong. *Not hundreds of them. There are thousands! No, Millions!*

Billions.

Some were scared, some were curious, most were confused. *What is this place?*

Cassandra's voice said, "Bear with me, everyone, please. Right now, I'm a *little* bit busy. There'll be time for explanations later."

Then she added, "If there *is* a later. "

Colin blasted Krodin with the most powerful heat-ray he could muster, but it didn't slow him down. Four meters from Victor's craft, he melted the ground at Krodin's feet, then, when the immortal had sunk to his knees in molten rock, he froze it again. That bought him a few seconds, at least.

Cassandra—what's going on?

"Colin... we can't avoid the Chasm. But Victor built a time-machine. It's designed to jump fifty seconds into the future. The Chasm will only take a few seconds to pass: we just jump over it. But the machine can only transport one person, and it only works once."

One person? Cassie, that's no good at all!

"It is if that person is Victor Cross, and he's carrying the minds of every human on the planet inside his head. That's what I've done, Colin. They're all in here with me. We disintegrated Victor's mind and now there are over seven billion minds in here. Look around you."

Colin looked. The other New Heroes were all on the ground, unmoving. "Are they OK?"

"They'll be fine, Colin, I promise. Time is running out. You're the last one out there, except for Krodin—and his mind just won't *go*. That's because he was connected to Lance and Max and Ragnarök, I think. All four of them shared a different part of the process. They... The others are *gone* now. I'm sorry."

"What? No, you don't mean—"

"Colin, time is *short*. We'll use Victor's machine, jump into the future and avoid the Chasm. And I'll put everyone's minds back."

OK, Colin thought. *You're certain that they will be all right?*

"Yes! Enough questions! The Chasm will be here in eight seconds so I'm taking you in *now!*"

At Krodin's feet, the solidified rock started to crack.

Go without me, Colin thought. He dropped down in front of Krodin, fists clenched.

"No, there's still time! He might not get free!"

Aloud, Colin said, "I can't take that chance. Do it."

Krodin broke free and Colin crashed into him with every iota of energy, forced him back.

They grabbed for each other at the same time, and their hands locked together.

Krodin roared, and Colin screamed.

They both sensed a flare of energy from the spherical craft.

Then the Chasm was upon them.

Epilogue

Five months later...

They sat on the roof of Sakkara, looking out at the devastation. This had been their first chance to take some time for themselves.

Most of the human race didn't know or understand what had happened. Only a few remembered the gray void.

In North America, the war had raged on, but the surviving New Heroes had worked hard to defeat Krodin's armies. Now, finally, it was done. The last of the mercenaries and hate-groups had been tracked down and apprehended.

Renata hated this. Sakkara had been their home, now it was a shell. The rubble had been cleared from inside, the ground tilled and a lawn planted.

Danny said, as he often did these past weeks, "We saved the world."

She loved him, she truly did, but sometimes he didn't know when to stay silent. After it was all over, Cassandra had told her about the time she'd spent linked to Danny's mind. "He would *die* for you. You know that. Every time he sees you, his heart races and he falls in love with you all over again. And he blames himself for not being around to save your brother from Krodin's armies."

When Renata learned that Robbie had been killed, her first instinct had been to blame Danny. He had saved thousands of others; why not Robbie Soliz? But she'd known that was wrong even as she was accusing him, and Danny had stood there and taken her screams and accusations and was still there when her rage subsided and she needed someone to hold.

Renata had spent the morning with her family. They wanted

her to move home full-time, but she wasn't ready for that. She'd been using the excuse that she had to wait until her ankles healed, but that one was wearing thin.

Nathan said, "Your father doesn't much like us, does he?"

"Can you blame him?" Renata replied. "He's been through a lot. After what happened to me and then Robbie, he's never going to trust any of us again."

Danny scratched at his beard. "We did what we had to do."

"You keep saying that," Renata said. "You weren't there, Dan. You don't know what it was *like*."

Nathan began, "Mina said—"

"Shut up about her!" Danny yelled. "She's gone, all right? Just forget about her. She ruined everything."

Nathan said, "No. It wasn't Mina. It's *your* fault."

"How? *How* is it my fault? Mina's the one who told Krodin that Victor was betraying him! Because of *her*, Colin had to stay outside to make sure Krodin didn't kill Victor."

"It's *your* fault because you can alter time and you won't bring him back!"

Renata said, "It doesn't work that way, Nathan. Colin knew what he was doing."

"They're all dead now! Alex and Roman and the others... And Colin... He was my *brother*!"

Danny and Renata looked at Nathan, identical to Colin in almost every way, and Danny put his hand on the younger boy's shoulder. "He was our brother too."

At sunset, Nathan took hold of Renata's hands and gently flew her down to the ground. Danny was already waiting for them: as always, he had simply run down the sloping side of the building.

They walked inside, where Abby, Brawn, Razor, Stephanie

and Cassandra were sitting on the grass in a small circle. Plates of food were spread out on a blanket between them.

"Picnic?" Renata asked, as she and Nathan and Danny dropped down among their friends.

Razor shrugged. "Can you think of a better place?" He leaned back and looked up at the roof. "They sure made this building tough. It's survived a *lot* of damage."

"We *all* have," Brawn said. "They wouldn't want us to grieve. If they were here now, they'd tell us to get over it."

Stephanie said, "Colin wouldn't."

"No, you're right. He'd be sympathetic. But *Lance*..." Brawn smiled, then gave Razor a playful thump that nearly knocked him over. "Your old man was one of the good ones, Razor."

Razor smiled. "Yeah."

Abby said, "He knew, didn't he?" She turned to Cassandra, "He knew that he wasn't going to make it."

Cassandra nodded. "He knew. Only a superhuman mind could survive that process, and *his* mind was human. Same with Max. He had been superhuman once, but that wasn't enough."

Renata stood up, and carefully walked over to the two small headstones. The one on the left simply said, "Colin Wagner. Hero." The headstone on the right said, "Lance McKendrick. Annoying but kinda funny sometimes."

Stephanie joined her, and they stood in silence for a moment, until Renata gently bumped her shoulder against Stephanie's and said, "Colin loved you."

"I know. But we never got around to *doing* anything about it. All those sly glances and secret smiles and hints and flirting... It was great fun and very exciting, but I'd trade them all in for one proper kiss!" She started to move away, then almost immediately she turned back. "Well, no, I wouldn't. But promise me you won't make the same mistake with Danny."

Renata smiled. "We're going to be OK. I have him well trained."

They looked back to see Abby approaching them. "I never got to know Colin," she said, "but I fought alongside him at the end. He was *fearless*. And Lance was, well... he'd have approved of the headstone. I'll always regret that we never got a chance to catch up. I never got to thank him for what he did for my brothers."

"What about Max?" Stephanie asked.

"Roz—his sister—told he they're going to scatter his ashes in a field near their childhood home."

Renata said, "Everyone wants me to take Lance's job, Abby."

"You should. Krodin and Cross are gone, but the world will always need heroes. And I would follow you to the end of the world. Again."

"I don't have any powers."

"Never stopped you before," Stephanie said.

Abby nodded. "You should do it, Renata. Losing your brother and your friends hurts, I know, but we have to be heroes so that maybe we can prevent other people from being hurt in the same way. So that they can have hope."

"Now you're starting to sound like your brother-in-law."

Abby exchanged a smile with Stephanie and said, "I can live with that."

Renata nodded, then turned back to face the others. "OK, folks. You've had your picnic. Time to tidy up, put on your work clothes, and get out there and fight the bad guys." She clapped her hands together. "Come on! Let's *go*, boys and girls—the world isn't going to save itself!"

The New Heroes / Quantum Prophecy series:
The Quantum Prophecy / The Awakening
Sakkara / The Gathering
Absolute Power / The Reckoning
Super Human
The Ascension
Stronger
Hunter
Crossfire
The Chasm

E-books:
The Footsoldiers
Flesh and Blood

Limited-edition short-story collection:
The New Heroes: Superhuman
(Includes "The Footsoldiers" and "Flesh and Blood")

For more information, see the Quantum Prophecy website:
www.quantumprophecy.com

or the author's website:
www.michaelowencarroll.com

CPSIA information can be obtained
at www.ICGtesting.com
Printed in the USA
LVHW011453150920
666085LV00008B/834

9 781547 067794